MW00390071

The Emerald Gate

by
Matt Heppe

Published by Matt Heppe
2020

ISBN: 9781704804767

Contact:
MattHeppe+EternalKnight@gmail.com

Cover by Dallas Williams

For my daughter, Amelia

Chapter One

Ayja and the Blade of Darra ran across the tortured, broken landscape, desperate to put as much distance between them and the Dromost Gate as possible. How many demons had been called by the explosion that had closed the gate? She'd seen movement in the distance as they'd fled — massive, misshapen forms surging closer and closer.

They ran three arrowflights across a twisted field of jagged black rocks before Ayja slowed and ducked behind a boulder. Her lungs heaved, drawing in the poisonous air of Dromost. She choked and coughed as she shifted her vision into the aether. There she saw the strands of magic and of the elements that were the fabric of existence. She also saw the poison choking her, and even as she gagged, she twisted the aether to cleanse it.

Clean air filled her lungs, but still, she coughed. Darra stepped close to her. He'd lost his helmet, and his mail coif had fallen back over his head, revealing lank, black hair. His breath didn't come in ragged gasps. It didn't come at all. Transformed by the twisted magic of a lych, the undead knight was sustained entirely by the life force he stole from others. "Keep moving, my queen," he said. "We have to find a place of hiding."

Ayja nodded, staring into the iron black eyes of the pale-skinned pyren. "I need a moment," she said, still breathing deeply. "I couldn't clear the poison while we ran."

Darra looked out from behind the rock that hid them. He wore a Saladoran coat-of-plates under a ragged blue kaftan and held Ayja's longsword in his hands — her mother's sword — the only thing Ayja owned linking the two of them. Ayja was just as well armored, wearing a long scale coat taken from the Temple of Forsvar. More importantly, though, she bore two of the Gifts of the Gods; Forsvar, the Godshield, and the warhammer, Dromost.

For all of the good they will do me. She and Darra were trapped in the world of Dromost with no hope of escape.

"They are coming," Darra said.

"Wait a moment," Ayja said. She twisted her working, weaving the strands of the aether so that the cleansed air would follow her as she moved. It wasn't complicated, but she'd never attempted it before, and it took some time to get it right.

"We must move, my queen," Darra said, shifting his grip on her sword.

She finished twisting the last strands of the aether, hoping the working would hold. "Ayja," she said. "Call me Ayja. I'm no queen."

"It wouldn't be proper," he said.

"Ayja," she said again, creeping out from their hiding place. The clean air moved with her, although she had to nudge it from time to time to keep it in place. *I have to make it permanent. Bind it to something as we did with Orlos's fire arrows.*

Her thoughts went to her friends. Had they made it clear of the Temple of Dromost? She hated to think they'd perished after the closing of the Dromost Gate. *Let them win their way free.*

"Something is coming," Darra said from behind her. "It's fast."

Ayja ducked behind another boulder, taking a better grip on Dromost. The hammer hummed with a desire to strike out and take the life force of an enemy. She'd only had the Godhammer for a very short time and was unnerved by the weapon's bloodlust. It *wanted* to kill.

"Perhaps we should hide," she said, pulling her eyes from the hammer. "I wonder if it can track us."

"I don't know, my queen. Too late now, though. It's coming right for us."

Ayja heard it now, claws scrabbling against stone. Which side of the boulder would it come around? She nodded to Darra. "Watch that side."

Then the sound stopped. Whatever demon it was, it lurked just on the other side of the boulder. Claws scraped, and something rasped as it dragged across the ground. Ayja's heart pounded in fear and anticipation as Forsvar's rim crackled with ethereal lightning. A pebble bounced off her shoulder.

It was above her.

The demon, a massive dog-headed wyrm, lunged down at her, its gaping maw filled with ebony teeth and a blue tongue. Without conscious thought, Forsvar slammed into the demon's head, the shield throwing its attack off. She raised Dromost, but the creature's mass of coils slithered over the boulder, falling on her and crushing her to the ground before she could swing.

The head rose again, poised to strike. Darra struck at one of the demon's claws with his sword. The two-handed blow cut through the

2

demon scales, slicing deep into its flesh. With a howl, it turned to face the pyren.

Ayja freed her arm from under the crushing coils, but had no leverage to swing the Godhammer. Instead, reaching into the aether, she sent a jet of fire at the demon's head. The flames washed over the demon, seemingly doing little harm, but distracting it enough that its strike went awry.

The demon lunged for Darra again, seizing him in one of its massive claws. The head darted forward, its maw wide, but Darra's blade was there, stabbing deep into its mouth. The demon recoiled, howling in pain.

Still trapped under the demon's coils, Ayja threw another blast of fire at it. It was futile, though. Fire meant nothing to this demon. It threw her a baleful glance and turned back to Darra. Still pinning the pyren with one clawed hand, the demon stabbed at him with the other, dagger-like blades plunging deep into the pyren's body.

The wounds would have killed a mortal man, but Darra's life was sustained by magic, not blood. He hacked at the demon's arm, but there was little force behind his blows, and his sword glanced off of the demon's scales.

The demon's jaws opened wide. It would surely tear the pyren in half if it sank its teeth into him. Desperate, Ayja reached within herself and touched her silver fire. It was on her in an instant. Her world went silver and power coursed through her veins. She channeled aethereal lightning through Dromost and touched the warhammer to the demon's sinuous body.

Brilliant light flared as aetherial power surged into the demon. It screamed and thrashed, losing its grip on Darra as it flailed. Ayja rolled free of the demon's coils as it turned on her, and then she struck it a heavy blow with Dromost. The demon's head rocked to the side as bones shattered under the hammer strike. She swung again, bringing the Godhammer down on the top of the demon's skull, this time unleashing a bolt of aether as the blow struck home. The demon screamed in pain as it recoiled, raising its head high above her and out of reach.

Its long body was still close, though. Ayja leaped forward and swung Dromost again. The god-forged weapon, driven by her silver fury, punched through the serpent scales, penetrating deep into its body. The demon's body jerked wildly, hurling Ayja prone.

The creature fled as she scrambled to her feet. She couldn't breathe. Poison filled her lungs as her silver vision faded in a coughing fit. She'd lost her working during the fight. As she choked, the dog-headed demon rapidly slithered away, grievously wounded. She was desperate to strike it another blow but fell to her knees instead, unable to breathe.

3

As quickly as she could, Ayja twisted the aether into another working. She knew it better now and rapidly bound the strands of air and aether to filter out the poison. She gasped as fresh air filled her lungs again.

Even as she gulped in air, she heard movement nearby and instinctively raised Forsvar to defend herself. She breathed a sigh of relief when she saw it was Darra. "Are you wounded?" he asked as he stepped closer.

She shook her head. "What about you? It impaled you." She saw three large holes in the front of his coat-of-plates where the talons had punched through.

"I am sorely wounded, my queen," he said. "If I don't find a source of life soon, I will perish."

"I can only give you a little," Ayja said. "My silver fire drains me."

"No. You cannot spare it. I can go a little longer."

There was a roar nearby, followed by a series of high, shrill screams. Ayja looked out from behind the boulder, searching the landscape for the source of the sound. She saw the retreating demon now engaged in battle against six or more spider-like creatures with long barbed tails. The struggle was at once horrifying and fascinating, but after a few heartbeats, she turned away.

"Let's get away from here. Quickly," she said. "Can you manage it?"

Staying low, they crept away from the sound of battle. They moved as fast as they could, but the rugged terrain made it impossible to run, or even jog. Heat radiated from the very earth beneath them, and Ayja wiped the sweat from her brow. Her well of power was depleted but not yet empty. When would she have a chance to rest again? When had she last rested? She'd never grown completely used to sleeping at sea aboard the *Summer Swan,* but now it seemed to her to have been the very height of luxury.

There were strange cracks and pops from the rock deep beneath her. She knelt and touched the ground. It was warm — almost too hot to touch. Through a crack, she saw a red glow. Touching the aether, she let her senses probe deep into the rock. She gasped at what she saw there. The rock itself was molten. What force of nature could melt stone? Or was it magic?

"What is it?" Darra asked. "We should keep moving."

Ayja nodded and started forward again. Nearby a small, scaled creature skittered away on long claws. Ayja raised Dromost, but the creature was gone.

"Stop it if you can," Darra said. "I need whatever strength I can take."

"Are you certain you don't want some of mine?" Ayja asked.

"No. Not yet, my queen."

4

Very abruptly, the area of jagged black rocks ended. The terrain rose slightly, and they entered a boulder-strewn field. There was soil here, and the rocks were granite, not the porous boulders they'd left behind them. There were no plants, however. Not the smallest bush or even a weed poked up from the dry, sandy soil.

They climbed up the slope, and Ayja glanced over her shoulder. The area of jagged black rocks flowed like a river down from the mountains to their right. It was dark, and a haze obscured everything in sight. She thought she saw the still form of the giant, snake-like creature that had attacked them, but she saw none of the spiders that had slain it.

Further off would be the bowl where the Dromost Gate was located, but the haze was too thick and the distance too great. It didn't matter, did it? The gate was closed and couldn't be reopened. Not by her, at least. Darra climbed up next to her and turned to follow her gaze.

"What do we do now, Darra?" Ayja asked.

"Survive, my queen," he said. "Find a way home."

"Ayja," she corrected. "Just Ayja. And there is no way home."

Darra looked up towards the mountains and then over the rocky landscape behind them. "If we are to return, it will be through your magic, my queen," he said.

She shook her head at his stubbornness. "And so we are doomed. I don't have the magic to open the gate. To cross between worlds is beyond me." She took a deep breath. Her working still held, keeping the poisons from her lungs. Hunger gnawed at her, and she desperately wanted a drink of water.

"Is there even water here?" she asked. "Or food? The very air is poison to me."

"Let's search." Darra glanced around. "This way," he said, pointing. "There won't be any in the black rocks we crossed."

They turned away from the mountains and started downhill, away from the river of molten stone. Three times as they walked, they saw motion. All three times, the creatures fled.

"Everything here is a demon," Ayja said. "Or at least that's what Telea told me. Large demons consume smaller demons and become more powerful. Dead demons are reborn as worms. Small serpents, I think."

"How did she know this?"

"Telea had a demon in her. She learned much from it."

"She did?" Darra asked, his pale face unreadable. "She was possessed?"

"Yes. Ever since she crossed into Salador. I think it entered her when she was a prisoner in Del-Oras." Did it matter that she was betraying her friend's trust? Ayja glanced around the broken landscape. Did it even matter anymore?

"All this time, she's been your companion, and you knew a demon possessed her?"

"The demon was in her, but it didn't control her. It was very weak. Some of what she learned from it, she taught to me."

"It's still in her?"

Ayja frowned. "It is, I think. If she still lives, at least."

They came upon a narrow gully. At the bottom, a trickle of liquid formed a black pool. It stank of rotten eggs, and she was certain she'd have to clean it. She paused. She had no container. Nothing at all to hold water in. Given time she could form a canteen out of clay. Time and strength. She peered over the edge, and some of the soil underfoot fell away and slid into the pool.

"Here, take Forsvar," she said, sliding the Godshield from her arm and handing it to the pyren.

"You're certain?" he asked as he accepted it.

"At this point, I'm fairly certain you aren't going to betray me, Darra," she said, forcing a grin. "Keep a watch out while I'm down there." Ayja shoved Dromost through her belt and slid into the gully. It was four strides deep and very narrow. She skidded to a halt at the bottom.

Her boots sank a handspan into the mud at the edge of the pool as she landed. There was nothing to be done for it; there was no place to stand that was dry. Ayja crouched by the water's edge. She wrinkled her nose at the stink. A slick sheen covered the dark water.

Shifting her vision into the aether, Ayja peered at the water and shook her head at the polluted, poisonous mess she saw there. Reaching out, she twisted the strands of the aether, separating the bad water from the good. It was simple work, but she begrudged the use of her energy. She had precious little of it to waste. It was just the slightest draw from her well of power, but it was necessary. She had to drink.

Ayja caused a globe of clean water to gather itself atop the pool. She took it in her hand and raised it to her mouth, greedily sucking it in. It was warm, but she didn't care. She couldn't spare the strength to cool it. For a moment, she thought to offer some to Darra and then grimaced at the foolishness of the thought. *To envy a pyren.*

She bent close to the water, prepared to draw out another globe of water, when several bubbles emerged from the pool, causing ripples to eddy outwards. She frowned. Sulfurous gas emerging from deep under the ground?

The pool exploded into Ayja's face, blinding her. She threw her hands up as something struck her, wrapping itself around her arms and head. She tried to push the creature from her, but it was too strong and dragged her face-first into the pool. Her left arm was trapped between her face and the creature, but her right was free. She pushed it deep into the mud as she fought to keep herself from being submerged.

A tentacle coiled around her neck, drawing tighter and tighter. She fought for a breath, but poison filled her lungs. Her working was gone, shattered by the attack. Stars and bright light filled her vision as her consciousness faded. She tried to call out, but her voice caught as the coil around her neck tightened even further.

She reached for the aether, but couldn't find it. She saw the strands of magic, but couldn't focus on them. She knew she had only heartbeats to live. Her silver fire was just a memory. She needed Dromost. It connected her with the aether in a way she'd never felt before. She scrabbled for the Godhammer, but without her hand to support her, she was drawn into the pool, her head completely submerged.

Ayja touched Dromost's shaft just as consciousness left her. Her world went black as fluid filled her lungs.

She choked and coughed as Darra hauled her from the pool. "I have you, Ayja," he said. She felt his hands uncoiling the creature's limp tentacle from around her neck. She drew in a deep breath, but then the poison assaulted her lungs, and she went black again.

Something struck her face. "Wake, Ayja!" Darra's voice was desperate. A surge of warmth filled her. She opened her eyes to Darra's pale hands touching her face. She saw the glow of magic there. "Drive off the poison air," Darra said. "Hurry."

Coughing, Ayja pushed his hands away. Twisting the aether, she quickly remade the working. She was barely able to do the work through the choking fit wracking her lungs. She took a breath when she was done, nodding to Darra that she'd finished.

He touched her again, pulsing life into her. His face was drawn — even more pale and sunken than it normally was. The sheen of his smooth skin had gone to a dull grey. She pushed his hands away again. "Enough," she said. "I'm all right."

Ayja sank back away from the pyren, resting her back against the dirt wall of the crevasse. She was soaked from head to toe, covered in the stinking filth of the ditch. The demon's tentacle lay right next to her. It reminded her of the octopus she'd seen while on the *Summer Swan,* but scaled and spined and even more horrible.

7

Even as she watched, the demon's skin bubbled and sloughed away, melting into the fetid pool beneath her. She gagged and wanted to retch, but held it in. Pushing with her legs, she scrambled away from the muck.

A sob escaped her. Grimacing, she clenched her fist, pushing her fingernails painfully against her palm. She would not break down. She would not fall apart in front of Darra. *No matter how desperate the situation, a leader must always show strength,* Cam had taught her. *A leader's fear spreads like fire through kindling.*

Ayja raised her eyes to the livid, lightning-streaked sky of Dromost. *Where are you, Cam? What will strength do for me now?*

Chapter Two

Nidon stared up at a mountain valley backlit by the rising sun. The Dragon Pass. He'd nearly died here on several occasions some twenty years ago. Back then, he'd been fighting the remnants of Akinos's armies after their defeat at the Battle of King's Crossing. Now he prepared to fight the survivors of Cragor's army after their defeat at the Battle of Sal Oras. *A pass of defeated armies. A pass for last stands.*

Perhaps this would be the last time a battle would need to be fought here. If Nidon had his way, the Army of Salador would push over the pass and into Rigaria. They'd defeat the last of Cragor's varcolac and unluks, ending their threat once and for all.

For seventeen years, the varcolac king, Cragor, and the Eternal Knights who'd served him as slave soldiers, had ruled Rigaria. Cragor was dead now, and the eternals destroyed. Humans made up the majority of Rigaria's population — not Akinos's twisted creations. From the Rigarians the Saladorans had captured, it appeared they would welcome King Handrin as a savior from the varcolac and others who preyed upon them and ruled over them.

Getting ahead of myself. First, we must clear the pass.

The morning light revealed a crudely built stone wall extending from one cliff to another less than an arrowflight away. Unluks, varcolac, and a few giant urias crowded it, waiting for the Saladoran assault. The approach was broken ground, but for a single narrow track — a deathtrap.

With siege machinery and enough time, the flimsy wall could easily be taken down, but they had no time. The snows would come soon and close the pass. Even then, there were few places to situate catapults or trebuchets. The wall had to be taken by storm. Seventeen years ago, they'd done it over and over as they'd worked their way up the pass — each time at terrible cost. In the end, they'd never been able to break through.

All because Queen Ilana wouldn't trust me to wield Forsvar. With the Godshield in his hands, Nidon could have led the knights of Salador over the pass and into Rigaria. Cragor would never have learned how to control the Orb of Creation and the eternals. The wars that followed never would have happened. The free Eternal Knights wouldn't have learned to turn themselves into lyches. *Hadde wouldn't have died.*

It would be better this time, though. Nidon glanced over his shoulder at the hundreds of knights crowding the valley behind him. Closest to him were the newly reformed Knights of the House in their red tabards. Just behind were the Lancers and Squires of the House. Beyond a bend, four thousand more soldiers of the Army of Salador waited. They even had human Rigarians with them — those who'd been captured and willingly turned sides to fight against their oppressors.

It wasn't numbers that would make the difference this time, though.

In the deep of the night, the Saladorans had launched a false attack on the wall. Men had paid the ultimate price in that attack, but it had been a success. Hidden at the base of the wall, sheltered from view, were King Handrin with the Orb of Creation, and four of his elementars. Nidon had argued that the plan was too bold — too dangerous. That they shouldn't risk the king and the Orb. They had the army to force the position. Even more so with elementars supporting them.

King Handrin hadn't wanted to pay the butcher's bill. He knew many soldiers would die in a frontal assault. So instead, he and the elementars would lay down a wall of fire, killing and driving back the defenders so that the knights of Salador could cross the difficult slope unopposed. Without the advantage of the wall, the creatures of Akinos could be defeated.

Not defeated. Destroyed. Broken and routed. They'll never march on us again.

Brilliant silver-gold light flared near the base of the wall where the king hid. Fire exploded on the parapets and raced down its length. Nidon heard the anguished cries of the defenders but hardened his heart to them. These monsters had issued from Rigaria, murdering, raping, and plundering the length of the East Teren to the bridges of Sal-Oras. They had neither chivalry nor honor — just simple bloodlust and greed.

They deserve everything coming to them and more.

"Forward, knights of Salador!" Nidon shouted. He didn't wait for a reply, charging up the rocky slope, his shield on his left arm, but his right hand free. He wanted to be able to pick his way over rocks and debris and climb the wall when he got to it. He stayed to the narrow trail, and he and the others on it soon pulled ahead of those to either side.

The fire still burned the length of the wall, but the flames were dimming now. Nidon wanted to get to it before they were completely extinguished. Would the Rigarians attempt to retake the works, or would they flee?

A couple of younger knights pushed past Nidon in their eagerness to get to the wall. He hated to admit it was more than eagerness. He'd lost a step on the younger men. They were thirty strides from the wall when Nidon saw King Handrin raise the Orb of Creation over his head. There was another bright flash, and a twenty stride wide section of the wall collapsed outward.

Nidon ran into the cloud of dust and smoke thrown up by the falling stones. The treacherous footing slowed him as he stumbled forward. He saw figures moving in front of him and drew his falchion. It wasn't a true knight's sword, but he'd grown used to it in his years in exile. He liked its weight and cutting edge. A butcher's weapon.

Steel rang on steel ahead of him. Unluks surged into the smoke. Squat, long-armed, and boar-faced, the unluks only vaguely resembled the humans they'd once been. They carried short, broad-bladed spears and heavy javelins they hurled as they approached. Nidon turned two javelins on his shield and then threw himself into the fight.

The unluks weren't skilled, but they were strong and fast. He cut one of them down and then stepped up to the left of the knight in front of him. "Forward! Forward!" Nidon shouted. They couldn't let the unluks eject them from the breach in the wall. Putting his shoulder into his shield, Nidon pressed forward into the unluks, trusting his excellent coat-of-plates and heavy, visored helm to keep him from harm.

Over and over, he landed overhead blows on the shorter unluks. He felt the press of knights behind him and pushed further forward. They'd pierced the enemy defenses, but the valley seemed full of them. The further they pressed into the enemy, the more their flanks were exposed.

A wedge of varcolac appeared out of the haze in front of them. Big, bearded men with silver eyes and the power of the aether running through their veins, they crashed into the knights with berserk fury. The knight to Nidon's left fell to a heavy axe blow, and for a dozen heartbeats, it was everything Nidon could do to keep himself alive. He parried spears and axes with shield and falchion, unable to land a single blow himself.

From off to his left, he heard a cheer. Trapped in the fierce melee, he had no idea what was happening. Had the Knights of the House pushed over the wall somewhere else? They were too late to save Nidon and those around them if they had. Another knight fell, and Nidon's enemies surrounded him. All he knew was that someone had his back. A spear

11

thrust over his shoulder took one of the varcolac in the throat, sending him toppling to the ground.

An axe blow clipped Nidon's helm, stunning him for a moment. He lashed out with his falchion and struck something, but in the chaotic melee, never saw where his blow landed. All he knew was that he couldn't let them push him back. They had to hold the breach.

A column of fire erupted just strides in front of him. Varcolac howled in pain, their bear and wolf cloaks catching fire. Nidon stabbed one through the chest and then nearly decapitated another. He pushed forward into the gap and found a clear space where the flames had burned. Knights came with him, and they charged into the faltering enemy.

With a roar, an urias pushed through the unluks. Misshapen, but three strides tall and with limbs corded with muscle, the urias raised its maul over its head. For an instant, Nidon remembered the last time he'd faced an urias in these mountains. The creature's club had broken eight of Nidon's ribs and sent him flying ten strides into a boulder. Only the heroics of a half dozen Knights of the House had saved him.

Nidon leaped aside and raised his shield as the maul swept down at him. The glancing blow was enough to stagger him and send him to his knees. The urias's maul had become lodged between two stones, and the beast was too dumb to let it go. Nidon leaped to his feet and chopped down on the urias's arm with his heavy blade, severing it near the elbow. The urias shrieked in pain as blood showered from the severed arm.

A second blow from Nidon's falchion took the urias just above the knee, and its leg buckled. It fell into two unluks, crushing them to the ground. Nidon ran past them, letting those who followed deal with the downed foes.

The enemy, having seen their elite varcolac broken by elementar fire and their urias felled by Nidon's blade, turned and fled. Nidon followed, cutting down enemies one after another. Some turned to fight, but most simply clawed at those in front of them in their desperation. Finally, Nidon had to stop. He'd killed a dozen of the fleeing enemy warriors, but his lungs heaved, and he could hardly raise his sword. He paused and let fresher knights and men-at-arms come up from behind and keep up the pursuit.

Enemies crowded the mountain pass above them. The slaughter would go on for hours, but Nidon wouldn't be there. His part in the fighting was over.

"Champion Nidon, some water?" He turned to see his squire behind him, offering a wooden canteen.

"Thank you, Squire Fress." Nidon traded his falchion for the canteen and, after raising his visor, drank deeply. He handed it back and took his freshly cleaned blade back. "Have you seen King Handrin?"

"He's coming, Champion."

Nidon noted his squire's bloody spear. "Was that you behind me in the fight?"

"It was, Champion. Sir Tormus fell, and I took his place."

Nidon grimaced. "He's dead? A good man."

"Not dead, Champion. Wounded."

"You did well, squire. You kept them off of me."

"Thank you, Champion." Fress beamed in pride through his fatigue.

Nidon looked up the valley. The Knights of the House had been replaced by the Lancers of the House, men-at-arms who'd come over to Handrin after serving in Queen Ilana's guard. He made way as even more East Teren knights passed through, greeting those he'd gotten to know over the past two months. Seventeen years of exile was a long time to be away. Many of the knights were the sons of men he'd served with under King Boradin.

"Make way for the king!" someone shouted below. Escorted by picked Knights of the House, Handrin made his way to Nidon. Four elementars walked with him, Baron Fendal amongst them.

"It worked, Your Majesty," Nidon said. "Your plan saved many lives."

"Thank you, Nidon. High praise from the Champion of Salador. You were the first through the breach?"

Nidon shook his head. "Third. Two young knights beat me to it. Sir Belefor and Sir Peleon, I believe. They should be lauded for their bravery, Your Majesty. I don't know their fate."

The king nodded. "I'll summon them to me after the battle."

"I know the Lancers of the House will have things well in hand," Nidon said, looking up the valley again, "but I'm anxious to see what's happening."

"Let them have their glory," Handrin said. "What advice could you offer in this valley? There's no maneuvering, just hard fighting."

Handrin held the Orb of Creation at his side, but it was dimmed from what it had been before. Nidon knew something of magic. He'd raised Ayja and had been around her magic all of her life. Before that, he'd been Champion to the Elementar King, Boradin. He knew that the Orb would need time to regenerate itself after having been used in such a tremendous display of magic.

"It galls me not to lead from the front," Nidon said. "To send others into harm's way while I am safe."

13

"You were one of the first men over the breach, Nidon. You showed great valor. Come, we'll advance with the army. They'll want to see us."

Nidon joined the young king as they marched up the slope with the men of the East Teren. *Young king. When did I start thinking of men of near thirty years as young?*

It did great good to march alongside the soldiers and encourage them as they climbed towards the fighting. *They want to see their king. They want to see their champion. Men strive harder when under the eyes of those they respect.*

The slaughter was terrible. The broken creatures of Akinos, trapped by others ahead of them, were mercilessly cut down by the Saladorans. No quarter was asked. The unluks knew surrender was not an option. From time to time, the Saladorans reached chokepoints and were forced into difficult assaults. They never lasted long, though. After a short resistance, the rear ranks of the unluks would break, leaving those in the front ranks unsupported.

Finally, late in the day as the sun sank towards the horizon behind them, the fighting ended. Crossbowmen loosed bolts at the last of the scattered unluks as they ran for the highest reaches of the pass. How many had died? A thousand? More? All day Nidon had climbed past the corpses of unluks, varcolac, and urias.

Nidon placed the knights of the West Teren in the van, ordering them to fortify the pass in case the enemy might return and launch an attack during the night.

"It will be a cold night," Handrin said.

"We aren't far above the tree line," Nidon replied. "I'll have our Rigarians bring wood up so that the men will have fires. Porters are already bringing up tentage and camp gear."

"I'll camp here," Handrin said to his escorts.

Nidon nodded. He approved of this king, even if it wasn't his place to approve or disapprove of the monarch. Handrin's mother, Ilana, had been a tyrant queen. She'd hunted down the elementars who'd emerged after the unlocking of the Orb of Creation, believing them a threat to her rule. In the end, it was her son who'd overthrown her, recognizing her evil for what it was. And now, when he could retreat down the slopes to stay in greater luxury, he chose to sleep among his exhausted soldiers.

Squires and pages rushed to set up the king's camp. Their Rigarian allies brought up wood, and fires soon dotted the slopes. For a time, Nidon and Handrin walked from mess group to mess group, the king lighting their fires with magic and spending a few moments speaking to them of the day's events. But then Nidon separated himself from the entourage to meet with the army's captains.

14

"How many did we lose, Nidon?" Handrin asked when they later met outside the king's pavilion tent.

"One hundred eighty-three, Your Majesty," Nidon said. "The Knights of the House were hit the hardest."

Handrin nodded. "They were the first in." He paused a moment. "We did it, though. The enemy has broken. We enter Rigaria tomorrow."

A voice spoke from close behind them. "Sulentis... King Handrin, I bring word from Belen."

Nidon turned to find a lanky, tall young man standing close behind them. He wore baggy dark blue trousers tucked into tall boots and a lighter blue tunic that crossed in front in Kiremi style. Nidon thought he recognized him, but it only hit him when Handrin said, "Orlos!"

Nidon drew in a sharp breath at the sight of the young man. Before he could get his wits about him, Handrin spoke again. "How are you here?" the king asked. "Are you back from the Empire of Belen? Isn't the East Pass snowed in for the winter?"

"I made it through," Orlos said. "I was in my spiridus form, but even then, the journey nearly killed me."

Orlos's face was drawn, and there were dark circles under his eyes. He looked even skinnier than Nidon had remembered. "Come here," Handrin said. "Stand by the fire. Have you eaten?"

Orlos shook his head as he joined them at the fire. "I came straight to you," he said.

"We had no word of your arrival."

"I outran the news," Orlos said. "When I reached the army, they wanted me to wait, but I couldn't stand it." He cracked a slight smile. "It's not like they could stop me."

Nidon glanced from Orlos to the king's nearby guards, who'd been evaded by the invisible spiridus.

"What of Ayja?" Nidon blurted out. "What of your task?"

A shadow crossed Orlos's face. "She defeated the demon at the Dromost Gate," Orlos said. "The Dromost Gate is closed."

"That's good news!" Handrin said. "Why is your face dark, though? What's wrong?"

Orlos nodded, and then his face contorted in a grimace. "She's gone," he said. "Ayja passed through the Dromost Gate and into Dromost itself. She's — she's trapped there. She's gone."

Nidon stepped close and took Orlos by the shoulders. "What do you mean? What happened?"

Handrin put his hand on Nidon's shoulder. "Give him a moment, Champion," he said. Then he turned and called out, "Bring a camp chair!

15

And wine!" Turning his attention back to Orlos, he said, "Take a moment, young man. We'll hear your story when you're ready."

The king glanced at Nidon and he released the spiridus's shoulders. *Ayja's gone? She went to Dromost? My Ayja is dead?* Nidon wanted to grab Orlos and shake the news from him but restrained himself. It was all he could do not to shout out. He'd spent sixteen years raising Ayja from a baby, only to see her stolen from him.

I should never have let her go. I should have gone. He pounded his fist into his palm with a sharp crack.

Three folding chairs were brought up, and Handrin pressed Orlos into one. A silver cup of wine was pushed into the young Landomeri's hands, and then Handrin and Nidon sat close to him in their chairs.

Orlos took a gulp of wine and wiped tears from his eyes. "I'm sorry," he said. "I've had over a month to think about this moment, and now that it has come, I can hardly speak."

"Take your time," Handrin said.

Orlos took another drink of wine, glanced from Handrin to Nidon, and then stared into the fire. "I'll tell you the story in full," Orlos said, "but let me get to the heart of it first."

Nidon leaned forward in his chair, his fists clenched, and his knees bobbing. He bit his lip to keep from shouting his frustration. *Where is my Ayja?*

"When we reached the Dromost Gate, the good summoners still held it — the Gatekeepers. They were allied with the Emperor of Belen. The other summoners, the Doomcallers, had the temple under siege. They were the ones who wanted to open the gate and let the demons through.

"The Gate itself was surrounded by a magical shield, one that kept anything from leaving. Inside the shield was a shadow demon and the Godhammer, Dromost. Ayja and the Blade of Darra entered—"

"The Blade of Darra?" Nidon exclaimed. "The pyren? What was he doing there?"

"He followed us over the pass. He came to serve Ayja."

"Why would he do such a thing?" Handrin asked.

Orlos glanced at the king. "He, ah, he called her his queen. He said she was the rightful heir to the Throne of Salador. He came to serve her."

"How could you trust him?" Nidon asked. "He was a pyren — a creator of ghuls! A servant of lyches!"

Orlos drew a breath. "He served Prince Morin, who he thought should be king. I know it sounds strange, but he was absolutely faithful to Ayja. He saved all of us on several occasions."

Nidon sat taller in his chair. "Go on. What happened?"

16

"Ayja and Darra killed the demon guarding the Dromost Gate. But when the old summoner tried to close the gate, it didn't work — the gate wouldn't close. Ayja and Darra went through the gate to see why it was still open. It was being held open from the other side."

Orlos paused and took a deep breath. He stared into the fire for a few heartbeats and then leaned forward, covering his eyes with his hands. "She knew she'd be trapped, but she went back anyway." He choked back a sob. "Before she left, she said that the gate had to be locked." Orlos looked up, his eyes shining. "She said only the Orb of Creation could keep the gate closed forever. Otherwise, the demons could reopen the gate and unleash an invasion that would destroy the world. We should have taken the Orb with us."

"She closed it from the other side?" Nidon asked. "She couldn't get back out?"

"I went through, but she made me go back. I — I couldn't breathe. The air was poison there," Orlos said. "I wanted to stay with her. I would have gone with her. I swear I would have."

"She could breathe?" Nidon asked.

Orlos nodded. "With her magic."

"We have to get her out," Nidon said, standing. He faced Handrin. "We have to save her."

Handrin frowned. "She had Forsvar and Dromost with her?"

Orlos nodded. "The Blade of Darra as well."

"I don't care about those things!" Nidon exclaimed. "I care about Ayja!"

"Quiet, Nidon!" Handrin commanded. "We must think this through. There's nothing we can do in this instant."

"Use your magic!" Nidon shouted, his anger too great to hold in. "Use the Orb of Creation! Open the gate and get her out."

"Calm yourself, Champion," Handrin said. "We will find a way."

Orlos wiped tears from his eyes. "The old summoner said that the gate must be locked. That it isn't enough that it's closed. It can be opened again, and all the hosts of Dromost will pour through."

"If it can be opened, then Ayja can be saved," Nidon said.

Orlos shook his head. "He said that she's... that she's already gone. That no one could survive in Dromost."

"How does he know?" Nidon demanded. "Has he ever been there?"

"He was the leader of all of the summoner priests. He knows better than anyone." Orlos paused a moment and took a deep breath. "I want Ayja saved as much as you do. I love her. But she's gone, and the gate must be sealed. The Dromost Gate can still be opened. They could be doing it this very moment."

Chapter Three

Telea walked on the white sand beach as waves gently rolled ashore. The sun was low on the horizon, and she was alone. There were boats pulled up above the high tide line, but the night fishermen hadn't arrived yet. Not far away, she heard children laughing. She glanced that way, but tall coconut trees blocked her view of the village.

Walking towards the surf, she stopped as the first waves lapped over her bare feet. She stared out at the red sun as it sank to the edge of the world. There was a rocky promontory nearby they'd have to cross to get from the fishing village back to town. It would be best for her companions not to walk the path in full darkness. She'd have to fetch them from the village soon before full darkness fell.

As dark as Dromost. It was a common saying, but not true. Dromost was a world of perpetual twilight and a sky filled with clouds and lightning storms. There was no life. No plants. Just demons. A world full of demons. Telea's demon had told her this, and more. None, not a word of it, good.

And Ayja was there.

Telea knew there was no way her friend had survived this long. It had been weeks since the Dromost Gate had closed behind her. Even with Forsvar and Dromost, how could someone survive in that world? The Blade of Darra was with her, but what difference could one pyren make?

If the demons hadn't taken Ayja, hunger surely would have. When demons died in Dromost, they left behind no flesh to consume — they just dissolved into the sludge and soil of that world. The very thought of it horrified her.

No, there could be no survival. Ayja was dead.

Untying the single knot holding her silk scarf dress together, Telea pulled it from her body and threw it up onto the dry sand. Naked, she walked into the surf. The waves in the little bay were gentle, and she easily walked through them until she stood waist deep in the warm water.

18

Telea was a water singer and had always felt an affinity for the element. Not as comfortable as most Etheans, who'd grown up their entire lives on the islands, but comfortable nonetheless. Her mother had made certain that she'd learned to swim off the beaches near Aftokropoli.

Facing out to sea, Telea drew in a breath and sang the *Song of Hope*. She saw the aura of the song surround her, a gentle blue that was almost invisible in the late afternoon sunlight. She turned the song inward and felt its magic deep within her. Courage and hope filled her, body and soul.

She stopped singing after two verses and then plunged forward, diving under the surface. She kept herself underwater as long as she could, luxuriating in the feel of the water as it flowed over her body. Finally, she emerged, unable to hold her breath any longer. Her feet could no longer touch the bottom, but she was a strong swimmer and wasn't worried.

She pushed further out, swimming on the surface now. Then she stopped and trod water. It was utterly peaceful. There was nothing to disturb her here. She floated on her back for a time, propelling herself just enough to keep above water. She felt a calm she hadn't felt in a long time.

The sun sank into the horizon. She didn't want it to end but knew she had to leave. Slowly, deliberately, Telea swam for shore.

There were two figures there. Calen and Sindi, she realized. Telea saw the Landomeri woman point out at her, and then the two stripped naked and sprinted out into the surf. Telea heard their laughter as they splashed through the waves. Both could swim — neither well. The two Landomeri paddled towards Telea but stopped where they could still stand. Telea quickened her stroke and swam to them.

"We were wondering where you'd gone off to," Sindi said. They'd stopped just beyond where the tiny Landomeri woman could stand, and she paddled over to Calen and put her hand on his shoulder for support. Telea was taller than most women, and the water only lapped up to her shoulders.

"I was thinking about Ayja," Telea said. "I wanted to be alone for a little bit."

"Don't worry for her," Sindi said. "It does her no good. It does you no good."

"How can I not worry about her?" Telea asked.

"To worry about something you can't do anything about is a waste of your energy. It brings down your spirit. If Ayja is dead, she is with Helna now. If she is not, I fear for the demons who cross her."

"You're right, I suppose," Telea said. "It's hard to let go."

19

"We didn't want to let Orlos go off by himself," Calen said, "but it was the right thing to do. We're concerned for him, but we can't let it affect us."

"Knowing a thing and doing a thing are different," Telea said. "We should go to shore. It's getting dark." She said it for the benefit of the Landomeri. Her demon gave her the gift of darksight. It didn't turn night into day, but nearly so. "How fast can Orlos travel when he's in his spiridus form?"

"Not as fast as a horse can run, but he'll need little food and rest," Calen said. "And no one can see him to bar his travel."

"It's so hard to judge the distance," Telea said. "I imagine it will take him another week to reach the Great Salador Pass."

They'd dropped Orlos off on the coast of Belen before sailing south to the Ethean Islands. It had been a hotly disputed decision. Telea's mother, Unxusa, hadn't wanted to risk the journey to Belen in a damaged ship and with a decimated crew. Calen and Sindi didn't want to let Orlos make the journey without them. Telea had wanted to immediately go to the capital, Aftokropoli, to see what was happening there.

In the end, they'd let Orlos go. He was the only one who could cross the Great Salador Pass in the dead of winter. And he had to get word back to Salador if King Handrin and the Orb of Creation were to cross in the spring. The rest of them had sailed on the *Summer Swan* to the Ethean Islands. They would repair their ship, get supplies and money, and return to Belen as quickly as they could.

There'd been one other reason to head for Ethea as well. They had the summoner, Muaz, with them. He'd been the only person with enough knowledge of summoner runes to help them create a lock that would close the Dromost Gate forever. The entire journey to Ethea, and more time while there, Telea had worked with him creating the design for the lock. Now she knew the secrets of the gates as well as he did. She hoped.

Recapture the gate and lock it forever. It's all that matters.

They emerged from the water and shook the sand from their clothes. They had no towels, so put their clothes on wet. It didn't matter. They'd dry by the time they walked back to town.

"Where are Tharryl and Isibindi?" Telea asked.

"They went into the forest to find bananas," Sindi said as they walked along the beach. "He's crazy for them."

"He can have them for free at the lodge."

Sindi shrugged. "It's just an excuse to be alone with her."

Telea snorted. "What does she see in him? He's an ass."

"He's a big, bold, handsome ass. Some women like their men that way."

"Like you?" Telea asked with a smile.

"Ha! I like my men dark and brooding," Sindi replied, taking Calen's hand.

"We could talk about something else," he replied with a frown.

They made their way across the rocky promontory to the town beyond. There was a small bay there, with good anchorage for small ships like the *Summer Swan*. A fort guarded the entrance to the harbor, but other than that, the town was defenseless. The islanders lived in long, low houses built very close to the beach, but raised on stilts. More were built on the steep, wooded slopes behind the bay.

Telea had never lived in her mother's homeland and was continuously amazed by the sights and sounds of it. The jungle grew right up to the beach, more dense than any vegetation she'd ever seen in Belen. Wildflowers and fruits grew everywhere. So much so that it seemed one could live each day off of a short walk into the forest to forage.

The steep hill behind the town rose to towering cliffs, often shrouded by clouds. You could walk a few dozen stades and be surrounded by mist and rain, and then walk back down to sunshine all in a quarterday. The sounds were just as amazing as the sights. Every imaginable noise came from the forest — the constant chirp of insects and the songs of birds and monkeys calling to each other from the treetops, seemingly having conversations of their own.

It was a paradise she didn't want to leave but knew that she'd have to.

She walked with the two Landomeri down a dark path through the forest towards the torches lighting their lodge. Not far away, she saw the *Summer Swan* careened on the beach awaiting the morning tide when it would be launched again.

They walked up the steps of the lodge and around the patio that surrounded it. There was singing coming from the front of the lodge, and when they got there, Telea saw that an impromptu party had formed on the beach in front of the lodge. Tables were set with fruits and seafood, and the crew of the *Summer Swan* were gathered around, eating and drinking as they sat on mats set on the sand.

Four people, two women and two men, sang songs in Ethean as one of the men tapped on a drum with his hands. It was a joyful song about a happy fisherman and his mermaid wife. Telea knew it from her childhood in the Ethean embassy in Belen. She remembered always hoping she'd one day see a mermaid, and how crushed she'd been to learn they didn't exist.

She'd learned that fact from her mother — a woman who had little time for the frivolity of silly myths.

Telea saw her mother, who nodded in greeting and approached. "The work is finished," Unxusa said. "The *Summer Swan* is ready to set sail. I invited the crew to come and eat and celebrate."

"That was kind of you," Telea said. They spoke in Ethean, as had been their practice ever since she'd been a child.

"They've worked hard. It is good to reward those who serve under you. People will always do more for those they respect than for those they fear." She looked past Telea to Sindi and Calen and speaking in Saladoran — the Language of Song — said, "Come, eat. We must talk about our plans. The ship is ready to sail."

"Thank you," Sindi said. Together they all filled wooden platters with steamed crab and grilled fish as well as a salad of mixed fruits. They walked to the beach where a woven mat had been set out, and they all sat down there. A smiling crewmember brought them wooden cups of strong, alcoholic fruit punch.

For a little while, they ate and drank to the sounds of Ethean music and waves crashing in the background. The moon had risen full and shone brightly down upon the proceedings. The crew laughed and some of those who had already eaten danced to the music. And why shouldn't they be happy? How could someone be here and not be happy?

"You are certain you wish to go through with this?" Unxusa asked, looking at Telea. She spoke in Saladoran for the benefit of the two Landomeri.

Telea nodded, wiping her mouth on a cloth. "I have to. If the Saladoran King is coming to Belen, we must find out what is happening in the capital. Emperor Niktonas behaved very strangely, don't you think? We must see if the Saladorans will be well received."

Unxusa nodded. "It was unlike the emperor to order Forsvar to be seized, but remember, Kyvern Psertis sorely misled him. He thought Princess Ayja had come to overthrow him. Perhaps he's learned the truth by now."

"I still find it hard to believe," Telea replied. "I think there is something more going on."

"It was greed," Calen said. "Psertis, High Priest Kopanos, the emperor... they were all desperate for the power Forsvar would bring them. Power corrupts."

"It's true," Unxusa said, "but some of Niktonas's strange decisions came even before the presence of Forsvar was known."

"So I will go to the capital and see what I can discover," Telea said. "I'm not known well there. I won't be discovered."

"If you are, there could be a high price to pay," Unxusa said. "The *Summer Swan* sank two imperial galleys. The emperor will want blood."

22

"Which is why you shouldn't go," Telea said. "Let someone else command the *Summer Swan*."

"I'm not going to send you into danger while I sit on the warm summer sand," Unxusa scoffed. "I'll take you there. But how do you think you'll discover anything? You won't be allowed into court. You have no contacts there."

Telea paused a moment, wondering how much she should say. She'd learned very dark magic from her demon. She had *ways* to get information from people if she needed to. "Ayja and I learned a lot about magic in the time we were together," Telea said. "There are things I can do now that will let me learn more about the affairs of court."

"What things?" Unxusa asked, giving Telea an inscrutable look.

"It is best that I don't tell you," Telea said. "You can't speak of things you don't know."

"You fear the *Summer Swan* could be taken?"

No, I fear that you'll learn that I'm a powerful summoner. That you'll learn I have a demon imprisoned within me. That I'm far more dangerous than you could ever have imagined. "The *Swan* could be taken," she instead said. "Just trust in me. I can find out what is going on."

"And you?" Unxusa said to Calen and Sindi. "What will you do? Will you go with Telea, or will you remain here?"

"We will go with Telea," Sindi said. "We will pass ourselves off as her Koromoi guards."

"What about Sir Tharryl?"

"If it were up to him, he'd never leave Ethea," Calen said. "He was sent by King Handrin to protect Ayja and to guard Forsvar. Both are gone now. He has no attachments."

"There is little need for a professional soldier here, on this island," Unxusa said. "He could make his way to a bigger island and find service there. I'd even take him on my ship. He's strong and a good man in a fight."

"Not so easy to get along with," Telea said.

"I don't have problems with discipline on the *Swan*."

"The only reason he'd spend time at sea would be to follow Isibindi," Sindi said.

"I was going to send Isibindi with you," Unxusa said. "I want Telea to have another protector."

"Then Tharryl will insist on coming as well," Calen said. "I'm certain of it."

"Because he loves her so much he'd follow her to war?"

"Because he won't stay behind while a woman goes off to war."

The *Summer Swan* set off two days later laden with supplies and over half the crew new to her. Unxusa drilled her crew tirelessly as they made their way across the clear, shallow seas between the islands. They sailed and rowed for three days, arriving at a larger island with a vastly larger city.

The city was smaller than Aftokropoli, but still, a far larger city than Telea had expected. For some reason, she'd thought every Ethean island would be a quiet paradise like the one they'd just left. Of course, she should have realized it couldn't have been the case. Ethea was a powerful country, well, a powerful alliance, capable of challenging the Empire of Belen for control of the seas.

Several times the Belenese had attempted to add Ethea to their empire, only to have their fleets smashed and their hopes crushed. They were friendly towards each other now — a friendship built out of respect, mutual benefit, and the fact that neither could ever hope to conquer the other.

A castle guarded the harbor entrance — a narrow passage between the coast and ship-wrecking reefs — and another, larger castle protected the city. A massive wall of black rock surrounded the city. It seemed in good repair, although the forest did grow up to the very edge of it. Telea imagined it had not been deemed worth the effort to continuously cut back the rapid growing jungle. After all, Ethea had been at peace for many decades.

When they entered the city, Telea was just as surprised as she'd been when they entered the harbor. There were broad, paved streets and houses built of stone with thatched roofs. Beyond that, it seemed the jungle had invaded the city itself. Fruit trees grew everywhere, and wildlife seemed just as comfortable residing there as the people. A river and many canals cut through the city, and it seemed boats were the most popular form of transit.

"We will go to the council first," Unxusa said. "They wish to hear everything I've already told them from you. It will be a long day. Tomorrow we will shop. We must purchase proper Belenese clothing and equipment for you so that you don't stand out too much when you arrive in Aftokropoli."

It turned out to be much longer than the single day Unxusa had hoped for. It was a week before the council gave them leave to depart. They had grilled Telea on every aspect of her journey, from even before the crossing of the Great Salador Pass to the destruction of the Dromost Gate. Calen and Sindi were interrogated endlessly on the history of Landomere and Salador and everything they knew about Forsvar and the Orb of Creation. Tharryl, who hated every moment of the experience, was treated as if he was an official representative of King Handrin, and not a newly minted knight. It was a role he didn't enjoy.

"What do I know of court?" he asked that night as they gathered for dinner. "I met the king once. They acted as if I knew him well enough to wipe his arse."

The summoner, Muaz, was interrogated as well. The council wished to know everything he could tell them about Drommarian intentions and the various factions there. In the end, it was decided that Muaz would remain behind. He was not exactly a prisoner, but neither was he free.

The council officially dismissed Unxusa as Ambassador to Belen. They had no choice. She was also forbidden from returning to Belen for fear of escalating conflict with the empire. "And I won't return," she said to Telea. "Technically. If my feet don't touch Belenese soil, I haven't returned."

"I don't want you to get into trouble," Telea said.

"If they knew you were going, they'd forbid it as well. It must be done, though. Events are moving too quickly for us to wait any longer."

The following day they entered the city and went to the bazaar. Every imaginable good was for sale there, including items from Belen and every part of Ethea. Although bearing arms in the city was forbidden, it was not forbidden to purchase them. They bought a scale hauberk for Tharryl, as well as a heavy spear and an Ethean tulwar. He still had the light Drommarian axe he'd taken from the temple fight. Calen and Sindi both received mail haubergeons, Ethean longbows, and tulwars as well. Isibindi already had her own weapons and a mail haubergeon. They bought bolts of green silk to make matching kaftans so that the four might appear as proper guards for Telea, who would play the part of a wealthy Ethean merchant.

Walking through the bazaar was an odd experience for Telea. Belen was so diverse in cultures and races that she never felt out of place there. In Ethea, nearly everyone had the same ebony skin and long-limbed grace her mother had. Women wore their hair close-shaven, just as the men did. With her hair recently redone in dozens of braids and her lighter skin, Telea felt like everyone she passed gave her a second look. It was even more the case with Tharryl, Sindi, and Calen.

The two Landomeri embraced the attention, cheerfully greeting everyone, and doing their best to speak with them in the few Ethean words they spoke. Tharryl, taller than everyone they passed, drew more attention than the rest of them combined. He stood out the most and enjoyed it the least. Isibindi did her best to keep his mood light, but it was a daunting task.

There were a few Belenese merchants in the market. Olive oil, wine, and metal goods seemed to dominate their stalls. A few tried to engage with Telea and her party, but she steered them clear. What good would it do if word got back to Belen that companions of Princess Ayja had been seen in Ethea? And she knew that not all of the merchants were simple merchants. Some were eyes and ears for their empire.

Finally, after their extended delay, the *Summer Swan* set sail for the north. They stopped three times in Ethean ports over the next four days, before heading out into the deep green for the long passage to Belen. The late fall weather wasn't pleasant, and the xebec was pummeled by high seas day after day. The further north they sailed, the rougher the seas became until Telea could hardly bear it any longer. All she could think about were the white sand beaches of Ethea.

"How far from Belen are we?" Telea asked Induna as she walked onto the raised command deck one morning. The grizzled pilot seemed permanently affixed to the steering oar.

"One day less than yesterday, singer," he replied, barely sparing her a glance as he looked up into the ship's triangular sails. "The answer is always the same."

She gave him a smile. "Some days, we sail faster than others."

"Some days faster. Some days slower. My answer is still the same."

Telea looked out over the bow. "So one more day?"

"Was it two yesterday?"

"Yes."

"So, you have your answer."

Unxusa joined them on the command deck, a hot mug of bitter chaf in her hands. "How much longer, Induna?" she asked.

"I don't know. Ask your daughter."

Telea's mother gave her a quizzical expression. "Tomorrow," Telea said. "He's in a mood," she added.

"Dumb questions put me in a mood." He faced Unxusa and said, "You wished to land on a beach, but we can't do that if this weather holds. The surf is too heavy. We'll need a port."

"I don't want to enter a harbor," Unxusa said. "The *Summer Swan* will be recognized. I'm sure they've declared us pirates, or worse."

"Then we stay at sea for a few days until this clears," Induna said. "It's too bad your wizard friend is not with us, Telea. I liked her. She could calm the seas."

Telea looked out over the ocean. "I liked her as well." She faced him again. "How long will this weather hold?"

This time he gave no sarcastic response but stared up into the clouds overhead. "Weather comes in patterns," he said. "This one has several more days in it."

A few more days at sea. Telea groaned. She'd had enough of it. The Landomeri and Tharryl had as well.

"There is a place — a beach," Induna said. "Not far. With the wind out of the west like this, it will be in the lee. We could land there, perhaps. Most ships steer clear, though. It's a pirate haven."

"We don't need trouble," Unxusa said.

"Not many pirates in this season and in this weather," Induna said.

"We could take a look, at least, couldn't we?" Telea said.

Unxusa nodded. "Let's try it. We've been lucky so far and have seen no imperial ships. I want to be safe away before any spot us."

"Very well," Induna said. He shouted out orders to the crew and changed course as the sails were adjusted. The weather lessened during the night but was still rough. In the morning, Telea and her companions packed their gear and prepared to depart. They saw the shoreline of Belen now. Rocky and normally dry, the fall rains had drenched it. It was far, far different from the lush beaches of Ethea.

"Should we wear our armor?" Tharryl asked. For much of the journey, he'd been an unpleasant shade of green. Only in the past few days had he gained his sea legs. Just in time to land, Telea thought with some pleasure.

"Yes," Telea replied. "There is a town a day's walk from the beach we'll land upon. If you are to play the part of my bodyguards, you should be armed."

Induna brought the *Summer Swan* within two arrowflights of shore. There was a sharp promontory off the port bow, and he steered around it. Steep cliffs hid anything beyond from view. As they rounded the headland, a beach came into sight. There was a ship there, drawn high up on the sand. Too high to quickly launch.

"Who is it?" Telea asked. "It looks like another xebec."

"It is," Unxusa replied. "Which, to me, is not good news. The Belenese use galleys for war and sailing ships for trade. Xebecs are a blend of both. We Etheans like them, but so do pirates."

"I don't see anyone," Telea said.

Unxusa shook her head. "It's lost its mast. It might be a wreck. Look how high on the sand it is." She called up to a lookout high on the mainmast. "Do you see anything?"

"No, captain. No one there."

"What do you wish me to do?" Induna asked. "It will be a hard row, and harder still if we keep sailing down the coast."

27

"Take us in," Unxusa said.

"Sails down! Oars out!" Induna shouted as he brought the ship around and into the wind.

"I want four archers in the forecastle as soon as the sails are in," Unxusa shouted. She turned to Telea and said, "Gather your things. You'll go ashore soon. And Telea, there is no more embassy in the capital. There is no one you can go to for aid. I will land here in two months, and again in four. Be here if you wish to go home."

"Belen is my home," Telea said.

Unxusa shook her head. "Perhaps not any longer. We have not made any friends here by our actions. Be careful."

"I will, mother," Telea said. Unxusa offered her a stiff embrace, and then Telea ran to gather her pack. The ship was under oar now. Four to a side, each pulled by two rowers. It had nothing like the speed of a galley under oar, but the *Summer Swan* had a shallow draft and was unladen by cargo. They made good time even rowing into the wind and against the current.

Telea joined Sindi, Calen, Isibindi, and Tharryl at the bow. All wore their kaftans and armor and had packs on their backs. Four Ethean archers stood there as well, their long black and red bows held ready. They scanned the rocky coastline for any sign of danger.

The seas were rough but not as bad in the lee of the headland. The rowers pulled for shore, but then, just outside the breakers, Induna called out, "Starboard oars full stop. Bring her around. Landing stern first."

As she ship heeled about and the four Ethean archers ran down the deck to the sterncastle, Tharryl said, "What's happening?"

"Let's go," Telea said. "We're landing stern first. It will make getting off the beach much easier once we're gone." The five of them made their way down the deck, carefully avoiding the hard-working rowers. The ship rocked as they made their way through the heavy surf.

"It will be a wet landing," Unxusa said to them. "We can't risk breaching on the beach. You'll go over the rails where you are."

Telea heard the keel scrape on the sand. She looked over the rail as a wave swept past them and felt a moment's trepidation for what they were about to do. They'd be soaked to the skin getting ashore. The ship lurched, and she grabbed the rail to keep from falling.

"Now!" Unxusa called from above them. "You must go now." She spoke in Saladoran, and at her first word, Tharryl was over the rail, leaping into the surf. One after another, the others followed them, Calen, Sindi, and Isibindi doing their best to keep their bows above their heads.

The water was waist deep, but as soon as she was in it, a wave struck Telea from behind, drenching her. She struggled forward, her kaftan and clothing wet and heavy. The fall water was still warm, but the wind chilled her to the bone. Finally, they dragged themselves from the sea. Behind them, the *Summer Swan* struggled to pull through the breakers. Telea spotted her mother at the stern rail and gave her one last wave goodbye.

"There is someone in the beached ship," Sindi said.

Telea looked towards the vessel, but a dune partially blocked her view. "You're certain?" she asked.

"I'm certain. He was careful to remain hidden."

"They could be here to escape the storm," Calen said.

All five now looked in the direction of the beached ship. "Bad men," Isibindi said. She'd only learned a few Saladoran words since she'd met Tharryl and the others. When she spoke, it was a mishmash of Saladoran, Belenese, and Ethean. "They no good."

"I agree," Tharryl said. He walked a few strides up the dune. "They would have greeted us otherwise."

"Maybe they fear us," Calen said.

"Then they would have run. They're up to no good."

Telea looked around for some way out of their predicament. The beach was half a stade wide and hemmed in by rocky cliffs on either side. The only way out was to walk past the other ship and up a steep slope beyond. "We don't have much choice, and we have to get up to the top of the cliff before we can get out of here." The *Summer Swan* was well off the beach now. If they called it back, would they even be able to get on board again?

"It's more than one man," Tharryl said. "They're coming out."

Chapter Four

Orlos ran through the Great Forest of Landomere shrouded by his spiridus cloak. His feet flew over the ground as he ran for Belavil and home. All around him white everbloom grew, their fragrance floating through the air and filling his lungs. Three spirit birds flew with him, their silver wings flashing in the dappled sunlight shining through the canopy of giant Landomeri oaks.

Little more than a week had passed since he'd left King Handrin and Sir Nidon at the Dragon Pass. He'd spent nearly the entire journey under his spiridus cloak, racing unseen across the Saladoran countryside. As he ran, he hoped the Lady of the Forest might appear to him. She'd once been his mother's friend, Hadde, but had given her life rescuing the infant Orlos and Ayja from mercenary raiders. The Great Spirit of Landomere had transformed Hadde into the ethereal Lady after her death. Now the physical embodiment of the Great Spirit, her presence caused Orlos's heart to soar every time she was near.

He would see her soon enough; he was certain. Maybe he'd search for her after visiting his family for a time. His family. He smiled. What a shock they'd get when he appeared! He wasn't supposed to come back until late spring, after the snows melted on the East pass.

Time meant little to a spiridus, and the arrowflights quickly passed under his feet. The sun was low on the horizon as he ran through the gates of Belavil and started up the winding roads to the plateau where his family lived. He was surprised at how much Belavil resembled the places he'd visited in Belen. He saw Belenese architecture everywhere now that he knew what to look for. All around him stood tall stone pillars and graceful arches. All ruins, though, destroyed centuries ago when the veden had laid waste to the spiridus city.

No one saw him under his cloak, and the spirit birds had flown off as he'd approached the open gates. Open gates in that there were no actual gates at all. Just a tall arch sculpted with vines and leaves in relief.

30

Landomere didn't rely on walls and gates for defense. Its defense relied instead upon the vast forest itself and on the rangers and hunters who lived there. And on the Spirit of the Forest as well. In truth, no enemy had reached Belavil since the veden attacked so long ago.

Orlos didn't feel hunger while shrouded in his spiridus cloak, not real hunger at least. Even so, the scent of dinners cooking wafted out onto the street, making him realize just how long it had been since he'd last eaten. He hoped his family hadn't yet dined. Or that they weren't visiting friends somewhere else in the city.

He dashed past the four wardens guarding the terrace gardens. There were few true soldiers in Landomere as there was little need for them. His stepfather, Kael, commanded those in Belavil. Kael had been one of the mercenaries who'd kidnapped Orlos and Ayja as infants, but he'd fallen in love with Maret and helped in their rescue. They had three children together — Orlos's half brother and sisters.

Orlos's father by nature was Earl Waltas, a terror of a man who'd raped his mother and mutilated her face with a knife. She'd survived the attack and had given birth to Orlos. Waltas had lived only hours past the attack, hunted down and killed by Hadde.

In truth, Orlos had a third father — his namesake, Orlos the Ancient, a spiridus who'd lived in Salador since before the destruction of Belavil. The ancient spiridus had saved Maret's life after the attack and transferred his immortal spirit into Orlos before passing away.

Orlos ran through gardens that in Belen would have been filled with olive trees, but here were covered in everbloom. The white flowers grew amidst the fallen columns and stone blocks that had once been temple buildings. In summer, there'd be vegetables as well, but it was winter now, and everything was out of season.

Bright lights glowed in the windows of his home, causing his heart to soar. *They're home!* Letting his spiridus cloak flow away from him, Orlos threw open the front door and rushed into the entranceway. Off to his right, in the great room, he heard laughter and then Kael's voice calling out, "Who's there?"

Smiling, Orlos stepped through the archway, suitably pleased by the clamor that resulted at his appearance. His family had guests over for dinner. He recognized the Saladoran family that King Handrin had rescued from Del-Oras. Tomin was a young baron, and his wife Wenla and daughter Varen were both elementars.

The guests smiled at his sudden appearance, but his family raised an uproar. His mother shrieked with pleasure, Kael gave him a hearty, "Hello!", while his twin sisters shouted in unison, "Orlos is back!" The eight-year-olds leaped off their chairs and dashed to embrace Orlos. They were followed by his mother, only heartbeats behind.

"How are you back so quickly?" his mother asked.

"I had to come back and bring a message to the king."

"A good message?"

"Good and bad," Orlos said, struggling to keep the frown from his face.

"Isn't the pass closed?" Kael asked.

"To anyone but a spiridus it is. And even then, I almost didn't make it. The Dromost Gate is closed."

"That's wonderful!" his mother exclaimed.

"It is," Orlos agreed, "but there's more to be done before we're safe."

"And the bad news?" she asked, concern crossing her face.

"Should wait until later," Orlos said.

"Very well, then," she said with a frown. But then she smiled and tousled his hair. "I'm so glad you're here!"

"It is good to see you again," Sir Tomin said. "My family won't forget the role you played in rescuing us."

Orlos tried to wave off their thanks. "It was King Handrin and Sir Rayne who saved you."

"But you warned us of those Inquisitors. Who knows what might have happened if they'd attacked? In any case, we are very happy to see you safe at home. I think, though, we should depart and give you time to be with your family."

"No! Don't leave," Orlos said. "You are welcome to stay." Orlos glanced at the table and said, "Just squeeze over a little bit and give me some room at the table. I'm starving!"

"Yes, you must stay," his mother said to their guests. "After all, this is your farewell dinner." She turned to Orlos and said, "They're going to Sal-Oras. King Handrin wishes to assemble every elementar there so that they can learn from each other. They're going to start a college of magic."

"I have some things I can share about magic," Orlos said, taking the chair Kael offered him. "Apparently magic works very well in circles, or something like that." And so, for a quarternight, Orlos regaled them with stories of everything he'd seen in Belen, leaving out the worst of it to spare his younger brother and sisters. He'd tell his mother and Kael of those things later.

Finally, well after his sisters had been put to bed and his brother had fallen asleep with his head on the table, their guests departed, amazed at the stories he'd told. Kael easily picked up Melas and carried him up to his bed while Orlos and his mother cleared the table. They were halfway through when his mother quietly said, "There was more to your story."

"The food was good," he said, trying to smile.

"You don't have to talk about it," she said. There was a brief pause before she asked, "What was it that bothered you?"

"She's gone," Orlos blurted out. "Ayja's gone."

Suddenly his mother was holding him and he was bawling uncontrollably. Sobs wracked his body as he sank to the floor, his mother cradling him as she hadn't since he was a child. All his grief, pent up through weeks and weeks of travel, rushed out of him in a flood. He wanted it to stop, but it was beyond his control. She was gone, lost in a world of demons. Ayja was dead.

Vaguely, Orlos heard one of his sisters say, "What's wrong with Orlos?" and his mother reply, "He had some very bad news. Now you go back to bed. No, no arguments." Then two pairs of skinny arms wrapped around him. "We love you, Orlos. We're glad you're home again."

Orlos's face was buried in his mother's neck. He only nodded in reply as his mother shooed his sisters off to bed. Then, after some time had passed, he told his mother the other parts of the story, the parts he'd only hinted at during dinner. His mother was strong. Orlos had always known that. How could she not be, having survived all she'd gone through? Through his story, she never shed a tear, but supported him and encouraged him the entire time.

"I have to go back," he concluded. They still sat in the same place on the cold tiles of the kitchen floor. The room was warm, though, heated by the cooking fires from dinner. "King Handrin is crossing the East Pass in the spring, and I'm to be his guide."

His mother touched the side of his face. "You've done enough, Orlos. Stay in Landomere."

He shook his head. "I have to go. The Dromost Gate must be locked. We are all in peril until it is."

"You aren't an elementar. This is a task for others."

"It will be safer this time. I'll be with King Handrin and Champion Nidon. They're taking the Army of Salador over the mountains."

"And when this task is done you'll come home for good?"

"For good. I'll never leave Landomere again."

She smiled. "That's what I wanted to hear."

"I'm sorry for looking like such a fool, crying on the floor like this," Orlos said, glancing around the kitchen.

"There's nothing wrong with being sad. Only a fool would say that a man can't cry."

Orlos stood and helped his mother to her feet. She was still a young woman, only fifteen when he was born, although the scars that crisscrossed her face made her age hard to read.

"You've had a long journey, Orlos. Why don't you go to bed?"

"The dishes aren't done."

"When did you start caring about dishes? I'll make Kael do them."

Orlos laughed. "Very well. I think I'll go out and walk the city for a little. I've been away so long."

"It's very late, Orlos. Nobody will be out."

"I don't mind. I don't really want to see anyone. I just want to see home."

"Take a cloak. They're by the front door."

"I know, mother," Orlos said with a smile. He gave her another hug. "Thank you. I love you."

"I love you too, my son."

With a last hug, Orlos strode down the hall and, taking a green cloak from a peg by the door, headed out into the chilly winter air. With his spiridus vision and the starlight, the darkness meant little to him. Colors faded to shades of gray, but otherwise, he could see nearly as well as during the day. One difference, though, was that the white everbloom shined under his spiridus vision, giving off an aetherial glow.

For a time, he walked amongst the glowing blooms, slowly making his way to the old, fallen temple that dominated the plateau. Then he saw the tunnel, and a chill crept up his spine. Here was the source of nightmares that had driven him from the borders of Landomere on several occasions. Nightmares that had made life in Landomere nearly unbearable for the past year. Only free of the Great Forest had he found peace, but always he was drawn back again.

Just months ago, he'd found the source of his nightmares, the Emerald Prison. Trapped in the stump of the destroyed Emerald Tree were thousands of spiridus, imprisoned by the veden centuries ago. Curious, he walked closer to the tunnel entrance. Two wardens stood guard there, but before they spotted him, Orlos drew his spiridus cloak around him.

Over dinner, his mother had told him that the Emerald Prison had changed. The thousands of skeletons piled on the floor had been removed and buried in the Great Forest. Beneath the skeletons, they'd discovered the shards of the Emerald Tree. Some dreamed the tree might one day be rebuilt from the shards, but no one had any idea how it might be accomplished.

Orlos paused just twenty strides from the entrance. His heart pounded in his chest, his thoughts filled with his memory of the place. He'd nearly

34

died there. Not just from being trapped in a tiny crevasse he'd attempted to crawl through, but by the prison itself. The evil of the veden magic had drained his life from him and pulled his spiridus from his body.

Before he knew what he was doing, Orlos crept past the guards and down the stairs. *I'll just take a look.* He remembered the spiridus, trapped in the stump of the tree. Would he be able to see them again? He was stronger now. The prison wouldn't be able to draw him in like it had before. He hoped.

The tunnel was pitch black, but Orlos's spiridus vision let him see vague shapes. The prison chamber would be lit by the stump's vivid red light. Unlit brass lanterns hung on the tunnel walls, but he passed them by. He had no tinder in any case.

Down he plunged, deeper and deeper under the crag of Belavil, under the Temple of Helna. That was where he was, wasn't he? Under the ruins of the Goddess's temple. Dromost and Forsvar had their own temples, across the East Pass. But Helna's was here.

Orlos passed the places where rockfalls had once blocked the tunnel. Masons and miners had cleared the passage and restored it so that, in the darkness, he couldn't even tell where it had been broken. Then, finally, at the end of a long passage, he saw the red glow of the Emerald Prison. Orlos stopped then, uncertain. What if he couldn't stop himself? Nobody knew he was here. There would be no Telea to save him with her singing. He turned to leave but halted after taking only a single step.

I have to see it. I have to see the spiridus.

Slowly, trembling, Orlos made his way to the end of the passage. He steeled himself against what he might see, but as the chamber slowly came into view, it was nothing like he'd seen before. Only the glimmering red stump remained the same. Sparkling green light shone down from the ceiling

Above him stretched a canopy of emerald branches and leaves. The trunk might be gone, but the branches clinging to the ceiling gave off a bright green light that drove back the red glow of the stump. Instead of being drawn to the stump, Orlos's eyes were drawn to the ceiling. *If only the tree were whole! What a sight it would be!*

The bones were gone. They'd once been piled so deep you could walk across them without touching the floor. Instead, the floor was a beautiful mosaic of swirling tiles all in greens and earth tones. It was as amazing as any of the art he'd seen in Belen. Along the walls, carefully arranged, were the shards of the emerald tree. Some pieces were as big as split wood for the fireplace, while others were as tiny as gems that might be strung on a necklace.

Finally, Orlos's eyes went to the Emerald Prison. In all the restored beauty of the chamber, it stood out as an ugly red scar. He felt drawn to it, but not in the same way he had been before. The last time he'd been out of his mind, pummeled by nightmares and overwhelmed by the evil of the place. Now he felt at peace — more in control of himself.

He crossed the chamber, carefully approaching the jagged, broken stump. There was motion within it — swirling lights whirling through the red stone. A shiver ran down his spine. *The spiridus.*

Stopping five strides away, Orlos took a knee. He didn't trust himself to go any closer. What if he touched it? Would he be drawn into the prison? As he stared at it, Orlos's vision seemed to plunge deeper and deeper into the ruby light. It seemed almost as if the spiridus were all around him.

How could it be so deep? The stump was only a few strides across. And yet there were thousands and thousands of spiridus within it. How could it be so large and yet so small at the same time? It made no sense. The dimensions were all wrong. As it came to him, the world spun wildly, and Orlos sat heavily, clapping his hands to the side of his head. He closed his eyes.

The prison isn't here. The spiridus aren't here. They're in Dromost. The Emerald Prison is a gate. Telea had told him that before. The veden had opened the gate with the blood of the Landomeri people. Their spiridus had been banished through the gate. Telea had said that the gate could be opened again — that the spiridus could be freed.

If that was so, could Ayja also be saved? If she still lived, could she escape through the Emerald Prison? No, not an Emerald Prison — an Emerald Gate.

What had Telea said? *A chorus could free the spiridus.* But could they free Ayja as well? How would Ayja even find the gate or know to go there? Telea was the only one who could answer his questions, but she'd gone to Ethea. How would he find her?

Orlos opened his eyes and stared back into the Emerald Gate. All these fantasies were based on the idea that Ayja was even alive. He knew Telea said it was impossible, but he couldn't give up hope. *She can find a way. Ayja is alive. She has Forsvar and Dromost. She has to be alive.*

Much later, he departed the tunnels under the ruined Temple of Helna and headed for home. Smoke still rose from the chimney, and he wondered who could be up. He opened the door as quietly as he could manage, but it still creaked on its hinges.

"Orlos?" Kael asked from the sitting room.

"Yes." He walked to the room and stopped in the arched doorway. There were three couches there. Day beds, really. It was an extravagance

36

few Landomeri had. They weren't without purpose. His family often hosted leaders of the community when important matters had to be discussed.

Now the room was occupied only by Kael and his mother. They'd pulled one of the couches close to the fire and sat under a blanket, the yellow light of the flames dancing on their faces. "Why are you up? What's wrong?" Orlos asked, but then he saw the tears on his mother's face. "What's wrong?" he asked.

"Nothing," his mother said just as Kael said, "She's very upset."

His mother wiped the tears from her face as Orlos approached. He knelt on the floor next to her. "What's wrong, mother?"

"Nothing, Orlos."

"She's upset about Ayja," Kael said.

Maret shot him a glare. "You don't have to say everything, you know. You can keep some things private."

Instead of speaking, Orlos leaned close and drew his mother into a hug. "She is a hero," he said. "She closed the Dromost Gate."

"I know, but I still want her here. I so desperately wanted to see her again. To hold her again." She let him go. "I wish you'd stopped here before going to Belen. You don't know what it did to me that you departed on such a dangerous journey without seeing me."

"I'm sorry, mother," Orlos said, a wave of guilt washing over him, "but the East Pass was about to close. We had to beat the snow."

"Don't do that to me again, Orlos. I can't take it."

"I do have to go again, mother. I told you so earlier."

"In the spring, though, right?"

He paused a moment. He had to find Telea. He had to get word to her. *How much time did Ayja have? Did she have any time at all?*

"Right, Orlos? Not until spring?"

He nodded. "A month at least. The worst of winter is on the pass. I don't even think I could cross it right now. I'll stay and study the Emerald Tree. I'll seek guidance from the Great Spirit."

"I worry for you, Orlos. I couldn't bear to lose you."

"I'll always come home to you. Don't worry. I'll always come home."

Chapter Five

Ayja awoke in complete darkness, buried in a tomb of her own making. With the slightest flick of the aether, she made a flame appear. Stone pressed in all around her, barely giving her room to move. Her stomach rumbled as she scrunched herself into a sitting position. When had she last eaten? How long had she been in Dromost? Weeks? A month? Time had no meaning here. There was no sun. There was no day. Just dismal, unchanging twilight.

Reaching to her side, she fumbled for her clay canteen. Besides Forsvar and Dromost, it was her most precious possession. She pulled the stone stopper and drank deeply. Possessions... besides what she'd brought with her to Dromost, she had only two. The canteen and the silver ring she wore on a chain around her neck. The two were as necessary for survival as the Gifts of the Gods.

She'd made the canteen from Dromost clay and her elemental power. It wasn't pretty, but it worked. She was happy for the time she'd spent making stoneware back in the East Teren. It had made making the canteen far easier. She'd had little time for trial and error. The canteen hung from a braided cord made from Darra's tattered Kaftan, or what remained of it at least.

She'd crafted the silver ring from a clasp taken from her armor and forged it with her magic in the heat of molten rock. She'd bound a working to it to keep the air she breathed clean. It had been a desperate, difficult effort, but one she'd had to complete. Without it, she surely would have perished. Nearly every time demons had attacked before, she'd lost her focus on her working and breathed the poison air of Dromost. And the demons attacked all the time.

Ayja drank again. At least for a little while, her stomach would have the illusion of being full. It wouldn't last. She could drink, and she could breathe, but there was nothing in Dromost for her to eat. If not for the life force Darra stole from demons and transferred to her, she would already be dead.

38

It was time to get moving. For whatever reason, the demons couldn't find her when she slept. She was invisible to them. At least her soul was. But awake, her soul was a beacon, summoning the demons to slay her. She reached toward the rock that sealed her hiding place. She'd used her magic to fuse it in place so that no demon could easily push it aside. Twisting the aether, she broke the rock loose.

Crawling free, she dragged herself out the narrow opening and under the livid purple and green skies of Dromost. The cloud-filled sky gave no indication of the passage of time. Sudden nausea overcame her, and she bent double and retched. Water and bile splattered the ground, soaking into the dusty soil. Pain gripped her stomach, a stomach that had known no food for too long.

Not again, she thought as she stood and leaned against the rock face. She'd been sick too often since entering Dromost. Had some poison or disease entered her that Darra's touch could not detect? He'd healed her of injury many times since they'd arrived. It always restored her strength, but then the nausea would come again.

She glanced around. Where was he? Fear gnawed at her. Had he gone hunting? She didn't fear for him, or not much, at least. The demons, to their misfortune, tended to ignore him until it was too late. With no soul, he had nothing the demons desired. But they had something he wanted — the life force keeping Ayja alive.

She, on the other hand... the demons wanted her. And now that she was awake, they'd sense her presence and come for her. Again and again, always the same. It never ended. Ayja knew she wouldn't last a day without Darra.

Ayja drew Dromost from her belt and started upslope, hoping to get a better view. They'd kept to the mountains, hoping that they might keep better hidden there. Hoping also that there might be fewer demons. She wasn't certain if the second was true. There were demons everywhere. They took all shapes and forms. Some were grotesque misshapen combinations of different beasts as if some madman had taken parts of many creatures and randomly assembled them. Others were sleek and beautiful serpents. Still, others looked like plants but weren't. She'd learned her lesson. If it looked alive, it wanted to devour her.

Higher on the slope now, Ayja hid behind a rock and looked down the valley behind her. She saw her hiding place and would reveal herself if Darra appeared. He had to come soon. The demons sometimes arrived just heartbeats after she awoke.

She caught a glimpse of movement in the rocks below her sleeping place. Her hopes that it was Darra were dashed the moment she saw them. *Imps. Poison imps.* Like all imps, they were small and walked on two legs. Poison imps had short, bowed legs and long forearms ending in curved hooks. As they scampered forward, they propelled themselves with their arms just as much as with their legs.

What made them fearsome, besides their speed, was the long, jointed tail curving forward over their backs. It ended with a long stinger oozing with venom. They latched onto their prey with the front claws and then hung on as their stingers struck over and over. She'd seen it. One had leaped onto Darra's back and struck him five times. The dagger-like strikes had done him greater harm than the poison, which hadn't affected his undead flesh.

Ayja shrank back behind the boulder, for all the good it would do. Hiding meant nothing. The demons *always* knew where she was.

Running wasn't an option. Some demons were slow, but not imps. They were fragile, at least. A single strike from Dromost would destroy one. Her fire would ravage them as well. She had a better weapon, though. Ayja pulled the cork from her canteen and took a big pull. The closest imp was only some thirty strides away.

She dropped her canteen and felt a tug on her shoulder as the strap took its weight. Then she cleared her voice and sang...

I sing a song of light
I sing of dark dispelled
I sing of life awakened
I sing of danger quelled

Silver light streamed out from her in every direction. She touched her well of power and added its magic to the song, strengthening it and projecting it towards the imps. The first imps bounded into the light and screamed their infernal agony. Light flashed, white fire flared, and they were reduced to ash.

The death of their companions did nothing to deter the remaining three imps. They charged up the slope, arms outstretched as if to embrace her. Ayja held Dromost behind her, ready to swing, but doubting she would need it. She stepped out from behind the rock and strode closer to the onrushing imps. Her music engulfed them, and they too were reduced to ash. She finished her verse and let the song fade from her lips. Not all demons were so easily slain. The more powerful could resist the *Song of Light*.

A hot breeze flowed down the valley scattering the imp ash. It had been easy enough. But she'd scarcely awakened, and this had only been the first attack. The day was young.

Ayja turned at a sound behind her. A dark shape flew at her, wings wide, long talons held before it. She swung wildly with Dromost, striking the demon at the very moment it slammed into her. Thrown from her feet, Ayja tumbled down the slope. She heard the snap as her arm broke, and Dromost flew from her grasp. Searing white pain flowed over her as she rolled, and her head struck a rock. Her world spun.

The demon, a feathered serpent the size of a large dog, lay crumpled on the mountain slope some twenty strides from her. It righted itself, but one wing was broken and torn. It faced her and gave an angry hiss from its beak.

Ayja tried to rise but fell to her knees. The pain from her fractured arm was unbearable. Blood dripped over her wrist. Ayja reached for the aether, but she couldn't focus her mind. The strands of magic swirled all around her, but she couldn't touch them.

The demon righted itself, raising itself on its serpent hind legs and the wing claws of its unbroken wing. Dragging its broken limb, the demon approached. Desperately, Ayja looked for Dromost, but it was nowhere to be seen.

"I sing a song of light," Ayja started, but there was no music in it. There was no *song*.

The demon was only five strides from her. It hissed as it stared at her with malevolent red eyes. She staggered to her feet, her vision slightly clearer now.

"Dromost take you, demon," Ayja muttered. She punched herself in her broken arm. A spike of pain shot through her skull, and then the world erupted in brilliant silver light. Her pain and fear left her, replaced by anger and the power of raw aether.

The demon threw itself at her — its jagged beak open wide and talons grasping for her. Ayja leaped forward to meet it. Grasping raw aether in her good left hand, she jammed her fist down the demon's throat.

With a primal cry, she unleashed her power within the beast. The explosion ripped the demon's head from its body and sent Ayja flying. She fell hard, but there was no pain. Only anger. She stood and unleashed a blistering bolt of power into the dead demon, shredding its still form.

"More!" she shouted. "Where are you? I'm ready to die! Are you?"

A figure ran towards her from above. She saw the brilliant display of aether and launched another bolt at it. Lightning crackled but then was torn to shreds by the attacker's shield. She poured more power into it but could make no headway against the creature's potent defense.

"Ayja! Stop!"

She drew more power, but then paused and drew a deep breath. She'd drawn tremendous power from her well, and her breath heaved at the effort. Still, the attacker came on.

"My queen! It's me, Darra!"

Darra. The Blade of Darra. He stood twenty strides from her, Forsvar blazing with its argent power.

Ayja lowered her hand and fell to her knees. "I've lost Dromost," she said.

Darra ran up to her. "I'm sorry," he said. "My hunt took me far from you."

"My arm is broken," she said, clutching it as her silver fire fled. Waves of pain threatened to overwhelm her. Darra caught her as she sagged and helped her sit with her back to a large rock.

"We have little time," he said as he unfastened the buckles on the front of her scale hauberk. "Demons are coming. They know of us."

"What do you mean?"

"Easy, now," he said. "I must see your wound." Gingerly, he pulled the hauberk from her, but even then, the pain nearly caused her to faint. She wanted to vomit but had nothing in her.

Blood covered her arm, the green silk of her shirt sleeve completely soaked through. Hidden by the sleeve, her arm canted at an ugly angle, the bone pushing at the fabric. "I'm sorry for this," Darra said as he tore her sleeve open. Ayja looked away before he exposed the wound.

"They know of us," Darra said again. Ayja felt him pull at her arm. There was an instant of pain, but then warmth flowed over her arm, and the pain vanished. She gasped with relief.

"One of the demons spoke to me," Darra said. "I heard it in my mind. It offered to feed me many spirits if I would give Forsvar to its master, although it didn't know the shield's name. It asked for Dromost as well."

Ayja looked at her arm. Darra still held it. It was whole now, and there was a scar where a jagged wound once was. She shuddered at the thought that a bone had once protruded there.

The demons rarely spoke. Well, it wasn't really speech. Some of them could reach into her mind and project their thoughts there. Some used their thoughts as a form of attack, but none had been able to break through the barriers of her memory walk. And Darra's soulless mind seemed to be unassailable to them.

"It spoke of a master?"

"And I fear they have some structure — some organization." He released her arm. "You lost Dromost?"

She pointed up the slope to where the flying demon had struck her. "Over there. I dropped it when my arm was broken."

42

"Put on your hauberk, my queen," Darra said. "I'll find it."

Ayja stood and made a fist with her right arm. There was no pain. Darra had healed it completely. *If only Telea had taught me to heal.* It was a foolish thought, she knew. Telea had explained it to her. To learn the *Chant of Healing* would have required her to learn Drommarian, and there just hadn't been enough time.

Pulling on her hauberk, Ayja scoured the skies for any sign of flying demons and then looked down the valley to see if any others approached. Tightening her belt, she went to help Darra find the Godhammer. As she walked, she refastened the buckles on her armor.

"Here," Darra said, raising Dromost. He approached and gave both Gifts of the Gods to her. "We shouldn't leave you without Forsvar again. You must always have both on you."

"I don't know if I like the idea of you hunting without one of them, at least."

Darra shook his head. "Forsvar makes my hunting more difficult, my queen. When I get close, they sense the Godshield's presence."

Ayja drank from her canteen. "You've restored me, Darra. Thank you once again." She swished the nearly empty canteen. "Which way? We must find more water."

"I think it's time we leave the mountains," he said. "I'm afraid that we might get trapped in a valley. I think they'll search for us in larger numbers now."

"What happened to the demon who spoke to you?"

"I slew him and took his life force. He healed you."

"How strong are you now?"

"Strong enough, my queen. I can heal you, or give you more strength if need be."

"Your magic sustains me, Darra. But I am so hungry all the time. And I still get sick."

"The only way to save you is to escape this world."

Ayja shook her head as they started down the valley. She was so tired. No, not tired. She felt hollow. Weak for lack of food. Even with the strength Darra shared with her, constant hunger still consumed her. How long could she go like this? "I can barely survive, let alone even think of how to escape. I fight only to live. Tell me more of what the demons said to you."

"It was a poor offer," Darra said. "Their souls mean nothing to me. I can't feel them or touch them. It's only their strength I want. And even then, there's only so much I can take."

"When we rest, I will try to teach you to create a well of power again," Ayja said, carefully picking her way downslope. Unable to eat, her sleep only restored a tiny fraction of her well of power. Not a day went by without her silently thanking Telea for teaching her how to craft one within her memory walk. Without it, and the life force Darra poured into it each day, she would have died shortly after their arrival. She was totally dependent on the pyren, but each time he gave her strength he was diminished. If he had a well of power of his own, it would allow him to feed her and to have a full store of life force for himself.

"We've tried, my queen," he said. "I don't think it's possible."

"We'll try again." They had one more steep descent to make, and then the land would flatten out below them, for a few arrowflights at least. She was about to start forward when she saw movement in the ravine below. A centipede-like demon crawled up the rocks. Only this one was twenty strides long. "Demon," she said, stepping back. "A huge one."

"One?" Darra asked.

"One that I saw. Coming this way."

"Will you sing?"

Ayja nodded. "Take Dromost. I can't sing and fight at the same time." She traded the Godhammer to him for her mother's sword and backed away from the edge.

Ayja raised Forsvar. She heard the clack and scrape of the demon's claws as it pulled itself up the cliff. They were a few strides from the edge. Not far at all. The demon would come upon them quickly.

The demon's hideous insect head appeared over the edge. It had four eyes spaced evenly around a mouth with four mandibles. Layer after layer of teeth filled the creature's maw. It paused for only a heartbeat and then lunged at Ayja.

"I sing a song of light—"

The magic of her song struck the demon a physical blow, driving it back. It raised itself high in the air, its first six rows of claws flailing high above her. Unlike the imps and other small demons, this one wasn't instantly destroyed by the power of her song. Instead, the argent light burned at the creature's flesh, searing it and driving it back.

Darra ran forward. He held Dromost two-handed, and while Ayja distracted the demon, he landed a crushing blow on its back. The demon twisted violently at the blow, and Darra was knocked down by one of its flailing legs. He rolled and leaped back to his feet as the demon turned to face him.

As the demon gathered itself to strike the pyren, Ayja advanced on it, still singing the *Song of Light*. She let the music support itself, not using any power from her well to strengthen it. Life energy was too precious to use unless she had to.

44

The demon quailed as she closed on it. One of its eyes burst, and the legs on the left side of its body began to smoke. It wailed in pain, but before it could flee, Darra ran up to it and struck it another two-handed blow. The demon's segmented carapace cracked, and dark blood spouted from the wound. Again he struck it, breaking more of its hard outer shell.

It could take no more. The demon threw itself from the cliff edge, tumbling out of sight. "After it," Darra called out. "We need its life force."

Ayja ran to the edge and saw the demon writhing on the ground, thirty strides below her. It was wounded, but not mortally. Darra scrambled down the cliff near her, but the demon would right itself and flee long before he could get there. Without another thought, Ayja threw herself from the cliff. Twisting the aether, she caused the wind to catch her and deposit her near the demon.

"Here!" she called out to the demon. "I'm right here."

The demon righted itself and charged her. She raised Forsvar and sang.

Her magic struck the demon, but its momentum drove it forward. Ayja slammed Forsvar into the demon's head. She heard mandibles snap on the Godshield as the impact rocked her back on her feet. She lost her song as she recoiled.

The demon reared for another strike. Again Ayja sang. The demon screeched out in pain, drawing away from her, unable to bring itself to attack through the light. She backed it against the cliff and it twisted. Its forelegs grasped the cliff face, ready to climb away. Ayja stepped even closer, her song covering the entirety of the creature now.

From the rocks above, Darra leaped atop the demon's back. He didn't swing Dromost; instead, he clutched at the demon's carapace with his hands. In the aether, Ayja saw the magic in his touch as he drew the life force from the beast.

The demon slowed. Still, it turned on Darra. Ayja ceased her song and dashed forward. "Here! Here!" she shouted. She hammered its head with the Godshield. It reeled back, and then its legs gave out under it, and it fell limp to the ground.

"I have it now," Darra said.

The demon twitched under Darra. Several of its legs still moved, but try as it might, it couldn't rise. Finally, it lay still. Almost immediately, the demon's flesh began to rot and slough off. Darra leaped free and took Ayja by the hand. Life force rushed into her — the pleasure of it rushed down her spine. She let his power fill her limbs and then directed the rest into her well.

45

"That's enough for now," she said, not wanting it to stop, but knowing they had to flee. "Let's get away from here."

They turned and ran down the slope, trying to make as much distance as they could. The longer she stayed in one place, the more dangerous it became, almost as if the scent of her soul spread in ever-growing rings. If she kept moving, she'd keep ahead of the scent, although demons could still follow behind.

The trail became rougher and then descended through another steep section. They were in a ravine now, but Ayja knew the terrain beyond was much easier. They turned a corner around an outcropping, and Ayja's heart stopped in her chest.

Hundreds of demons filled the gentle valley below them. The demons were of every variety, from imps to great lumbering beasts. Their eyes glowed in the darkness, all facing her — all moving in her direction. The closest were a hundred strides away.

"Back up the valley," Darra said.

They were doomed. How could they escape so many demons? "We'll never get away," Ayja said.

"We must hide. I will mask you."

"How?"

"No time to explain. We just have to hide. Trust me."

"Let's lower the odds a little, first." Stepping back out of view, Ayja twisted a ring of fire. Magic was strongest in a circle. The discovery had opened tremendous avenues of power to her. No longer did she have to feed her magic only with the strength she had within her, but she could cause the strands of magic to loop around and sustain themselves. They could even draw in power from existing strands outside of her.

The key was time. To twist and braid the strands of aether took time, skill, and concentration. In many fights, there just wasn't the time. Now, there was. She'd give the demons a wave of fire. She took her ring of fire and elongated it until it became a tube between her hands. If she was careful, she could cause a ring of fire to sustain itself for days without any support from her. That wasn't what she wanted now. Her earliest efforts at creating a ring of fire had been unsustainable and resulted in dramatic explosions. That's what she was after.

Ayja stepped out from behind the rock so that she could aim her cylinder down the valley. The demons saw her, but she ignored them. Darra touched her shoulder. "They're coming," he said. She nodded in reply, unable to talk.

Not looking up, Ayja maintained her focus on her working. Instead of exploding, she wanted it to unsustainably feed itself, growing wider and

46

taller until it exhausted its potential. She wanted a wave of fire that would roll over the demons, killing them and driving them back.

It was complicated. Too complicated. She was losing it.

"They're close now," Darra said. "Fifty strides."

The fire didn't want to be contained. She poured her energy into the working, not to make it stronger, but to hold it until it was ready. There were just too many moving elements.

I should have just made a wall. She'd been too greedy, wanting to destroy as many demons as possible.

"Now," Darra said. "Now or never."

Ayja raised her eyes and released her working. Orange-yellow fire washed down the valley in front of her, but she could barely make it out, so blinded was she from staring into her creation.

Darra took her by the arm and pulled her back. "Now's our chance," he said. "We have to hide."

Ayja wanted to watch her working, but Darra pulled her away. She turned and ran up the valley with him. They ran to where they'd killed the demon centipede, and Darra slowed. "There are crevices and caves here," he said. "Or we could go higher."

"It will take too long to scale the cliff," Ayja said. "We can't let them see us." She looked around and pointed. "Up there. On the cliff face. That gap. Can you get to it?"

They ran to the wall, and Ayja slung Forsvar on her back. There was a narrow crack she could hold and used it to pull herself up. She climbed a little higher and waited for Darra. He struggled at first, his armor less flexible than hers, but then he managed to join her.

Ayja looked over her shoulder, down the valley. If a single demon saw them now, it would all be over.

"Take off Forsvar," Darra said as they squeezed into the crevice. He pulled Dromost from his belt. "I will keep both Gifts next to me but will touch neither. If they are untouched, the demons won't sense them."

"You know this?"

"Yes. I'm certain of it. I've done it."

Ayja gave Forsvar to the pyren and scrambled deeper into the rock. It was much shallower than she'd hoped — only four strides deep. It was dark and narrow, though. And it would have to do. They'd committed to it now.

Darra pressed in close behind her. There was no floor. The crevice simply narrowed to a wedge beneath them. She couldn't sit or lay down, but could only rest her back against the wall.

She heard a scrape as Darra wedged Forsvar into the crack at his feet and then placed Dromost beside it. She couldn't see anything at all with

47

the pyren beside her, blocking her exit. He pushed against her and twisted, and she could see his pale face in the dim light.

"It is time for you to go to sleep," he said, placing his cold, dead hand on her face. She didn't resist, but let the darkness overcome her.

Chapter Six

"The *Summer Swan* is too far out to help us," Telea said.

"Then be ready to fight," Tharryl responded, "because they're coming for us."

Sindi, Calen, and Isibindi quickly strung their bows and nocked arrows while Telea ran up to join Tharryl. She'd hoped he'd been exaggerating the danger of the men — that maybe they were just stranded merchant sailors. She knew at first sight that it wasn't the case. These were hard men and women with ill intent. They held axes and javelins, and four had bows or crossbows. Most wore padded aketons, some with mail patches or metal plates sewn on.

Still, Telea hoped to avoid a fight. Twelve to five were bad odds. She took several more strides until she stood in clear view of the pirates, for that's what she knew they were. "We mean no harm," Telea called out to them as they approached. "We just want to head up the road to Aftokropoli."

"Oh, ho, is that the case?" a man asked from the center of the group. He was bigger than the others and had a long, black braided beard. He held a curved Belenese sword and wore a brigandine of plates over mail. He stopped twenty strides from Telea, his companions forming a half-circle stretching out on either side. There were four women with them, just as rough-looking as the others. "Then why didn't you just sail your fine vessel up the coast?"

Tharryl moved up to stand next to Telea. "We have business to attend to in a nearby village," Telea said.

Their leader laughed. "Is that the case? Or is it that you're a bunch of spies? Or maybe assassins come to kill the emperor? There are a lot of rumors about you Etheans. They say you kidnapped the Bride of Forsvar and stole the Godshield."

The two archers and two crossbowmen held their weapons at the ready — their eyes focused more on Tharryl than on Telea. Telea took two steps forward, opening her hands to show she was unarmed. Pitching

49

her voice to sound as agreeable as possible, she said, "That's not true. We were with the *nafai amas*. We went with her to the Dromost Gate on that very ship. She closed the Dromost Gate."

"What kind of a fool do you take me for?" the man scoffed. "Look, I don't really care about you or your lies. I was really hoping to take that ship of yours, but it looks like that won't happen now. So here's the deal. Give us everything you have, down to your last stitch of clothing, and we'll let you go free."

A skinny man with a scarred face to his right giggled and said, "Yep. Set you free."

The leader glared at scar face before turning back to Telea. "Tell your skulking friends to come up here and drop their bows. And you can drop your spear, big man."

"What does he want?" Tharryl asked. "Why'd he look at me?"

Telea knew he didn't have the Belenese to follow the conversation. "He wants you to drop your spear," she said in Saladoran. "He wants us to give them everything we have."

"Fuck that," Tharryl said. "I'm going to kill him."

"What are you saying?" black beard asked.

"I'm telling them we have to surrender," Telea said.

Tharryl shrugged, and then his spear fell to the ground at his feet. *"I give up,"* he said in Belenese. He took off his helmet and tossed it to the ground as well. *"I join you."*

"What are you doing, Tharryl?" Telea asked, her heart thudding in her chest. Without the big Saladoran knight, they'd have no chance against the pirates.

Tharryl turned to Sindi, Calen, and Isibindi. "Their archers are the most dangerous right now, understand?"

"What 's he saying?" Black beard asked.

"Tell him that we surrender," Tharryl said to Telea.

"But — "

"Just do it. Tell him we surrender and that I wish to join them."

Telea faced the pirates. Fighting their way out had never had much hope; they were so outnumbered. At least it was a chance, though. She held little hope for them if they surrendered. If she could get close enough to their leader, they might have a chance. If she could touch him, she could possess him and maybe get them out of this.

"Tell him," Tharryl said.

"We surrender. My companion says—"

Tharryl's spear was suddenly in his hand. In one smooth, powerful motion, he flung it at the pirate leader. The heavy spear struck with such force it punched through the pirate's brigandine and his body as well. Tharryl was already charging before black beard hit the ground.

A crossbow snapped, and a bolt whistled past Tharryl. The other crossbowman and two archers never had a chance to loose — three long Ethean arrows struck them before they could aim.

Telea was unarmed, so she sang. If she'd been a fire singer, she could have dismayed her foes. An earth singer could have flung them aside with his voice. She lifted her voice in the *Song of Hope,* directing her magic at her companions. It would give them heart and steadiness. It was all she had.

Tharryl drew his axe and hurled it. The axe hit scar face, splitting both his grin and his head. In three strides, Tharryl made it to the pirates, his tulwar in hand. In two quick strokes, he'd killed as many pirates. Another two fell to Ethean arrows, while a third was wounded.

As fast as the fight had begun, it was over. The pirates — those who could still move — broke and ran. "Kill them!" Tharryl shouted as he pursued the one nearest him. He slashed the man's leg from behind, causing him to fall, and then stabbed him through the throat where he lay on the ground. Three more fell to arrows — only a few made it past the dunes. Sindi and Calen ran after them with the others close behind. Telea saw them pause and loose two arrows before disappearing beyond a dune.

Telea passed the wrecked ship to her left and then crossed the crest of the dune. The sand soon ended in rocky, scrubby ground sloping upwards towards a ridge. Two cliffs hemmed them in on either side. Fifty strides ahead, Sindi and Calen made their way up the steep slope. Telea ran to catch up to Tharryl and Isibindi.

"Did any of them get away?" Telea asked.

"None from that group," Tharryl said. "There could be more. The Landomeri are taking a look."

"You think there could be more?"

"Takes more than a dozen to crew one of those ships, doesn't it?" he asked. "Let's clear it."

"How did you do that with your spear?" Telea asked as they warily approached the ship.

"I flipped it up with my foot. You don't spend your whole life fighting without learning some tricks."

"I thought you might really be surrendering."

Tharryl snorted. "They would have killed Calen and me and kept you women for sport."

"You're an impressive soldier, Tharryl."

"I'm the best knight in Salador. You, however, were as useless as tits on a bull."

Telea flashed him an angry glance. "I can do other things. You know that. I can heal."

"None of us were injured," he said as he continued to advance on the wreck. "Oh, maybe you could heal this scratch on my little finger. It's a real ouchie."

"You don't know the things I taught Ayja," Telea said, growing angrier with each passing heartbeat. "She never could have succeeded without the things I taught her."

"Sure, I know that. You can sing. You can heal. You do all that magic stuff. No excuse not to be able to fight. I used to think women couldn't fight at all. Still think they aren't as good as men. Sindi and Bindi sure know how to shoot a bow, I'll admit. And Bindi knows her way with a sword as well."

"I was forbidden from learning how to wield weapons when I went to the College of Healers," Telea said, hard-pressed to keep up with his long strides. "I took a vow not to kill."

"Pretty stupid vow if you ask me."

They were close to the ship now. It had lost its masts, and Telea saw a fracture in its hull where some rock or reef had staved in some of the strakes. Otherwise, it seemed the ship was in decent shape. Given some work, it could be made seaworthy again.

Isibindi put down her longbow and drew her tulwar. She nodded to Tharryl and then motioned towards the ship. "Maybe you should stay behind," Tharryl said to Telea. He didn't wait for a reply but turned and cautiously approached the ship with Isibindi at his side.

Flushed and angry, Telea followed behind them. She hated the big Saladoran. He was as arrogant and mean-hearted a man as she'd ever met. What frustrated her, even more, was that there was some truth to what he said. He didn't understand the true strength of her magic. He didn't know what she was capable of. But she'd been no help at all in that fight. If she got close enough to touch someone and possess them or draw their life from them, she was also close enough to be stabbed by them. She needed some way to reach out and touch them with her magic.

She paused in her tracks, just a few strides from the ship. Tharryl and Isibindi were already stealthily climbing aboard, but Telea was frozen in thought. What if she *could* reach out with magic? Maybe she could twist her magic, or alter her song, in such a way that she could affect people from a distance. Certainly, her songs could. Why couldn't her chants?

"You coming or not?" Tharryl whispered.

"No." She turned away from him. "I'm going to check on the wounded."

"Bah, let 'em bleed out."

Telea walked away without another word. When Ayja had unlocked the Orb of Creation, she'd unleashed a tremendous potential for magic in the world. The two of them together had already learned so much, but there were still infinite opportunities open to them. She just needed time.

Wasn't that what Ayja had always longed for? She'd told Telea over and over how she longed for a life of peace where she could explore all the paths of magic. *Not anymore, though. You're gone now.*

She came to the scene of the fight. Tharryl had left none of his opponents alive. One woman, an arrow in her shoulder, had crawled off a short distance, a trail of blood in the sand behind her, but had seemingly bled out.

One of the crossbowmen was still alive. He lay curled in the sand, his hands wrapped around an arrow in his guts. Telea cautiously approached him. His eyes were open, and tears streamed from them. Telea held her hands open to him. "I'm a healer," she said. "I can help you. Can I approach?"

He gave her a gap-toothed grimace and nodded. The man was wiry, with close-cropped hair and a long scraggly beard. He had a long dagger in his belt, but Telea didn't think he had the strength to use it. Still, she had to take care.

Moving towards his bare feet, she crouched and took him by the ankle. As soon as she touched him, she began to chant, pushing her mind into his body, dominating his thoughts, and paralyzing him. He had no memory walk and no defense against her. His mind resisted for just a moment, but weakened by his wounds and filled with pain; he quickly folded under her assault.

Don't resist, Telea thought. *I can heal you.*

She began the *Chant of Healing*, not healing yet, but probing his wound with her magic. He'd lost a lot of blood, and the arrow had pierced his intestines. It had narrowly missed his spine, though, which was fortunate. His wounds weren't beyond healing.

Letting a pulse of her life force into him, she stopped the bleeding and stabilized him for the moment. The wounds would reopen when she drew the arrow out, but she could quickly heal the wound then.

When did you get here? she asked.

How are you doing this? he replied. She could feel his fear. It was palpable. *How are you in my mind?*

When did you get here? She was more insistent this time, demanding an answer from him.

Four days ago.

He wanted to resist her questions, but couldn't. *Were there more than the twelve of you?*

Yes. Thirty. They've gone off.

To do what? His resistance grew now. She felt it. *To what?* She pushed harder, and his consciousness flinched back from her.

To raid a nearby village.

What have you done? How bad a person are you? He didn't reply, his consciousness desperately fleeing her. *How bad a man are you?*

Telea took a deep breath. She was doing nothing now she hadn't done before. But there was another step she could take. While she'd pushed her thoughts into the pirate, her conscious mind was still within her own body. But if she wanted to, she could completely possess him — remove her mind from her own body and place it in his. She'd never done it before, and her heart pounded at the thought of it. What if she couldn't get back?

She knew one way to get the answer. Within her memory walk, she gave her imprisoned demon awareness of the outside world. *Demon, speak to me.*

Free me, it said. *I grow tired of this prison.*

When my task is done, not sooner. Now, tell me, if I possess this man, is there anything that could stop me from returning to my own body?

Is he a singer or a summoner? Could he contest your will? He looks weak. An easy target. Give him to me. Let me possess him, and I will be your ally.

No. Now tell me. Is there any other danger?

Your own body will be defenseless while you are gone. Make certain that it's safe. He is a weak thing and wounded. Take him and devour his soul. Make your well of power greater. Grow into the great summoner you could be.

Be gone. With a thought, she locked the demon away, blind to the outside world.

She looked back to the pirate. What other chance would she get to do such a thing? And she wanted to know... what kind of man was she dealing with? Gathering her strength, she pushed her mind inside the pirate's. Her vision went black, and her world spun. Then images flashed before her eyes. She saw people and places she'd never seen before. She saw events — fights, feasts, gulls flying over rough seas. Moments of laughter, but also moments of fear and pain. The images whirled around her and she thought she might be sick. Then they slowed and she could see again, but now she was looking at herself from the pirate's eyes.

His will — his sense of self — faded as she took complete control of him, mind and body. She lifted her hand, and his bloody hand appeared in her vision. She felt a moment of panic as she made him flex his fingers. He was totally under her will.

She looked at herself. She was soaked and sandy. Half her braids had come loose from her bun and hung in her face. Her own face was blank — calm and devoid of any emotion. If she got up and walked away in the pirate's body, how long would her own body remain there, unmoving? The thought terrified her, and she was tempted to flee back into her own body again for fear of somehow losing it.

She calmed herself. She could get back. She was in complete control of the pirate and could, in an instant, return to her own body. The man's mind was a chaotic mess, with nothing like her memory walk to keep it organized. Thoughts and memories jumbled together, connected with threads that sometimes made sense, but other times seemed bizarrely unrelated.

The chaos and unfamiliarity were overwhelming at first, but then she made some order of it and began to explore. Within a few heartbeats, she wished she hadn't. He was a monster. His memories were filled with hate, violence, and lust. He was a thief, a murderer, and a rapist. She saw his victims in horrible detail and felt his pleasure as he harmed them. She recoiled from his thoughts, but couldn't escape them entirely.

Everywhere she looked in his mind, she saw pain and vicious cruelty. Her consciousness fled his mind and returned to her own, although she remained in contact with him.

You are a terrible person. You cause so much pain.

Get out! Get out! Get out!

You are evil.

Everyone is. Leave me! Go away! I'll kill you.

No, you won't. You'll never kill anyone again. Telea began to chant, drawing the man's life force from his body and into her well of power. When her well was full, she used the surplus to heal herself of fatigue and to restore the strength to her limbs.

He didn't have much strength to him, having lost so much blood already. As the last of his life force left his body, she said, *I could have made it hurt. I give you that mercy, at least.*

Telea glanced around to see if any of her companions were near. Seeing none, she continued her chant and probed deeper into the body and mind of the now-dead pirate. She'd had time to speak with Muaz about more than locking the Dromost Gate. She'd been deeply curious about the silent brothers — the undead defenders of the temple that the summoners had reanimated. Even when their souls have departed, he had told her, there remained in a body the memory of life. That memory could be utilized to turn a dead person into the undead. An obedient, animated corpse. *A silent brother.*

The summoners had seen it as a wonderful thing — the idea that they could serve the Temple of Dromost even after death. Telea knew it wouldn't be seen in the same positive light outside the Summoned Lands. In Belen, a corpse was to be treated with reverence and given a sacred burial. The idea of taking a dearly departed one and then animating them as some sort of servant would be seen as abhorrent.

She looked down at the corpse. *You are no dearly departed one, however.*

Muaz had told her that the silent brothers had, of course, no life force remaining to them. It was necessary to donate life force to them to give them motive power. However, they required very little life force compared to a living person to remain active. How long? He hadn't been able to say. How could one measure the quantity of life force?

Telea took hold of the pirate's memory of life, and using her well of power, donated some life force to him. There was resistance. A barrier pushed back against her efforts. The barrier was soft and yielding, but she couldn't penetrate it. She pushed more life force at it, hoping to batter her way through with sheer strength, but the barrier gave like mail armor under a blow. She withdrew her life force and sat back to think for a moment.

How could she get through? She knew there was a way. Then a thought came to her. She'd served in the Summoner War as a healer. She'd treated many kinds of wounds. Soldiers in mail rarely suffered slashing wounds. Mail armor absorbed the impact of a long blade. Soldiers in mail suffered from piercing wounds.

Telea resumed her effort. This time, though, she focused her assault into a narrow point of light. She'd pierce the barrier like an arrow pierced mail. There was resistance, but only momentary, before it gave way. She pushed her life force through the gap and touched the pirate's spark of life. She recoiled as his dead eyes moved and looked at her.

She'd done it! Pride and horror touched her at the same time. Shuddering, she said, "Raise your right arm."

With a moment's hesitation, the pirate raised his hand until it pointed straight up to the sky. Telea's gasped at the sight. She'd made a dead person move! He had understood her and obeyed her. There was something deeply wrong with it, but fascinating as well. Was this something that had always been possible? Or was this yet another element of magic that Ayja had unleashed when she'd unlocked the Orb of Creation?

"Put your hand down," Telea commanded.

The dead pirate's hand slowly fell to the ground. She crouched close to him. "Can you speak?" she asked.

"Ungh. Agh urgh."

Telea frowned, trying to understand. Were they words? The pirate had clearly attempted speech. It had heard her question and responded. "Raise two fingers," she said.

The pirated raised his hand, holding up two fingers. Telea nodded in satisfaction. "What is seven minus four? Show me with your fingers."

His hand remained where it was, unmoving, still showing two fingers. She frowned. "Hold up three fingers."

A third finger joined the other two. Then the pirate's hand slowly lowered to the ground, and all sign of animation disappeared. Telea chanted and touched him again. The life force she'd given him was already gone. It hadn't lasted long, but she'd only given a tiny portion to him. Within her memory walk, she spun life force into a ring and then pushed it into his memory of life. His body twitched as soon as she did so.

She stood and took two steps back from him. "Stand," she said.

The pirate got to his feet. He did it easily. She'd seen only a few silent brothers at the Temple of Dromost. The one she'd seen more than others had been quite dumb, only able to shamble around from place to place, seemingly unaware of what was happening around him. Tharryl, however, had seen many of them defending the walls. They'd been very vigorous and capable, he'd said. While they wore their armor, he'd hardly been able to tell the difference between a silent brother and a living man.

What accounted for the difference? What made one barely functional and another a capable warrior? The pirate stood in front of her, face pale and expressionless. It still had an arrow through its abdomen but paid it no heed.

"Telea! Where are you?" Sindi's voice called from beyond the dunes.

Telea reached out and touched the pirate's face. With a quick chant, she drew the life force from him, and he collapsed like a sack of oranges. Sindi's head appeared from over the dune. "We must go," Sindi said. "There are more of them coming."

"I'm coming," Telea replied, her hand shaking as she looked at the corpse at her feet. Then, at another call from Sindi, she ran up the dune and away from him. The five soon gathered at the base of the slope.

"There are two dozen of them coming up from the south," Calen said. "If we are fast, we can get away to the north before they return."

"They'll search for us when they find the bodies," Tharryl said.

"We'll have to keep ahead of them."

"Go ahead," Tharryl said. "I'll catch you. I want my axe and my spear."

They started up the slope. It wasn't so steep that they needed to climb, but it was challenging. Telea began to sweat with the effort. She welcomed the warmth, though. They were all still soaked, and although Belen was warmer than Salador, it was still a cool, overcast day. She glanced over her shoulder and saw Tharryl coming up behind them, spear in hand.

At the top of the slope, they found themselves on a wide swath of rolling hills. In the distance, the hills rose to become a low mountain range. There was a road here, running along the coast. It appeared well maintained. Telea looked out over the sea and saw the *Summer Swan* barely visible in the haze, sailing south into the deep green. They were alone now, with only themselves to rely upon.

"This way," Sindi said, leading them northeast along the coastal road. "The pirates are the other way."

A good thing, Telea thought. The pirates weren't blocking their route to Aftokropoli. The three women went ahead while Calen stood watch and waited for Tharryl to reach the top. He soon arrived, and the two men ran to catch them. They ran the first few arrowflights, trying to gain as much a lead as they could.

"They will think the attack came from the sea, won't they?" Telea said at one point. "They might not even pursue us."

"It depends if they have any good trackers amongst them," Sindi said. "Better to be safe."

They pushed themselves well into the night until they were stumbling through the moonless darkness. The sky was still overcast, and a light rain fell upon them. They found a sheltered place and made camp, lighting a fire to keep off the chill. They had some provisions with them — dried fish and fruit and some salt pork for the most part. It seemed like a feast to Telea.

No one accosted them during the night, and the following dawn arrived with sun and warmer temperatures. By midday, they were fairly certain they weren't being followed, and that evening they arrived in a town of a few thousand residents. They found lodging and purchased horses, but also discovered that the pirates weren't the only people who thought less than kindly of Etheans.

It was a fact reinforced each night over their several-day journey to Aftokropoli. The rumors Telea heard were rampant and contradictory. The most common was that the Etheans had raided the Temple of Forsvar, captured the *nafai amas*, and stolen the Godshield. Telea feigned ignorance, claiming that she was only a merchant and knew nothing of anything that had transpired. The fact she was free with her money helped smooth things over, but their antipathy was palpable.

The Temple of Forsvar was the most sacred place in Belen. To think that it had been attacked was horrifying to the Belenese. Many people they ran across called for open war with Ethea. "This doesn't bode well for our mission," Telea said as they rode on the final leg of their journey to the capital. "Orlos has gone to bring King Handrin here to form an alliance with the emperor. Does the emperor truly believe these rumors? What will he do when the King of Salador arrives?"

"You need to tell the emperor the truth," Sindi said. "Tell him that the Dromost Gate has been closed. We can convince him."

Tharryl laughed and shook his head. "He already believes the story Kyvern Psertis told him. He thinks Princess Ayja came here with Forsvar to overthrow him. We sank two of his ships and killed hundreds of his Children of Forsvar. And you think he'll believe our story?"

"I don't understand why the emperor would be so quick to believe Kyvern Psertis," Telea said. "And why did he send men to the Temple of Forsvar with orders to seize Forsvar when the High Priest told him of our true mission? It doesn't make sense. And why, if it is clear that the summoners have betrayed us, hasn't the emperor called up the full might of Belen?"

"It's what happens when you put people in power because of who their fathers were," Tharryl said. "It has nothing to do with talent. Maybe he's just a bad emperor. Or, more likely, he's a greedy bastard, just like the rest of them. He's in it for himself."

They approached the capital in the late morning of their fifth day since landing and were surprised at the amount of traffic on the road. Aftokropoli was the only walled city in all of the Belenese Empire, it having been decided a century ago that walls only encouraged rebellion against imperial authority.

Telea and her companions rode through ten stades of pleasant suburbs before arriving at the city gates. Here the homes were larger; some reached three stories in height. Vendors had set up stands along the road, selling food and wares to travelers entering the city. As they'd been on the road since dawn, and it looked to be some time before they could enter the city, they dismounted and purchased grilled chicken and cheese wrapped in flatbread and ate it while they waited.

"It will be dark before we can enter the city," Tharryl said. "We should find a place to stay outside the gates."

Telea shook her head. "Let's not add another day of travel. I want to get inside the city and find a place to stay."

"What's the hurry? Your mother's ship won't return for seven weeks, and the pass is closed until spring."

Just then, the traffic ahead of them began to move more quickly. Telea smiled and said, "See? No problem. We'll find an inn in no time."

They remounted and followed the line of carts and pedestrians towards the gates. It was odd to have waited so long. She'd been to Aftokropoli on many occasions. Traffic usually flowed right through the gates. There were guards, but they were there only to prevent crime. They rounded a gentle bend, and the gates came into sight. Only one side of the double gates were open, severely restricting the passage of traffic. There were more than just a few guards there as well. She saw two dozen on the road and more on the wall above.

"Is it always like this?" Telea asked the man in front of them. He drove a cart piled high with heavy sacks, pulled by a sad old draft horse.

"You should know, Ethean."

"I'm not Ethean," Telea said. "I'm Belenese. I was born here."

He glanced past her at Isibindi and shrugged. "You look Ethean to me."

"What does that have to do with the gate?"

"Ever since your people raided the Temple of Forsvar, there have been more guards on the gate. Maybe they think you'll go for the Emperor next."

"I'm sure the Temple of Forsvar wasn't raided by any Etheans," Telea said. "Just rumors."

He spat on the ground. "They say your fleet sank five galleys. We got you back, though, and sank six of yours."

"It didn't happen," Telea said. "And stop saying *you*. I'm loyal to the Emperor. I'm Belenese."

He turned away to her and flicked his reins. "So you keep saying."

As they approached, the large square in front of the gate came into better view. Telea could see more clearly now and was shocked at the number of guards. Everyone who passed through the gate was interrogated. To her dismay, she saw at least a dozen Etheans separated form the rest of the travelers and held off to one side with a heavy guard on them.

"Will there be trouble?" Sindi asked.

"I have papers," Telea said. "They should be more than adequate to get us through. I have coin if the papers fail."

"You're certain?"

"Just remind Calen that the two of you are Koromoi riders who are in my employ. And Tharryl is a hillman from near the Great Salador Pass. Let me do the talking."

"Maybe we should turn back and find another way," the Landomeri said, glancing over her shoulder.

Telea glanced towards the gate and shook her head. "If we turn back now, it will be noticed. Don't worry. We'll pass through." She said it with more confidence than she felt.

They finally reached the inspection point in front of the gate. Several of the guards had clearly taken notice of Telea and Isibindi and were heading towards them. The man on the cart in front of them was waved through without a second glance, but he paused his horse and motioned a well-appointed guard closer. As soon as the guard was close, the farmer leaned close to him and whispered something to him. The guard frowned and turned to glare at Telea. Behind his turned head, the farmer shot Telea an obscene gesture and lashed his horse into motion.

The guard, his hand on his sword hilt, faced Telea and said, "You there! Ethean. Dismount, and don't give me any trouble."

Chapter Seven

Nidon pulled his heavy fur cloak closer over his shoulders as wind-whipped snow swirled around him. Winter was refusing to let go of its grip on the East Pass, even though they were a month into spring. He stamped his feet, only partially to get the blood flowing into his toes.

When would they clear the pass? When would they find the Temple of Dromost? When would they free Ayja?

There was a sharp crack, and a chunk of cliff face split off and toppled into the seemingly bottomless gorge. As the rocks and ice tumbled, he wondered how many heartbeats it would take for them to hit the valley floor. How many times would a person bounce off the side? Or would it just be a clean descent to a sudden halt? He preferred it hidden by snow. He preferred not knowing.

Better than dying like Sir Galan, who had turned back from Ayja and then frozen to death in a way station. They'd found his body the day before. Orlos had mentioned the coward when he'd reported to the king everything that had transpired in Belen. He'd spoken of those who'd fought so bravely and loyally for Ayja, and those few who'd betrayed her trust.

And so Nidon stomped his feet with impatience, waiting for Handrin and his elementars to finish their work. There was another crack, and yet another piece of the cliff face fell into the valley. Nidon stepped closer to watch the king at work.

There were three elementars there now, making a new cliff road the Saladoran Army would use to cross the East Pass. When they'd first arrived, they'd seen the flimsy rope bridge Ayja and her companions had used to cross into Belen. There'd been no way the army could cross that way. It would have taken an absurdly long time and the bridge wouldn't have stood up to the strain.

King Handrin and Lady Wenla had the lead now, with Wenla's daughter, Varen, close behind them, observing their work. Four more elementars remained back at the way station, resting and waiting their turn. Handrin had the Orb of Creation in his right hand and his left hand on the back of Wenla's neck. Nidon knew Handrin was feeding the Orb's reserves of power into Wenla, giving her the strength to keep at her work far longer than she otherwise would have been able to.

Wenla placed her hands on the stone in front of her. Nidon saw fine gold lines spread out from her fingers, working themselves up and down the cliff face, and then, with a sharp report, the rock shattered and fell into the valley. She'd done in seconds what men with hammers and hand drills would have taken a quarterday to do.

Handrin could have done the work himself, but ever since he'd taken the throne, he'd spared no effort to find every elementar he could and bring them to Sal-Oras. He taught them everything he knew of wielding the aether and working the elements. He didn't want magic to hide in the shadows but believed it to be a powerful force for good in the world. Now he put them to work battling the stone that blocked their route to the Belenese Empire.

Only by exercising and practicing could they get stronger. All of the elementars had listened with rapt attention when Orlos told them what Ayja and Telea were capable of. Orlos had mentioned rings of fire, memory walks, wells of power, and crafting fire arrows, but so far, no one had been able to duplicate what the young spiridus had told them. It had been frustrating for everyone to hear of such potential but not to be able to do it. And, as Orlos wasn't an elementar, he couldn't adequately describe what should be done. He'd only been able to say what he'd heard and tell them what he'd seen.

Crack! A huge piece of stone fell over the edge. The path was less than a stride wide. The idea was to make it wide enough for foot soldiers to pass through and then broaden it later.

How long for ten thousand men to pass through? They'd done the math over and over until Nidon's head had pounded with the strain of it. Each way station could hold perhaps sixty men if they had no horses with them. Each way station was a halfday's march from the last. At sixty men a day, an army of ten thousand would take over one hundred and sixty days to cross the East Pass. No wonder the histories never told of wars between Belen and Salador. The East Pass was too big an obstacle to cross.

There were options, though. Once the weather cleared, soldiers could sleep on the road. The number of men crossing each day would increase dramatically. But then there were issues of supply and horses and camp followers and so much more. Nidon would leave Earl Livran to deal with the logistical nightmare.

Nidon's page had set a fire in a crevasse in the cliff face, and he went to warm his hands there. He would have preferred to rest in the comfort of the way station, but it wouldn't be appropriate to take his ease there while the king was out in a snowstorm.

Handrin had said it would be another three days before the path would be finished. At least this phase of it. Once the narrow path was completed, Nidon would cross the pass while King Handrin remained behind to widen it so that more soldiers might pass through. Nidon would take Baron Fendal with him so that he'd have an elementar with the advanced guard. The rest of the elementars would remain with Handrin, working on the road.

Hopefully, they'd find Orlos waiting for them at the far side of the pass. The spiridus had been too impatient to wait for better weather and had sent word to the king that he was going to cross the pass ahead of the army. Orlos's message had said that he was going to find Satrus Exonos, who had hosted Ayja and her company of knights in his manor, and who had been their greatest ally in Belen.

Spiridus or not, Nidon couldn't imagine how the young man could have crossed the pass. It was a rash decision, not waiting for the army.

Just as Nidon left the fire, he saw Handrin, Wenla, and Varen approaching. "Finished for the day, Your Majesty?" Nidon asked.

"We are exhausted. The Orb is exhausted. We made good progress, though. Lady Wenla and Young Lady Varen did excellent work," he said as they walked down the path to the way station.

"You are too kind, Your Majesty," Wenla said. "My daughter accomplished far more than I did."

"Be that as it may, I am still impressed."

The way station had a proper door now. When they'd arrived, it had only a simple curtain to keep both the wind and rain out. Pages and squires rushed up to them as they entered, taking cloaks and jackets from them. Folding camp chairs were set by the fire for those who'd just returned from outside.

"Three more days," Handrin said as he sat down. "Three more days, and you'll take the advanced guard over the pass, Nidon. That is if this snow doesn't close it."

"This snow won't stop me," Nidon said. "We'll dig our way through if we have to. With your permission, I'll send word for the advanced guard to arrive here in three days."

Handrin nodded his assent and waved for his squire to approach. "Bring the orders for the First Advance to me. I wish to sign and seal them."

While the king wrote at his camp desk, Nidon called for a Royal Messenger. "Take word to Sir Dalaman at the next way station that I want him here three days from today. Make certain that orders for the First Advance are taken to the army encampment and given to Earl Livran."

"Yes, Champion."

Nidon's advance company would consist of five lances of the Knights of the House and twenty Landomeri archers. Forty men wouldn't be too many for the way stations to handle, but still made up a strong detachment. There'd been some grumbling about sharing the honor of the advance with the Landomeri, but Orlos had warned them of both the terrain they would cross and the enemy they would fight. Nidon wanted light troops with him — soldiers who could fight in the rough terrain of the wooded mountains. He also needed archers. The Landomeri fit the bill.

They were bringing twenty builders with them as well — carpenters for the most part. Orlos had told them of a chasm spanned only by a rope bridge. That wouldn't do for the passing of any army. Once Nidon had secured the crossing, the workers would construct a wooden bridge fit for cavalry and large numbers of men.

For three more days, the elementars labored at carving a path for them. Nidon never tired of watching them work. Ayja had tried on many occasions to explain to him what it meant to see the aether and all the strands of magic that made up the fabric of the world. She'd told him of how she could twist those strands, moving them to change the shape of air, earth, fire, and water. It never failed to mystify him. He was blind to how it worked, but he loved watching the result.

The weather turned for the better, which was a relief to everyone braving the mountain road. Meltwater flowed down the face of the cliff, creating beautiful waterfalls, but at night the cold would set in, and the water would freeze, making the narrow trail deadly when they rose. Everyone wore hobnailed boots, and each morning they'd cleared the path of ice for fear someone might slip over the edge.

On the evening of the third day, four lances of the Knights of the House arrived, along with a dozen Landomeri and four donkeys laden with supplies. The remaining Landomeri and the woodworkers would arrive the following day, keeping one way station behind the lead party. No more would cross until Nidon sent word that the bridge was secure and that he'd made contact with Orlos and the Belenese.

If the young man made it. The spiridus had gone over the mountains two weeks before. He'd been counseled to wait but had been impatient to be on his way, swearing that he could make the crossing alone.

Nidon was surprised at first to see that nearly half the Landomeri were women. Then he shook his head at his own cluelessness. Why would it shock him, when the only Landomeri he'd ever known was Hadde, and she was the finest archer he'd ever met? It brought a lump to his throat, seeing them as well. These were Hadde's countrymen. He'd once intended on them being his own countrymen. They would have been but for his failure to save her life.

How much different would his life have been if he'd arrived thirty heartbeats earlier? What if the two of them, fighting side by side, had killed the last of the varcolac and taken Ayja back to Landomere with them?

A foolish dream. She didn't even know that I loved her. She never knew.

Three Landomeri approached him. All wore mottled cloaks thrown back over their shoulders. The air might be cold, but the late sun was still warm on the cliff face. Two, a man and a woman, wore mail haubergeons, but little other armor. They carried longbows and had quivers stuffed with arrows at their belts. The third hardly looked Landomeri at all. He wore a long mail hauberk, split for riding, and had an expensive Idorian crossbow slung over his shoulder. His clothes, though, were Landomeri.

"Greetings, Champion Nidon," the woman said, "I am Doree of Wind Tree, a ranger of Landomere. This is ranger Teladan of Running Brook, and Kael, a warden of Belavil. We have come with our companions to help you in your task."

"It is good to have you," Nidon said. "Thank you for coming. I have the highest regard for the Landomeri. Your countrymen were instrumental in closing the Dromost Gate. I knew Hadde the Landomeri, as well. She was a great woman."

"I met her as well," Kael said, speaking with a strong Idorian accent. "Although I'll add, it was at the wrong end of an arrow. She was, as you say, a great woman."

"The wrong end of an arrow?"

Kael smiled a lopsided smile. He was a big man, although not quite as tall as Nidon. Scars crossed his face. "I am married to Maret, Orlos's mother. Although when I met Hadde, I was a sergeant in Captain Saunder's company of *contractos*."

Nidon frowned. "The mercenary company that took Ayja and Orlos?"

"The very same."

"What you did led to Hadde's death," Nidon said, anger growing in the pit of his stomach.

"It was wrong. I came to know it even when it was happening. I did what I could to protect Maret and the children. If I could have held off the varcolac for fifteen more heartbeats, Enna and Orlos would have been saved."

Nidon narrowed his eyes. "So much is a matter of heartbeats. Hadde fought those same varcolac to save Princess Ayja. I arrived just moments too late."

"I regret the part I played in taking the children," Kael said. "I've tried my best to make up for it. I am a good husband to Maret. I am a good father to our children, and I include Orlos when I say 'our children.'"

"It would be easy for me not to like you," Nidon said. "But Orlos is a fine young man, and I'm pleased that you've made a good life for the Maiden Maret. At least that's how I remember her. It is hard for me to imagine her as a grown woman."

"Besides Orlos, we have three children together."

Nidon nodded. *Would I have children now, if I'd arrived thirty heartbeats earlier? Would I be a Landomeri like this Idorian?* "When this is over, I would like to go to Landomere. I would like to see Lady Maret and meet her children."

"You would be welcome in our home. I hope you will stay with us."

"I accept your offer. Now to the task before us."

The way station was filled to overflowing with the new additions. So much so that the donkeys were covered with blankets and left to stay outside. It would be cold, but not so cold they couldn't bear it. After dark King Handrin returned, announcing that the path had been cleared. It had taken longer than expected, but it was finished, and the advanced party could pass through in the morning.

Nidon stayed up for a time, planning the coming days with Baron Fendal, Sir Dalaman, and the leaders of both the Landomeri and the builders who would accompany them. Finally, when all the others had gone to sleep, Nidon asked Kael to sit with him and to tell him the story of how the children had been kidnapped, and of how they'd been pursued. He'd heard the story from Calen, but he wanted now to hear it from Kael's point of view. Nidon couldn't help but smile as Kael related his tale. Kael described Hadde as a relentless and fearless hunter. No matter their best efforts, the mercenaries had been unable to shake her or to kill her, although they thought they'd succeeded on a few occasions.

"And in the end, you returned with the Landomeri to live in Belavil?"

Kael nodded. "I'd fallen for Maret by that time. Her scars meant nothing to me." He paused. "No, that's not true. Her scars were a sign of her strength and her devotion. Through all the fighting and all the terror, she'd remained strong and true to the children."

"She was just another silly maiden-in-waiting when I knew her," Nidon said. "I am impressed at the woman she's grown to be. I look forward to seeing her again."

"She always spoke glowingly of you," Kael said. "That's not strong enough. She and the other maidens worshipped you."

Nidon brushed him off with a wave. "It was Prince Morin they worshipped. He was the one the maidens wanted to marry." *Not just the maidens. Hadde had fallen for him as well.*

"Well, she thought very highly of you. I am, in fact, a little bit in awe. You are six times the Champion of Salador. No man has ever won the Champion's Tournament so many times."

"Seven times if you include my fight with Ilana's varcolac," Nidon said. "But I'm not the knight I used to be. I'm a man of middle years now. If I had to fight for the title again, I'm certain some young warrior would take it from me. In truth, I hope this is my last campaign."

"Mine as well, I hope."

The following morning the company rose before dawn and prepared for their departure. "You are in command of this expedition, Champion Nidon," King Handrin said. "Baron Fendal is your second, and Sir Dalaman your third. We don't know what we will find or if Orlos was successful. I will not throw away the Army of Salador on some fool's mission. I will not take the Orb of Creation to Belen only to have it captured by enemies there. It will be up to you to assess the situation you find. I put my faith in you. Send word as quickly as you can. The path will be widened, and the army ready to march in a few days."

"You can trust us, Your Highness," Nidon said.

"I know I can. Farewell and good luck."

Nidon was the first across the newly constructed path. It was narrow, and the precipitous fall to his left was utterly terrifying. He kept his fear in check, taking a deep breath when he finally made it to the far side and the wider road there. Once across, four fleet-footed Landomeri were sent ahead to scout the way.

They'd only gone three arrowflights when two of the Landomeri returned. "There is ice blocking the way," a tall, stick-thin woman said. She carried an unstrung longbow that had to be over two strides tall.

"Blocking it? How?" Nidon asked. "The path is covered in ice?"

She shook her head. "It is like a frozen waterfall. A wall of ice. There is a narrow gap behind it, but it is too small for a knight or a donkey."

"I'll take a look," Fendal said, flexing his fingers. "Perhaps my magic can break it."

68

The Landomeri woman shrugged. "It's a lot of ice."

"Bah, take me there."

As they departed, Nidon called for Master Hod, the lead carpenter. "Spring is coming too slowly to the mountains. Take your men ahead. There's a wall of ice blocking our way, and we might need you to break through." And so, Nidon found himself marching behind the backside of a donkey as a crew of carpenters led the Saladoran advance into Belen.

The ice waterfall did, in fact, turn out to be too much for Fendal's magic to handle. He shattered more than half of it before he ran out of strength. When he retired, the builders went to work on it with their hammers, wedges, axes, and picks. Nidon soon began to worry that they'd have to beat an ignominious retreat back to the way station.

In the end, the delay cost them an eighthday and an injured worker but didn't destroy their schedule. A falling chunk of ice struck a carpenter in the shoulder, shattering it and nearly throwing him off the cliff. A litter was constructed for the wounded man, and four crossbowmen were dispatched to carry him back.

Three hundred strides and our first loss. It did not bode well for the coming days.

The frozen waterfall wasn't their only obstacle that day. Twice more ice blocked their path, although in neither case was it as severe as the first. The delays did give the four crossbowmen time to rejoin the company, however. Finally, much behind schedule, the company crossed the top of the pass, finding the ruined camp Orlos had mentioned would be there. The four bodies were still there as well, having spent the winter under snow, but now partially thawed and decomposing in the spring warmth. There was no wood for a cairn, and they were already delayed, so Nidon had the bodies left to be taken care of later.

The delays caused them to arrive at the next way station well after dark. This cold, dark station had no door and only a meager supply of wood. They had a small supply of wood with them, and Nidon ordered it used as the men and women of the detachment were cold and wet after a long hard day. He also knew from Orlos that the next way station was better supplied with wood.

When they woke, they found that the previous day's melt hadn't refrozen. And soon after they started, they discovered that the Belenese side of the pass had received less snowfall than the Saladoran side. They were only stopped twice for ice and snow, and in neither case was it difficult to clear.

As promised, the next way station was better supplied, and they enjoyed a much more comfortable evening. Nidon went to the crossbowman who would be their messenger and said, "When you go,

69

tell the king that we will need twice as much wood as we planned for. Especially if the army is to camp on the road."

The next day, by midday, they'd fallen below the tree line. It was noticeably warmer here, with snow standing only in places where the deepest shadows lay. By that afternoon, they arrived at the rope bridge. It was a sorry looking thing, having taken some abuse over the harsh winter. It hung a little off-kilter as well, which didn't give Nidon the greatest confidence in it.

He looked across the gap at the tree-filled slope beyond. *This is where Ayja was ambushed.* Orlos had told them how she'd leaped the gap, only to be attacked by men with imp jars. Nidon had fought creatures of Akinos, like the varcolac and urias, and Morin's pyren and ghuls as well, but the thought of fighting demons summoned by sacrificial blood somehow seemed far worse. He shook his head. *A sword kills them all the same.*

Nidon ordered archers and crossbowmen to take positions covering the far slope, and then he started across the swaying bridge. He was halfway across when the thought came to him that perhaps sending the biggest man in the heaviest armor across first might not be the best idea. How could he do otherwise, though? He could never send a man into danger in his place.

Nidon felt ridiculously exposed with his shield and his Idorian axe strapped on his back so that he could hold onto the ropes with both hands. How easy would it be for a few archers to knock him from the precarious crossing? They'd scanned the trees for any sign of enemies but had seen nothing.

Finally, he was across. He slipped his shield onto his arm and took his axe in his right hand as he pushed forward. Unlike the other men in his company, Nidon's shield was plain red, as was his tabard. It was the sign of the Champion of Salador that his shield should be unadorned. All of the others had the crossed silver lightning bolts of Forsvar depicted upon their shields and tabards. None had any personal coat of arms. These were the Knights of the House, the king's picked soldiers, and loyal to the throne above any family ties.

Each lance of the Knights of the House normally had two knights and two squires, but Nidon had added a crossbowman from the Company of the House to each lance as Orlos had warned him how common archery was in Belen. As soon as his five lances were across, the Landomeri followed. Together, they swept the slope to be certain no enemy waited for them there. Then he placed two lances and six Landomeri to guard the narrow bend in the trail ahead of them, while the rest returned to set up camp and to begin construction on the bridge.

Tents, camping gear, and building supplies all had to be brought across the rope bridge by hand. It simply wasn't steady enough for the five donkeys to cross. Almost as soon as the equipment was across, the ringing of axes on trees could be heard.

"How long?" Nidon asked Master Hod.

The bald, broad-shouldered guild master wore a bronze chain of office around his neck. He looked up at the trees on the hillside and back to the crevasse. "I'll have a working bridge for you tomorrow evening, Champion Nidon. I'll have a bridge fit for an army the day after that."

Nidon nodded, impressed. "That fast?"

"You have twenty of the highest recommended, best workers in Sal-Oras here with you, Champion. We'll have it done."

When to send word to the king… that was the question. Nidon didn't like the uncertainty they were walking into. Ayja's reception hadn't been the one they'd hoped for. How much had changed in the intervening months? Had the Emperor of Belen realized the errors of his ways? That he'd been tricked?

The Landomeri built a strong abatis and placed it across the road. Any force that tried to turn the corner against them would find itself up against a withering hail of crossbow bolts and arrows coming from the slopes above with no ability to counter it. It would take a very large, very determined force to take the position.

The night came early and cold, but at least now they had unlimited supplies of wood to keep them warm. They woke at first light and once again axes bit into tall trees. Nidon left Master Hod to his work, knowing better than to advise a man who was a professional in his trade.

"Baron Fendal," Nidon said, "I am leaving you with half the company while I continue down the pass. We will return before dark. If you don't hear from us, expect the worst. If we don't return by tomorrow night, burn the bridge and return to King Handrin."

"Very well, Champion. I wish you good luck."

The man hadn't objected to being left behind, not that Nidon had expected him to. He might be a baron and an elementar, but knightly bravery was asking much of him. Fendal was too cautious by half, but he was intelligent and organized and would see that the bridge would be built.

Nidon took three lances and ten Landomeri with Kael at their head and marched down the trail. The day was the brightest and warmest they'd seen yet, which gave him some encouragement. The slopes were shallower on either side of them, and the trail was tree-lined. The pines were different than any he'd seen before, with long, thin needles, but otherwise, the land reminded him of his mountain home of the past fifteen years.

It was midmorning when they saw a party approaching them. The Belenese, two men and two women, one very young, waved at them from a distance of a hundred strides. They wore no armor, although the two men carried short spears, and the woman carried a bow. As he looked closer, it seemed to Nidon that the two men were quite old.

The Belenese hurried closer. To Nidon, they seemed no threat, but he'd take no chances. "Kael, take your people into the woods and make certain we aren't about to be ambushed."

The former mercenary nodded and sent half his number down the slope to their left while taking the other half uphill with him. Nidon waited on the trail with his three lances. He kept his shield on his back and placed the butt of his axe on the ground next to him.

The Belenese never slowed their pace but marched right up to the Saladorans. Nidon was fairly certain they must have seen the Landomeri enter the woods, but they showed no concern at the threat. The eldest of the Belenese stopped and bowed when he was five strides from Nidon.

"You are the king of Saladorans? King Handrin?" he asked in heavily accented Saladoran. "I for to give apology. I learn Language of Song long ago — when young man." The two men were dressed in short, belted tunics of undyed wool that went down to their knees, but no trousers at all, just sandals on their feet. They had short capes over their shoulders, but bare arms. The woman and the girl wore sleeveless dresses that went to their calves, although the woman's was a pale yellow and the girl's a very faded green. All had black hair, all but for the eldest man, whose hair was white. Their skin was dark, as if tan from the sun, even though winter had just ended.

"I'm not King Handrin," Nidon said. "I am Nidon, Champion of Salador and commander of the king's army."

The man nodded, his head bobbing up and down and his wispy white hair floating in the wind. "Yes! Champion Nidon. Orlos spoke of you." He looked past Nidon up the pass. "You bring army with you?"

"It is coming," Nidon said, unwilling to reveal too much to the stranger. "When did you see Orlos?"

The man cocked his head in thought. "A month ago? He is with Satrus Exonos. Come! Satrus Exonos need you." He gave an enthusiastic wave down the pass.

"He needs me? Why does he need me?"

"Kyvern Psertis is coming. There will be a battle."

Chapter Eight

Ayja and Darra sat across the polished wooden table from each other. The window shutters were thrown open, letting bright afternoon sunlight into the sturdy house. Cool spring air wafted into the room, bringing the sound of singing birds and the scent of pine trees with it. Behind her, a glowing ember popped in the fireplace, sending sparks up the chimney.

Darra was a handsome man. Middle-aged, maybe a few years older than Cam. His dark brown hair, somewhat streaked with grey, was pulled back in a ponytail. He had a trim beard with two patches at the corner of his mouth that had gone salt and pepper. He wore a parti-color arming coat of black and yellow. A black bear rampant decorated the yellow half.

Ayja wore her favorite red kirtle. She'd worn it often as a child, and it would never have fit in reality, but in her memory walk, she could wear anything she wanted. She'd even worn a silken Belenese dress once, but it had seemed somehow out of place, and she hadn't worn it again. Her hair was loose, and she brushed it back from her face.

"I can't do it," Darra said. "I don't understand how it works."

"But it's in you," Ayja said. "I feel it. You touch the aether all the time. It is all that sustains you." She stood and went to the kitchen counter and returned with a cutting board of bread, hard cheese, and venison sausage. It was delicious. Wonderful. And she would pay for the fantasy when she returned to Dromost. The memory of the food would torture her until she entered her memory walk again.

She glanced over her shoulder and stared into the fire. Just embers now. Her well of power was nearly empty. They couldn't stay much longer.

"I'm a creature *of* magic," Darra said. "I don't wield magic. I can't see it."

"If only I could enter your memory walk," Ayja said. "I'm certain I could help you create a well of power there. You already have the ability

74

to draw life energy from other creatures. You just need a place to hold it."

"We've tried," Darra said. "I can't make the doorway."

Ayja shook her head. "Another thing I wished I'd learned from Telea. If only we'd had more time." She should have studied more with Telea. She begrudged every wasted moment.

"You were busy, my queen. You could not do everything." He took a piece of sausage and ate it. "You don't know how much I've missed eating."

"Really? Don't I? Think about it for a moment, Darra. And you chose your path," Ayja said, her frustration seeping through. "No one forced you to become a pyren."

"Of course. I'm sorry, my queen. Caught up in all this," he said, glancing around her memory walk, "I forgot, for a moment, our reality outside. And... as to becoming a pyren... I was dying. Morin gave me a second chance. And before you say it again, I am deeply remorseful for the things I did when I was in his service."

"This house was destroyed because of you and the other pyren and ghuls who attacked. This house. All of my friends and neighbors. You killed so many."

"I know," he said, turning away and looking out the window. "But I am different now. Everything I do, I do in your service. You are my queen."

"Queen of Dromost. A doomed queen."

Ayja stood and walked to the window. She looked across the open yard and the stone well that stood there. She remembered the pyren and ghuls charging across the yard and assaulting her home. She remembered her friends, slain, or taken as ghuls. She remembered the destruction of her village and the deaths of everyone who lived there.

"I would have died a hundred deaths by now if not for you, Sir Darra," she said. "The Dromost Gate would not be closed if not for you. Still, it is hard to forget. It is hard to forgive."

"Until my last moment, I will give everything for you, my queen."

Ayja saw movement off to her left and spotted Jef the Donkey eating grass near the barn. She smiled. As a child, she'd never known that Cam had named Jef the Donkey for Earl Jef over some unknown slight years long gone. Earl Jef was dead now, slain holding the rearguard as Ayja had escaped the Temple of Forsvar.

She owed so much to so many.

"There's a demon nearby," Darra said.

Ayja glanced out the open door as if he meant the demon was present in her memory walk. It wasn't, of course. He meant in the real world. In the world of Dromost.

"You can see it?" she asked. She glanced at the hearth and the flickering coals there. She had very little strength remaining in her well of power.

"I hear it scrabbling along the cliff. Be ready. The moment my touch leaves you, you will awaken, and it will know we're here."

"I'm ready. I have little strength, though."

"I have some to offer," Darra said. Life force surged into her, and the fire blossomed in the fireplace. "The last demon was generous, but its strength will not last forever."

The host of demons that had approached them up the valley had dispersed long ago. Her wave of fire had worked, giving the two of them time enough to hide, and time enough to put Ayja into a sleep-like trance. Unable to track her, the demons had moved on. How long ago had it been?

"If we can take the demon at some advantage, we must do it," Ayja said.

"I can't leave you to look. There could be more than one."

"Do you want to attack?"

Darra shook his head. "Let's wait a little longer. Perhaps it will move off. I want to wait as long as possible. It... it seems to be moving away."

It was a strange feeling to be in her memory walk, seeing the home she'd always lived in, while Darra was in two places at once. He was with her in the great room, but he was also in Dromost, keeping watch and looking out of the crevasse they'd tucked themselves into.

Ayja walked to the doorway of her home. There were pegs on the wall where she and Cam had hung their cloaks and coats, but there were also three spears there, and two bows and quivers as well. Near them, Forsvar and Dromost were propped against the wall. Ayja picked up the Godhammer and, after pushing the cutting board aside, placed it on the table.

Forsvar was barren of any markings. There were no words or inscriptions. It was an old-fashioned round shield, painted red, with the god's crossed lightning bolts emblazoned upon its face and a band of silver around its rim.

Dromost was the opposite. She let her fingers trace down the length of the Godhammer's steel shaft. Every fingerlength of it was covered either by Drommarian runes or with delicate scrollwork. She shifted her gaze to the hammer's head. On one side, it was a pronged hammer and on the other, a blade-like spike. There were runes on the head, and six engraved circles as well.

"Can you read it?" Darra asked. He still sat at the table across from her, watching.

"Some of it," Ayja said. "It was one thing Telea did manage to teach me besides singing. She thought it very important that I learn Drommarian runes."

"Why was that?"

"I've told you how magic runs in streams all around us, connecting everything and binding everything, right?"

"Yes, the very lines I cannot see and cannot touch."

"I can see them, and have always been able to. I can twist and shape those lines with my thoughts. It's not that I'm actually touching the lines. It's simply that my fingers make my thoughts more accurate — more precise."

She looked up from the Godhammer and into Darra's eyes. So strange to see brown eyes staring back at her instead of iron-black orbs. "Telea's magic is different. Singers use their voices to shift the strands of magic. They don't pick out specific strands but move many strands together all at once. Because they don't touch individual strands, they can't manipulate the elements the way I can. They can't create fire or shape the earth. But, before she taught me to sing, she could do things I couldn't do. By harmonizing many strands together, she could affect emotions and touch the souls of creatures and demons. Earth and fire singers could cause great shifts in the strands that had physical force."

"It is a shame I have no voice," Darra said. "I never had one."

"I don't know if it is that, or if it is because you are a pyren. Or maybe it's that I'm not a good voice instructor. Telea told me that not everyone could become a singer."

"I can draw the life force from others, and give it to them as well," Darra said, holding his hands out before him and staring at them. "I can enter their minds and manipulate their actions and even their dreams. But I don't know *how* I do these things. It is just who I am."

"You could become a summoner," Ayja said. "Telea said that anyone could do it. It is just a matter of study." She pointed at Dromost. "See these runes? They are simply the twisting of the strands of magic in physical form. They are empowered by life force. By blood in most cases. Summoner chants are used to twist the aether, but also activate the runes they draw. Telea's healing magic was the combination of summoning magic and the magic of song. I wish I'd learned more of it."

"Could you do a summoning?" Darra asked. "Do you know that magic?"

Ayja shook her head. "The little I know of their magic has to do with the binding of magic to items and how to make magical workings last longer. It was Telea's knowledge of summoning that taught me the power of the circle. I know almost nothing of actual summoning or of healing. If I did, I would be able to enter your memory walk and maybe help you create a well of power."

"I've seen the circles on Dromost." He pointed to the three small circles engraved on the Godhammer's head. "What do they mean?"

Ayja nodded and turned the hammer over. There were three matching circles on the other side. "I only know what a fraction of these runes mean." She pointed to one on the shaft. "That one is strength. This one means permanence — it is very important. This one means lightness." She looked closer at the six circles on the hammer's head. All were identical. "The symbol in the circle means spirit, or soul."

"When Dromost kills, it binds the soul of the victim inside it," Darra said. "I've felt it."

"I have as well. It is those souls that empower the Godhammer with its most powerful strikes. The souls are consumed."

"Forever?"

Ayja shrugged. "I don't know. We have souls that depart this earth and join Forsvar in the heavens above when we die," Ayja said. "At least that's what we've always been told."

"Yours perhaps," Darra said. "I gave up mine when I became a pyren. It was... consumed by the magic of my transformation."

"I'm sorry if that's true. I mean — I don't doubt it's true. It's just hard for me to fathom."

"Trust me. It is. When I am eventually destroyed — and I say destroyed because I am already dead, my soul will not go to live with Forsvar. I will become nothing. It was my choice. I knew it as it happened."

"When you die, there will be nothing? You are certain of this?"

"It's why the demons ignore me. I have no soul for them to consume."

"Telea told me that spiridus and demons are different. They have eternal spirits instead of souls. When their physical form dies, they are reborn to live another life."

"For how long? How many times?"

Ayja shrugged. "I have no idea."

He stared at the warhammer. "So does Dromost consume the souls and spirits that empower it? Or are they just released?"

Ayja frowned. "I don't know. I just don't know."

Darra leaned back and rubbed his chin with his hand. "Those six circles are empowered by the souls that Dromost takes when it kills? And the runes that form the, what do you call it, the working? They are permanently engraved on the hammer. Those circles are just waiting to be empowered."

"Yes."

"Can you do the same thing with the workings you cast?" he asked, waving his fingers in the air in front of him.

Ayja laughed. "I don't look that way when I make a working."

"You do to me."

"But what are you saying? I've bound my magic to the ring that cleans the air I breathe. I've bound magic to arrows so that they'll explode."

Darra shook his head. "No, that's not what I mean. I've seen you use very powerful workings, but the most powerful take time. Like the wave of fire you threw at the host of demons. I've seen you make rings of fire you throw at demons and jets of air you blast them with."

"Right. Circles are very powerful. Before I met Telea, I would use raw energy, raw life force pulled from my own body, to twist the elements to my bidding. Together we figured out how to twist a working into a circle so that it would feed itself. Those workings are powerful, but take time."

"Couldn't you do what the summoners do, and create the framework for the working ahead of time and then empower it later?"

"I did that before. Remember Orlos's fire arrows?"

"No, not that. I mean, do it here. In your memory walk. You taught me how to make my own memory walk and how to store my memories there. Couldn't you pre-make these complicated workings and store them here? Then you could fill them—"

Ayja stood so suddenly the bench crashed to the floor behind her. "You are brilliant, Darra!" Unable to contain herself, she paced the floor of the great room. "I could do that! It would still take time to fill the working with power, but it would be much faster than before."

Smiling, Darra stood and walked to the door. "Couldn't you pre-fill it with power and then use a chant or a rune or whatever to unleash it? Then it would take no time—"

Ayja ran up to Darra from behind and hugged him. "You should be a wizard!"

She felt him stiffen with surprise at the sudden assault. "A what?"

Ayja let go of him and backed away. "I'm sorry. That wasn't very proper." She couldn't read the inscrutable look on his face. "A wizard," she said. "It's an Ethean word Telea taught me. It means a wielder of magic. In just a few heartbeats you've given me two brilliant ideas." She began pacing again. "This is all I wanted to do after the Orb of Creation was unlocked. I just wanted to explore magic and all of its possibilities. I've learned so much, but everything I've learned will perish with us in Dromost. In the end it will all be meaningless."

Darra shook his head. "It won't, Queen Ayja. We will free ourselves from this place. You will find a way. Look at everything you've learned so far. We just need to keep surviving long enough to figure a way out of here."

"Were you always this positive?" Ayja asked. "Even..."

"Even before I was a pyren?" He stepped into the sunlight coming through the front door. "Yes. Even when I became ill, I thought I'd recover. And when I did finally succumb to despair, Morin came to me and offered me hope."

He pointed out the door. "The demon is here."

Warm, potent life force surged through Ayja, and she was suddenly awake. Darra was pressed close to her, but in a heartbeat, he turned and threw himself at some barely seen demon at the entrance to their hiding place.

Ayja followed him. She saw Forsvar and Dromost at her feet and struggled to pull the Godshield free in the confined space of the crevice. Just in front of her, Darra struggled with the demon — a man-shaped, horned beast. She could do nothing though, so close were the walls on either side of her.

Darra dragged the demon closer and threw it against the wall. He held its throat with one hand while his other grasped its clawed hand. The demon's free hand raked across Darra's face, tearing at his flesh, but then the strength went out of it, and its red eyes grew dim. Ayja saw the aetherial glow as Darra drained the life from it.

"Hurry," he said. "There are more of them. We have to fight free."

Ayja slid Forsvar onto her arm and handed Dromost to Darra. As soon as he had it in his hand, he leaped out the entrance, disappearing from view. Ayja stepped over the rapidly decaying demon and stood at the cave opening. Darra was below her, facing two more of the demons and three spiked imps.

Dromost flashed as Darra struck one of the imps. The Godhammer passed through the imp, spraying broken spikes and ichor in a wide arc. The rest of the demons rushed him.

Ayja reached to her belt only to discover that Darra had both Dromost and her sword. Despite the strength Darra had given her, her well of power was not nearly full.

Darra struck down another of the imps, but then the two horned demons were on him, grasping at him with their clawed hands. Ayja threw herself into the melee, swinging Forsvar and striking one of the demons a heavy blow. Bones shattered at the impact, and the demon flew five strides, landing in a crumpled heap.

An imp whipped its tail, flinging three spikes at her, but she raised Forsvar and batted them away. Another imp threw itself at her, but she hurled a jet of fire at it, incinerating the little demon mid-flight.

Darra struck the remaining horned demon, shattering its arm, but still it grasped on to him. The demon's head flashed forward, and it bit into Darra's neck. At the same moment, the last imp's tail flicked, and two spikes punched through Darra's coat-of-plates and into his back. The heavy armor turned two others.

Running forward, Ayja swung Forsvar like an axe, slamming the Godshield's rim into the demon's back. There was a snap like a dry branch breaking, and the creature folded back upon itself. With the last blast of fire, she burned down the remaining imp. Within her memory walk, the fire dimmed.

Darra knelt over the demon, his hand on its face, drawing what little life force remained from it. "Don't let that one escape," he said, nodding toward the demon she'd sent flying. "But don't kill it."

The demon was only then struggling to its feet. It hissed at her as she approached, its right arm hanging limp at its side. Ayja charged it, Forsvar held high in front of her. The demon turned to flee, but she was faster and struck it in the back. Overbalanced, the demon topped forward. With only one good arm, it was unable to catch itself, and its head slammed into a jagged rock.

Darra ran past her and put his hand on the demon's back. There was no glow. "Dead," Darra said. "I needed its strength."

"I couldn't stop it. I tried." Ayja sank to her knees, gasping for breath. "I have little left, Darra."

He touched her face, kindling a small flame in her well of power. "It's all I have. Can you pull these spikes from me?" he asked, turning his back to her.

She grabbed on, but cried out in pain and pulled her hand free. It bled from a score of tiny slices. "It's barbed," she said.

"Take my glove." He held his left hand to her. He wore only one, keeping his right hand free to touch his victims.

Ayja took it and put it on her hand. "This will hurt," she said.

Darra shook his head. "I don't feel pain. At least not the way you do. Pull it free before it burrows in and does any more harm to me."

81

Putting her bloody right hand on his back to brace herself, she grasped the spike with her left and yanked it free. It took flesh and thick, black, shimmering blood with it. She shuddered at the sight.

"Hurry," Darra said. "We must get away from here."

She pulled the second spike free and threw it on the ground.

"I cannot heal myself," Darra said. "These wounds took a lot from me. Every passing heartbeat I grow weaker." He handed Dromost to her. One of the hammer's circles glowed with a purple light. "Any foe I face, I must try to steal their life. Try not to kill if you can avoid it."

"I will try. My well of power is nearly empty, Darra. I have only the strength of my body, and that is fading."

Lightning licked across the sky as heavy raindrops began to fall. He looked her in the eyes. "If we cannot defeat the next demon we face, we are lost."

Chapter Nine

Telea dismounted, motioning for the others to follow her lead. The gates to Aftokropoli stood open just fifty strides away, but dozens of soldiers stood between her and the entrance. She gave her horse's reins to Tharryl and stepped up to the guard in front of her. "How can I help you?" she asked in perfect, unaccented Belenese. The man had to believe she was one of his countrymen.

"Who are you and where are you coming from?" he asked. Most of the guards wore leather cuirasses and carried spears and round shields. This one was clearly an officer. He wore a bronze scale cuirass and bronze greaves. His polished helm held a tall panache of yellow feathers. *Feathers from Ethea, of course.*

"I am a merchant," Telea said. "My name is Penelea of Makedan. What is the meaning of this delay?"

"A merchant? From Makedan? You look Ethean to me. And she's certainly Ethean," he said with a nod towards Isibindi.

"She is one of my guards. Yes, I hired her on my last trip to Ethea. They make good soldiers. I, however, am Belenese, even if my mother was Ethean."

"Where is your caravan? You have no wares?"

"My ship was damaged in the recent storms and had to put in at Limanis, just down the coast. We hired horses and rode for the city. My ship shall soon arrive." Telea removed her bamboo scroll tube from her belt and uncapped it. The papers were legitimate, issued by the Ethean council just for this purpose. The man would find no flaw with them. Removing the papers, she offered them to the guard.

After glancing at them for only a moment, he shook his head. "This will require more time. You'll have to wait with the others."

Telea's mind raced. The Etheans held near the gate were being treated as prisoners, and from all appearances, some had clearly been there all day. Was the emperor attempting to arrest every Ethean in the country? Surely there were too many.

"How long a delay will this be?" she asked the guard as he motioned her towards the other Etheans. "I have important business to attend to."

"We have to be certain we can trust you," he replied. "Now, take your retinue and join the others."

How do I get out of this? How do I control this man's mind to make him set us free? Telea asked her demon. *Remember, serve me well, and I will set you free.*

When? You say that so often it is meaningless.

When the gate is sealed, and we are free of the demon threat.

When will that be?

Help me, and it will come sooner!

Let me possess him. He will suddenly become very amenable.

No. There must be another way.

Touch him. Touch his mind. Offer him something he wants.

Money?

You. He wants you. Offer him that. Be subtle. Do not let him feel your presence.

"Get moving," the guard said. "Good people are waiting."

Telea stepped close to him and reached out for her papers; however, instead of taking them, she took his hand in hers. The moment they touched she let her mind brush his. He had no memory walk, and his mind was defenseless to her. He was hot in his armor. He was angry at his job. He wanted it to go back to the way it used to be. He was worried about war.

"Perhaps you could let me through, and we could talk about this later?" she said.

"Later?"

"Dinner, perhaps?" She floated an image in his mind. Of the two of them sitting at one of the expensive restaurants overlooking the harbor. Telea knew the city well and, as the daughter of an ambassador, had dined at some of the finest establishments in the city. The image she sent was very clear. In it, they were together, at a candlelit table well off from the others. She showed herself in a diaphanous white gown with a plunging neckline. In the vision, she stared longingly at him.

"Dinner? I don't know if I — "

"Business," she said. "Purely business." She showed herself leaning across the table to kiss him full on the lips.

"I'd love to dine with you," the guard said, a confused wrinkle on his brow.

Subtle! Be subtle! The demon said.

"Perhaps we could meet at the *Sun and Sky* just after nightfall? Wait for me there." Within his mind, she looped the image of them seated across the table, and her leaning across it to kiss him.

"That would be lovely," he said.

"Thank you for letting us through," Telea said.

He turned to the guards standing nearby and said, "Let Penelea and her escorts through. Her papers are in order."

"But captain — "

"Her papers are in order," he said, more sternly now. "Go ahead, Penelea. I'll see you soon."

"Thank you, captain," Telea said, taking her papers from him as she let go of his hand. "Come along," she said to her companions. Mounting their horses, they started forward. Telea glanced towards the gathered Etheans and felt a pang of guilt. She'd done nothing to help them. Some of them looked at her with envy in their eyes — others with hope.

I should go back. Perhaps I can free them.

No! Her demon replied. *You did too much already. You were too strong.*

As they rode into the gate tunnel, she heard the captain call out behind her, "Sotoros, you have command. I'm off to the *Sun and Sky*."

"Captain? That's a long way off. When will you be back?" the soldier replied. Telea didn't look back to see who was speaking.

"I won't be back. She said to meet her there. We are to dine tonight."

"I don't understand, Captain. It's not even time for the noon meal."

"She said to wait for her there!" The captain's voice rose in anger. The heavy clip-clop of their horses' hooves in the gate tunnel prevented her from hearing the other soldier's response. They soon exited the tunnel and were inside the city. Three broad avenues led off from the gate square. Telea took the leftmost — the one leading towards the University District. She knew the area well, or at least better than most, and there would be people of many backgrounds there, making it less likely her odd group would stick out.

Aftokropoli was four times the size of Sal-Oras but was far more open and spacious. The Saladoran capital had felt incredibly cramped and overwhelming to her, with its narrow streets and press of humanity everywhere. Aftokropoli had wide roads and broad, open squares. There were areas of the city where people lived closer together, but they were the exception. The Great Death had also taken its toll on the population. It would be decades before the population was what it once was.

"What happened back there?" Sindi asked. "How did you get us out of that?"

Telea shrugged. "He really wanted to go out to dinner."

"There was more to it than that. He mimicked your every word. You had him in the palm of your hand."

"He really, really wanted to go out to dinner."

"Did you do something to him?" Sindi lowered her voice to a whisper. "Did you use some of your song magic on him?"

"Just a little," Telea said, glancing around to make certain no one was in hearing.

"It seemed more than a little."

Telea shrugged. "It got us through the gate. I'm very worried about the reception we've received. Well, that Isibindi and I have received. I'd hoped to speak with the emperor, but it seems he is poisoned against Etheans. Perhaps you and Calen can speak for us?"

"What do we do if the emperor won't listen?"

"We'll have to leave it to powers beyond us. We'll have to get word to King Handrin and the Ethean Council. It will take diplomacy. Emperor Niktonas thinks he's under threat and doesn't even realize he's been saved. He doesn't even know the Dromost Gate is closed."

They searched into the afternoon for a place to stay in the University District, but no one would rent them rooms. More than a few rude words were cast their way, and it seemed everyone in the city had turned against the Etheans.

Finally, just before dark, an older woman gave them rooms in a poorer section of the district. "My grandmother was Ethean," she explained as she ushered them into the foyer. "I've heard the ugly rumors. I'm only a quarter Ethean, and people I've known for years are treating me like a traitor."

"I don't want to call more attention to you," Telea said. In truth, only the woman's wavy hair gave away any hint of her Ethean ancestry. And it was still enough to cause those near her to mistreat her.

"I feel for you, dear," the landlady said. "And, to be honest, I could use the coin."

"We thank you for your kindness," Telea said, paying the woman for a week's lodging in advance.

The residence was a typical city villa that had been converted to apartments. The front facing the street was plain and more than a little weathered, the old columns having not been scrubbed in quite some time. However, once they entered the courtyard, the rest of the establishment appeared clean and tidy. The villa formed the shape of a hollow square, with the landlady's residence in the front and apartments on three sides. A small stable took up half of the first level in the back.

A young boy and girl came out to take care of their horses, while a young woman led them upstairs to their rooms. Telea had paid for three rooms — one for Calen and Sindi, one for Tharryl, and one for Telea and Isibindi. Or at least that was her plan. Isibindi and Tharryl had different ideas. Telea shrugged as they entered the adjoining room together.

"You've been on the road a long time it seems," the landlady said. "I have a small bathhouse. Six would be a crowd. I, ahem, do frown on mixed company in the baths. We aren't that type of establishment."

"It would be welcome," Telea said. "I will let the others know."

"I will serve dinner in the dining room at dusk. Very soon, as it is."

"Thank you," Telea said. After she'd departed, Telea called the others to her room. Old frescoes depicting a bucolic vineyard decorated the walls. The furniture was sturdy, if somewhat plain. An ink-stained desk stood by the courtyard window. The room had spent some time as a student residence.

"There is a bath downstairs. No mixed company," she said, crossing her arms in front of her. "Understand? It was hard enough finding a place to stay."

"I'm souring on Belenese hospitality," Tharryl said.

Ignoring him, Telea said, "We can bathe and eat and rest. Tonight, after dark, I am going to the palace. I want to see what I can learn there."

"You are going unannounced?" Calen asked. "Will they even see you?"

"I am not going on an official visit. I'm going to spy around and see what I can find."

"No offense," Tharryl said, "but people seem to be paying a lot of attention to you. It might make sneaking around difficult."

"I won't be seen. I have magic that will hide me."

"Really? Like Orlos?" Sindi asked.

"Not quite as well as Orlos can manage. I can only make it work at night, or where it is very dark."

"You wish I come with you?" Isibindi asked in heavily accented Saladoran. "Your mother ask me to watch you."

"No," Telea replied. "I have to do this alone."

"Be careful," Isibindi then said in Ethean. "We can't afford to lose you. You know the secret to closing the gate."

"The summoner, Muaz, knows it as well."

"That may be true, but we still don't want to lose you."

In turns, the women and then the men bathed. They then took their dinner in their rooms, rather than eat in the dining room. There were other guests in the villa — all students, but Telea didn't want to them be aware that they were foreigners from beyond the Great Salador Pass. Who knew what the students might say to someone? Better to remain safe and out of the way.

Before she left, Telea gave Sindi her coin purse. All but for a small portion she might need if something arose. The coin purse was heavy with gold and silver. Isibindi held an equal sum. It was a small fortune, but they hadn't been certain how long they'd have to stay, or what expenses they might have.

"I don't know how long I'll be," Telea said to her companions. "I'll be back before dawn. Stay out of sight and don't draw attention to yourselves."

"You are certain you don't want us to come?" Calen said. "Sindi and I won't draw much attention here."

"What good would it do? You can't bear weapons on the streets. And even a little attention is bad attention. Don't worry. I'll be fine."

"What if you don't return?" Tharryl asked.

"She'll return," Sindi said, glaring at Tharryl.

"It needs to be asked."

"I would send Isibindi to Ethea," Telea said. "Pay for passage on a ship. It isn't safe for you here. The rest of you should go to the Great Salador pass and make your way to Salador. Use your best judgment. I'll see you soon."

Telea exited the villa onto the street. It was dark and cool, and there were few people out. She glanced around to make sure that no one was in sight, and then stepped close to the wall and drew the demon's cloak of shadows around her.

The night was dark and the sky was overcast. She couldn't have wished for better conditions. She had the demon's sight as well, and while it didn't turn dark into day, and everything was shades of grey, she could see well nonetheless. She walked down the street, confident that she would not be accosted. It was pleasant. She listened to snippets of conversations as she passed. Talk of business and friends, lovers and entertainments. She walked down the street unnoticed by others, even though they were within a few strides of her. It filled her with a sense of power. If she wanted, she could reach out and touch them. *And oh, the things I could do with a touch.*

She left the University District and started uphill towards the Imperial Palace. She'd been there before, long ago with her mother. Had she only been eight or nine? She remembered being awed by the spectacular wealth of the palace. Everything gleamed of gold and silver and was reflected in mirrors. Long marble hallways stretched forever with arched ceilings supported by smooth pillars. Even the grounds were amazing. Acres and acres of gardens surrounded the palace, some with mazes one could get lost in for hours.

A wall surrounded the palace, but it was more for privacy than defense. In places, the wall was covered with vines or ornamental stonework that would make it easy to climb. The emperors hadn't feared anyone in nearly a century. Not an assault, at least. There had been assassins, but the elite palace guards had not allowed an emperor to be killed since before the Traitor's Rebellion.

Telea didn't know what to expect when she arrived. Would she attempt to enter the palace? She should if she got the chance, she thought. Who knew how much she could learn by simply listening in to those outside? The streets were more brightly lit as she approached the palace. There were lamps here, casting circles of light onto the street and sidewalks. They weren't so bright that she had to avoid them, but she did so out of caution. She'd only used the cloak of shadows a few times and wasn't certain how far she could trust it.

The broad avenue she followed opened onto a large square in front of the palace itself. There were expensive villas here as well as restaurants for the richest residents. Across the square was the main gate to the palace. Unlike the city walls, no buildings were pushing up against the walls here. There were things that had changed, though. There used to be trees growing near the palace walls, shading the sidewalk there. All had been cut down. The flowering vines that had grown up the walls were gone as well, ripped away by someone who'd not cared about the damage done to the wall's facade or to the beauty of the palace.

There were guards as well. Dozens of soldiers were posted in front of the towers guarding the gate. More stood atop the towers. These were the Imperial Timari — picked men in good armor. Not a force to be trifled with. Inside the palace, she'd find the Emperor's Axes — Blood Drinkers who'd left their mountain homelands to become the emperor's elite bodyguard. Her father had been one of them until he'd met and fallen in love with her mother. When they'd married, he'd been forced to leave the Axes — his loyalty placed in doubt.

There was no way, even under the cloak of shadows, that Telea would attempt to get close to the main gate. There were other gates, though. The palace had several, and some smaller sally ports as well. She backtracked and went down some side streets, approaching the palace from another direction. The streets were darker here. It was late enough now that there were few lights in the surrounding villas.

The wall curved ahead of her, and Telea paused as she approached the turn. She heard voices and peered carefully ahead. There was a small gate here with maybe six soldiers in front of it. A dim lamp hung nearby. It cast only a faint glow over the gathering. Telea crept closer.

"I heard someone say it was the *nafai amas*," one of the guards said.

"Bullshit," replied another. "Why would the Bride of Forsvar go to the Temple of Forsvar and attack it?"

"They say she had the Godshield with her."

"Who says? Who?" a third guard chimed in. "Bring them here, and let's hear their crap first hand."

"Yeah, what do you think happened?"

"It was an elementar. They tried to overthrow Kyvern Psertis, but when they failed, they turned south and tried to sack the Temple of Forsvar."

"Dromost take them!"

"They were trying to link up with their Ethean allies."

"What if it was the Bride of Forsvar?"

"You idiot. Why would the *nafai amas* attempt to overthrow the Emperor?"

"None of you knows shit. All just rumors."

"I'll tell you what's not a rumor. Captain Trelos at the South Gate went mad."

"What?"

"Yeah, I heard it as well."

"What in Dromost's name are you talking about?"

"A couple of Etheans came through. Apparently he sees 'em and falls madly in love with one."

"Bullshit."

"It gets better. He lets them through the gate and then drops everything and heads off to meet her for dinner."

"What do you mean he dropped everything?"

"Just up and leaves. Puts someone else in charge and heads off to meet her at a fancy restaurant."

"Sounds stupid, but not mad. Shit, he sounds possessed."

"In the bright light of day? A possession?"

"Who knows what those Etheans are capable of?"

"Well, get this. She doesn't show up. He waits for her the whole day. His relief hears about this and sends some men to get him. He won't leave. He says he'll wait there forever until she arrives. Keeps insisting that she told him to wait. When they try to get him to leave, he draws steel on them."

"Dumb bastard. What happened?"

"They beat the crap out of him and drag him back here. He's locked up at the main gate raving like a lunatic. 'I have to get back,' he shouts. 'I have to wait. She told me to wait'."

"Must have been a real looker. I go for those Etheans."

"This is beyond lusting for some looker. He's lost it. Mad."

90

"Possessed."

"Head's up. They're coming."

From the far end of the street, another party approached. Telea expected soldiers, but it was a group of eight women led by two well-dressed men. Unlike the liveried soldiers, they wore traditional short tunics with fine capes over their shoulders to fend off the chill. The women all wore long, revealing gowns of Ethean style. None were Ethean, however. Even in the dim light, Telea saw they were all long-limbed and beautiful.

"This is a special engagement, ladies," one of the guards said. "You'll be well paid. You understand that pay extends to your silence?"

"We know our business," one of the women replied.

"You understand that this might be an extended stay? None of you have any pressing business that you might need to leave for? Because you won't be allowed to leave until the engagement is complete."

One of the women laughed. "Is that what you're calling it?"

Telea now saw there were porters behind the women. They were laden with leather travel bags and small trunks. The guards ushered the women through the door, and Telea saw her chance. She approached the crowd at the door, staying as close to the wall as she could manage. The dim lantern hung from a peg on the far side of the door. Several people stood between her and it.

Some of the guards preceded the women into the palace, while six remained outside. The guards stood aside, making way for the porters. Telea followed close behind the last porter. The man carried a huge trunk on his back, and she did her best to keep it between her and the light. They were almost through when the top of the trunk hit the lintel, and the man nearly dropped it. Telea ducked low as a guard moved up to help the porter. His foot kicked hers, and she held her breath in fear, thinking she'd be caught. Burdened by the trunk, he barely glanced in her direction before moving on. She slowly let out her breath.

With a few choice curses, they got the trunk through the door. Telea slipped in behind the guard and flattened herself against the wall. The guardroom was crowded, but a far door was open, and the women streamed though it into another room beyond. The porters were paid and ushered out with several warnings not to speak of the work they'd done.

"What of our bags?" one woman asked.

"Palace servants will bring them in," a guard said. "For now, we'll take you for some late evening refreshments. Who knows who might show up?"

Nervous laughter and sidelong glances followed. "Do you think he'll really come to see us?"

"Who knows?" the guard said.

The outside door was closed and barred as the last of the guards entered. The women passed out of view into the next room. Telea kept herself pressed against the wall. There were too many guards to risk crossing the room, but after a few heartbeats, and more than a few ribald comments about the women, most of the guards departed.

Telea didn't wait. She followed the last of the departing guards out the door before anyone thought to close it. The next room was a cluttered mess. Crates, food stores, bolts of cloth, and tools were strewn about in utter disorganization. Two doors exited. She heard female laughter through one and followed the sound. A short hall led to a small kitchen. Too small to be the palace's main kitchen. This was clearly a servant's wing.

She passed a hallway of iron gated alcoves. Bottles, casks, barrels, and clay jars of every imaginable alcoholic beverage filled each alcove — all under lock and key. The women were just in front of her now, escorted by only two guards. Were they really being brought in for the emperor's pleasure? She found the thought hard to believe. She'd seen Niktonas before, but not as emperor. Then he'd been commander of the Belenese Army of the East. He'd always been a stern, serious man, not given to pleasures of the flesh. The man she remembered was totally devoted to defeating the summoners and protecting the empire. And despite the contents of the hallway, she'd always heard that he didn't imbibe intoxicants either, liquid or otherwise.

But who else could the *he* the guard mentioned be? Perhaps some high ranking officer of the court? If so, the man was truly bold to sneak so many women, so obviously, into the palace. General Niktonas would have had the man's head.

Telea followed as they left the storage hall, passed a larger, better stocked, kitchen, and then entered a finer hallway. The floor here was polished marble, and the walls decorated with fine frescoes. Lamps lit the hall, and Telea let herself fall far behind the women, lest she be seen. The light wasn't bright, but if she were caught now, there'd be no escape.

She was curious now. What was going on within the palace? She had to know more. She had to know what was going on in court. The women and their escorts disappeared through a brightly lit doorway. Telea crept closer and listened around the corner. They'd apparently arrived at their destination. She heard the clink of glass and the scrape of knives on plates. Servants offered food to the women while they chatted about the identity of their secret guest. Clearly they thought him to be the emperor, but even they didn't know for certain.

Telea didn't dare enter the room. It was far too bright. The hall she was in ended in a closed door. She'd explore beyond, see what she could discover, and make her way out of the palace. The night was late, and the palace dark. She didn't imagine she'd have too much difficulty making her way from place to place undetected. As she crossed the open doorway, she glanced in and saw the women in two clusters, talking and eating from finger plates. There were two well-dressed female servants in the room, as well as three escorting guards, one more finely attired than the others. She didn't pause to look closer — instead going to the closed door and listening at it. She heard nothing beyond. She didn't want to risk opening it, for fear some quiet guard might be lurking just beyond. Still, it was this or accomplish nothing at all.

Glancing over her shoulder to make certain no one was looking out from the dining room, she turned the door handle and pulled it ajar. She peered through the gap, but there was no one there. The door led outside, to a small garden with a fountain in the middle. A covered walkway circled the edge of the garden. Vaguely, from her childhood memories, she recalled that there had been many of these gardens in the palace, each more beautiful than the last.

Telea slipped through the door and into the garden. Even in the darkness, she saw that it hadn't been maintained in some time. It surprised her. Perhaps the recent war with the summoners had left the treasury bare.

Closing the door behind her, she made her way along a covered walkway to another door. She listened at it for a moment before passing through. This corridor was even wider than the last and more ornate. The ceiling rose high over her head and was supported by beautiful marble arches. Windows looked over gardens to either side.

Telea wandered the halls of the palace, becoming lost in their twists and turns. It was empty. Hundreds of people usually lived there, and she knew it was late at night and they'd be asleep, but the palace seemed cold and hollow. There should have been some signs of life.

She turned a corner and saw an intersection ahead of her. She heard the stomp of boots and two timari crossed in front of her. Hurrying as quickly as she dared, she caught up to them.

"...they say he's in a mood tonight. He's got three of them in there with him. He doesn't like to be disturbed."

"Orders are orders. We're to tell him if anything unnatural happens. Anything that might be magical. Captain Trelos going mad fits the bill."

Telea followed behind them. There were no sounds but those the two men made, her cloak of shadows silenced her steps as well as shrouding her from view.

What did I do? How do I help him? She asked her demon.

Too late for him now. I told you to be more gentle.

Can I heal him?

You'll never get to him. He's under guard, they said.

Perhaps-

"You know some of the women don't come back out again. What do you think he does with them?"

"Don't start with that idiotic talk. He gives them a good ride and then ushers them out the back."

"I've heard rumors."

"Best keep them to yourself. Speaking poorly of the emperor is treason to some."

"I don't like it. He's sent all the singers east, but he hasn't called up the army."

"There's already an army there. Don't underestimate him. He's a great general. He probably figures they only need a few more singers to handle the summoners."

"Or maybe he wants them out of the way."

The second timari suddenly halted and grabbed the man who'd just spoken by the arm. "Watch your mouth! Seriously. Listen to yourself? You want to be arrested? Say that crap in front of the Emperor's Axes, and your head will soon depart your shoulders."

"Something's not right."

"Best you leave now, then. Keep this up, and you're a dead man. I'm serious. Now, are you going to come with me and do your job? Because I don't need to lose my head because you made some dumbass comment to an Axe."

"I'm coming."

Telea followed until they came to an intersection guarded by four Emperor's Axes. The huge Drinkers wore long scale hauberks like the one Ayja had worn. They wore tall helms with nasal guards and long mail aventails. Bushy beards overflowed their armor and hung halfway down their chests. They leaned on their long axes and watched the two men approach.

The two timari stopped a few strides from the Axes. "I've brought an important message for His Imperial Highness, Emperor Niktonas."

"Show me the scroll tube," one of the Axes said in heavily accented Belenese.

Telea hadn't seen it as they passed, but the older Timari pulled out a silver scroll tube and handed it to the Axe. The huge man looked it over but didn't open it. "Any of you recognize them?" he asked his companions. His eyes never left the two timari as he spoke.

"They guard the front gate," another of the Axes said. "I recognize them."

The first Drinker handed the scroll tube back and gave the briefest nod to the timari. Both timari saluted with open hands and continued down the intersection. Telea followed behind them. It was hard to stop looking at the Drinkers. She'd spent the five years living amongst them before she'd gone off to the College of Healers. To her, they'd always been the strongest, most noble people she'd known. Utterly incorruptible. If something were wrong, they'd fight it. She hoped it was still the case.

They went another fifty strides before coming to a large double door guarded by six Axes. Once again, the timari presented his scroll case. "His Imperial Highness, Emperor Nikontas, asked to be informed of any unusual events, day or night," the older timari said. "This is such a case."

The captain of the Axes nodded, and without a word, rapped on the door three times, twice, and then once. He repeated the pattern again and then stood, silently staring at the two timari.

One of the double doors was suddenly yanked open, revealing an elderly man with scraggly gray hair. Not the emperor, but one of his servants. He wore a fine silk tunic trimmed in red, very similar to the ones the Children of Forsvar had worn. Telea almost lost control of her cloak of shadows at the sight of him. But not for his appearance or his attire.

The man was demon-possessed.

Chapter Ten

"What do you mean, 'there's going to be a battle'?" Nidon asked the old Belenese man.

"Kyvern Psertis is bad man. He attacked the *nafai amas*. He try to steal Forsvar. Satrus Exonos is good man. He help the *nafai amas*." The old man smiled a broad smile. "I touched Forsvar. *Nafai amas* has returned!"

Nidon knew of the legend of the Bride of Forsvar, although he didn't approve of it. But Orlos had warned them of Belenese beliefs, and not to challenge them for fear of driving off their allies. "Why is Kyvern Psertis attacking?"

The old man shrugged. "He still want Forsvar. He be angry at Satrus Exonos."

"What about the emperor? What does he think?" Nidon wasn't certain he wanted to become involved in a Belenese civil war. And Handrin was only bringing ten thousand men across the East Pass. They were intended to be allies with the Belenese, not to battle them.

"I do not know Emperor Niktonas. You speak with Satrus Exonos."

Nidon took a deep breath. What was he getting himself into? "How many men does Satrus Exonos have? How far away is he? How many does Kyvern Psertis have?"

The old man shrugged again and then spoke with his companions in Belenese. It was clear that none of them had the answer even before he spoke again. "We only messengers. Exonos is... two days away."

What would happen if his small force engaged a much more powerful army? There would be no rapid escape up the pass. "Can Satrus Exonos come here?"

"I not think so. Battle is near."

If some enemy took the pass, even as far as the crevasse where they were building the bridge, no Saladoran force would ever be able to break through. It would be an impossible, uncrossable barrier if held by enemy soldiers. And the Dromost Gate had to be closed. There was no other way about it. He'd promised King Handrin he'd keep Salador's needs first in his mind. To be cautious now might cause a delay that could not be overcome.

And Ayja must be saved.

"Kael!" he called into the forest. "Come here! I need you."

The Idorian jogged out of the forest, his crossbow held easily in his hands. "What do you need, Champion?"

"Would you send two of your men — people — to Baron Fendal and ask him to bring both lances and the rest of the Landomeri down the pass? We are going to meet with Satrus Exonos. He's to follow as quickly as he can."

Kael nodded. "And what of the rest of the army? Should we send word to the king to bring the army over the pass?"

Nidon thought for a moment. He couldn't risk committing the entire Saladoran army. "Send word to the king that I am asking for the First Plan — that we occupy each way station and start bringing supplies. The main army is not to advance."

"Very well."

Nidon turned to the four Belenese. "Take us to Satrus Exonos."

By early afternoon they arrived in a small mountain village. It was a poor village of herders, but it was tidy, and the people were friendly. They all rushed out to greet the foreigners. Through the interpreter, the villagers asked about Ayja and the god, Forsvar.

Nidon didn't have anything to offer them except his assurances that they were here to help. It was less than the people wanted to hear, but they were gracious hosts, feeding the company a hearty, simple meal before they set off further down the mountain pass. The old man wished them well, but couldn't accompany them any further. He was as hard as an iron nail, but the long journey had taken a toll on his joints. His son, the younger man, agreed to continue on as a guide, although he barely spoke two words of Saladoran.

They'd been told that if they pushed hard they'd make the next village after nightfall. Otherwise they'd spend the night out of doors. Nidon paid the villagers in silver Saladoran nobles for their hospitality, hoping to spread some good favor for all of the Saladorans who might soon follow.

After noon they passed through the ruins of some long-abandoned village — a memory of a more prosperous past. There was evidence that the previous village had once been larger. Nidon saw old stone walls and building foundations that hadn't been used in centuries — or at least since the East Pass had been closed.

It was well after dark when they stumbled into their destination. Their arrival was greeted at first with fear, replaced quickly by wonder that Saladorans had once again crossed the pass. Over and over, Nidon heard the words *nafai amas* spoken, but with no one to translate for them, communication was nearly impossible. Through signs and silver, Nidon made it clear that they needed food and lodging, and the village roused itself from slumber to provide both.

Two of the village's young men were sent off into the darkness, tin lanterns and spears in hand. "Go Satrus Exonos," their guide said. At least that was all Nidon could make of it.

The company was slower to start the following day, the previous day's journey having taken a toll on them. Nidon had yet to see a horse in Belen, even though Orlos had mentioned how much cavalry they had and the quality of their horses. As they marched, dark clouds gathered in the sky overhead. The day was cool, and a soaking rain would make the journey more difficult and far more unpleasant. Spring had definitely arrived in Belen, though. As they marched, they shed their coats and heavy cloaks, the hard march and their armor being more than enough to defeat the cool air.

They'd just turned a bend when four riders appeared on the forest trail a mere fifty strides ahead. The riders reined in at first, and then one drew his sword, and holding it by the blade, raised it high above his head. It seemed a friendly enough greeting, but Orlos hadn't mentioned anything about Belenese salutations.

"Where's Orlos when I need him?" Nidon muttered.

Two of the riders dismounted and approached on foot. Both wore scale brigandines over mail hauberks, with leather and plate reinforcements on their arms and legs. Over their armor, they wore loose robes of intricate patterns in red and yellow, much like the kaftans the Kiremi wore, although finer. They left their conical helms and shields on their horses, bearing only their sheathed swords and maces with them. Both wore trinkets of gold and silver sewn into their kaftans and strung from their armor. In the case of one of the two, it was a fortune in metal and gems.

"Join me, Sir Dalaman," Nidon said to the knight beside him as he handed his axe to Squire Fress. With Dalaman at his side, he marched out to meet the two Belenese.

The leader of the Belenese, or at least the man Nidon assumed to be the leader by the ornateness of his armor and equipment, sheathed his sword as they approached. He stopped a few strides from Nidon and said, "Welcome, knights of Salador. I am Satrus Exonos. This is my second,

Okwesi." His Saladoran was nearly perfect, spoken with just a bit more of an accent than Telea.

Exonos's second took Nidon by surprise. His skin was nearly as dark as charcoal, darker even than Telea's. Okwesi gave Nidon a bow and smiled, his white teeth standing out brilliantly against his dark skin.

"I am Champion Nidon, commander of the Army of Salador. This is Sir Dalaman."

"Champion Nidon!" Exonos said. "You raised the *nafai amas,* Princess Ayja. She told us of you. It is my pleasure to meet you in person."

The man's smile and words seemed genuine to Nidon. "Orlos sang your praises," he said. "He had nothing but the kindest words for you. Have you seen him recently?"

"He is too kind," Exonos said with a bow. "I only wish everyone Princess Ayja had encountered had treated her with the respect she deserves. Orlos is further down the valley. He volunteered to do some scouting. I hope it is not a problem."

"To be frank, I'm not certain. Am I walking into a war? King Handrin thought we were coming as allies to the Belenese Empire. "

"No, not a war. Kyvern — you might call him governor — Psertis attempted to seize Forsvar from Princess Ayja. It was a devious, terrible act. When he failed, he spun a lie to the emperor. He told Emperor Niktonas that Ayja was here to take his throne."

"Orlos said that the High Priest at the Temple of Forsvar also attempted to take Forsvar."

Exonos nodded. "He was in league with Kyvern Psertis."

"This is all very worrisome to King Handrin," Nidon said. "He has no wish to take part in a Belenese civil war. Where does Emperor Niktonas stand? Does he know the true nature of Ayja's mission? Wasn't it he who invited us to cross the East Pass and close the Dromost Gate?"

"In fact, it was his father who sent the embassy. Emperor Niktonas, his son, is a great man, though. I know him. I fought under him during the Summoner War."

"Can we not get word to him? To let him know the truth of the matter?"

"I have tried. As of yet, I am not certain if any of my messengers have gotten through."

Nidon took a deep breath and let it out slowly. He didn't like this. Any of it. "Has the emperor taken any part in your war with Kyvern Psertis?"

Exonos shook his head. "None. It has been my satrusal forces and the populace against the kyvern's soldiers."

"The people are with you?"

"They know that I am an ally of the *nafai amas*. They know that she would never do the things she is accused of. They met her. They saw her magic. They touched the Godshield. They believe in her. Just as I believe in her." Exonos paused. "I see your concern. I understand it. But Orlos told me that the *nafai amas* has said that the Dromost Gate must be locked. That our peril is not ended."

"Did he tell you where Princess Ayja is?"

Exonos nodded gravely. "In Dromost."

"We must close the gate," Nidon said. "And somehow, it is my hope, save Princess Ayja."

"I do not believe the *nafai amas* can be trapped anywhere she doesn't want to be," Exonos said, his voice filled with conviction. "Perhaps when she is saved, and the Dromost Gate locked forever, Forsvar will return to us."

Nidon held little faith in the Belenese belief that Forsvar still walked Helna's world. Like all Saladorans, he believed the Three Gods to have been banished by Helna long ago. He also knew better than to challenge Exonos's beliefs. This was an ally he had to have. "Tell me the situation that faces you."

"There is a village a few stades — what you call arrowflights — from here. My men are there, but we are few in number: just a dozen timari and as many freemen. Timari are my knights, like my escort here. Freemen are light horse. I also have nearly one hundred hillfolk who will take up arms. More if I get word to the villages you passed.

"Kyvern Psertis's son, Prodidos, has perhaps fifty timari with him and twice as many freemen. He has reinforcements behind those, but they are days away."

"You are outnumbered," Nidon said.

"The pass is easily defended," Exonos replied. "When the Army of Salador arrives, we can drive Prodidos from the pass and break through. Then we can get a message through to the emperor and join forces with him against the summoners."

The pass could be easily defended, Nidon knew. If the very worst was to befall them, the Army of Salador could retreat over it with few losses. Everything fell on the emperor and how he'd react to the arrival of King Handrin. "Can the emperor be convinced that we are allies?"

"I am certain of it," Exonos said. "He is a good man."

Nidon glanced up the pass behind him. The Dromost Gate had to be locked, and it couldn't happen with the Army of Salador and the Orb of Creation on the wrong side of the East Pass. "We will aid you," Nidon said, making a decision that would put the lives of thousands of Saladorans at risk.

"Kael!" Nidon called out, waving the man closer. "Satrus Exonos, this is Kael, one of my lieutenants. He commands the Landomeri archers who are with me. He is also step-father to Orlos."

Exonos gave Kael a curt bow. "Your son is a good man," he said.

"Thank you," Kael said. "He spoke very fondly of you."

"Kael," Nidon said, "send another pair of messengers back directly to King Handrin. Ask him to bring the army over the pass without delay. The army must cross as quickly as possible."

"I will."

As he departed, Nidon turned back to Exonos. "Where will we hold?"

"The village is indefensible. There are too many approaches. I held my men there as it is the last village on the pass that offers another route of retreat."

"There's a strong point up the pass from here," Nidon said. "We passed it just an arrowflight ago."

Exonos smiled. "You and Princess Ayja think alike. That's the position she held when she first met me. She has an eye for terrain."

"I taught her well," Nidon said, proud she'd earned the praise of the Belenese warrior.

"I will order the village abandoned," Exonos said. "The people and all of their livestock will move up the pass behind us. Their warriors will stay behind and hold the strong point with us. How long until your army arrives?"

"Eight knights and ten archers will arrive in a day if they move quickly. We are just the advanced guard, though — a scouting party really. The army won't arrive for another six days and will be few in number at first. The crossing of the East Pass is not easy."

"Kyvern Psertis's main force will arrive before then."

"We can retreat up the pass further," Nidon said. "There are other strong positions, although none as strong for a force as small as ours. We can fortify the position and hold it until help arrives."

Exonos nodded. "That would be my choice."

"Kael!" Nidon called out. "Did those runners depart? Well, send someone to sprint after them. When the bridge is completed, tell Master Hod to bring his men down the pass. I have more work for them."

"I must get the villagers moving," Exonos said. "There's not much time before Prodidos arrives."

Nidon and his company followed Exonos's men to the village. It was the largest of the three they'd seen so far, but still only had a population of a few hundred. For the most part, the villagers took the news of their departure seriously and hastily gathered their livestock and most treasured possessions. Even as they worked to depart, the Saladorans drew a lot of attention. And once again, Nidon heard the words *nafai amas* mentioned more than once. Whatever superstitious beliefs the people had about Ayja, it was working in Nidon's favor. They seemed willing to do almost anything asked of them if the name of the Bride of Forsvar was invoked.

Nidon saw what Exonos meant when he said that the village was indefensible. Wide fields bordered the road approaching from the south. There were no fortifications — Orlos had mentioned that defensive walls were outlawed in Belen. The river bordering the east side of the village was wide and shallow, although it was running fast with spring runoff. A broad, wooded slope bordered the town to the west.

Exonos loaned Nidon, his five knights, and six squires spare horses from those of the timari. The timari rode fine coursers, although Nidon found the high stirrups and low cantle of the saddle uncomfortable and unstable. The horses of the freemen were light, quick hobbys, too small for armored men in full harness.

Nidon sent his three crossbowmen and six remaining Landomeri across a field and into the tree line. From there, they'd be able to cover the approach to the village. He and the mounted Saladorans remained in the village with Exonos's timari, four of whom, Nidon was surprised to see, were women. Exonos's freemen had been sent down the road to harass any approaching enemy.

Orlos arrived in the midst of all of the confusion, running up to Nidon and giving him a cheerful, "Hello."

"Where have you been?" Nidon asked. "Or should I ask, what have you seen?"

"Just having a little look-see," Orlos said with a smile. "Satrus Prodidos's men are coming. Some of Exonos's light horse are waiting in ambush."

"How long do we have?"

"If they want to be here before nightfall, they will. They are several arrowflights away, but moving cautiously."

"Your countrymen are in the woods to the right of those fields," Nidon said, pointing. "You can join them there if you wish. I'll tell Exonos what you've reported."

"I'll join them."

"Aim true."

"I will do my best," Orlos replied, although with little enthusiasm.

By late afternoon the village had mostly been cleared. Only a few herders waited to take their goats up the trail. It would take some time, though, as the pass narrowed quickly and the villagers who'd gone before slowed progress for those who followed. It wasn't encouraging when thunder rumbled up the valley. A good rainstorm would add even more delay, not to mention a miserable night spent out of doors.

Nidon had begun to think them home free when the trouble began. Across the open field in front of the village, ten of Exonos's freemen suddenly emerged, riding at a gallop. As they rode, they turned and loosed arrows behind them. "They are early," Exonos said, joining Nidon. "Prodidos pushed his men harder than expected."

"We need to buy time," Nidon said, glancing up the pass to where the villagers were still escaping. It would be a disaster to be caught at the tail end of the retreating column.

Prodidos's freemen raced onto the open fields, loosing arrows as they pursued Exonos's men. Exonos shouted orders to his timari, who immediately moved to the edge of the village.

"Where do you want us?" Nidon asked.

"Stay in the village. I don't want the kyvern to know that you are here. Support us only if our need is great."

Nidon watched the advancing freemen. Twenty had already emerged, but he couldn't tell if more were coming. It galled him to be left behind, but this was Exonos's fight. "We'll cover your advance," Nidon said.

Exonos's timari sortied from the village just as his retreating freemen entered it. The attackers, overextended and too focused on their foes, were caught strung out in loose order as the timari charged into them, loosing arrows as they rode. For an instant, Nidon remembered Hadde at the archery contest when she'd outshot the squires of Salador from horseback.

The timari only loosed two arrows each before sheathing their bows and drawing curved swords. Their arrows had plucked four riders from their saddles before the enemy freemen realized what they were up against. Too late, they reined in their horses and tried to flee, but the momentum of Exonos's timari was too great, and they crashed into the light horsemen to devastating effect. Close in, the heavier armor and bigger horses were too much for the freemen, and those they caught were quickly cut down.

Even as the fight went on, more of Prodidos's freemen and even some timari entered the field. "Ready yourselves," Nidon said. "Knights to front."

Exonos saw the danger of the enemy reinforcements and ordered his timari to break off the attack. It wasn't easy to reform in the swirling melee, though, and the enemy timari were advancing.

"Forward!" Nidon called out. The Saladorans emerged from the village's main street and immediately formed up. They started across the field at a trot. Exonos's timari had just broken free and were fleeing their way. Seeing the Saladorans, they split, flowing to either side.

"Advance!" Nidon shouted. Their horses cantered towards the enemy. It wasn't a proper charge. They had no lances, their saddles were wrong, and their horses were unbarded, but it would have to do. Their armor was heavier, and they were Knights of Salador.

"Charge!" The twelve Saladorans leaned forwards in their saddles, their shields held high and their swords outstretched. The kyvern's men, a mix of timari and freemen, outnumbered the Saladorans. Confident in their numbers, and unaware of the weight of Saladoran armor or the skill of their foes, they came on.

The two bodies of horsemen were just forty strides apart when a volley of Landomeri arrows and Saladoran bolts tore into Prodidos's cavalry. They weren't many, but the range was short and the enemy flank open. Two horses fell, throwing their riders violently to the ground. Arrows plucked two riders from their saddles.

The Saladorans crashed into the Belenese. Nidon impaled a timari with his falchion and almost lost it as the man fell. He turned a sword blow on his shield as he wrenched his sword free and then slashed at a freemen, cutting his arm to the bone. A blow hit him from behind, taking his wind, but his coat-of-plates held, and he spun his horse. The unfamiliar beast was clearly trained for war and turned in place so quickly Nidon nearly lost his seat.

A gaudily attired timari swung at him, but Nidon caught the blow on the edge of his shield. For several heartbeats, the two men hammered at each other, their horses turning in a tight circle, their shields pressed against each other. They locked blades, and Nidon leaned into the smaller man, shoving him so that he began to slide from his saddle. As he tried to recover, Nidon laid a heavy blow on the side of the man's helm, and he toppled to the ground.

Thunder pealed across the sky overhead, the crash so heavy it seemed to cause a heartbeat's pause in the fighting. Fat raindrops fell as swords and maces hammered on armored bodies.

More enemies joined the fight. Nidon still saw Saladoran red around him, but more and more, he saw the bright colors of the Belenese. A freemen woman rode up to him and shot an arrow at him from just two strides away. Nidon twisted his shield at the last instant, and the arrow hammered into it, punching a full hand-depth through it. Before he could reply, the woman was gone.

104

Lightning streaked across the sky, and torrential rain poured down from the heavens. Nidon spurred his horse at a timari, but the man turned and fled. Suddenly all the enemy fled as a rush of horsemen charged into the battle. Exonos's timari and freemen had returned to the fight. Their weight, the galling Landomeri arrows, and the crushing storm conspired to set the enemy to rout.

"Hold! Hold!" Nidon shouted. It wasn't time for pursuit. While they had the chance, while they had the cover of the storm, they had to escape up the valley. "Squire Fress," he called out, looking for his squire, and finding him a horse length away. "Tell Kael to retreat up the valley."

"Yes, Champion!"

Nidon looked to where the enemy was retreating. They were nearly impossible to see through the sheets of rain. "Who is down?" He scanned the ground for fallen knights. Seeing one, he leaped from his saddle. It was Sir Dalaman. Unconscious, but alive, having taken a blow to the side of his helm that had knocked him senseless. One of the squires hadn't been so lucky — an arrow had punched through a gap in his coat-of-plates, killing him.

Village warriors rushed out onto the field, taking the wounded from the field, rounding up stray horses, and looting weapons from the fallen.

"Your men fought well," Exonos said to Nidon. "The Knights of Salador live up to legend."

"Legend?" Nidon asked, wiping the rain and sweat from his face.

"Stories from the War for the Orb. The Saladoran Paladins of Forsvar rode into battle alongside their god. We tell our children stories of their exploits."

Nidon shook his head. "We're just soldiers, like you. Don't place too much hope in us."

"I'm placing all my hope in you."

Chapter Eleven

Ayja slammed Dromost into the skull of a bull-headed demon, releasing the power of Dromost's five contained souls. With a flash of purple energy, the demon's head exploded, sending horns and bits of skull and flesh splattering across the landscape. She raised Dromost, ready for the next attack, but none came. They were dead. All of them.

It had been the fiercest battle they'd yet fought. Two score demons had attacked when she and Darra had been at their lowest. If not for Forsvar and Dromost, they surely would have perished. She and Darra had fought side by side, Ayja creating a ring of death while Darra sought out individual demons to steal life force from. In the midst of battle, he'd managed to share some of their energy with Ayja.

Ayja turned to look for Darra and saw him lying on the ground behind her. His armor was burned away from the right side of his chest, exposing his burned flesh beneath. The rectangular steel plates were all that remained where his coat of plates had been. The plates themselves were pitted and brown. Beside him, a serpent demon decayed into mush, its head severed from its body. Ayja's sword lay on the ground beside it.

Kneeling beside him, Ayja said, "Darra, are you still with me?"

He shook his head. "I am near death. Destruction if you will," he whispered.

"Take some life from me," she replied, taking his cold hand in hers. "Take what you need."

"Just a little," he said. His hand became warm as he drew life from her. It didn't hurt. In truth, it felt good. Was that some condolence to those the pyren drained of life entirely? If she was drained completely, she knew Darra could turn her into a ghul. And there would be nothing she could do about it if he did.

The savage burns on Darra's face began to heal as Ayja's well of power drained to almost nothing. Within her memory walk, there were just glowing embers remaining in the fireplace. Darra removed his hand after only a few heartbeats. Ayja pulled him to a sitting position.

"My coat of plates is ruined," he said as it fell away from his chest. He pulled off his shredded kaftan and then started to work at the remaining straps of his armor. Ayja knelt beside him to help. Together they pulled it from his body and tossed it aside. He still wore his mail hauberk. There was a large hole where the acid had eaten through both it and his arming coat.

"It's damaged, but better than nothing," Ayja said, nodding to his hauberk.

Darra nodded. "I'll keep it on." He pulled his kaftan together and did up the ties. He gave the ruined coat of plates a little kick and said, "A shame. A good harness ruined."

"It did its job. You'd be dead without it."

"That I would. The demon was too strong to paralyze," he said. Darra's voice was low, and Ayja saw the weakness in his movements. "Still, I was holding it off and draining it of life. It had almost healed me of all my wounds and more. I would have had too much to give to you. But then it spewed some foul acid on me, burning away my armor and wounding me terribly. I had to slay it for fear it would spit more acid. We find ourselves where we were before."

He picked up Ayja's sword and inspected it. "Not damaged, at least. The acid must only have been in its spittle." He paused and looked around the ruined landscape. "Where do we go next?" he asked as he knelt and cut the leather lining from his ruined coat of plates. It made sense. They had nothing, and Dromost gave them nothing. Soon their armor would be so rent as to be unusable, and the rags they wore would fall from their bodies.

"Somewhere new."

Darra nodded and rolled up the scraps he'd saved and tied them to his sword belt. Together they headed off across another landscape of broken rock. Ayja felt the heat radiating from the earth beneath them and from time to time, saw the glow of molten rock in the cracks beneath her feet. She sloshed her half-full canteen. It might be some time before she could fill it again.

Hunger was a constant, aching pain now. Her body had no strength, and she survived only by using the life force in her well of power. If her hearth went cold again, she was certain she'd collapse and die. "I don't know what to do, Darra," Ayja said over her shoulder. "How long has it been since I've last eaten? Weeks? Months? I have no idea how much time has passed. My body exists on the magic you feed me, and I don't know how much longer it can sustain me. Each passing heartbeat I feel my well of power drained a little more."

107

She heard him scrabbling over the rocks behind her, but he didn't reply. Had he even heard her? She glanced up into the sky for a sign on any flying demon but saw none. From time to time, she did see small, shadowy forms slipping away through the tortured landscape. *Worms. Too small to take us on. They fear us.*

"There is a way, my queen," Darra said.

She marched forward, waiting for him to continue, but he said nothing more. "What is it?" she asked, pausing to take a pull from her canteen. She'd given up on him calling her Ayja. He just wouldn't do it. She looked at him and met his gaze for just a heartbeat before he looked away.

"I can turn you into a pyren," he said.

An icy chill flowed down Ayja's back. She imagined the wild, raging, skeletal ghuls — mindless, horrible beasts hungering for human flesh. "I won't be a ghul," she said, shifting her grip on Dromost.

Darra shook his head and then met her gaze. "Not a ghul. A pyren, like me. The demons would no longer hunt you. They wouldn't be able to sense you."

"Because I'd have no soul."

"You'd no longer have to depend on me. You would be able to steal the life force from demons. You would stop wasting away. You would live."

"As a pyren." Ayja turned away from him and continued through the jumbled field of broken boulders. She couldn't do it. There was no way she'd become a pyren — a soulless creature of undeath.

They passed over a broken area where molten rock oozed from cracks beneath them. It was almost impossible to tell what area was safe just by sight. The molten rock turned black as it cooled, leaving deceptively thin layers over the orange-red liquid fire below. It was the temperature that was the best warning. Ayja felt the heat radiating from it from a distance of ten strides or more.

She paused at a small stream of flowing rock. It would be easy enough to jump, but why take the risk? She knew now that a small detour would find a hardened bridge over the molten flow. Looking past the stream, she saw that the black field went for another arrowflight before a slope took them to older, solid land. Perhaps there they would find a puddle of water or a stream where she could refill her canteen.

The molten rock bubbled and rose in front of her. Some unseen pressure from the earth beneath them was causing the level to rise. "This way," she said to Darra, motioning off to her left. Once again, she glanced to the sky for any sign of flying demons.

"Watch out!" Darra shouted at the same moment Forsvar warned her of an attack. She whirled and raised the Godshield as a creature of molten rock rose out of the glowing stream. It stood taller than a man and had no legs, just a torso growing from the rapidly rising pool beneath it. It had a head, though, with two flaming eyes, and two long whip-like arms.

One arm, thick like the heavy cables Ayja had seen on the *Summer Swan*, whipped towards her, slamming into Forsvar. The blow rocked her back as glowing liquid rock splattered all around her. The limb, shorter now by two strides, pulsed and began to grow.

Even as she watched, three more arms grew from the creature. Two of them struck out at her. She dodged one and caught the other on Forsvar. Again, molten rock spattered everywhere. She felt searing pain as a glob struck her leg, burning through her trouser and into her flesh.

Ignoring Darra, the demon aimed its newly grown arms at Ayja. She wanted to flee but didn't dare turn her back on the assault. Twisting the aether, she sent a blade of wind at one of the demon's arms, severing it. Two more struck her, but she caught them on Forsvar. They exploded in fire and a spray of molten rock, burning her again.

The first strike to pass the Godshield would be the end of her.

Darra leaped forward. Wielding his sword two-handed, he slashed twice, severing two of the arms. "Flee!" he shouted even as the demon grew more arms.

Ayja aimed a lance of air at the demon. The tight spiral blew a hole clean through the demon, molten red rock instantly turning black. For a moment, the demon faltered, but then the hole filled in.

"Now, Ayja! Run!"

The demon lurched at Ayja, even as Darra sheared another two limbs from it. "Come with me!" Ayja shouted as she leaped away from the demon. She drew precious strength from her well of power as she jumped, drawing a gust of wind under her to cast her far from the demon's reach.

Even as she jumped, a molten arm lashed out at her. Forsvar took the blow, but some of the shattered arm caught the side of her face. The pain and power of the blow threw her off balance and sent her tumbling as she landed hard on the razor-like rocks. Her trousers tore open and deep gashes opened in her leg.

Silver flooded her vision, and strength filled her arms, but she fought it with all her will. Her rage would consume her last reserves of strength. It would kill her. For several heartbeats, she lay prone, battling against her silver fire.

She was out of range of the demon, though. Darra was still there, battling it. He cut off a limb and turned to run as the creature surged forward, trailing a stream of molten rock as it advanced.

Darra leaped out of its path, but an arm lashed out at him, catching him clean across his back. The pyren toppled forward under the impact but somehow managed to roll to his feet. He was on fire. His kaftan burned as he ran. "Run, Ayja!"

As the silver left her vision, it seemed a tremendous weight fell upon her. Her well of power was just a glowing ember now. She had nothing left. Still, by force of will, she managed to stand. She had to get away from the demon's source of power. She had to get away from the molten rock underfoot.

Staggering forward, she ran uphill, away from the demon. Darra had broken away from the demon. His kaftan no longer burned, but she saw glowing embers and smoke streaming from his back as he moved to join her.

The demon pursued Ayja for only twenty strides before receding into the cracks in the rocks beneath it. Still, she stumbled forward, not trusting the demon not to appear through the very ground beneath her.

Stumbling on the rough terrain, Ayja fell to one knee, tearing it open and causing blood to flow. She tried to stand, but couldn't. Suddenly, Darra was there, pulling her to her feet. "Come, we have to get off this field," he said.

"I have nothing left, Darra. My well of power is empty. I am dying."

"I can't heal your wounds," he said as he half-dragged her forward. "I don't have enough strength left to me. But I can put something into your well." Pausing for just a moment, he touched her face, and she felt the briefest moment of joy as life force pulsed into her. The embers of her well of power became the tiniest flickering flame.

Ayja nodded, and they stumbled forward. They were fifty strides from safety when a molten pool suddenly burst into being almost at their feet. "Run!" Darra shouted as the demon emerged, but Ayja didn't have the strength. She could barely walk. Darra dragged her forward for several strides as the demon emerged behind them. Then, when she fell, he picked her up in his arms and ran with her.

The demon hurled globs of itself after them, exploding in splattering flame. None of them struck Darra directly, but sticky, burning stone still splashed him. He ignored it though, running hard to put as much distance between them and the demon as possible. Ayja raised her head and looked over his shoulder to see the demon sink back into the flow again.

They reached solid ground again, and only then did Darra slow. There was a steep bank at the edge of the molten field, and he put her down there. "I can't carry you up and keep my balance."

Ayja stood unsteadily with her hand on his shoulder. "I can't climb that," she said.

"Take my hand. I'll pull you up."

She did as he said, and they scrambled up the crumbling dirt embankment. When they reached the top, Ayja sank down, unable to stand any longer. "I can't go on, Darra. I have no more."

"If I give you any of my strength, I don't think I'll be able to hunt. I don't even know if I can do it now."

"Take Forsvar and Dromost," Ayja said, surrendering to the inevitable. "You can survive here."

Darra knelt next to her. "My life has no purpose without you, my queen."

"Then hide the Two Gifts so that no demon will ever find them. If a gate opens to Helna's world, I would not have them used against my friends."

"Take my blood," Darra said. "Become a pyren like me. You will survive, at least."

"You're asking me to give up my soul. For what purpose? To live out the rest of my existence in this place?"

"It would give you time to find an escape."

Ayja shook her head. "I won't survive it even if I tried. I saw my father create three pyren. It's a terrible ordeal. One man didn't survive. He died a horrible death."

"I know. I remember. But you are an elementar. Perhaps it will be different for you."

"I am too weak. Even then..."

He took her hand in his. It was warm. Just a trickle of life force flowed into her. "I don't want to," he said. "I can't lose you. Sleep. I will hunt." He looked up as if hoping to see a demon victim walk by.

"It won't matter. They will find us again. How many times can I go through this?"

"Can you make yourself sleep? Stay asleep, I mean?" Darra said. "You told me about circles and magic. Can't you trap yourself in a circle of sleep? If you're asleep, no demons will come for you."

"I can make circles of elemental forces, or raw aether. I can't make a circle of sleep." She paused and frowned. "Unless I make... make a circle of song. The *Song of Rest.*

"If you're under the influence of the *Song of Rest,* will your well of power not drain so quickly?"

Ayja nodded, holding her hand up so that Darra would stop speaking. Could she do it? Twist the magic of the song into a circle so that it would never end? She'd never attempted such a thing, but it *seemed* possible.

"Where can I hide?" she said. "I think I can do it." She looked around, but they were on a relatively flat plain. There were no caves here.

"There is a boulder nearby. I will dig a shelter under it. I will cover you with rocks."

"It will serve as a cairn if this doesn't work," she said with a grimace as she struggled to her knees. Darra raised her to her feet and half-carried her the twenty strides to the boulder. He let her down and then, on hands and knees, dug at the stones and soil beneath the stone.

Ayja glanced around for any demon sign. How long did they have? They'd taken too long already. As Darra worked, she softly sang the *Song of Rest.* Looking into the aether, she saw the glow of magic. The song was a mix of soft blues and yellows and included strands of magic she wasn't familiar with. They were beyond the elemental strands she knew so well.

Still, she reached out and twisted the strands of the song so that they circled back upon themselves. It was hard both singing and focusing on the strands at the same time. She also had to push the song away from her so that it wouldn't affect her. It wasn't time yet for her to sleep.

Deep within her memory walk, her fire was just warm coals now. Her working, being song, drew almost nothing from her well, at least. Twisting and weaving the strands required only the slightest effort. Within the aether, she looked at her working and smiled. It was sustaining itself. It would last a very, very long time.

"It will work," Ayja said.

Darra stood. "I'm sorry, my queen. It will not be comfortable."

Ayja looked at the hole he'd dug. *A shallow grave.* "I'll be asleep," she said. "Don't worry for me." She took Forsvar from her arm and placed it on the ground. Then she took Dromost from her belt and placed it atop the Godshield. "Take them. And good hunting."

"I shouldn't take them both. You might be attacked again."

She shook her head. "It wouldn't matter, Darra. I am too weak to fight. You need them to hunt."

"I'll be back for you, my queen."

"Ayja," she said. She took a deep breath. "I'm ready."

Darra helped her squeeze under the rock. "I'm so sorry," he said. Ayja squirmed as best she could to help him. "Cover me after I'm asleep," she said. She didn't know if she could maintain her focus as she was buried alive.

"I will," he said.

Ayja took his now cold hand and lay back. She saw her working floating in the air where she'd created it. She gently touched the aether and moved it closer to her so that it hovered over her chest. "If the time ever comes to wake me, you might need to enter my memory walk to do it. If that fails, then move my body from this place. The working will remain behind."

"The time will come," he said. "I swear it."

Ayja closed her eyes and sang softly as she directed the magic of her working at herself. Darkness swept over her as she retreated to her memory walk. She stood in the doorway of her home. It was evening, and crickets chirped in the depths of the pine forest.

She imagined Orlos walking out of the woods towards her. She thought of him often, but tried not to. What good would it do? It was only torture knowing she'd never see him again.

In the distance she heard a demon roar.

Chapter Twelve

Against her will, Telea gasped. The man — the emperor's servant — was demon-possessed. Luckily, no one heard her over his ranting as he berated the timari. She quickly let her demon look through her eyes. *Tell me what you see,* she demanded.

A strong demon has complete control of him.

"What? What?" the man barked. "Why do you bother Emperor Niktonas at this time?"

The timari held out the scroll, and the servant snatched it away. "Something unusual has happened," the timari said. "An officer, a captain at the south gate, has gone suddenly and inexplicably mad. It happened after he met an Ethean woman and her party at the south gate."

"Mad? How? What did he do?"

"He abandoned his post and went to meet her at a restaurant. He would not leave and would not obey orders. He drew his sword when they attempted to make him leave."

"Did she touch him? Did she?" the demon possessed man spoke very quickly, his words tumbling over each other.

"I don't know."

"Find out! Find out and return to me!" He waved the scroll tube. "It is all in here? In the report? Tell me! Is it in here?"

"It is, simvolos."

"Hurry then, and come back to me. Is the man here? This captain? Is he here?"

"At the front gate, simvolos."

"Go! Find out if she touched him."

Telea wanted to shout out to the Axes that the man was possessed. The emperor's very own advisor. No wonder things had gone so wrong. She stopped herself, though. What would the Axes do when she suddenly appeared?

What if the emperor is possessed as well? her demon asked.

Impossible. It could never have happened. He is too well protected.

114

Is he?

Could it have happened? She thought of the things the emperor had done. Things she could never have imagined him doing before. He was a great man — a legend. But his decisions recently had been inexplicable. She had to see for herself.

"Any word from Emperor Niktonas's sister? Has she returned?" the simvolos demanded.

"No word yet, simvolos," the older timari replied.

Telea walked closer to the door. Two lanterns hung from either wall, but they were dim and were set well away from the door. The Axes stood well off to either side. She only had to get past the two timari and the simvolos. The timari held his lantern in his right hand, his body casting a shadow to his left. She'd go that way.

The simvolos stood in the center of the doorway, but it was wide enough she could get through.

Will he see me? Telea asked.

Probably not.

She had to do it didn't she? She had to know the truth. Walking as close to the Axes as she dared, and keeping as far from the simvolos as she could, Telea walked through the doorway. The hair on the back of her neck tingled as she passed within reach of the Emperor's Axes to her left. She forced herself not to look at them, for fear of meeting their eyes. She somehow *knew* that if she met their gaze, her shadows would be dispelled.

She pushed herself against a wall as soon as she was through the door, barely able to breathe. Her pulse pounded in her temples. This was it. She was in the emperor's chambers. Any mistake now and she was a dead woman. There would be no forgiving trespassing here.

The simvolos closed the doors and barred them. There were no lights in this part of the palace. Why would there be? Demons had no need for them. Clutching the scroll tube, the simvolos rushed down the short corridor. There were two doors on either side, and he took the one to the right. He was too quick for Telea to slip in behind him.

Telea stood there, not sure what she should do. She couldn't risk opening the door. What if he was on the other side? She went to the opposite door and listened at it. Hearing nothing, she cracked it open and peered in. The room was a large, opulent parlor. A circle of stuffed couches dominated the center of the room. Artwork of every variety covered the walls — most of them portraits of the members of the royal dynasty. There were weapons and trophies on the walls as well.

She entered and closed the door gently behind her. The room itself was disheveled. Furniture stood askew, and there was, under the strong

115

floral smell of scented candles, an odor of decay. As she looked around, she saw that one of the portraits had been slashed.

Only one door led out of the room. When Telea was just three strides from it a man came through. Another demon-possessed man in servant's clothes. He walked with a herky-jerky motion, his back and limbs contorted, as he rushed for the far door. Telea threw herself out of the way to avoid him. He missed her, but her foot caught on the leg of a couch, and she fell to the floor.

She knelt on her hands and knees on the thick rug. The man stopped and loomed over her. She shrank back from him, willing the cloak of shadows to hide her from his gaze. She didn't dare look up, but stared instead at his feet, just a stride away. He only wore one sandal. His other foot was bare, and claws had begun to grow where his toenails had been.

For a moment, he stood over her, sniffing the air. Then, just as suddenly as he had stopped, he rushed away from her and through the same door she had entered. Slowly, Telea got to her feet. She crept to the next door, fearing what she might find.

The emperor was possessed. She was certain of it now. He would not let his chambers have fallen to such disrepair. He'd have noticed the possessed servant.

The next room was a very small dining room. If anything, it was more disheveled than the last room. Rotten food sat on the table. Plates and cups lay smashed on the floor. She stepped carefully around the sharp pieces and exited into a dressing room. Clothes lay scattered everywhere. Many slashed and torn.

She heard a woman's voice from the next room. Double doors stood open, and Telea crept closer to them. Someone was crying.

"I hunger. I hunger. You don't understand," a man's voice said. "Why must I contain myself any longer?"

"Please, no," a woman begged. "Don't. Just set me free."

Telea peered through the door and into the emperor's bedroom. There was a gigantic bed there, larger than any she'd ever seen before. Veils had once hung from its frame, but they'd been shredded and torn down. In the bed was the huge bulk of the emperor. The demon-possessed emperor. At first, Telea couldn't believe it was him. She could see his face, though, and even distorted by the weight he'd put on, it was still him.

There were three women in the bed with him, all naked and chained with collars around their necks. The emperor himself was naked as well. The women's backs were to Telea, while the emperor faced her. "I hunger," the demon said. He reached out and took hold of a Koromoi woman and threw her towards the pillows at the head of the bed.

As he turned and pushed his bulk atop her, Telea was horrified to see spikes growing out of his back. *Get away,* her demon said. *It is a powerful demon. If he sees you, he will destroy you.*

I have to help them.

Get help, then. You cannot do this yourself.

Telea backed away from the door. From within the room, a woman screamed in pain. She had to get help. She turned and fled.

Telea ran through the emperor's apartments. How could this have happened? How could the emperor have been possessed? *Why does he look like that?* She asked her demon. *The Niktonas I knew was a fit and powerful man.*

He's eaten too many souls, the demon replied. *He can't contain them any longer.*

What do you mean?

When a demon eats souls, it uses their life force to grow. To physically grow. He's eaten too many, but he's also trying to appear human and contain his size. He can't do it. He can't contain himself. The pressure is building up within him and is driving him mad.

Anyone who sees him will know that something is wrong.

Soon he will be beyond caring. He will lose all control, and the demon within him will be unleashed. He will be a grotesque. I can see it.

She paused at the closed parlor door and listened, but heard nothing. She cracked it open and peered through, only to see the twisted demon standing on the other side, staring at her. Telea froze. Did it see her? Or was it just peering at the door that had just opened?

Just as she began to back away, the demon lunged at the door, slamming it into her. She stumbled back and fell, striking one of the couches. The demon threw itself on her grasping her neck with one hand and her wrist with another. The possessed man's eyes glowed red as he pressed down on her.

"Master!" he called out. "Come!"

Telea tried to pry his hand from her throat. She needed to be able to chant. Only then could she paralyze him or draw his life from him. Suddenly, she felt an assault on her mind as the demon tried to force its will upon her. The shields of her memory walk held, though, and the demon snarled in frustration.

A shadow moved behind the man, and the simvolos appeared. He grabbed Telea's free hand and pinned it to the floor. "Who is this?" he demanded. "How did she get here?"

"Emperor's woman," the twisted man said. His head jerked as he spoke. Not just his head, but his whole body spasmed.

117

"This isn't one of the emperor's women," the simvolos said. "This is a spy."

Once again, Telea felt a mind assault hers. She poured strength from her well of power into her defenses. The simvolos flinched back. "This one has power," he snarled. "A singer, I'll bet."

"Eat her soul?" asked the twisted man.

"No. The emperor can break her. Her walls won't stand against him."

Darkness closed in as the demon continued to choke her. "Don't kill her," the simvolos said. She heard fabric ripping, and then cloth was shoved into her mouth. She tried to resist, but they were too strong. Soon a gag was tied tight, and her hands were bound behind her back.

The two possessed men lifted her roughly to her feet. "Lets put her with the other ladies," the simvolos said with a smile. "The ones who've already visited with the emperor. When he's finished with the others he can have this one for dessert."

The twisted man giggled. "Yes! Good!"

They dragged Telea across the hall. She smelled the sweet, sickly stench of death here. They passed through a library and into another room before the simvolos opened a door. Without a moment's hesitation, they threw her into the room and slammed the door behind her.

Telea tripped and fell on something soft. The smell of death was overwhelming. The room was pitch black, but her demon's sight allowed her to see the source of the stench. Bodies, dozens of bodies, lay strewn across the floor. Some bloated and rotten with time, others fresh and newly dead. All were women, and nearly all were naked.

Telea rolled off the body she'd fallen upon and got to her knees. She'd seen death before. She'd caused it. This was worse than anything she'd seen before. The smell. The contorted bodies. The open eyes were staring from faces filled with horror. Her stomach heaved, and it took all her will not to throw up. With her mouth gagged, to vomit would be to choke and die.

Carefully, Telea backed from the bodies until her back was pushed up against a wall. The room had once been a study or a map room. There were desks and chairs, and cubbies stuffed with rolled scrolls filled one wall. She saw a map of the empire painted on another.

Twisting and writhing, she got her hands free of the fabric bonds that had tied her wrists. The moment she did, she took the gag from her mouth. It was a relief to breathe through her mouth and save herself, to some degree, from the horrific stink of the room. For a few heartbeats, she closed her eyes against the scene in front of her and took slow, even breaths.

She could sing now, at least. But alone and against two demons, she didn't know how much it would do. If they were imps, she'd easily destroy them, but these demons were more powerful. Perhaps she could defeat the demon possessing the twisted man. It was the weaker of the two.

How had the summoners done it? How had they put a demon into the Emperor? Niktonas had been the commander of the Belenese army fighting them. By possessing him, they'd taken him out of the war. Did they know his father would die, and he'd become emperor? Or was that also part of the plan? She'd heard his father died in his sleep.

Perhaps that wasn't the case.

The Doomcallers had won the battle for the Temple of Dromost. Now their greatest enemy, the Empire of Belen, was under demonic control. What would have happened if Ayja hadn't closed the Dromost Gate? There would have been nothing to stop the demonic invasion that would have followed.

Telea had to escape before the emperor came for her. Shuffling along the wall, she reached the door. How long would the demon remain outside? She reached for the door handle and tested it, but it didn't turn.

Telea paused, listening for any sound beyond, but there was none. The door itself was heavy and well-constructed. Was it barricaded from the outside? She pushed on it, but it didn't budge.

She saw no way she could break through. Certainly not without making a great commotion. Telea looked for the hinges, but the door opened outwards. There was no way to remove them and pop the door free of the jamb. Moving carefully to avoid the dead, she crept around the room, exploring for anything that might help her. She found quills and inkwells and a few pen knives, but nothing that would help her get free.

She tried her best to keep her eyes from the dead as she searched. The demon emperor had stolen their souls and cast their useless husks away. She looked across the jumbled, naked bodies and shuddered. How long until she was one of them?

Something moved among the corpses, and her heart lurched. After a few heartbeats, she saw it again. A rat. She shuddered. Rats were eating the corpses. She saw another, but at first, it seemed the corpse had moved, chilling her.

But the bodies could move, couldn't they? She could make them move. Did she dare do it? Did she have a choice? She saw no other hope for escape. Telea carefully walked towards the freshest bodies near the door. Crouching low, she touched the cold flesh with her bare hand and began to chant.

119

The woman was dead. Long dead. More than a day. As a healer, it was wholly disheartening to search a body for signs of life and to find absolutely nothing. She'd touched people who'd died before. Some who'd died just moments before. A couple of times, she'd managed to bring someone back because, while their heart had stopped beating, there was still life in their vital organs or their brains.

It wasn't the case with this woman. Everything about her was dead. Still, Telea let her healing vision explore the woman. Soon, as she'd discovered before, she found a spark of motivation. Even after death, the body retained some memory of life. Drawing from her well of power, Telea pushed life energy into the body, sparking that memory of life.

"Raise your arm," Telea commanded.

The arm resisted the command. It didn't want to move. The death stiffness had taken it — the blood clotted and cold. Then, ever so slowly, the arm lifted until it pointed at the ceiling. A chill crept down Telea's back.

Then, just as with the pirate, Telea crafted a circle of life force and laid it over the spark of motivation that remained within the woman. Energy flowed from the circle and through the woman's limbs.

Removing her hand, Telea stepped back and said, "Rise."

Slowly, stiffly, the woman stood. She turned and faced Telea, slightly rocking in place. It shouldn't be possible. No blood flowed through her muscles. She shouldn't be able to stand. Her eyes shouldn't see. Her mind shouldn't be able to think. Were all these body functions sustained by Telea's donated life force?

The woman continued staring at Telea. It was as if she *knew* her. "Stop staring at me," Telea said.

The woman turned away, but Telea still had the feeling that the two were connected. It felt as if an invisible thread linked the base of Telea's spine with the dead woman.

"Stand by the door," Telea said. The woman obeyed. Her movements were ungainly and off balance — almost like a toddler. The thought made Telea cringe. *This dead thing is not my child.*

The dead woman stepped on and over other corpses as she made her way to the door. *How can you see?* For she clearly could see. She avoided tripping on any of the other bodies and walked directly towards the door. *You don't have my demon's sight.* Was it another function of Telea's magic?

When she reached the door, the dead woman turned and faced Telea. Once again, Telea had the chilling feeling that the two of them were connected. *The eternals were connected to the Orb of Creation. Ghuls are connected to their pyren and their pyren to lyches. Is this the way of magic? The created is linked to the creator.*

Gods! Stop staring at me!

And then, to her horror, the woman turned away. Telea staggered back, tripped on a body, and fell atop the dead. Quickly, she scrambled to her feet and pressed her hand against the wall to keep from falling again.

She can hear me. She can hear my thoughts.

Telea had a chance now. She looked over the heaped corpses. Alone, she couldn't take on the two demons, but she had allies now. She knelt by another of the fresher corpses — the body of an Ethean woman.

Touching the woman, Telea drew from her well and animated her. Again she felt the invisible connection between the two of them. With a thought, Telea sent the woman to stand by the door. How many could she create?

And how long would they remain animated? Given enough time, she could test them and see how much life force remained in them. She shuddered as she looked at the two naked corpses swaying by the door. Test it? She never wanted to do it again.

A wave of revulsion passed over her. Was there some other way? How could she escape without desecrating the dead? What she was doing was wrong, she knew it in her heart. But she needed them. She had to escape.

Never again — after tonight.

Steeling herself to what she had to do, Telea went from body to body, reanimating them each in turn. It started to take a toll on her well of power, but more than that, it took a toll on her mind. She *felt* them in her. And with each additional link, she felt a growing tension. They didn't like what she'd done. It wasn't anger. It was pain. It was longing for release. They were in agony.

Telea tried to close her mind to them. It was only temporary. She *had* to have them now. But no matter how she tried, she couldn't block them out. Retreating to her memory walk gave her no respite. Their presence followed her even there.

How many did she need? She'd animated half of them already. Would there be enough to fight the demons? One by one, she animated the rest — twenty-eight in total. The longest dead were the most difficult to bring back.

Back? I'm not bringing them back. It wasn't that they took more life force — they were more resistant. Their pain was stronger as well. No, it was more than pain. Anger filled them. They resented her power over them.

With only her mind, Telea commanded them to make way for her, and she retreated to the back of the room. She crouched behind a heavy desk, her back against the wall. Then she ordered her undead to lay down, unmoving, on the floor.

How long until the demons would come for her? And would it be all three of them? She didn't know how strong her undead were. They had no weapons. They could only grapple and punch and choke.

When the demons came for her, she could sing the *Song of Light*. It would weaken the demons, at least. If they came close enough, she could draw the life from their possessed bodies, but that would mean touching them.

She needed a way to draw their life without touching them.

It had to be possible. She just had to work out the correct chants. If only she had more time. The thought brought Ayja to her mind. It's all her friend had wanted — peace and time to study magic. She'd never get it now.

Telea waited. It seemed she'd been there an eternity, but had no idea how much time had passed. How long would it take for the demons to come for her? She tried to rest but couldn't. Her undead were too much in her head, a constant whisper she couldn't quite hear. A whisper of pain and anger that filled her with foreboding.

There was a scrape at the door. Telea drew her cloak of shadows around her at the sound of a key entering the lock. It turned, and she saw the two possessed men there, the simvolos and the twisted man. *No emperor.*

The two men peered into the room. "Come out, spy," the simvolos said.

Telea didn't move. She needed them to enter.

"Come out. Or do you wish to spend more time with your dead companions? I can lock you in here forever."

"But the emperor," the twisted man objected.

"Silence!"

"Must get her."

The simvolos cuffed the twisted man. "You don't want us to come in. You might think your wards will protect you, but there are other things we can do to you. The emperor doesn't need you intact."

"Likes them fresh," the twisted man objected again.

"Go in, then! Get her!" the simvolos said, contempt filling his voice.

The twisted man stepped into the room, peering left and right as he searched for her. "Hiding?" he cackled. "Maybe eat you? Eat your soul?"

Telea held her breath as he came closer. The simvolos still stood at the door. She needed him to enter as well. It would be too easy for him to close the door and lock her in again where he stood.

Grab his ankle, she commanded the woman closest to the door. The twisted man shouted as one of the undead grasped his ankle in both hands. "Ah! She is here!" he shouted. He tried to pull free, but the animated corpse held on tight.

The twisted man bent down and struck the corpse in the head. Still, she held on. "What? Not her!"

"Drag her out here!" the simvolos shouted.

"Can't!" the twisted man reached down and tried to pull the grasping hands from his ankle, but Telea commanded another corpse to grab his other ankle as well.

"Fool! Get her!" The simvolos took two steps into the room.

"More than one!" the twisted man called out, looking around in confusion.

Seize them. Kill them, Telea thought to all of them. The writhing mass of corpses rose as one, falling upon the two possessed men. The demons struck out at their attackers but were overwhelmed by the mass of women and their grasping hands. *Grapple them. Pin them to the floor!*

Then she began to sing the *Song of Light.*

The demons shrieked as the aura of the song touched them. Their shouts were so loud she feared the emperor might hear them. She quickly ordered the undead to clamp their hands over the men's mouths and to choke them. They were only partially successful, but at least the sound was somewhat muffled. The men thrashed and fought, the demons within them pushing them to fight harder than they ever could have otherwise, but the undead were too much for them.

Telea continued her song. She wasn't an air singer, but her voice had the range to sing the song well. The twisted man gave one last terrible spasm and suddenly lay still, his dead eyes open and staring at the ceiling — the demon within him destroyed and banished to Dromost. She stepped closer to the simvolos.

This demon was stronger, its defenses deeply embedded within the man's mind. She focused her song on him, trying to drive the demon out. The simvolos's body jerked and spasmed as he fought, his voice screeching through undead fingers.

Finally, the demon could take it no longer, and its defenses crumbled. The *Song of Light* struck the demon full force, and it was ripped from the man's body and disappeared. The simvolos sagged in the grasp of the undead.

"Hold him! Stop choking!" Telea commanded. She knelt beside him as the undead obeyed her orders. Touching him on the cheek, she began to chant. As she did, her mind entered his.

He was a singer — she knew it the moment her mind touched his. She entered his memory walk — a grand villa hidden deep in a verdant valley. There'd once been defenses there, but they'd been shredded. Had the demon been that powerful? How had it gotten through?

She found the man crumpled on the floor of the villa's breezeway. She sang the *Song of Hope*. It had no effect on him. Within his memory walk, she knelt by him and touched him. "You are safe now," she said.

He flinched and jerked away from her. "Who are you? What are you doing? How are you in my mind?"

Telea held up both hands to show him she meant no harm. "I just drove the demon from you. You are safe now."

"What demon? How did you get past my defenses? Why can't I wake up?" He stood and stared wildly around, clearly distraught at her presence within his memory walk.

"You've been possessed for some time. Maybe a month or more. You, the emperor, and another man I don't know."

"Why can't I wake up?"

"I'm keeping you asleep for now. You won't like what you see when you awaken. Can't you remember anything?"

"Of course I do! Emperor Niktonas just returned. His father just recently passed away."

Telea shook her head. "That was months ago."

"Wake me!"

"I will," Telea said. "You will find yourself in a room of dead women. The demons feasted on their souls and left their bodies here."

"And who are you?"

"I am Teleana Telas Tarsian. I was on the embassy to Salador."

"Yes! I thought I knew you. I saw you before you left. You are a healer."

Telea nodded. "We returned with Forsvar and Princess Ayja and went to Drommaria. Ayja closed the Dromost Gate."

"You came back already? The gate is closed? You just left."

"Months ago."

Telea commanded the undead to carry the simvolos's body from the room and place it on the floor outside. Then she commanded them to return to the room and lay unmoving on the floor. All the while she kept contact with the simvolos, chanting the *Chant of Healing* and keeping him asleep. Finally, she removed herself from his mind and stopped her chant.

124

The simvolos's eyes opened and he sat up. Without the demon inside him, he appeared older and frailer. Deep wrinkles lined his forehead and the corners of his eyes. His disheveled graying hair had started to go bald on top. "I can hardly see," he said. "What's that stench?"

"Be glad it's dark," Telea said. "The smell is that of the dead."

"You can see?" he asked.

"I'm young and have good eyes. Let me help you to your feet." She lifted him and guided him to a door. The next room had a garden just outside, and the barest glow of moonlight came through the windows.

"Where are the servants? Where are the Emperor's Axes? What are you doing here?"

"The Axes are just outside. I don't think they know what has happened. The servants... I don't know. I think they've been sent off."

"And you?"

"I came to check on the emperor to see if he really had been possessed."

"But how did you get in?" The simvolos backed a few steps away from her as he spoke.

"I had to sneak in."

"I have to call the Axes."

"Yes!" Telea said. "We need to tell them the emperor is possessed."

"Chomenos?" a deep voice called from behind the far door. "Where are you? Where is the prisoner?"

The simvolos turned at the sound of the emperor's voice and called out, "Here, Your Majesty! Call your guards!" Then he ran for the door.

Telea took three steps after him. "Stop!"

Even before he reached the door, it swung wide, and Telea saw the naked bulk of the emperor standing there. The simvolos halted in shock before turning away. The moment's delay was too long, though, and the emperor's hand shot out and took him by the wrist.

Telea ran.

Chapter Thirteen

For two days, Nidon's men battled both relentless rain and Prodidos's soldiers. They built rough shelters to protect themselves from one and a wooden palisade to defend themselves from the other. Their position was strong, though, and Prodidos could make no headway against them. Nidon's left was protected by a steep ravine and a flooded river, his front by a steep slope, and a heavily wooded ridge rose to his right. It didn't help his enemy that the road took a sharp right turn, preventing them from bringing many bows to bear, while those who turned the corner faced all of Nidon's archers and crossbowmen.

Welcome relief came with the arrival of Baron Fendal and his half of the company and the builders. They were further reinforced by hillfolk warriors who, while lightly armed, were skillful archers and slingers. Conditions were poor, though. They'd turned the ground to a muddy quagmire, and many had gotten sick in the cold and damp. At least the village's children and elderly had retreated up the pass to the villages above.

"We are at a stalemate," Exonos said. "He has too many men for us to attack, but our position is too strong for him to assail."

"How many men can he bring to the field?" Nidon asked. The two men stood at the palisade, looking down over the valley below. There were no enemies to be seen, although his Landomeri said there were a few well-hidden freemen keeping watch over them.

"Normally Kyvern Psertis could muster ten thousand. He's lost the faith of his satruses, though. In time he might muster five thousand. At the moment, he has five hundred at the most. Two hundred timari and perhaps three hundred freemen. Soon he'll have several hundred foot as well."

"King Handrin is bringing ten thousand men over the mountains," Nidon said. "It will take more than a month, and they'll be strung out over the pass."

"We must break Psertis before he can call all of his loyal satruses to arms. It is in our favor that Psertis doesn't enjoy great favor among his followers. If the Orb of Creation is revealed, they will come over to us."

"My concern is that their numbers will grow faster than ours," Nidon said.

"You have an elementar as well."

Nidon nodded, glancing at the fire where Fendal warmed his hands. "He isn't the elementar Ayja is. He won't turn the tide of battle. We need the king and the Orb of Creation."

"How long until he arrives?"

"I haven't had word. He's on his way."

The night fell cold and wet, but the sky was clear, promising a better tomorrow. When dawn finally arrived, it was better than expected, warm weather having followed the storms. Nidon rolled from under the damp lean-to that had been his home for the past three nights. Squire Fress arrived with boots warmed and dried next to a fire and some terrible tea that tasted of bark. Nidon pulled on the boots, grateful for their warmth, but knowing they'd be soaked through in a quarterday. All in all, Fress was a good squire and a capable man-at-arms.

Nidon's thoughts went to Rayne, who'd been his page and then King Handrin's squire. More than the king's squire — his friend. It had been so strange for Nidon to meet him again after so many years. Rayne had become a skilled knight and fearsome warrior, but now he was gone — killed by a demon while fighting at Ayja's side.

So many had died. So many more would die.

Nidon stood and stretched. His back ached from where he'd been struck in the skirmish. The blow had hurt at the time, but twice as much the day after. He had a huge welt on his thigh as well, but for the life of him, he couldn't remember when he'd taken the blow. As Nidon buttoned his arming coat, Fress gathered up his mail hauberk. It was tarnished, despite the squire's best efforts. He could hardly blame the lad — the conditions had been impossible. The weather was better today, with a cloudless sky overhead. "This shirt will gleam tomorrow, Fress. Understand? A knight's life depends on his harness, and I won't tolerate it falling into disrepair."

"Yes, Champion," Fress said as he helped Nidon into the hauberk. *At least he has the sense not to make excuses.*

With his coat-of-plates finally buckled, Nidon took his helm under his arm and marched off to inspect the lines. Food and fire hadn't been a problem, both were plentiful, although he was growing somewhat tired of roasted goat. The village herds would feed them for some time yet, although as the army arrived, their supplies would rapidly dwindle.

They'd only planned on bringing so much over the mountains. They were supposed to be supplied by the Belenese, not to go to war with them.

Nidon found the watch well situated and the carpenters already at work reinforcing their palisade. They'd also created a spiked abatis to be staked at the far side of the wall. He praised them for the work, the abatis in particular. "More of them," he said. "Anything to slow their approach."

He found Exonos speaking with some of the hillfolk leaders. Nidon worried about their morale. Their village was occupied, and they'd spent the better part of three days soaking wet. Fighting for a *nafai amas* and the Orb of Creation had inspired them to join Exonos, but neither was in sight, and some had started to realize that they were in open revolt against their kyvern.

Exonos caught Nidon's attention as the hillfolk departed. "We need your king to arrive soon. They grow worried."

Nidon glanced up the pass. Where was he? What had the storm done further up the pass? "He's coming. That's all I know."

It was late morning when Prodidos sent three emissaries up the hill. Nidon, Exonos, and Fendal went to meet Prodidos and his two captains halfway down the slope in front of their works.

"You must surrender, Satrus Exonos," Prodidos said after introductions had been made. The handsome young man in a fine scale hauberk and silk kaftan looked haggard. Dark circles under his eyes spoke of little sleep. *The weight of command on a young man's shoulders,* Nidon thought. "And the Saladorans must retreat over the pass and not return to Belen again." Prodidos spoke in fluent, but accented, Saladoran.

"Why is your father doing this?" Exonos asked, his tone reasonable, and his expression calm. "The *nafai amas* has returned to Belen with Forsvar. The Saladorans come as allies to help us in our battle against the Summoned Lands."

"You are a fool and a traitor, Exonos," Prodidos replied. "The Saladorans are here to conquer the empire."

Exonos sighed. "Why keep up this charade, Prodidos? You have an audience of two," he said, nodding at the two captains. "We know the truth. You know the truth. Your father knows the truth. And when the emperor learns the truth, your father will be executed. He tried to steal the—"

"He did not! Ayja of Salador led an army of beguiled citizens in an effort to overthrow my father."

"Princess Ayja succeeded in her mission," Nidon said. "The Dromost Gate has been closed. We are here to see that it is locked forever."

"Emperor Niktonas does not need or want your help. He told us to throw you back over the mountains. We shall deal with the Summoned Lands without you. Return to Salador immediately."

"You have a message from the emperor?" Exonos asked. "Show it to us."

"It was relayed to me by my father's couriers."

"We wish to speak with an Imperial Officer," Exonos said. "I have no reason to trust you or your father."

Prodidos shrugged and said, "I cannot produce one. Unless you'd like to wait for a month for one to be summoned."

"This is just a trick," Fendal said to Nidon. He spoke Low Saladoran, the language of the commoners. Even then, he spoke it with the most outrageous South Teren accent. *"His officers are spying on our works."*

The Belenese frowned as they glanced at Fendal, clearly not comprehending him.

"You're right," Nidon said. He'd seen it as well. The two captains had paid little attention to the discussion, instead doing their best to examine the palisade behind them.

"Speak plainly," Prodidos said. "This is a parlay."

"We must speak further on this," Nidon said. "Let us meet tomorrow for further discussion."

Prodidos shook his head and stood taller. "There's nothing to discuss. My father's demands are clear."

"So it is not a parlay, then. It is an ultimatum."

"You wish to delay so that you might gain more reinforcements from over the mountains. It is unacceptable."

"You grow stronger each day as well," Nidon said. "Give us a day to consider."

"We shall meet tomorrow at midday. Satrus Exonos will surrender to us, and you will return to Salador. This is your last chance at a peaceful resolution."

"Until tomorrow, then," Nidon said.

As soon as they entered the palisade, Nidon turned to the others and said, "They will attack tonight."

"Ordinarily, I would disagree," Exonos said. "We Belenese honor our agreements. However, Prodidos and his father have already shown their willingness to break with norms. They will attack tonight."

"Can we hold them?" Fendal asked.

"They will take heavy losses assaulting this position," Nidon said. He turned to Exonos. "How willing are they to die?"

"How willing will they be to die when I call my fire down upon them?" Fendal asked, rubbing his hands together.

"They have numbers, and numbers bring courage," Exonos said. "The timari are courageous, professional soldiers. They won't easily give up. The freemen will be less willing. If they have singers, which they might, they will fight even more fearlessly."

Nidon glanced up the pass. *Where is the king?*

"We will be ready," Nidon said. "We will hold."

Later in the afternoon, Nidon received answers to some of his questions, but there was little good news in them. Twenty Landomeri arrived with two lances of the Knights of the House. They told Nidon that what had been rain in the valley had been snow in the mountains. All progress had been halted. King Handrin, they said, had been one way station behind them, but they didn't know how close or how quickly he'd followed.

The reinforcements were welcome, the news less so. Nidon needed more men. The enemy, secure in the shelter of the village, knew that Nidon's force had weathered the storm out of doors. They knew they had a numerical advantage as well. What they couldn't do was starve them out. Nidon had a line of supply coming over the mountains that couldn't be cut.

Nidon's left was unassailable. The palisade to his front would be difficult to assault. He'd place his knights and Exonos's timari and freemen behind it. His right was vulnerable, though. The woods and steep slope would make it a challenge, but it wasn't impassable. He'd placed his Landomeri there, supported by the hillfolk warriors. More of the hillfolk would support the palisade, although he had little faith in them if the line folded.

"Master Hod," Nidon called out to the lead builder. "What can we do to make the slope up there even more difficult?"

"Too steep and too rocky to build on, Champion," Hod said. "Unless... how much time do we have?"

"Until nightfall."

Hod shook his head, drawing a breath through his teeth. "I can make an abatis of felled trees. The enemy will have Dromost's own time trying to get through."

"Good," Nidon said. "Do it."

There was little else Nidon could do. He made his presence known, moving from place to place and giving encouragement or lending a helping hand. He let everyone know he expected an attack that night, and they did their best to prepare. He had confidence in everyone except for the hillfolk.

"They need to see the Orb of Creation," Exonos said. "They need their faith that they are on the side of right restored."

"I can't give them that," Nidon said. He thought a moment. "I can give them a display of magic, though." He sent Squire Fress off to find Fendal. When he arrived, Nidon said, "I have a request of you, Baron Fendal. I wish to introduce you to our allies, the hill warriors, and for you to show your elementar powers to them."

"For what reason, Champion? I'm not an entertainer. I would prefer not to waste my strength on displays when we are expecting an attack tonight."

"I'm not asking you to waste all of your power. I wish for you to inspire our allies with your strength. We will tell them that you are Princess Ayja's cousin — "

"But — "

"You are," Nidon said, holding his hand up. "Close enough, at least. You both have the blood of Handrin the Great in your veins. The hillfolk believe Ayja to be the Bride of Forsvar. I need you to be her proxy. To show them that you possess her magic as well."

"Bride of Forsvar? Silly superstition," Fendal said.

"It is not," Exonos said, glaring at the Saladoran nobleman. "The *nafai amas* has returned to us."

"She has," Nidon said, giving Fendal a hard look. "And we need to remind the hillfolk of it."

And so, for a time, the three of them made their way amongst the men and women of the hill tribes, speaking of Ayja and Forsvar, while Fendal put on displays of elementar magic. He caused dramatic jets of fire to streak out from his hand, blasted the warriors with gusts of wind, and picked globes of water out of puddles and threw them like snowballs. The effort, combined with sun and warmth, seemed to have the desired effect. To Nidon, it seemed the attitudes of the warriors turned for the better. Of course, the real test would be on the field of battle.

"I should refrain from doing any more," Fendal said. "If we truly expect an attack tonight, I must rest and restore my powers."

"Go and take your ease, Baron Fendal," Nidon said. "I appreciate your efforts."

Nidon ordered a double ration of food to be prepared for the soldiers and then took one last look at their defenses as night fell. Walking up the wooded slope, he spotted Kael. "The felled trees will make life difficult for any attacker," Nidon said. All afternoon he'd heard the ringing of axes and the crash of falling trees.

"They will," Kael replied. "They obstruct our view to a degree, but it will be worth it."

131

"They'll come hard for you, I think," Nidon said.

"And pay dearly for it."

"If they turn you, the palisade will be flanked. It will be the end of the defense."

"We need you just as much as you need us, Champion. If they overrun your palisade, we'll be trapped on this slope and unable to escape."

Nidon grinned. "True. We must stay in contact. If either of us is about to fall, we must warn the other so that we can retreat up the valley and set up another line of defense."

Kael offered his hand. "You can count on us," he said.

"I know I can," Nidon said, shaking hands with the former Idorian mercenary.

Nidon returned to his lean-to where Squire Fress brought him a meal of goat and garlic bean paste. The flavors were far different than those of Salador, but Nidon enjoyed them. Well, all but the goat.

A cloudless sky and a half moon meant a decent amount of light to see by. Nidon wondered if the Landomeri on the slopes above him were all as uncannily night-sighted as Hadde had been. They certainly seemed as stealthy, as he couldn't make out a single one of them. If he didn't know better, he'd have thought they'd all departed.

Not wanting to backlight their defenders, Nidon ordered all fires near the palisade doused, keeping only a few lit well behind the lines. Still in full harness, Nidon pulled a blanket around himself and settled back to rest. Exonos would command the defenses for now.

"Champion Nidon," Squire Fress said, waking him after what he thought had only been moments. "Exonos says the enemy is approaching."

Nidon rose. No, it hadn't been a few moments rest. They were well into Exonos's watch. He stretched and slipped his shield's strap over his shoulder. "How late is it?" he asked as Fress helped him with his helm.

"Half night. I was just about to wake you."

"You didn't sleep?"

Fress shook his head. "I couldn't, Champion. The coming fight had me up."

"You have to learn to sleep anywhere, any time," Nidon said as Fress handed him his axe. "Now you won't get any sleep at all."

"That's alright, Champion. I don't need it."

Nidon shook his head. "Youth," he muttered, heading for the palisade. "What does Exonos say? What's happening?"

"The enemy is attempting to be stealthy. They've sent some freemen into the tree line. Their dismounted timari are gathering just at the bend."

"Get Baron Fendal and make certain all our lances are on the palisade."

Fress saluted and jogged off. *A good squire. He just needs a little seasoning.*

Exonos's ten timari and eight freemen were on the shooting step behind the palisade. All crouched low behind it, not exposing themselves to anyone beyond. Nidon spied Exonos with them.

Behind the wall knelt three lances of the Knights of the House with their pole-axes and war hammers. When Squire Fress arrived with the remaining two lances, he'd have twenty-three Saladorans in total, almost the same number of men as Exonos had on the shooting step. Nidon saluted his men as he joined Exonos.

"Are they advancing yet?" Nidon asked, keeping low so as not to expose himself.

Exonos shook his head. "Perhaps two dozen freemen entered the woods, but I've had no word from your Landomeri. A large force of timari is just beyond the bend, but they haven't turned the corner yet. Our scouts had to pull back when the freemen advanced."

Exonos spoke to the timari near him in rapid Belenese. The men and women nodded, some hands going to their quivers. All of his soldiers, freemen and timari, carried powerful horn bows like the one Hadde had carried. Around a third of the Landomeri carried similar bows, the rest, the eastern Landomeri, had longbows.

An anguished shout of pain caused Nidon to turn. Someone downslope had taken an arrow. More shouts followed. Nidon peered over the wall, but only saw shadowy forms moving in the moonlight. The Landomeri were engaged. A skirmish to start things off.

Down the hill, at the bend in the road, a strong force of soldiers appeared. Marching quickly, they pushed up the road towards the palisade. "They're coming," Nidon said.

Exonos gave an order in Belenese, and his timari and freemen all rose. Almost as one, they drew and loosed their powerful bows. Arrows whispered into the night, disappearing in the darkness. Heartbeats later came the cracks and thuds of arrows striking metal and wood. There were shouts as well, some of pain and others of surprise. Nidon heard commands as well. The enemy came on.

The defenders loosed four more volleys before the enemy made any reply. Arrows suddenly smacked into the palisade or whipped by close overhead. It was unnerving, not seeing the arrows loosed, or even in flight, and having them suddenly arrive with deadly violence.

The enemy had made it a third of the way up the hill when the Landomeri began to loose at the main column. Nidon heard more shouts then, as the Landomeri took Prodidos's soldiers in the flank. The damage wasn't as much as Nidon had hoped for, though. The soldiers in the front ranks of the enemy column all carried large pavises — huge body shields that provided cover not only to the soldier carrying it but to those nearby.

Never underestimate your foe. Always assume they're smarter than you think they are.

"Have your men shoot over their front ranks," Nidon said. "Shoot into the heart of the column." That was where the enemy arrows were coming from — the back of the column, where the timari had slung their shields and loosed arrows instead. Their shots were hasty, though, the archers only stopping long enough to loose an arrow and move on. There was no place for them to set themselves on the narrow road.

Exonos's arrows were taking a toll, but it wasn't enough to stop the column. More and more freemen pushed up into the wooded slopes as well. Had they reached the felled trees yet? Nidon wasn't certain. It was impossible to make anything out in the woods.

The enemy was halfway up the hill, and their arrows were more frequent and more accurate now. Not far away, a freemen fell screaming from the shooting step, an arrow in his face. There were no archers to take his place. Two of Nidon's squires pulled him back from the palisade, while a knight took his place on the wall.

"Do I hear singing?" Nidon asked. He thought he'd heard voices from the slope below.

Exonos paused as he nocked an arrow, cocking his head to the side. "Dromost take them," he said. "They do have singers."

"What does that mean?" Nidon asked. He knew of Telea and a little about her magic. "They have healers?"

Exonos shook his head. "Not healers, necessarily. They'll have earth singers who can strike with their voices, fire singers who can intimidate their foes, and water singers who can inspire their own warriors. They shouldn't have any at all. The emperor called for them to be sent off to the east to fight the summoners. Psertis must have kept some of his behind. What it means is that this fight just got harder." Exonos turned and shouted commands in Belenese. Then he said to Nidon, "Kill the singers if you get the chance. It pains me to say those words, but it is our only hope."

The enemy timari were three-quarters of the way up the hill. Their archery — uphill and into a palisade — was greatly reduced in effect, but it still took a toll. Two freemen and a timari took wounds and had to be replaced by Saladorans. The enemy came on. The close range was deadly for them, but they had numbers and the inspiration of their water singers. Finally, only thirty strides from the palisade, they dropped their pavises and charged. A last volley of arrows took down four of them, but then the defenders had to put aside their bows and draw their swords.

The palisade wasn't tall — just a little over two strides in most places. High enough to make climbing difficult and to give an advantage to the men and women fighting from above. The attackers thrust up at the defenders with spears and light lances, but they'd also brought ropes and hooks. Instead of climbing, they hauled on the ropes, trying to rip the palisade logs free of their moorings. Other attackers hacked at the palisade's lashings with axes and swords.

Nidon took his Idorian axe and cut down into the attackers, driving those nearest him back. A grapnel hooked the top of the palisade near him, and he cut its line. Next to him, a freemen who'd kept his bow in hand loosed it into the attackers, the arrow easily punching through both scale and mail at such short range.

Some attackers, those further back, had kept their bows as well, shooting the defenders who exposed themselves to fight. An arrow clanged off Nidon's helm, and he quickly threw down his visor. In the dark, he was nearly blind, but it was better than being shot through the eye.

Nearby attackers had wrenched one of the logs free of its lashings and pulled it down to make a gap. Nidon pushed aside the freemen next to him and slammed his axe into a man's hand, severing his fingers. The timari screamed and fell back, but then another drove a spear at Nidon, catching him in the chest. Nidon stumbled back, almost falling from the shooting step, but his coat-of-plates held.

The spearman thrust at him again, but this time Nidon caught the spear in his hand and yanked it towards him. The owner, instead of letting go, was pulled closer. Off balance and exposed, he was an easy mark for the freemen who shot him through the throat.

The enemy singers were closer now. Nidon heard high voices inspiring his enemies, and beneath them, lower voices that attacked his spirit and causing him to want to fall back from the gap in the wall. He felt what they were doing. He *knew* what they were doing, but he couldn't help himself. Gritting his teeth, he pushed through it, forcing himself forward as if wading against a powerful current.

Swinging his axe, he drove off another attacker. More spears were thrust through the gap at him, but he parried one aside and snapped the second with his axe. Still, the music assaulted him. There was fighting all around him, but he could only focus on the fight in front of him. The darkness, his visor, and the intensity of the fight limited his world to the gap in the palisade and his foes there.

"They're over the wall," Exonos shouted nearby.

Nidon spared only a moment's glance to see enemy timari clambering over the wall to his left. "Bring up the hillfolk!" Nidon ordered, hoping they'd come, but not certain he could rely on them.

Brilliant flames exploded off to his left. For a moment, the enemy's song faltered, and the men facing Nidon fell back. Baron Fendal was on the wall, his right hand pointing towards the enemy, guiding the magic fire erupting in their ranks.

The enemy fell back from the wall nearest Fendal, the breach temporarily contained. Nidon took shelter behind the palisade as the enemy in front of him fell back. He leaned heavily on his axe, drawing in great lungfulls of air. A third explosion of fire lit the night air.

How much did Fendal have in him? Nidon knew he wasn't as powerful as Ayja or Handrin. For now, his display of power had the enemy on their heels. Nidon looked uphill towards the Landomeri position. He heard fighting there as well. Were the Landomeri holding?

A dozen or so hillfolk joined them at the wall, but it wasn't enough. There were more behind their position, but they were holding back, wary of joining the bitter fight. "We need more of the hillfolk, Exonos," Nidon said. "They can't hold back. We don't have the numbers."

"I'll see what I can do," Exonos said. He jumped from the shooting step and strode towards the cautious hill people. Nearby, his remaining timari and freemen drew their bows from their cases and began to loose arrows into the attackers who'd retreated from Fendal's fire.

"Fendal, how are you?" Nidon called out.

"I don't have much more in me," he replied, ducking behind the wall. "I can't put that display on again."

"Strike them as soon as they advance. Let them fear you have more." The singing began again, and moments later, a shout went up among the attackers. "They're coming!"

Nidon took his axe in both hands and waited by the gap in the wall. Just as the enemy struck, Fendal's fire fell upon them again. Men screamed out in agony, falling back from that section of the palisade, but everywhere else, they continued their assault.

A man appeared in the gap, forcing his way through. Nidon's overhand blow took the timari in the shoulder, cutting deep, shattering his collarbone, and sinking deep into his chest. Nidon yanked his axe free, readying it for the next man. A spearman stabbed at him, but Nidon parried the blow aside.

There was another man next to the spearman. The big man had a shield and a sword, but he didn't push forward. Instead, he sang. The music struck Nidon in the chest with the power of a warhorse's kick. He

136

flew backward, losing his axe and landing hard on the ground behind the shooting step.

The air driven from his lungs, Nidon lay on the ground with the dark sky whirling overhead. He tried to draw a breath but could do little more than gasp. Slowly, he rolled to his side and then to his knees. He looked up to see men pushing through the breach.

Staggering to his feet, Nidon slid his shield from his back and slipped it onto his arm. The gap in the wall was narrow and hard to push through. Only two men had made it so far — neither of them the big singer.

Drawing his falchion, Nidon staggered forward. He fended off a sword thrust and then swung at the timari's leg, just missing as the man dodged backward. His two opponents stood on the shooting step above him, raining blows down on him. Nidon raised his shield and continued to strike at their legs. Finally, he aimed an overhand blow at one of their feet, nearly severing it in half. The man howled and fell to the ground, but was immediately replaced by two others.

The wall had been breached in other places now. "Fall back!" Nidon shouted. "On me!"

The Knights of the House and Exonos's timari joined him, but there weren't many of them remaining. The enemy charged their thin line. They held, but only barely. And soon they'd be outflanked. "Exonos!" Nidon shouted. "Now!"

The singers were over the wall. Nidon felt the magic of the fire singers wash over him, sapping his strength and will. They couldn't hold. There was no use in it. Then he saw the big earth singer again. This time Nidon was ready and leaned into his shield as the song struck him. Still, it nearly drove him from his feet.

The enemy redoubled their attack. The ends of Nidon's line folded. Soon there'd only be a small ring of defenders fighting for their lives. Where was Exonos?

Nidon risked a glance over his shoulder. High on the slopes behind them, he saw a brilliant light moving through the trees. Hope filled his heart and he turned back to the enemy.

"Stand fast, Knights of Salador! Stand fast, soldiers of Belen!" he shouted. "The Orb of Creation is near!"

Nidon cut down a timari with a heavy blow to his helm that knocked the man senseless. He parried a spear from another and then broke the man's arm with a blow that didn't penetrate his armor, but shattered the bones beneath.

They only had to survive a short time. The enemy could not stand in the face of the Orb and King Handrin's magic. But their attackers were everywhere and his line was collapsing around him. How many would die before the king arrived?

Nidon turned two more attacks on his shield, but then the song struck him again, bowling him and the man next to him backward. He would have fallen but ran into someone behind him. A timari leaped forward, taking advantage of the collision, and swung his sword at Nidon's head. He barely raised his shield in time. The sword glanced off the shield and struck the top of Nidon's helm, staggering him.

"Stand fast!" Nidon shouted. Two men formed up on either side of him. For a time they held, the blows coming so fast Nidon could hardly tell one from another. They held, though. Every heartbeat mattered. Many more would die if the line broke.

Two timari spearmen attacked. Nidon parried one, but the other struck him in the shoulder. His coat-of-plates held, but he was driven into the man behind him again, and this time, both stumbled and fell. Nidon tried to stand, but the two timari were on him, hammering blows down upon him. It was all he could do to fend them off.

Silver-golden light filled the night. The two men above Nidon reeled back, blinded by the assault. For a hundred strides in every direction, it was brighter than the brightest sunlit day.

Then a cheer that sounded more like a roar washed over him, and the enemy turned to flee. Suddenly, there were hillfolk everywhere, charging and attacking the fleeing enemy. More than hillfolk. There were Knights of the House in a wedge, with King Handrin at their head.

In the king's hand, held high over his head, was the Orb of Creation, blazing with the light of the sun.

Chapter Fourteen

Telea crept into the villa as the earliest dawn light brightened the horizon. Sindi stood on the balcony, waiting as Telea dragged her way up the stairs, exhausted and demoralized by the night's events. She still felt the presence of the undead within her mind — twenty-eight half-souls linked to her, never giving her peace. She felt as if they were with her, following her, everywhere she went. Just thinking about it made the hair on the back of her neck stand up.

Could she still command them? Separated by all this distance? She wished she could sever her ties with them, but despite her best efforts, it had been impossible. Did she have to draw the life force out of them to free herself? Eventually, it would fade on its own — the magic that sustained them wouldn't last forever. But how long? The sudden thought that even then their undead spirits might be connected to her filled her with dread. What if she could never free herself from them?

"What happened?" Sindi asked as Telea topped the last stair. "You were out all night."

"Our worst thoughts came true," Telea said. "Are the others awake? We must talk."

"Calen and I took turns waiting up. He's asleep now. Isibindi stayed up well into the night, but went to bed as well."

"And Tharryl?"

Sindi shrugged. "He said it wouldn't do anyone any good to stay up."

Telea grunted. "He probably had the right of it." She drew a deep breath. "I must rest and think. Come for me when everyone is awake."

"You said the worst had happened."

Telea nodded. "The emperor and his closest advisor are demon possessed."

Sindi drew in a sharp breath. "You're certain?"

"I saw it with my own eyes."

"And nobody knows? He still rules with a demon within him?"

"For now." Telea raised her hand before Sindi could ask another question. "When everyone's awake," she said. Sindi nodded and backed away as Telea entered her room. There was a pitcher of water on the dressing table, and Telea poured it into a bowl. Stripping off her clothes, she washed the stink of death off of her. All the while, images of walking corpses ran through her head.

What should she do now? What would the emperor do, now that he knew he'd been seen? How could she convince others that he was possessed? Everything was worse than she'd imagined.

What would happen if her undead were discovered? Would they just lie there? She focused her mind on the lines connecting her to them. *Lay still,* she thought. Then she pictured the emperor in her mind. *If you see him, kill him.* She had no sense that they had heard her or if they would obey. What sweet revenge it would be if the women he'd slain were his undoing. Then she cringed at the thought. It was horrible — all of it.

After drying herself, she pulled on her spare Koromoi trousers and shirt and sat at the edge of the bed. What could they do? The simvolos was certainly dead. Could the emperor maintain control without him? Certainly, anyone who saw the emperor would know that he was a demon. Did he have other servants who could speak for him?

All the singers have been sent east. Telea drew in a sharp breath. Of course. The demon had removed his most powerful enemies by sending them out of the city. But even then, there were more than enough soldiers to fight the emperor. He might be a powerful demon, but he couldn't fight all of the Emperor's Axes.

She had to get word to them. How could she do it in a way that would be believed?

Outside, Telea heard the distant call of strident horns. She listened closer. She'd been with the army for over a year. This one was *alarm.* Then another followed it — the call to arms.

It's because of me. She pulled on her boots and walked out onto the balcony. The villa didn't have many guests, maybe four besides Telea and her companions. They all stood outside their doors, listening. Sindi and Calen were already outside. Tharryl and Isibindi soon followed.

"What is it?" Calen asked.

"The call to arms," Telea said. "They are mustering the army."

"Why?"

"Come here — into my room. I'll tell you." Telea ushered them inside and shut the door. "The emperor is a demon. He saw me. They also have the captain I enchanted at the gate and know that I did something to him. They are hunting for me right now."

"Hunting for us," Sindi said. Telea nodded in reply.

"The emperor's a demon?" Tharryl asked. "Why did you let him see you?"

"If I could have avoided it, I would have."

"Well done," Tharryl said. "Aren't we trying to lock the Dromost Gate? How are we going to do that with a demon ruling Belen? And, more importantly, how are we going to save our own hides?"

"We have to get word to Ethea and to Salador," Telea said. "I think we should leave the city as soon as we can. Tonight. Sindi, Calen, and Tharryl should make their way to Salador. We'll send you north, through the Koromoi Steppes. You'll avoid Kyvern Psertis's land that way. I will go south with Isibindi. We'll wait for the *Summer Swan* and head to Ethea."

"Why not tell someone?" Tharryl asked. "Tell them he's a demon."

"Who will tell them?" Telea asked. "And tell them what, exactly? Hey, the emperor's a demon! Go check it out!"

"Yes!"

"It wouldn't work, Tharryl," Telea said. "No one would believe it. The army is already in the streets, surely told that a spy or assassin has attempted to kill the emperor. No one will get close to him now."

"There must be a way of exposing him," Sindi said. "Someone we can tell."

"This isn't Salador," Telea said. "The emperor's rule is absolute. He can stay in his apartments and give orders through his simvolos, and they *will be* obeyed. No one can challenge him. It's been that way ever since the Traitor's Rebellion."

Tharryl shook his head. "Well done, everyone. Great success."

"We'll stay inside for the day," Telea said. "I'll have our meals brought up to our rooms. We'll make our way out in the evening."

Dawn was breaking when Telea found the innkeeper at the front of the villa looking out to the street. "Good morning," Telea said. "We'll take our meals in our rooms today."

"I wonder what's happening," the innkeeper said, ignoring Telea's request. "The alarm is sounding all across the city."

"Some drill, perhaps?"

"No," the innkeeper said, her concern clear on her face. "This is real. Are the summoners up to something? It is war again?"

"Perhaps." Telea kept in the shadows of the doorway. There were others in doorways and windows all along the street looking out as well. "We'll be leaving this evening. I've decided to return to Ethea. There's a ship departing at dusk."

"Of course. It might be best. You paid a week in advance, though."

"Keep it," Telea said.

141

"That's too generous," the innkeeper said. "Let me return some of your money." She turned away from the door and headed toward her chambers.

"No. That's not necessary. You've been very kind to us."

A timari on horseback galloped down the street. Telea stepped out of view as he rode past. The innkeeper looked down the street in the direction the rider had gone. "I do wonder what's happening. I'm worried."

"I'm sure it will be fine," Telea replied. She made her way to her room, and a short time later, the inn's three servants, all of them the innkeeper's relations, brought their food. They ate together, crowded in Telea's room. Telea could hardly eat, however, given what she'd seen.

After a while, the horns stopped sounding, but several times she heard the echo of rapid hoofbeats on the streets. They retired to their rooms, but through her open door, Telea could hear a commotion out on the streets all through the morning. There were shouts and marching soldiers, but she didn't dare go out and look for fear of being seen. And still, she felt her connection to the undead women in the palace.

The sun was high overhead when Telea heard rapid footsteps on the walkway outside, and the innkeeper appeared in her doorway. "You must leave," she said. "Immediately!" Without waiting for a reply she went to the next room and hammered on the door. "Out! Out! You must go!"

"What's going on?" Telea asked, stepping into her doorway. The noise had gotten the attention of some of the other guests, who stood in their doorways or looked out their windows to see what was going on.

"You Etheans have to leave," the innkeeper shouted. "The army is rounding up all the Etheans in the city, and I don't want any trouble. Get out of my villa! Now!" The innkeeper stormed down the stairs, shouting orders for their horses to be readied.

"What do we do now?" Calen asked.

"Head for the docks," Telea said. "Earlier than planned."

"We won't make it an arrowflight out of here," Tharryl said.

"We have no choice." Telea said. "Gather your things."

She went to her room and stuffed her few belongings into her bag. As she stepped out onto the balcony, she heard horn calls nearby.

Telea went to check on the others. They all had arming coats and mail to don. She entered Tharryl's room to help Isibindi buckle his brigandine.

"Could you be any slower?" he asked.

"Shut up and let me work, you oaf," Isibindi replied.

They gathered their packs and rushed down the stairs just as the last of their horses were led out to the street. They entered the breezeway and were about to head out to the street when the innkeeper stepped in front of Telea.

"What are you doing?" Telea demanded.

The innkeeper nodded to someone behind Tharryl. Fearing some trick, Telea spun to see who was there. A servant boy stood by the door to the courtyard and slammed it shut behind him.

"Follow me," the innkeeper said, closing the front gate. She opened a door revealing a staircase leading down into the darkness. "Hurry! You can't go out onto the street. You'll be arrested in no time."

"I thought you were throwing us out," Tharryl said in his broken Belenese.

"I'm saving you, fool! Get in the basement before someone sees you."

"Why are you doing this?" Telea asked.

"They are arresting all of the Etheans. Some have been killed. Get in the basement!"

"You trust her?" Tharryl asked Telea.

"Do we have a choice?"

Tharryl was the last to follow as the innkeeper led them down the steps. She held a small oil lamp she'd taken from a hook by the door. Its dim glow lit smooth cut stone walls. The wide stairs led into a large, vaulted storage room filled with a jumble of tools and old furniture. Lumber was stacked in a corner, as well as fired bricks and roof tiles.

"This way," the innkeeper said, leading them to a narrow passage at the back of the room. There were two barred alcoves here, one with barrels stacked high on the back wall. The innkeeper pulled out a heavy key ring and unlocked the barrel chamber.

"If she locks us in, we're doomed," Tharryl said in Saladoran.

"You are free to go if you want," Telea said. "I wish you the best of luck." With that, she followed the innkeeper into the cell.

The innkeeper twisted the tap of a large barrel and pulled it open, revealing an empty interior. She stuck her body halfway inside, gave a muffled grunt, and the back of the barrel opened to reveal a dark chamber. "A hidden room," the innkeeper said. "Some of these old villas keep secrets that go back to the Traitor's Rebellion."

Telea looked into the keg and saw a short passage leading into a hidden chamber beyond. "All this because your grandmother was Ethean?"

"All this because it's the right thing to do." The innkeeper gave the oil lamp to Telea. "Go ahead. I will come for you as soon as I can."

"What of our horses?" Sindi asked.

"My granddaughter is taking them to a stable. I'm telling anyone who asks that you left."

143

"Why didn't you tell us about all of this upstairs?" Telea asked.

"I had to make the other guests believe you were leaving. Hurry now. Who knows how long it will be until they come to find you?"

Telea took the lamp and climbed through the barrel. It led into a small, dark chamber. The room was bare, although in good repair. It was only three strides deep and maybe four strides wide. She set the lamp on the floor and took off her pack before turning and helping the others into the room.

"Now she goes and tells the town watch that we are here," Tharryl said. "I wonder how big her reward will be?"

Telea closed and latched the trap door at the back of the barrel and then sat down with her back against her pack. "We'll wait until dark and then make our escape," she said.

They had no way of knowing how much time had passed but for the diminishing reservoir of the lamp's oil. Then they heard a sound outside the barrel. Taking up their weapons, they stood by the trap door, ready for whatever might appear.

There was a knock and the door swung open and a pile of blankets fell through. The innkeeper's head appeared. "It's safe for now. Can someone come out and help me? I have some straw mattresses and other supplies for you."

"We aren't staying," Telea said. "We have to leave the city."

The innkeeper climbed out of the barrel. She was quite spry for her age. "No," she said, shaking her head. "There are soldiers everywhere. You wouldn't make it past the end of the street. Better to hide until this has passed over."

"Until what passes over?"

"Until Ethea makes peace with Belen." She threw her hands into the air. "Everyone's gone mad. Talk of the *nafai amas,* and of Forsvar, and elementars. Claims that the Temple of Forsvar was sacked. Nobody knows anything for certain, and it's putting everyone on edge. Just stay with me until it all passes over."

"Could we be smuggled out?"

"I don't know anyone who could do such a thing."

With their help, the innkeeper brought in enough conveniences to make their stay more comfortable. And so they waited. For the next three days, the innkeeper reported more and more alarming news. Soldiers were searching homes door to door, dragging out any Ethean they found. There were rumors of massacres, but the innkeeper didn't want to believe them.

"A Saladoran army has marched over the mountains," the innkeeper said the next time she returned. "There was already a battle. Kyvern

Psertis was driven back, and now the Imperial Army is marching out of the city and heading off to fight the Saladorans. They say there are elementars with the Saladorans, if you can imagine that!"

"The army is leaving?" Isibindi asked. "Does that mean we can leave?"

The innkeeper shrugged. "I don't know how many soldiers are leaving. I'm worried, though. My neighbors don't look at me the same way they used to. I don't see any Etheans anymore."

"Perhaps you should leave as well?"

"Where would I go? My only family is my granddaughter and my grandson. I lost my husband and sons long ago."

"Be careful," Telea said. "If we can help you escape, we will."

"It is kind of you. I can't believe it has come to this." Then she departed, closing the secret door behind her.

"Perhaps King Handrin can defeat the Belenese army and unseat the demon emperor," Tharryl said.

"The Imperial Army is far larger than any force Salador could bring over the mountains," Telea said. "It's not supposed to happen this way! The armies were supposed to unite and march on the Summoned Lands together." She shook her head. "The demon emperor is tearing Belen apart."

"King Handrin will retreat over the East Pass," Calen said.

"The demon has to be destroyed," Telea said. "Belen and Salador must unite."

"We'll get right to that," Tharryl said. "Just march in and kill the emperor."

"He can't lead the army in person," Telea said. "Anyone who sees him will know he's a demon. The emperor must stay in the palace."

"Soldiers surround the palace," Sindi said. "You said so yourself."

Telea paced the little room. "But the soldiers are leaving for war. The palace won't be as well guarded."

"Does it matter if it's fifty men or five hundred?" Tharryl asked. "I can only kill so many of them."

"I can do it," Telea said.

"What do you mean *you* can do it? Alone?"

"Yes. Alone."

Tharryl crossed his arms in front of his chest. "If you can do it alone now, why didn't you do it before? You could see him, couldn't you?"

"I can do it. Just let me think."

"This is grand," Tharryl said. "I want to hear this."

Telea ignored him and closed her eyes. Entering her memory walk, she went to the well where she'd imprisoned her demon. *Demon, I need your knowledge of runes. I want you to help me create a working.*

For what purpose?

I need to create an army of the dead.

Telea sank deep within her memory walk, blocking out Tharryl's grumbling and Sindi and Calen's whispered conversation. The war between Belen and Salador had to end. The demon emperor had to be destroyed. And both had to happen immediately.

Telea feared what she was about to do. She still felt the horrible connection with the undead she'd made before. Each one whispered to her, although she could never quite make out the words. They were miserable, though. They hated her for what she'd done.

I'll release you when it's over. Soon, she thought. She had no idea if they understood, or even if they heard her.

She had to do whatever was necessary, however terrible. Good people would die. People who had no idea they were following a demon. An image of the Blade of Darra flashed in her mind. Was she any better than Prince Morin and the other lyches and their pyren? They'd created an army of ghuls to serve them. They'd been convinced their cause was good.

But her cause *was* good. Prince Morin created ghuls because he thought he was the rightful king. It had been about him. About power. Her undead would serve a truly good cause. The Dromost Gate had to be locked.

She pushed any more thoughts from her mind and focused herself entirely on crafting her complex working. It was the only choice.

Some time later, she wasn't certain how long, Telea was pulled from her memory walk by someone shaking her shoulder. She heard Sindi whisper, "Be quiet. Someone's outside."

Telea nodded and stood up. The lamp wick was turned very low, and only the barest glow lit the room. Tharryl and Isibindi stood near the barrel door, their weapons held ready. Calen was a few strides back, an arrow nocked.

"The innkeeper?" Telea whispered.

Sindi shook her head. "Too loud. A man's voice."

Telea nodded. There was little she could do except prepare herself to sing and hope they wouldn't be found. "They're searching the villa," Isibindi whispered.

They waited for a long time, but no more noises came. "I think they're gone," Telea finally said.

"Why hasn't the innkeeper returned?" Calen said. "We should stay alert."

"She hasn't returned because she's dead," Tharryl said.

"You don't know that," Telea replied.

He shrugged. "We'll see."

They waited what had to be a quarterday before some of them took their ease while one stood guard at the barrel door. All the while, Telea and her demon crafted her working. Eventually, they ate a cold meal and then went to sleep, convinced that no one was coming.

"It's been too long," Tharryl said after they'd roused themselves. "We should go out and see what's happening."

"A little longer," Telea said. "She'll come back."

Tharryl just shook his head. Eventually, even Telea relented. It *had* been too long. They quietly opened the barrel door, and then the second door into the basement. It was dark and silent.

Telea held their little lantern and turned the wick higher. The basement was still the disheveled mess it had been before. Was it even more so now? Then she saw the open gate to the wine room. There were broken bottles and jugs, and the smell of spilled wine filled the air.

Tharryl handed his spear to Isibindi and drew his tulwar before heading up the stairs. Calen and Sindi followed him with Isibindi and Telea at the rear. It was only when Telea had reached the top of the stairs that she realized it was full night outside. She blew out the lamp so that the light wouldn't give them away. There was enough moonlight streaming through the front windows to see.

Sindi motioned her forward, and as Telea stepped into the foyer, she saw Calen and Tharryl crouched low. She stepped closer and saw the dark stain spread across the marble floor. Blood. A lot of blood. A long, wide streak of it led from a wide pool towards the door.

Calen motioned across the room, and Sindi nodded. "There were two," Sindi whispered. "They were dragged out the door."

Stepping carefully to avoid the blood, Tharryl went to the door, glanced to his left and right, and closed it. He waved them closer. Telea and the others crouched low as they moved past the windows and joined Tharryl in the breezeway.

"At least she didn't give us up," Tharryl said. "Good on her."

"She was only a quarter Ethean," Telea said. "She lived her whole life here."

"Her granddaughter didn't look Ethean at all," Sindi said.

Telea looked back to the foyer and the second pool of blood there. *They killed her granddaughter as well. What of the others?*

"The street is quiet," Tharryl said.

147

"What about the boy?" Telea asked. "Her grandson."

"Who cares," Tharryl said. "He's not our concern. We have more important things to think about."

"Like saving your skin?" Telea asked.

"Like war between Belen and Salador. Like the Dromost Gate. Let's get out of the city while we can."

"We're not leaving," Telea said. "I'm not, at least. Those massacres the innkeeper told us about. They happened because the emperor saw me."

"That's not true," Sindi said. "The emperor was arresting Etheans even before we arrived."

"The killing started the day after I entered the palace. I have some responsibility in this. And I'm not going to let all those Ethean deaths go in vain. Those victims will get their revenge."

Chapter Fifteen

Ayja sat at the dinner table, six arrows laid out on the table in front of her. It was late evening, but the blazing fire in her fireplace brightly lit the house. Her well of power was full, or near enough to it.

Her well could never be full for more than a heartbeat — the demands of keeping her own body alive constantly drained life force from it. Asleep, as she was under the working of the *Song of Rest*, the drain on her well was minimal. She knew that when she awoke, the draw on her well would be much stronger.

And so she continued to sleep. How long? Forever? The Blade of Darra had seen no sign that any demon had come close to finding her hidden body. Sleep shrouded her soul, but still, some slinking worm might come upon her by pure chance. What would happen if she was attacked? Would she awaken from her working and be able to defend herself? Or would she be devoured in her sleep and her soul consumed?

She shuddered and pushed the thought away, turning her attention back to the arrows in front of her. She looked past their physical form — the illusion she'd created in her memory walk — and at their true, ethereal form. The arrows weren't arrows at all, but workings she'd created. She'd already made a dozen others — fire rings of varying sizes. She'd placed them in her quiver. The workings were unlike anything she'd ever done before. These were just a *framework* of magic.

The newest were wind arrows. Three were lances of air, and two were spinning maelstroms. She'd created them without actually empowering them with aether. They were simply models of what she hoped they'd become when she poured power from her well into them.

Would it even work at all? She hoped so. Twisting the aether into complex woven circles was slow, but took far less of her energy to unleash than wielding the elements raw. She'd be able to touch these workings with a small draw of energy from her well, and they'd be instantly available. She glanced at the door, wishing she could wake for just a short time and test her new creations.

Was it even possible for her to break the bonds of sleep she'd imposed upon herself? The crafting had been hastily made, and simple. If she'd spent time on it, she could have added a word that would free her. Or perhaps even a rune in her memory walk she could touch. Perhaps she could do it even now. She shook her head, frowning. Could she execute a working in her memory walk that had power in the real world?

She tapped one of the arrows on the table in frustration. There were always more and more things to explore. She had time now, unlimited time, but the boundaries of her memory walk limited her. Even tinkering with her induced sleep might be dangerous. As long as her conscious mind remained within the boundaries of her memory walk, she was safe. Well, relatively safe.

Yawning, Ayja stood and gathered up her arrows. She needed true sleep. Her mind could not remain conscious forever, even in her memory walk. Her bed upstairs beckoned. It scared her a little, though. She hated the idea of true sleep — of not being ready if something happened. She walked to the door and placed her new arrows in Cam's quiver. She smiled. Just the smallest stream of aetherial power from her well *should* activate them.

She opened the door to the cool mountain air. Brilliant stars shone high in the sky above her. She couldn't see the sky from horizon to horizon as tall pines surrounded their home. *Their home.* She still thought of it as Cam and hers, even though it no longer even existed in the real world, and Cam couldn't visit her memory walk.

Does Cam know that we closed the Dromost Gate? Is he proud of me? He'll be proud when he learns of it, but he'll be sad as well. *We're not blood, but I'm his daughter.* It was hard to imagine the Champion of Salador crying, but she knew he would. *He'll try to save me, even though he can't.*

I'm back, Darra said.

She gasped in surprise and stepped back from the door. She lowered her guards and let him enter her memory walk. She saw him then, walking across the yard. He was strong and hale, his cloak billowing out behind him.

"Hello, Sir Darra," she said. "I'm surprised you're back. My well is nearly full." She wondered what he looked like now. Were there more rents in his mail hauberk? Had demons torn more flesh from his body, or had his magic restored all harm?

"Almost full? Let me fill it completely then."

Warmth coursed through her, and the fire — the illusory image of her well of power — flared brighter behind her. Stepping out of the way, she ushered him inside.

Out in the real world, Darra was touching her, feeding her his strength, saving her from having to draw on her well of power. She imagined him out there, lying prone on the ground, his arm shoved through some small hole in the rocks, touching her face or her hand.

"You are doing well?" she asked. "Why have you come back so soon? If it is soon." She shook her head. "I have no sense of the passage of time."

"I have Forsvar and Dromost, and demons don't notice me until it's too late for them." He stood by the fire, staring into the flames. "I have taken some of them into my service."

"You've what?" she spun to face him. "How? What do you mean?"

"They fear me and don't want to die. They've pledged themselves to me."

"You've talked to them? Made deals with them?"

"I hear their thoughts in my mind. And they hear mine if I let them. You've felt their minds brushing yours."

Ayja nodded. "I know. It just popped into my head that maybe they spoke. I wonder if they are even capable of it. Can you trust them?"

Darra smiled and brushed a lock of hair from his brow. "No, I don't think I can trust them much at all. But I use them to find more demons, and to warn me when danger is coming. So far it has worked."

"Why don't they just flee you if they fear you?"

"There is a structure to demon society, I've learned. It's a ruthless hierarchy of power. The strong consume the weak and grow more powerful. But as they grow stronger, they become a temptation for even stronger demons. So they subjugate some of the weaker demons, forcing them to serve them. They are paid for their service in souls."

"So why don't they flee you?"

"If they flee this area, they enter the domain of a stronger demon. They'll just become food."

"So you're a demon lord now?"

Darra shrugged. "Perhaps a lesser one."

"Does that make us safer?"

"For now. It makes you safer, at least. I've ordered my subjects to clear this area of demons. You are less likely to be discovered now." He turned away from the fire and faced her. "But I'm afraid I've also drawn the attention of far more powerful demons. They know of Forsvar and Dromost and want them."

Ayja grimaced. "That's not good. Maybe we should move on." She waved at the brightly burning fire. "That hasn't happened since before we arrived. We need to find a new place and hide again."

"I was thinking, my queen... what if we don't hide? What if we confront a more powerful demon and seize its domain? Force its subjects to obey us."

"They won't do that, Darra. They want to consume me."

"They'll recognize your power. If we show them how strong we are, they will respect us. We can't go on fleeing and hiding forever."

"Remember that demon of molten rock? We couldn't defeat it. How powerful are the most powerful demons?"

Darra crossed his arms in front of his chest. "If we can take dominion over some region, some defensible place, I can hold it and keep you safe. Once we take it, we can hide you and put you back to sleep again." He motioned around the room. "I will keep you fed with life force, and you will be free to work on an escape."

"I've created some workings, but they are tiny, insignificant things compared to the magic it would take to free us of Dromost. I don't think it's possible."

"I want to give you the conditions that make it possible, my queen."

"I know, Darra." She reached out and put her hand on his arm. "I know how hard you are working to keep me safe."

He looked down at her hand. "Your well of power is full. You could... you could become a pyren now if you wish. Survival would be much easier. Even if we never escaped, we could survive here together as long as we wished."

Ayja pulled away from him. "I'd rather die."

"You'd rather die than become a monster like me?" He gave her a crooked smile. "Or do you fear to spend eternity with me?"

"Neither. I'd rather die than live out eternity in this horrid world."

"I know, my queen. You will find a way," Darra said. He gave her a wan smile then turned to the door. "I have to go. I don't want to draw attention to this place. I might be away a little longer this time. I must patrol the borders."

"Thank you, Darra."

He disappeared. Normally he walked out the door and into the forest, maintaining the illusion of her memory walk. *I've upset the only other person I have in this world.* She blew out a long breath. *Well done, Ayja. Well done.*

She went to the table and slumped down with her back to the fire. She'd apologize to Darra. She knew how devoted he was to her. But even with his company, how much could she take? To live out eternity as a soulless pyren, sucking the life force from demons was no existence at all.

She folded her arms and laid her head down on them. She didn't want to contemplate an eternity in Dromost. She wanted to think of better things. She wanted to think of magic and all its possibilities. She'd make an empowered working next. She'd craft a circle, just as she did before, but this time she'd fill it with power. There'd be a trigger, though. The working would remain potent, but locked away, waiting for her to call it into being. She fell asleep, smiling at the challenge ahead of her.

The dreams were pleasant enough, at first. She dreamt of growing up with Cam. Of tending to their small fields, of caring for their animals, of him teaching her how to fight, and of her learning to be an elementar. But each dream ended horribly, broken by the arrival of some sinister force in the forest.

Some of the dreams ended with the arrival of Morin's ghuls and pyren, come to ravage the countryside and to turn the peaceful villagers into a host of ghuls for his army. Then the dreams turned even darker, with demons appearing, relentlessly chasing her in hopes of devouring her soul. She tried to fight back, but she couldn't touch the aether.

She dreamt of Orlos and the time the two of them had swum naked in the pool above the Temple of Forsvar. In her dream they approached each other, ready and willing to make love, but then she became aware of malevolent eyes watching them. Demons intent on tearing them apart.

Finally, she dreamt that Darra came to her in her memory walk, but this time as a pyren, and not as the man he'd once been. "I don't have to ask you to become a pyren," he said. "I can turn you into one in your sleep."

Ayja awoke with a start within her memory walk. How long had she been asleep? In her mind, dawn was rising, but it meant nothing. It was always dawn when she awoke within her memory walk.

She fetched eight candles from a drawer and returned to the table. Now she could begin a project she'd been looking forward to for a long time. She would create empowered workings.

Just as she had with the arrows, she started by making a framework of a working. However, this time she'd fill the workings from her well of power. It would diminish her well of power, but in the real world, she'd be able to instantly call up the working and not have to craft it or empower it.

The work was incredibly difficult. She was working the aether within her memory walk, not in a real space. What would happen if she lost control of it? Would her head burst into flames? Would it explode in a ball of fire? She stopped and paced around the room, unable to focus for the fear that suddenly consumed her.

Was it worth it to have a powerful working instantly available? Her fire wasn't quite the size it had been. The fire she depended upon to keep her alive. She could reverse the process, though, right? She could unravel the working and put the aether back into her fire. It should be possible, but it would take effort and time.

Slowly, carefully, she created her workings. She placed each one she finished within a candle, and then placed it on her fireplace mantle. The work was taxing, and when she had enough, she stood back to look at what she'd accomplished. Six brightly burning candles rested atop the mantle.

Six fully formed rings of fire, tied to the aether of her well of power, only needing a trigger to be loosed upon the world. Or so she hoped. She yawned. Tired again? Already? How long had she been working on the candles?

She stepped away from the mantle and into the great room's kitchen space, the skirts of her dress swooshing as she walked. How long had it been since Darra had last visited her?

She went to a shelf and pulled down two clay jars she'd created and took them to the dining table. Opening the smaller one, she removed her memory of the runic circle from the floor of the Temple of Dromost. This was the circle that had been filled with sacrificial blood and had opened and kept open the Dromost Gate.

Tracing her finger along the runes, she tried to make sense of them. She knew several from her lessons with Telea. There were just so many she didn't know. She had figured out some of them by context, but others were a mystery. The opening of the gate had been an incredibly complex act, and she just didn't have the knowledge to piece it all together.

She paused and cocked her head, listening. She'd heard some noise. *In the real world. Something was close.*

Chapter Sixteen

"An army of the dead?" Sindi asked. "What do you mean?"

"You remember the silent brothers at the Temple of Dromost?" Telea asked.

Tharryl nodded. "They weren't the best soldiers, but they were certainly hard to kill. They made hard work for the summoner fanatics coming over the wall."

"I can do it. I can create silent brothers of my own."

The others stared at her in silence.

"I learned how to create the undead at the Temple of Dromost," Telea continued. "I learned more from the summoner Muaz." It was only partially the truth. She'd worked out more of the puzzle with her demon.

Tharryl clasped his hands together and smiled. "That's our first bit of good news. Let them fight for us."

"Listen to yourself, Telea," Sindi said. "You're talking about raising a host of the dead!"

"Do you see anyone else rushing to help us?" Telea asked. "I can create an army. It isn't what I wish, but it is what I have to do." She had the magic to do it, at least. Could she handle the strain? She wasn't certain. She still felt the presence of the undead she'd created in the palace. They were still there, still alive. *Still undead.* Their presence in her mind was a pressure, a weight, pulling her down. Could she handle an army of the dead?

"Do I understand your Saladoran?" Isibindi asked in Ethean. "You wish to create an army out of dead Etheans? Out of our people?"

Telea frowned. "We must defeat this demon emperor," she replied in the same language. "Let our people get revenge in death for what was done to them in life. Let them have purpose again."

"It is a grim thing you are proposing." Isibindi held up her hand to stave off any objection. "To make the dead rise is a terrible thing."

"It is," Telea said. "But what choice do we have?" She faced Sindi and Calen and, in Saladoran, said, "Can you give me some other option?

The Belenese are marching to defeat King Handrin. They can't be stopped unless we kill this demon."

Sindi glanced at Calen, and he nodded. "We've seen so many terrible things on this journey," Sindi said. "I can't imagine Helna or the Great Spirit would approve of making the dead walk again. But the gods are gone and have left us to our own devices. We are with you."

"I'm glad," Telea said. "I need all of you. This won't be an easy task. Now let's see if we can find the servant boy — the grandson. Perhaps he can tell us more."

"I'll watch the door," Tharryl said.

"I stay as well," Isibindi added in her broken Saladoran.

Telea, Sindi, and Calen entered the dark courtyard and made their way towards the stables. The doors were open, but there were no horses there. It smelled of manure, though. Had the other guests kept horses there? The innkeeper had said that they were all students. Did students have that kind of wealth? Not those who lived in such a simple villa, she thought.

They entered the stable and looked around, but the boy wasn't there. As they departed, Telea saw the faint glow of light through the shutters of a first-floor room. *The other guests. Some are still here? Did they even know?*

She pointed the light out to Sindi and Calen. "We can ask whoever lives there."

"Not you," Sindi said. "I will ask. You stay out of sight."

"You speak enough Belenese?"

"Enough to ask what happened and where the dead were taken. You should stay out of sight."

Sindi was right. Best not to be seen. There was no knowing which side they were on in all of this. Telea hid near the breezeway, while Sindi gave her bow and sword belt to Calen.

The little Landomeri went to the door and softly knocked. There was no response. She went to the window and spoke through the cracks. Telea was a good distance away but saw the glow of lamplight disappear. It appeared Sindi was speaking to someone through the window, but it was hard to tell.

Finally, Sindi rejoined the others. As she belted her sword around her waist, she said, "I didn't want to look threatening. As it was, it didn't matter. She wouldn't open the window or the door."

"Did she tell you anything?"

"She's very afraid and won't come out. She saw large wagons in the street earlier today. They were filled with bodies and being drawn towards the city gates. She didn't see the innkeeper killed, but she heard

156

it happen. She doesn't know where the boy is. The soldiers questioned her. They wanted to know about the two of you — the Etheans. She told them she thought you'd left."

"I wonder if the wagons have already passed the gate," Telea said. "Let's hope they're still inside the city." She couldn't believe it had come to this — that Belenese soldiers would so remorselessly arrest and kill on the orders of the emperor. Belen was an enlightened society filled with people of many races and cultures. How could it fall apart so quickly?

They rejoined Tharryl and Isibindi. "We have to head down to the gate," Telea said. "There were wagons filled with the dead heading there earlier today."

"They will be out of the city by now," Tharryl said.

"We have to try. I don't want to wait another day."

They stole out of the villa and onto the street. The night was late, and there was no one to be seen. Aftokropoli wasn't like Sal-Oras. The streets were broad and had trees planted on them. Parks were frequent and filled with gardens. All made for stealthy progress.

Twice they dodged foot patrols, once by hiding in a garden, and the other time by ducking into an alley between two villas. How late was it? Telea began to fear they'd run out of darkness.

As quickly as they dared, they made their way towards the same gate they'd entered a week before. The final street before the gate was broader than the others they'd followed. At the far end they saw torchlight and gathered soldiers.

"It will be hard to approach," Sindi said.

Telea nodded. They hid behind a low wall protecting a garden. "I'll go down and see what's happening. I'll use my magic to keep out of sight."

"Be careful."

Telea crept over the wall, and drawing her cloak of shadows over her, made her way down the street. There were fewer soldiers than she'd first thought — maybe ten in all. As she came closer, she saw they guarded three large wagons. One had thrown a wheel and was canted off to the side. The back gate was open, and soldiers were unloading the wagon's cargo — dozens of corpses. Men, women, children. Etheans. All hacked to death.

Telea flinched and looked away. How was this possible? How easy had it been to turn people to such evil? She steeled herself against the sight and turned back.

The soldiers took the corpses from the crippled wagon and then heaved them up over the strakes of the next wagon — a wagon already

157

full to overflowing. They tossed the bodies as if they were sacks of grain, swinging them once, twice, and then throwing them up onto the pile.

As Telea crept closer, she heard two of the soldiers arguing. "That one there," one said, "that one's a danger?" The woman pointed as a child was thrown up onto the wagon.

"They sacked the Temple of Forsvar!" her companion said, his voice rising.

"That one didn't!"

"Look, we're at war with three countries now. You want to be in a battle and have some Ethean traitor stab you in the back? Better to be rid of them."

"Really? Again, was that one going to stab you in the back? That babe there? I don't think he could have lifted a sword. Was he five years old?"

The male soldier threw up a hand, dismissing her. "They resisted. There was a big fight in the Old Market. They should have come along peacefully."

The female soldier shook her head and was about to respond when someone shouted at them to help with the wagons. For a few heartbeats, Telea watched as they joined the others in their grisly task. All killed for a lie. All killed to serve a demon's purpose. But even if the lie was true, no soldier should have obeyed the orders. It sickened her that Belenese soldiers would be so quick to kill innocent Belenese citizens.

A body hit the side of the wagon and fell to the ground, the head striking the pavers with an audible crack. "Idiot! Pick it up!"

"I slipped. It was bloody!"

It — a young woman of maybe fourteen years. Rage boiled up within Telea. It was time for all this to end. And not in the way the soldiers expected.

Still wrapped in her cloak of shadows, she walked into the square and to the opposite side of the furthest wagon. It was stacked so high she was certain bodies would start toppling from it the moment it started moving.

There were no soldiers on this side. They were all busy moving the bodies from the broken wagon. Climbing the spokes of the big rear wheel, Telea pulled herself up to the edge of the strakes. She could hardly bear to look at the bodies there.

An elderly woman's dead eyes stared at her, and Telea felt the wave of anger again. *Wake up! It's time for your revenge.*

Reaching out, Telea touched one of the bodies. Chanting softly to herself, she unleashed the working she and her demon had created. The energy of the working passed down her arm and into the woman. Her eyes blinked, and at the same moment, a tendril of the aether connected them.

Telea commanded her to remain still and just to move her hand enough for the working to go about its task. The undead woman's hand moved just a finger length and touched a man's forehead. In an instant, he awoke as well.

Telea's heart hammered in her chest. *It works! The undead create the undead.*

Carefully, she moved to the front of the wagon and repeated the working, filling it with energy from her well. It took so little life force to create the undead that a single working could be passed on several times. How long would each living corpse survive? She didn't know for certain, but she still felt her connection to the women in the palace.

Long enough to do one last task. Then they can rest forever.

One undead touched four more, and those each touched another three or four. It took only heartbeats for the entire wagon to be filled with silent, still undead. Telea staggered from the wheel and fell to her knees on the cobbles. Souls once free were wrenched from whatever peaceful place they'd found and bound to dead flesh. The weight of their misery threatened to crush her.

What torment had she wrought on them? How long could she take this?

Go! She commanded them. *Kill the men who killed you. Take their weapons. We will end this!*

The undead spilled from the wagon in a confused, chaotic mass. They toppled onto the cobbles as soldiers cried out in surprise. At first, they thought the wagon had tipped, but then, very quickly, they realized their error. The dead rose and charged.

Soldiers shouted out at first in alarm and then in terror as the undead attacked. The soldiers drew swords and snatched spears from where they leaned on the wagon. They cut and thrust at the undead, severing limbs, slashing skulls, and piercing hearts, but the undead didn't care. They wanted only one thing.

The dead threw themselves at the soldiers, ignoring otherwise deadly wounds, and grappled them to the ground. Cold, dead hands reached for throats, throttling the life out of horrified men and women, who'd just moments before been flinging the dead into the back of a wagon.

Telea caught her breath as some of the slain soldiers rose as well, joining forces with those who'd just taken their lives. She ran around the back of the wagon to where the last soldiers still fought. It lasted only moments. The undead overwhelmed them with their fearless onslaught. Then she saw three figures running away, up the street — two men and a woman escaping the massacre. Using the trained voice of a singer, Telea called out, "Stop them! Don't let them escape!" Hoping her friends would hear.

From behind her, across the square, she heard the shouts of soldiers guarding the city gate. She'd forgotten about them, and now some sallied from the tower and charged to the aid of their companions, not realizing their fate. There were soldiers atop the wall as well. Some had bows and heavy crossbows, but none loosed their arrows or bolts. In the darkness, they couldn't be certain of what was happening.

"Kill them," Telea commanded the undead nearest her. Two dozen undead silently charged across the square, launching themselves full speed into the six soldiers who'd come to investigate. A couple of soldiers turned to retreat when they realized what was coming for them, but they were too slow and were tackled from behind. The City Guard atop the walls and gate towers now loosed a shower of missiles on the dead. The arrows and bolts struck the walking corpses, but none fell. Telea recalled them with a thought, needing them for another task. Like before, the soldiers they'd just killed rose up to join them. Her working was still spreading. She'd have her army.

Alarm bells sounded from the city gate. Would more sortie? She doubted it. Not until they could put together larger numbers. *Let them come. The more they send, the more soldiers I'll have.*

Even as the thought crossed her mind, more undead spilled from the two remaining wagons. She tried to do the math in her head. The working shouldn't have created so many. Then she saw the dead wagon guards in the back of the wagons, waking even more dead Etheans. Each soldier raised more than they should have been able to.

How was it possible? "Come here!" she commanded one of them. The dead soldier marched up to her and halted a stride away. *The woman who had argued against the killing of Etheans.* Telea hardened her heart and reached out to touch her. *You should have tried to stop them.*

Chanting, Telea reached out with her magic to explore the soldier's body. She saw the working within the soldier, but it was far stronger than it should have been. It held more energy than she'd put into the very first Ethean she'd touched. *You weren't dead to start with, were you? The working absorbed all of your life force when you died. Instead of creating four undead, you can create a dozen or even more.*

All the better. A larger army to assault the palace. She had seventy of the undead with her and another twenty-three in the palace. Only one of her undead lay unmoving in the street, his head split by a Belenese sword. *They feel no pain and can suffer the most terrible wounds and keep fighting. But how many will I need?* The Emperor's Axes weren't the City Guard.

"Telea!"

She turned at Isibindi's shout. A dozen of her undead rushed up the street towards her companions. "Stop!" Telea shouted. "Come back!"

The undead halted in their tracks, turned, and walked back towards Telea. Now her undead host surrounded her, staring at her with unblinking eyes. *Turn away!* She commanded them. They obeyed, but while it saved her from the torment of their eyes, it didn't save her from their presence in her mind.

Do not attack my companions, Telea commanded. She projected images of each of them to the undead. Then she walked out from among them and up the street. Four of the nearby undead had Ethean arrows deep in their chests.

"You'll be safe now," Telea called up the street. Her friends emerged from the shadows. Sindi, Calen, and Isibindi had arrows on their bowstrings, while Tharryl held his spear.

"You're certain?" Sindi asked. The four stopped thirty strides from Telea.

"They'll obey me," Telea said.

"We killed the soldiers running up the street," Tharryl said. "By the sound of those horns, more will be coming."

"There are people watching us," Calen said, pointing up towards the second-floor villa windows to their left and right.

Telea glanced where he was pointing and saw people hastily pull back from windows. "It doesn't matter," she said. "We aren't turning back now."

Tharryl walked closer. "Your friends need weapons," he said.

"We'll take them from the dead," Telea said. The undead stood motionless at the entrance to the square. "Come, I don't want this to last any longer than it has to."

"This is terrible," Sindi said.

"All of it is terrible," Telea replied. "I'd give anything for it to all be over." With a thought, she ordered the undead to start up the street. When they came upon the three soldiers who'd tried to escape, three of the undead knelt over them and transferred the working to them. "We'll kill any soldiers we come upon," Telea said, hating the words as they came out of her mouth. "We need more in our host."

They jogged up the street, the undead running silently with them. They didn't breathe or talk — there was only the slap of their feet and shoes on the pavers and the swish of their clothing. *They would run forever if I asked. To the end of the world and never stop.* More horns

161

sounded, warning of attack. How many defenders did the city have? The City Guard had several thousand, but they'd be manning the walls all around the city and looking outward for the attack. It would take some time for them to realize it was coming from within the city. The real threat were the Imperial Timari and the Emperor's Axes. How many had remained in the city when the army had marched off to attack the King of Salador?

There were shouts at an intersection ahead of them as Telea's undead ran into a patrol. A horn call cut off mid-blast. By the time Telea got there, it was over. Six guardsmen were rising to join the others, but one lay unmoving, a spear wound through his head.

It was the second time she'd seen one of her undead downed. The other had had his head split open. *If you destroy the mind... if you destroy the brain, the undead are unmade.* It made sense. The memory walk was in the mind. The well of power and workings were as well. *Yes. The undead still need a mind to think.*

"That way!" Telea said, pointing up a broad avenue. "Hurry!" The dead tormented her mind now. It wasn't a willful act. It was simply the result of what she'd done. Their minds were linked with hers. She got to feel what they were feeling. *This false life is torturing them.*

"What's our plan?" Sindi asked as they jogged up the street. "Do we try to turn the palace guards to our side?"

"Not likely," Tharryl said. His breath came heavy now, the run taking its toll on him in his heavy armor. "Not with the alarm sounded."

"They won't turn," Telea said. She was feeling the run now as well. Not the undead, though. They paced along behind her without a breath and without a drop of sweat. "The Emperor's Axes certainly won't. I hate the idea of it. They're good men."

"So, what's the plan?" Sindi asked again.

"Straight in," Tharryl said. "Don't pause. Don't stop. Don't speak." He took a deep breath. "Straight in."

"Straight in," Telea said with a nod.

They struck another patrol on the route to the palace. Sixteen men this time. Telea lost two of her undead but gained the sixteen City Guardsmen in compensation. She had a force of over a hundred now, a third of them armed.

As they entered the palace square, a hail of arrows flew at them from the gatehouse and the palace walls. The arrows tore into the front ranks of the undead, punching through leather cuirasses, but they didn't falter. The undead shielded Telea and her companions from the assault. She motioned for her friends to hold back at the same time she mentally commanded her undead to charge the palace.

162

Fifty Imperial Timari stood in front of the gate. When the timari saw the charging City Guard, they formed a shield wall instead of retreating through the gate. Perhaps they were confident in their skill or the support of the archers on the wall. Whatever their thinking, they didn't realize their mistake until it was too late.

Arrow after arrow struck, but only a single undead fell, struck through the eye by an arrow. Now the unarmored Etheans charged past Telea — men, women, and children alike.

"What do we do?" Isibindi asked.

Telea grimaced. "Kill the palace guards," she said.

The City Guard undead crashed into the timari shield wall with fearless fury. The timari stabbed at them with spears, only to find their blows ineffective. Spear thrusts that would have killed any living soldier only pushed the undead back for a moment.

Telea's companions had just nocked arrows to their bows when a score of riders appeared from a side street. The mounted timari lowered their light lances and charged into the flank of the Ethean undead, riding them down and trampling them beneath their horses' hooves.

Any normal fighting force would have broken at the sudden assault, but the undead didn't care. They picked themselves up off the street and charged the horsemen, grabbing both riders and horses by the legs and trying to throw them down. Men and women screamed as they were dragged from their saddles.

Sindi, Calen, and Isibindi drew back their Ethean longbows and loosed into the confused melee. Many of the timari had ridden through the mob and out the other side. They turned to charge again, but there was some disorder in their ranks. The foes they thought they'd broken were rising from the cobbles and charging them.

Some of the riders tried to pull their horses back from the charging mass of undead. Others snatched bows from cases and loosed arrows into the undead, only to see the missiles have no effect.

As the fight raged, Telea felt one strand and then another sever as her undead fell. But for every strand that severed, two or three more were formed. Her undead were still creating undead. Without her using the slightest thread of her power, her army was growing.

The riders shouted in fear and kicked their horses' flanks as they turned in panicked flight. Two dozen Etheans chased them. The timari at the gate weren't as lucky. They couldn't flee, at least not those in the front ranks. They held at first, their superior armor and training getting the best of undead. Slowly at first, and then more rapidly, the tide turned. More and more timari were killed only to rise and join the attackers.

"This isn't right," Tharryl said. "This isn't the way war should be fought. Men should fight men."

"Go then and fight," Telea snapped. The burden of the undead was crushing. Keeping track of them was overwhelming. "The demon emperor must die."

"Dromost take this, it's a grisly thing."

The timari broke and fled through the gate, the undead close on their heels. The archers on the gate tower and those on the nearby walls continued to loose arrow after arrow into the undead, desperate to take some toll on the undying invaders.

Whatever chaos reigned within the gatehouse, no one threw the lever to drop the portcullis. Nearly every undead passed through the gate, all but for those few who had pursued the escaping horsemen or the few chasing timari who'd fled across the square. Telea ran forward, commanding some of the undead to charge the palace doors and others to clear the walls.

Blood soaked the cobbles in front of the gate, but for all the fighting, there were only six dead there — four City Guard and two Etheans. Every timari that had fallen defending the palace was now assaulting it instead.

They ran through the gate tower and out the other side. Undead fought within the tower and on the walls now. Any timari who could manage it fled. Only those with no escape stood and fought, realizing now there'd be no surrender.

Immediately in front of them, the undead hammered on the palace doors to no avail. The palace wasn't a castle, though. If the front doors were closed to them, they could find another entrance. "This way," Telea said, pointing off to her left. She didn't know for certain that she'd find a way in there, but it would do no good to wait. Twenty undead ran off ahead of them, while dozens upon dozens trailed behind.

They ran through manicured gardens and came to a side gate, but it was locked. Tharryl kicked it four times, but it was heavily barred and didn't break. The next door they came to collapsed under the first blow. Tharryl rushed through, followed by six undead timari. The fighting was over by the time Telea made it into the guardroom. The five timari who had defended it were already rising.

More and more, it was happening now. She felt the threads connecting her to the new undead. These were further off. Her undead, beyond her control, were fighting soldiers elsewhere. There was nothing she could do for it. They were too far off for her mental commands to have any effect.

"Keep going," Telea said. "We can't let the emperor escape." At her command, the undead rushed through the door and into the palace proper.

"Which way?" Tharryl asked.

"I'm not certain." The undead poured into the hallway with them, and she sent them off in two different directions. She'd know if they started fighting nearby. Either by their deaths or by the undead they created. "This way," she said, mostly guessing.

She mentally pushed undead ahead of her, letting them find defenders. She heard a man give a terrified shout, and then a woman cried out in fear. Telea grimaced. There weren't only soldiers in the palace. There were servants as well. *Just kill the soldiers. Just kill those with weapons,* she commanded, pushing the thought out as far as it would reach. Still, she had no idea how many of the undead could hear the command. Did they even have the intelligence to understand?

They ran through several rooms and past a garden courtyard before coming to a broad hallway. Unlike the dark rooms they'd been passing through, bronze oil lamps hanging from the ceiling lighted this hallway. It looked familiar, like one she'd been in just a few nights before, but she couldn't be certain. A trail of undead followed her and her companions now, but there were no undead immediately ahead of them. She called out for them to find their way to her.

They'd just started down the wide hall when four Emperor's Axes rushed around a corner thirty strides in front of them. "Halt!" one of them shouted, raising his long axe.

"A demon possesses the emperor," Telea called out. "It must be driven out of him."

It was a foolish, useless attempt. The Axes charged. Bowstrings thrummed, and three arrows streaked towards the Axes. One glanced off the heavy scales of an Axe's armor, but two others struck home, both hitting the same man. Despite an arrow in his shoulder and another in his chest, he continued his charge.

Tharryl stepped in front of Telea, his heavy spear poised to strike. Before he had the chance, the undead rushed past on either side. The Axes tore through the undead, their heavy axes splitting skulls and severing limbs. Tharryl thrust his spear at an Axe whose weapon had become stuck in a timari corpse. The spearhead struck like a viper, plunging into the man's neck and out again.

Two more arrows struck the same Axe as before, rocking him back on his heels. A timari's sword slammed into his helmet before a third arrow struck him in the face, killing him. The last two Axes cut down five undead before those they'd already knocked to the ground grappled their legs, toppling them.

Telea commanded her undead to grapple the Axes, but not to kill them. It was too late for one — a City Guardswoman had plunged a dagger under his armpit and into his heart. The other was alive, though.

"I don't want to kill you!" Telea said to him. These were her father's people, the brave men of the frontiers who held the summoners at bay. "The emperor is possessed. He must be stopped."

"I am oathsworn!" the Drinker shouted. He grimaced as he tried to yank his limbs free of the undead grasping them, but there were too many. "What are these foul demons, summoner?"

Even as he spoke, two Axes rose from the floor, hefting their weapons.

"Summoner!" the Drinker shouted. "What have you done?"

"We don't have time for this," Tharryl said.

He was right. There was nothing she could say that would convince the Axe she wasn't a summoner. Pushing a timari aside, she knelt on the Drinker's chest and touched his face. Chanting, she drew his life force from him, filling her well of power, and putting him into a deep sleep. *Leave him in peace*, she commanded the undead. By the time he awakened, it would all be over.

She stood and commanded the undead to release the sleeping Drinker. Five undead and one Axe with an arrow in his skull lay on the floor with the sleeping man. It was the first fight where she'd lost more than she'd gained. The Drinker axes had taken a toll on the skulls of the undead.

They pushed down the hallway and made a turn. She kept the two undead Drinkers and the heaviest armored timari in front. At the end of the hall, a dozen Emperor's Axes stood in front of the double doors leading to the emperor's apartments.

Telea didn't wait this time. She sent her undead streaming down the hall to attack the Axes. There was no room for maneuver. The enemy couldn't be outflanked. The fight was a terrible, bloody brawl in a dark hall. Once again, Drinker axes took a terrible toll on the undead. Telea couldn't see the melee through the crowd, but she could feel her connecting cords being cut as her undead fell.

Only then did she realize how many more threads had been formed. Distant threads. Hundreds of them. The undead had escaped her control and were creating more and more undead in the city. And it couldn't just be soldiers. There were too many. Her undead were spreading unchecked through the largest city in Belen.

She stood there, overwhelmed at what she'd unleashed. How far would her undead plague spread? "I have to go," she said, stepping back from the fight.

"What do you mean?" Sindi asked. "Where are you going?"

"The undead are spreading through the city. Innocent people are being attacked." She turned to leave, but Tharryl seized her arm, stopping her.

"Finish this first," he commanded. "You're the only one who can command these things."

"That's right! I'm the only one! I have to go out and call them back. So many are dying." She grasped the sides of her head with her hands. *So much pain. So many dead.*

"How many more will die if this demon emperor lives?"

Telea shuddered, and tears ran from her eyes. The weight of the undead was crushing her. She'd killed hundreds of innocents. It would be thousands before this would be done. She turned and faced down the hall towards the Axes. "Kill them!" she screamed at her undead. "Kill them now!"

Driven to a frenzy by her commands, the undead fell upon the Axes with renewed fury. The tide turned as Axes fell and then rose again as undead. With every heartbeat, more undead were created in the city. Not one at time, but three or five or seven. "End this!"

The doors behind the last Axes flew open, and with fearsome cries, three creatures threw themselves into battle. The creatures had once been women but had been twisted into horrible monsters by the demons possessing them. Green scales covered them from head to toe, and long, dagger-like claws protruded from their hands and feet. Their limbs were stretched unnaturally long, and all that remained of their humanity were their tortured faces and manes of long hair. In the hall behind them, a massive shape loomed, its head nearly scraping the high ceiling.

The scaled demons tore into the undead. Their claws ripped heads from necks and limbs from bodies. Dead, partially coagulated blood splattered the walls and ceiling. The undead didn't care, though. They threw themselves fearlessly at the demons, hacking with axes and swords and stabbing with spears and daggers. The demon scales turned many of the blows, but not all. And the undead didn't tire; they struck each blow as hard as the last.

Sindi, Calen, and Isibindi loosed arrow after arrow at the demons. The heavy Ethean bows sent their arrows with tremendous force. The demons screamed with rage, lashing out at the undead and driving them back several strides.

Telea tried to sing, but she couldn't find her song. The crushing force of dead souls was too much for her to take. She could barely think, let alone summon her voice for song. The huge figure appeared in the doorway behind the scaled demons. It had once been the emperor, but no more. Naked, bloated, with orange-red skin, the massive demon filled the hall. Unable to contain all the souls it had consumed, their stored energy had erupted into a disfigured, misshapen mass.

Telea's undead fell faster and faster. The Axes and timari, the heaviest armored of them, were mostly destroyed, leaving only the City Guard and unarmored Ethean undead between Telea's companions and the demons. The demons had paid a price, though. Each bled from a score of wounds, and some of the fury had gone out of their fight.

Only thirteen undead still stood. *No, not thirteen. Thousands. The city is filling with undead while I am here.*

And all those thousands could do nothing for her. She needed them here. Then she remembered the slain women hidden away in the map room nearby. *Come to me,* she thought. *Slay the monster who killed you. Kill the emperor!*

Tharryl leaped forward, and holding his spear overhead, stabbed one of the demons in the chest. The demon grasped at the spear shaft for a moment before the light went out of its eyes. At the same moment, two arrows punched through the scales of a second scaled demon, and it fell as well.

The bloated emperor pushed into the undead, crushing them with his fists and slamming them into walls. Some, their bones shattered, could only twitch or crawl on the floor. Others picked themselves up and threw themselves into the fight again.

The last of the scaled demons threw itself at Sindi, but Isibindi intercepted it, and with a single blow from her tulwar nearly severed its head. The dying demon lashed out at the her, its claws slashing through her mail as if it wasn't there, carving deep wounds in Isibindi's side and down through her hip.

Tharryl leaped forward and hurled his spear at the emperor. The spear buried itself deep in the folds of the demon's flesh, but still, it came on. There were only a couple of undead left in the emperor's path. They mindlessly launched themselves at the emperor, not caring for the fate of all the undead who'd gone before them.

"Fall back!" Tharryl shouted as he drew his tulwar and Drommarian axe. No one obeyed. Telea sprang to Isibindi's aid while the two Landomeri loosed arrow after arrow into the emperor. Their arrows sank so deep into the demon's flesh that only the very last of their fletching showed, but still, the demon came on. It was strides from Telea now. Only Tharryl and a single undead stood in its path.

A moment of paralyzing fear gripped Telea as she placed her hands on Isibindi. *I can't sing. What if I can't chant?* Blood pooled under Isibindi as her heart pumped it from her wounds. She'd bleed out in heartbeats.

Telea tried to clear her mind, sinking deep into her memory walk and pushing away the thousands of undead threatening to overwhelm her. Within the temple of her memory, she found the *Chant of Healing*. At first, her voice failed her, but then the words came and the magic flowed out of her. She poured life force into Isibindi, closing her wounds and stopping the bleeding.

The demon emperor oozed blood from dozens of wounds. Opening its mouth grotesquely wide, its long forked tongue lashed out and wrapped around the neck of an undead, yanking the Ethean off her feet and dragging her close. The demon pulled the undead to his mouth, where he bit deeply into her neck. Thick, red-black blood dripped from the wound before the demon hurled the corpse against the wall.

"No soul!" the demon shouted, fury filling its voice. "No soul!"

Tharryl leaped forward and delivered a heavy blow to the demon's forearm, his blade sinking deep into its flesh. He almost lost his sword as the demon yanked its arm back. As the demon recoiled, Tharryl hacked deep into its leg with his axe.

The demon aimed a heavy blow at the knight, but Tharryl ducked it and struck the demon two more blows. And still, from strides away, Calen and Sindi loosed arrows at it, every one of them plunging deep into its body.

Twice, the demon swung at Tharryl. Once, he dodged the blow, and the second time he parried it with a vicious slash from his tulwar. Then a third blow struck him solidly, throwing Tharryl ten strides down the hall. He hit the floor hard and lay still. Sindi and Calen each loosed another arrow into the demon but dodged away as it charged the prone knight.

As the demon passed, Isibindi rose, her sword held two-handed. She brought it down on the demon's leg, severing muscle and tendon and sending it toppling face-first to the ground. Still, it lunged for Tharryl, grabbing him by the leg. Sindi and Calen dropped their bows and drew their tulwars, hacking at the demon's arm in hopes of making it drop the knight.

The demon opened its mouth again, and its tongue lashed out, wrapping around Calen's waist and yanking him closer. Isibindi dashed forward and cut at the tongue, but the demon backhanded her, sending her into the wall. Then, with the same hand, it knocked Sindi aside and dragged Tharryl closer.

The demon's orange-hued bulk nearly crushed Telea against the side of the passage. She reached out and touched it and began to chant, drawing the life force from it. The demon flinched from her, but she pushed forward, keeping her hands pressed against the demon's fleshy hide. It had taken scores of wounds, but it was so large, and had consumed so many souls, she realized that she could never drain it in time to save her friends. She'd only given Calen and Tharryl a moment's reprieve.

Sudden motion pulled Telea's attention from the demon. The undead female consorts had arrived. They scrambled upon the demon striking and clawing at it with their hands but to no effect.

Calen was drawn to the demon's mouth, but with his arms and legs, he fought being pulled to its wide maw. He had a dagger in his right hand and stabbed over and over at the tongue holding him. The demon flicked its head and sent him spinning to the floor.

Weapons! Take up weapons! Telea commanded the undead. In heartbeats, they had axes, swords, and spears in their hands and swarmed over the demon, hacking and stabbing it.

Sindi and Isibindi charged forward, slashing the demon's arm over and over until it finally released its grasp on Tharryl. All the while, Telea continued her chant, drawing life force from the demon into her well of power.

The demon lurched, throwing some of the undead from it, but one young lady, naked but for the flimsiest of garments, jumped atop the demon's back and managed to keep her balance. She held a huge Drinker axe in both hands and brought it down on the back of the demon's skull, splitting it with a sickening crunch.

With one last grunt, the demon flopped forward onto its face. Air escaped its lungs like a bellows slowly released. The undead, naked and covered in blood and ichor, turned to face Telea, awaiting her next command.

Telea staggered away from the dead emperor. "The undead," she said. "They're ravaging the city. They've escaped my control."

"What do we do?" Sindi asked as she helped Calen to his feet.

"Nothing. This is up to me."

Chapter Seventeen

The victory in the pass had been greater than Nidon could have hoped for. Not only had they captured Prodidos, but the following day they'd taken his father, Kyvern Psertis, as he'd ridden to his son's aid. With their capture, all local resistance had fallen.

Nidon waited two weeks at the entrance of the pass for more reinforcements to arrive and for word of Psertis's defeat to spread. They were in Exonos's satrusy, where the people, many having seen Ayja and Forsvar in person, willingly came to him to offer their aid. The presence of King Handrin and the Orb of Creation only solidified their support.

They had nearly all of their five hundred Landomeri archers with them now, as well as the entirety of the two hundred Knights of the House. They had another four hundred knights, mostly drawn from the South Teren, and an equal number of crossbowmen and spearmen supporting them. What they didn't have were horses. Exonos did what he could to find them, but it would take time.

Exonos had also called in every soldier he could find. He had nearly a hundred timari, three hundred freemen, and a similar number of volunteers on foot armed with javelins, slings, and bows. More important than all the soldiers he provided, Exonos supported the expedition with carts, wagons, and food supplies. It was paid for with Saladoran gold and silver, but it was Exonos who made it happen. He'd assured them Emperor Niktonas would repay it all, but at the moment, Handrin's purse emptied like a rushing stream.

It took a little more than a week for their small army to arrive at Prodopoli, the capital of Psertis's kyverny. Nidon was astounded, as he was at every stage of their journey, at the lack of defenses. There were no walls or moats — just an open city that started as villages and slowly grew to streets lined with villas. In Salador, every village had a tower or fortified manor, and every town had a stone wall or, if it was very poor, a wooden palisade. But here, everything was open.

For the length of their journey, Exonos had sent out messengers, spreading the word of the arrival of the King of Salador and the Orb of Creation. The messengers told the people how King Handrin would travel to the Summoned Lands to fight the Doomcallers in an alliance with Emperor Niktonas.

The army was greeted cautiously at first, but wherever the Orb of Creation was displayed, the caution turned to joyous celebration. Nidon made certain his army was on its best behavior, enforcing discipline with an iron fist. It wasn't the Landomeri he worried about or even the highly disciplined Knights of the House. His concern was with his South Teren soldiers, who might take advantage of the openness of the Belenese. They'd certainly taken note of Belenese attire, or lack thereof — a problem he'd already had to deal with on several occasions.

They entered Prodopoli with no opposition. Psertis had taken all of his regular forces with him, and without him, there was little enthusiasm for more war. The citizen militia, all of whom had military training and arms, formed up outside the city's boundaries, but it was a welcome parade rather than an effort at defense. The more he saw, the more Nidon realized Psertis's lack of popular support.

They stayed in the city for three days, resting, resupplying, and gaining reinforcements, both Belenese and Saladoran. Two satruses joined them with their own contingents. One, Kalos Koros Kamani, knew Ayja, having escorted her to the Temple of Forsvar. The other, a strong, gray-haired woman named Viatis Zarta Vartos brought nearly fifteen hundred timari and freemen with her. Together, the three satruses decided that Exonos should take up the role of acting kyvern until Emperor Niktonas could name a replacement.

Nidon, Handrin, and the three satruses all met in the grand kyvern's villa in Prodopoli, eating a feast as delicious as any Nidon had ever eaten before. "It is a shame I've missed this all my life," Nidon said. "You Belenese know how to eat."

"And how to bathe," Handrin said. "When I return to Salador, we shall be doing some construction. We'll build baths everywhere."

Exonos smiled. "You sound very much like Princess Ayja, King Handrin. I think she enjoyed the very same elements of our culture. I sincerely hope that she will be returned to us."

"As do I," Handrin said.

Nidon looked down at his plate, suddenly less hungry than he had been. Ayja was in Dromost. *Was she even alive? Could she have survived?* When he thought of it, only the most horrible images came to mind. And she was there with the Blade of Darra. He knew what Orlos

172

had said, that Sir Darra had been a faithful, loyal servant to her. In his mind, he only saw the pale-skinned ghul-creating monster.

"I've read many of Psertis's papers," Exonos said. "I've also spoken with his simvolos, Rastari. He, by the way, claims to have had no knowledge of Psertis's plans to steal Forsvar from Princess Ayja. He says that it was all a plot by Psertis and his son, Prodidos."

"A claim that is ridiculous on its face," Satrus Kalos said. "A simvolos knows everything that is going on in a kyvern's household. It's their primary responsibility."

"We should have him in chains as well," Viatis said, Exonos translating for her. "To have assisted in an attempt on the *nafai amas* is a terrible crime. Unforgivable."

"He has been a help to us, though," Exonos said. "He's been quite happy to reveal Psertis's every last secret. I'll have eyes kept on him. It is clear that Psertis was successful in convincing Emperor Niktonas that Ayja was intent on his throne. What is surprising to me is how easily the emperor was convinced."

"Psertis did have the support of the High Priest of Forsvar," Kalos said. "He's a powerful voice in court. Sadly, he's expanded the lie, spreading word that the Etheans have joined the Saladorans in the attempt to overthrow the emperor."

"How do we counter this?" Handrin asked. "How do we convince them of our good intentions?"

"I've sent messengers," Exonos said. "Now, we wait for an imperial representative."

"How long will it take?" Nidon asked.

"The Belenese Empire is very large. We are weeks away from Aftokropoli."

"Is there any reason to delay our journey?" Nidon asked. "Every day we wait is another day when the Dromost Gate could be opened."

Handrin nodded. "I'm in agreement. I wish for this task to be completed as quickly as possible."

"My only reason for caution is that to advance continues the story that this is an invasion," Exonos said. "If we remain here and await the imperial messengers, it will ease the emperor's fears."

"Everywhere he's gone, King Handrin has shown goodwill to the people of Belen," Nidon said. "They are clearly pleased with the arrival of the Orb of Creation and the idea that we will defeat the summoners. I say we push on."

Exonos looked to the other satruses, who nodded their agreement. "We should continue on," Kalos said. "The people are with us. The emperor will see how he's been misled."

"I agree," Viatis said.

Two days later, they departed Prodopoli with cheering crowds lining the streets. The army had doubled in size, mostly due to the addition of the two satrus' forces, but also to Saladoran soldiers continuing to stream over the pass. Exonos also made good on his effort to get mounts and nearly half of the knights now rode Belenese warhorses. They'd also gained an extensive baggage train and a contingent of camp followers.

For three days, their advance had the festive atmosphere of a parade rather than that of a military maneuver. At every village and town, people gathered to see the King of Salador, his proud knights, and the Orb of Creation. They cheered for him and for the end of the summoner threat. It was clear the majority of the population had come to believe that this was yet another omen that Forsvar would soon return and that the summoner threat would be ended forever.

On the fourth day out of Prodopoli, everything changed.

"There's an imperial army on the road ahead of us," Exonos said. "We are ordered to lay down our arms and surrender."

Nidon grimaced at the news. Everything following the defeat of Psertis had gone so well. *Too well, apparently.* Handrin, Nidon, and the three satruses gathered in Handrin's spacious tent. The sides were open, letting the cool night air blow through. A welcome relief from the heat that had set in ever since they'd left the mountains.

"Why would they make these demands?" Nidon asked. "Haven't they received your messages?"

"Apparently Kyvern Psertis was very convincing," Exonos said without humor.

"Your emperor impresses me less and less with each day," Nidon said. "You keep speaking of his intelligence and character, but all I see is a man being led by a nose ring."

"These are not the actions of the man I know," Exonos said. "Perhaps sitting on the throne has changed him. This is not how the general I knew would have behaved."

"The weight of a crown is heavy," Handrin agreed. "It can change a person. In this case, for the worse. The emperor's actions put us all in danger."

"How large is this force?" Nidon asked.

"We don't know for certain," Exonos said. "Certainly more than fifteen thousand."

"That's nearly three times the size of our army," Nidon said.

"The size doesn't matter," Viatis said. "We cannot fight them. These are imperial forces acting under the emperor's direct orders. It isn't some rogue kyvern. Our soldiers will not fight them. I will not fight them. We have to find another way."

"We won't lay down our arms," Handrin said. "I can't put myself and the Orb of Creation at the mercy of Emperor Niktonas. If diplomacy doesn't work, I must return to Salador."

"What of the Dromost Gate, Your Majesty?" Nidon asked.

Handrin ignored Nidon and looked to Exonos. "This is disheartening. You sent an embassy to my country seeking aid, and when we give it, you turn against us. You try to steal Forsvar, and now, I can only assume you are attempting to steal the Orb of Creation."

Exonos stood tall. "I've treated you in good faith at every turn," he said, "and I will pay a price for it. If the emperor's mind cannot be changed, I will be branded a traitor and lose everything."

Handrin pushed his hand through his hair. "I've endangered my own country, and spent its fortune on this endeavor."

"How far away is the imperial army?" Nidon asked.

"Four days," Exonos replied.

"Let's make one more effort at diplomacy, Your Majesty," Nidon said. "If they do not immediately send a representative to speak with you and to see the Orb of Creation, I suggest that you return with the mounted Knights of the House to the East Pass. I will remain with the rest of the army and attempt to extricate them as best I can."

"And so we just hope that no one opens the Dromost gate?" Satrus Kalos asked. "There has to be a way."

"Orlos told us that Ayja went to the Temple of Dromost by sea," Nidon said. "Couldn't we do the same? It would be daring, but perhaps it would work."

"Summoner allies held the Dromost Gate when she went by sea," Exonos said. "The Doomcallers hold it now. You wouldn't get near the temple."

"We have King Handrin and the Orb of Creation. Four other elementars as well."

"The risk is too great, Champion Nidon," Handrin said. "We can't take such a gamble." He turned to Exonos. "Let's halt here. The emperor's representative has two days to come and meet with me in person. If not, I return to Salador."

"I will send a message immediately."

"I don't like this, Nidon," Handrin said after the Belenese had departed.

"Perhaps you should leave sooner rather than later, Your Majesty," Nidon said.

"You think I should leave tonight?"

175

"For your own safety and for the protection of the Orb of Creation, yes."

"I like these Belenese," Handrin said. "Exonos is a good man. I hate to abandon him to his fate. I will depart tomorrow if there is no change. It will be your task to get the army to the pass, Champion."

"We will win our way free."

The next day dawned clear and warm, as it seemed nearly every day did in Belen. The Belenese said that it was the rainy season, but besides the storm at the East Pass, they'd seen little of it over the past two weeks.

The army halted for the day. The soldiers were surprised at the halt, having just departed Prodopoli; however there were few complaints. What soldier needed to be convinced to take a day of rest?

It was early in the afternoon, just after Nidon and Handrin had finished their mid-day meal, when Exonos rushed up to their tent with a man and a woman in tow. Both wore red kaftans over scale brigandines. White piping embellished their kaftans. Silver ornaments heavily supplemented the woman's. In fact, all of their garments were red, from their leather boots to the turbans wrapped around their conical helmets. Sweat and dust covered both of them.

All three were about to enter the king's tent when Handrin's six bodyguard Knights of the House stepped in front of them, swords drawn, demanding that they remove the swords and horn bows hanging from their waists.

"You must hear this message, King Handrin," Exonos said from the other side of the guards. "It is urgent. They come from the Imperial Army."

Nidon and Handrin stood from their camp table, the king drawing the Orb of Creation from the belt pouch where he kept it in those rare instances it wasn't in his hand. "Let them in," Handrin commanded.

The Knights of the House stepped aside, allowing the three Belenese to enter, but the knights followed them and stood close behind. The two exhausted visitors nodded in greeting, but then their eyes fell on the Orb of Creation, and they gasped. To Nidon, the woman had the looks of a Kiremi, with her black hair and high cheekbones. The man appeared Belenese, if shorter and leaner than most.

Exonos spoke to them in Belenese, and then the man said, "King Handrin, I am file-leader Mikos of the First Regiment of Imperial Light Horse. This is Captain Asimi."

The woman nodded again, saying something briefly to them in Belenese. Nidon thought he caught the word *greeting,* but wasn't certain, having only learned a few words of the language.

"King Handrin," the man continued, "my captain doesn't speak the Language of Song, and asks that I translate for her." He took a scroll from her and held it out to Handrin, but Nidon took it instead. Before he could open it, Mikos said, "We are under attack and ask that you come to our aid."

"You are under attack?" Handrin asked. "By whom? I was under the impression that you'd come to demand our surrender."

"It is an army of the dead," Mikos said. "They've come at us from behind, cutting our supply lines to Aftokropoli."

"What do you mean by 'an army of the dead'?" Nidon asked. "Demons?"

"We are certain that it is some act of the summoners, but they aren't demons. They are the dead. They are Belenese citizens and Etheans made moving corpses by some foul summoner magic. We fill them with arrows, but they keep coming. They feel no pain and fight with tireless strength."

"You fought a battle with them?" Handrin asked.

Mikos spoke with his captain and then said, "Two days ago. We heard reports that some enemy had cut our supply line. A rear-guard was detached to find out what had happened. Only the cavalry made it free. Every man on foot was killed and then... and then rose again to join the enemy."

"You were there? You saw this?" Nidon asked. In his mind he saw ghuls. Had the Blade of Darra or some other lych or pyren come to Belen? Even then, it didn't make sense. Ghuls could be killed. It took some doing, but they would die.

"Captain Asimi and I were there," Mikos said. "It was a terrible massacre."

"Did any of these undead fall? Could they be killed?"

"Only a few. Some think that maybe they must be struck in the head. That only then will they die. I'm not sure."

"Did they consume the dead they killed?" Nidon asked, leaning forward.

Mikos grimaced and shook his head. "No. Not at all. But those who were killed rose to fight again. For the enemy."

Nidon looked to Handrin. "It doesn't sound like ghuls, Your Majesty."

"What does your general want us to do?" Handrin asked.

"The Imperial Army will turn and fight. We hope that you will join us. You are an elementar and bear the Orb of Creation. We know there are more elementars in your army. We hoped that you might be able to destroy the undead."

"What of your mission to arrest us?"

Once again, Mikos spoke with his captain. "If you come to our aid, General Solis says that he will know that the rumors he's heard are true. That you have indeed come to battle the summoners and to close the Dromost Gate."

"And what will Emperor Niktonas say?"

"The undead march from the direction of Aftokropoli. Some wear the uniforms of soldiers there." Mikos swallowed. "We don't know if the emperor still lives. We must defeat this army of the dead and march on the capital."

"We are not an army of invasion," Handrin said, "despite what you've been told."

Mikos frowned. "Before this — before meeting you — I only knew what I was told." He glanced at Asimi and then back to Handrin. "Seeing with my eyes, you seem good men. Will you aid us?"

"We will," Handrin said.

"Thank you, King Handrin," Mikos said. He spoke to his captain in Belenese. She smiled and spoke to Handrin. Mikos translated, saying, "Captain Asimi thanks you. She asks when you might march. Our army will take a defensible position one day's march from here."

"Our army is ready to march," Handrin said, glancing at Exonos, who nodded his agreement. "We will leave before dawn."

Indeed, it was still dark when the combined Belenese-Saladoran army departed. Nidon, Handrin, and Orlos rode with the vanguard — the Knights of the House and a picked force of Exonos's timari. The Landomeri were held in reserve, Captain Asimi having warned them of the ineffectiveness of arrows at killing the undead.

It was afternoon when they arrived in the rear of the Imperial Army. There were baggage carts there but also wounded. The road they followed led through a break in a ridgeline ahead of them. Dust rose from beyond the ridge, and in the distance, Nidon heard the sounds of drums and horns and the clamor of battle.

Mikos rode up to them at the head of nine other light horse. "The battle has already begun. It is a desperate fight."

"Are we too late?" Nidon asked. He saw Belenese soldiers retreating over the ridge. To him, it appeared the beginning of a rout.

"The general asks that you take the center. He hopes that the power of the Orb of Creation and your elementars will break the enemy."

"How do you break a dead enemy?" Handrin asked. When no one replied, he said, "Where is your general?"

"In the center. On the road."

"Exonos, would you cover our flanks?" Handrin asked. Then he called out, his voice amplified by his magic, "The Knights of the House will form front by lances!"

"This is an audacious move, Your Majesty," Nidon said as the knights deployed to their left and right.

"Didn't you once famously say, *'Audacity! Always audacity!'*"

"I also once said, *'A bold man and his head are soon parted.'*"

"Your quotes don't seem to be very consistent, Champion Nidon."

"They are situational."

Handrin shook his head. "If we don't stand with the Belenese now, when will we? If we cannot defeat this enemy, how will we ever hope to get to the gate?"

Handrin raised the Orb of Creation overhead, and it began to blaze brilliant silver-gold light. "Advance!"

Nidon loosened his falchion in its scabbard. Just ahead of them, brightly clad timari on horseback fought an unseen enemy to their front. On the ridge to either flank, Belenese soldiers fought on foot, and for the first time, Nidon caught sight of their foe — men, women, children, soldiers, and shopkeepers. The undead were a cross-section of Belenese society. Those who were unarmed threw themselves at the imperial soldiers, grappling them and dragging them to the ground. Those who were armed fought with fearless, brutal strength. And they were winning.

Nidon saw undead run through with spears, or who had limbs hacked off, but still fought on. When they killed a Belenese soldier, the soldier soon rose to join their side. The losses were affecting the men and women of the Imperial Army. They saw their unstoppable foe and their fate in death, and they began to fold.

Some of the Belenese, though, caught sight of Handrin and the Orb of Creation, and a cheer went up. "It is now or never, Your Majesty," Nidon said. "The Belenese will soon collapse."

"Their heads," Nidon shouted. "Swords to the head!" The Knights of the House handed their lances to their squires, who tossed them on the ground behind them so that they wouldn't be in the way. The borrowed light lances, made of a tall, heavy reed, had been a welcome addition to the fine coursers they rode. But the lances would do little good against the undead, who did not care if their bodies were impaled.

The timari to their front expertly broke off from the undead host and divided, flowed past the Knights of the House. Handrin raised the Orb of Creation high over his head, where it blazed with a brilliant golden light. "Now, Nidon."

Nidon stood in his stirrups and, raising his sword, said, "Knights of the House... charge!" The knights put their spurs to their horses and surged forward. The sight of the charging knights had no effect on the undead, who rushed directly at the horsemen.

Nidon raised his sword high, poised to strike down at the enemy. Directly in front of him, he spotted an undead timari and was just ten strides from the man when he collapsed to the ground. Then, like a wave, all of the undead began to fall. First by the dozens, then by the hundreds, and finally by the thousands.

Nidon reined in his horse. All around him mounts balked at walking on the figures piled on the ground under their hooves. Nidon wondered if it was some trick, but the undead lay perfectly still.

"What happened to them?" Handrin asked. All around them, Saladorans and Belenese were asking the same question, milling in circles as they reined in their horses. For the first time, they had a good view of just how large the undead host was. It numbered in the thousands, but all lay on the ground as if truly dead. Nidon looked across the field of undead and saw five figures still standing. Four of them held swords over their heads, hilts held skyward. One stood hunched, her arms across her body.

"It's the Belenese sign for parlay," Handrin said.

"But who are they?" Nidon asked. He turned to Squire Fress. "Ask Exonos and the imperial general to join us."

As the squire rode off, Nidon looked at the undead again. In his mind, he'd imagined an army of ghuls, but these were just normal people. The sight of them was truly horrible. Just people. Regular people. All had some wound or another, some old and covered in dry blood, some fresh and terrible. Just heartbeats ago they'd all been actively fighting and now... now they were just dead.

What horror did this to them? He looked up again. An arrowflight down the road, the five figures still stood, waiting. Were they summoners? Living prisoners of the undead army? No, they were armed and armored — commanders of the undead.

Exonos and another man rode up with an escort of timari. "King Handrin, Champion Nidon, this is General Solis."

Solis was older than Nidon, with gray in his beard and lines at the corners of his eyes. His magnificent breastplate, entirely gilt in gold, was formed in the shape of a human torso, and his helm sported a high red crest of horsehair. He saluted Handrin and Nidon with a sweep of his sword.

"Thank you for coming to our aid," Solis said in clear, crisp Saladoran. "It seems you had a greater effect on the enemy than I ever expected. Was it some power of the Orb of Creation that caused the living dead to fall?"

"I wish I could say it was," Handrin replied, "but unless it was the very light of the Orb that caused them to fall, I have no answer."

"And some of them wish to parlay?"

"We can't go out there," Handrin said. "We must assume some trick. How do we know that the dead will not rise again?"

"Call them closer, Your Majesty," Nidon said. "We don't dare approach."

Handrin nodded, then using his magic, projected his voice, saying, "Come closer if you wish to parlay."

One of the men waved back and then the other, the largest in the group, leaned over to help the woman who was bent double. She looked up and waved her hand, and a swath of the dead lying on the ground suddenly began to crawl, leaving a clear path between the two groups.

"By the gods, they're just playing dead," Handrin said. "All of them."

Nidon shifted his grip on his sword as a cold chill passed down his spine. What would happen if the army of the dead suddenly rose up? Would he be able to protect the king? Would they be able to cut their way free?

"Prepare yourselves, Knights of Salador," Nidon called out. "They all might rise again." All around him, knights raised their shields and readied their weapons.

Three of the five enemies were women, Nidon saw as they approached. Twenty strides closer, Nidon drew a sharp breath and said, "I know them."

"How?" Exonos asked from just behind him.

"That is Telea," Nidon said. "You know her, don't you? And the tall man-at-arms is Master Tharryl. I see Sindi and Calen as well. Only the last woman is a stranger to me."

"Teleana Telas Tarsian?" Solis asked. "The healer who was part of the embassy?"

"It's her," Exonos said. "I recognize them now."

"What are they doing amid a host of the dead?"

When they were thirty strides away, Telea's knees buckled, and Tharryl let her down.

Nidon sheathed his falchion and worked the straps to his helm free and drew it from his head. "Telea? It's me, Nidon." She didn't look well. She was on her knees with her arms across her body. Sindi knelt next to her.

Telea raised her head. Nidon saw white streaks in her long braids. She seemed to have aged thirty years since he'd last seen her. "Is King Handrin safe?" Telea asked, her voice weak. "Is that truly the Orb of Creation?"

"He is safe," Nidon said, motioning to the king. "The Orb is safe. What happened to you?"

"Is he truly safe?" There was fierceness in Telea's question. And in her eyes as well. "They sent an army to capture him. I had to stop them."

"They did send an army," Nidon said, glancing at Solis. "But they stopped and asked for our aid when the army of the dead attacked. What do you know of this?" he asked, motioning to the fields of the dead.

"Who is this?" Telea demanded, pointing a crooked finger at the general.

"I am General Solis of the Imperial Army. Who are you?"

"King Handrin, you must tell me," Telea said, desperation in her voice. "Are you safe from this man? The demon emperor sent him to take the Orb of Creation."

"Demon emperor? There is no demon emperor!"

"Are you safe?" Telea shouted.

Nidon turned to the general. "Do we have anything to fear from you, General Solis?"

The general drew himself up and said, "My only concern is returning to Aftokropoli and Emperor Niktonas. By his actions, King Handrin has shown me that he is not an enemy and that the Belenese Empire should not fear him."

"Is that good enough, King Handrin?" Telea asked. "Can we end this?" Her face was a mask of pain.

"I take the general on his word," Handrin said.

"Good," she said. Then Telea lifted her hand, and the undead rose to their feet.

Chapter Eighteen

Orlos froze as the dead rose. Hidden by his spiridus cloak, he'd followed close behind King Handrin and Nidon as the Saladorans had advanced. Now he cursed his curiosity and wished he hadn't. For a moment, as the dead shambled to their feet, he lost hold of his spiridus cloak and shimmered into visibility. Desperate, he pulled it back around himself, willing himself to be unseen.

The dead raised their weapons as shouts of alarm went up amongst the allied host. Then an undead timari turned to a Belenese man, a baker or a cook by his clothing, and split his skull with a swing of his sword. Orlos shrank back, crouching almost to the ground as the undead began to massacre one another. They made no effort at defense. Those without weapons stood as others cut them down. In every case, the attackers swung for the head.

Orlos closed his eyes and turned away. Everywhere around him, he heard thunks and cracks as swords and axes slammed into heads. Skulls split and brains splattered as the undead ruthlessly destroyed one another. Orlos shrank deeper and deeper into his cloak, willing with all his might to remain invisible.

It seemed to go on and on, but really only took a short time for thousands to fall. In the distance, he heard a few more gut-twisting thuds, but no sound nearby. No cries of pain or distress. The undead had simply and quietly annihilated each other in a matter of a hundred heartbeats.

Orlos stood, looking for Nidon and Handrin. He saw them with the Belenese general and the five people who'd accompanied the undead. Shaking off the horror of what he'd just seen, Orlos approached the group, quickly realizing who they were. When he did, he rushed to join them. As he did, Telea slumped in Tharryl's grasp. He gently lowered her to the ground as the others gathering around her.

"What was that?" Solis demanded. "What did I just see?"

183

"The dead were taking a toll on her," Sindi said as she and Tharryl knelt by Telea. "They were killing her. She had to destroy them. She's fallen unconscious. She needs help."

"She caused them to attack each other?" Handrin asked. He stared down at the healer. "How?"

Sindi took some water and a cloth and wiped Telea's face, but she didn't stir. "She had control of them."

"She killed all of these people and turned them into walking dead?" Solis asked.

"Yes," Tharryl said. "She had to. A demon had possessed the emperor, and we needed an army to defeat him."

"What do you mean?" Solis asked.

Tharryl barked a laugh. "Your emperor was a demon, and he had more with him. You'll know the truth when you see his huge, bloated corpse."

"Emperor Niktonas is dead?"

"Very much so," Tharryl said. "And good riddance."

"Master Tharryl," Nidon said, "how did—"

"Sir Tharryl," Tharryl corrected. "Princess Ayja knighted me."

Nidon nodded. "Of course. Orlos told us. Sir Tharryl, how did Telea do this?"

"It was her magic," Calen said. "She learned how to make the dead rise and serve her."

"Can't we get her to a place of rest?" Sindi interrupted. "She needs to heal."

"She needs to heal?" Solis said. "Look at what she's done! Look at how many she's killed. Heal her? She should be executed!"

"Are you the commander of the Belenese army?" Tharryl demanded. "Maybe it's your head that should be on the block! Every Ethean dead you see out here was killed on your orders. Their blood is on your hands."

"The Etheans were making war on us," Solis said. "They were in rebellion. They had to die."

"What utter bullshit," Tharryl said. He stood and rested his hand on his sword hilt, as Sindi took Telea's weight in her arms. "It was a fucking massacre, and you know it."

"Sir Tharryl!" Nidon said. "If you want to be treated as a knight, you must carry yourself as a knight."

Tharryl pointed a finger at the general. "Your Majesty," he said, looking to King Handrin, "on the command of a demon, they butchered every Ethean in Aftokropoli. On the command of a demon they came to

184

attack you and steal the Orb of Creation. Telea raised an army of the dead to stop them. She isn't the villain. He is."

"How dare you!" Solis said, his face growing red. "I acted under lawful orders. The Emperor speaks with the authority of Forsvar. You are defending a summoner who raised an army of undead and who killed thousands of innocent civilians and faithful Belenese soldiers."

Isibindi looked up from where she knelt by Telea. "Many more would have died if not for Telea. A demon was ruling the Empire! You were obeying a demon."

"I should believe you? You are her conspirators!"

"Enough," King Handrin said. The Orb of Creation flashed in his hands as he spoke. Instantly, all eyes were on him. "Is what you say true? The Emperor of Belen was a demon, you saw him with your own eyes, and you fought him. Telea raised this army of the dead to fight the emperor and then brought it here to save the Orb of Creation."

Orlos watched as Tharryl slowly drew his sword, took a knee, and offered his sword hilt first to Handrin. "Your Majesty, on my word as a Knight of Salador, every word of what we've spoken is true. I swear to it."

"So we all say," Sindi said. "We were there. We saw it."

Calen and Isibindi nodded their assent.

"General Solis, these were Princess Ayja's faithful companions. They traveled with her to the Dromost Gate and closed it. I believe them."

"We don't even know that the gate was closed," Solis said.

"It was closed!" Orlos shouted as he dropped his spiridus cloak. "Ayja went through to Dromost and it was closed!" Those near him flinched at his sudden appearance.

"Calm yourself, Orlos," Handrin said. He turned to Solis. "If Telea had ill intent, she would not have caused her army to massacre itself. Let's assume all we have heard is true. What is our next move? Who rules in Belen when an Emperor dies?"

"Princess Kelifos, the emperor's sister, in next in line for the throne. Word must be sent to her. She is at the College of Healers."

"We should establish a camp, General," Exonos said. "And march for Aftokropoli tomorrow."

Solis nodded. Then he nodded to Telea, who still lay unconscious in the arms of her companions. "She is dangerous. She must be placed under guard."

"I will take her under my authority," Handrin said. "I wish to speak to her when she awakens."

To Orlos it appeared Solis was about to object, but then the general glanced at the gleaming Orb of Creation and deflated. What argument

185

could he make? Who better to watch her than the elementar king and bearer of the Orb?

"I must see to my army," Solis said. He saluted King Handrin, and taking Exonos with him, departed.

Orlos rushed up to his friends. "You made it!" Calen said, embracing him. "Well done."

"How is Telea?" Orlos asked, pulling free of Calen and kneeling by her.

"She's unconscious," Sindi said. "She won't wake."

Orlos looked up at the king and Nidon. "Do the Belenese have healers with them?"

Nidon shook his head. "We don't know. We just met them."

"The army will make camp," Handrin said. "I'll send my surgeon to see Telea. The Belense have many wounded. I'll send a request to them for a healer but doubt they'll send one soon."

For the most part, the soldiers of both armies were stunned at what they'd just witnessed. Slowly, with some units set to watching the undead for fear they'd animate again, the rest of the army dispersed and began to set up camp.

Handrin's rapid march had left their baggage train behind. General Solis had lost most of his supplies to the undead. He provided a single pavilion tent for King Handrin's use. The king eschewed its use and had Telea placed within it under a heavy guard of Knights of the House.

As it turned out, the Belenese army had no healers with it — no singers at least. All had been sent east by the emperor. Handrin's surgeons looked in on Telea but announced they found no physical injuries. Telea slept on a sleeping mat set on a carpet. She had blankets covering her, but she shivered as if in the throes of a terrible fever. Sometimes her eyes opened, but it seemed she didn't see anything at all.

"What happened to her?" Orlos asked, leaning close to Sindi and whispering so that Telea wouldn't hear. He and Sindi stood at the far side of the tent while Isibindi sat with Telea, holding her hand.

"You remember the silent brothers from the Temple of Dromost?" Sindi said. "She made an army of them."

"She did all that?" Orlos nodded outside the tent.

"She learned how to do it from the summoner apprentice. And she learned how to make the undead create more undead. She lost control of it, though. It started to spread through the city. Orlos, I've never seen anything more horrible. I'll never forget the screams as people ran from the undead. So many people killed. The undead didn't care. Children, elderly, the infirm. They were relentless." Sindi turned away from him and looked out the open tent flap and towards the sunlight outside.

186

"How did she stop it?"

"After we killed the emperor, Telea ran outside and called the undead to her. Some were beyond her touch and we had to run from block to block so that her thoughts could reach them."

"Her thoughts?"

"Yes. They were in her mind. I can't tell you that I fully understand. I think it was driving her mad, though." Sindi paused and took a breath. "We were very lucky, Orlos. If we'd spent more time in the palace... well, I don't know where it would have ended. They might have spread across the world for all I know."

Orlos looked back to Telea, shivering on the floor. "I don't think I've ever seen anything more horrible than what I saw today. I can't believe Telea was at the heart of it. Why didn't you just tell someone that a demon possessed the emperor? None of this would have had to happen."

"If it was that easy, don't you think we would have done it?" Sindi said, glaring at him. "We aren't a bunch of fools!"

"I'm sorry. Of course," he said, shrinking back from her anger. He paused a moment and said, "I need to speak with Telea. I think I've found a way to save Ayja."

"How could she even be alive? She's in Dromost!"

"She's a powerful elementar wielding two Gifts of the Gods. She had the Blade of Darra with her. If she's still alive, I need to get a message to her. I'm hoping Telea will know how. There's a way out."

"You could try," Sindi said, shaking her head. "Speak to her."

Orlos walked the few strides across the tent and knelt at Telea's side. Her eyes were closed and she rocked back and forth. Her face still looked younger in sleep, although creased by tension and fatigue. Her hair, however, was that of a woman decades older. Some of her braids had gone entirely to white, while others were mixed salt and pepper.

"Telea, can you hear me?" Orlos asked. "I need to speak with you." There was no reaction. "Telea?"

"I speak with her, but she does not hear," Isibindi said. "I worry for her."

"Telea, it's about Ayja," he said, leaning close to her. "She's alive. I must get a message to her."

Telea paused and then wrapped her arms around her head until he could barely see her face. "Dead," she muttered.

"She's not dead," he said, putting his hand on her shoulder. "She must find the Emerald Prison. You remember? The stump of the Emerald Tree in Belavil. She can come out through it."

Telea was silent for a time. Then she turned her body away from him, pulling her shoulder from his grasp. "Dead," she whispered.

"Please, Telea. Can you get a message to her?"

Telea lay there, unmoving now, her back to him.

Sindi approached and pulled him back. "Give her time, Orlos."

"But—"

"Give her time."

Orlos retreated, but all through the afternoon and evening, he hovered near the tent. Nearby, on the battlefield, soldiers began the grisly task of organizing the dead. There were thousands of them. Too many to bury and too many for a pyre. Orlos saw them being carried over a low ridge but didn't investigate. All he wanted was to speak with Telea.

Finally, well after dark, Isibindi exited the tent and came to him. "She will see you now. She is weak, but she's eaten and had some water."

Even before she was done speaking, Orlos headed for the tent. The Knights of the House let him pass without question. Telea sat on the carpet, a blanket drawn around her shoulders despite the heat.

"How are you, Telea?" Orlos asked.

She waved him closer, and he sat down on the carpet across from her. Her face was drawn and her cheeks sunken. She had dark bags under her eyes. "I've never been worse," she said.

"Is there anything I can do?"

She shook her head.

"Do you remember how you once told me that singers might be able to open the Emerald Prison and free the spiridus? Well, we might be able to free Ayja at the same time."

Telea met his gaze. "Orlos, it's impossible that she's still alive."

"We can try at least, can't we? I just want to know if it is even possible."

"The singers have all been sent east to Drommaria. It will take many months before a chorus could go to Landomere. And even then, I don't know if they can open the gate."

"But you said—"

"I know what I said. And when I said it I was in desperate need of your help."

"You lied?"

Telea looked away from him. "I don't know if the gate can be opened with song. There is so much we don't know."

"Maybe Ayja can find a way. We have to tell her, at least."

She closed her eyes and took a deep breath, finally saying, "If she's alive, I can get a message to her."

"That's great!" He wanted to jump up and shout but held himself still.

"Do you have something of Ayja's? Something she owned?"

"Yes! I have a marble cup she made with her magic at the Temple of Forsvar." He prized the cup as one of his only mementos of her. He remembered her pride at how well she'd crafted it.

"That will do," Telea said. She rubbed her bleary, red eyes. "Bring it to me. And a quill and a sharp knife. We must also find somewhere with a stone table or a flat piece of marble. It doesn't have to be big. Maybe a half a stride across."

"A stone tablet?"

"It can be thin. It just has to be very smooth. I have to be able to write on it."

"Is that it?" Orlos asked as he stood.

"That's all. We can do it tonight."

"Thank you!" Orlos ran out and went in search of King Handrin. One of his aides would have what he needed. It took some time, but Orlos caught up to the king and his staff in the Belenese army's camp. The King and Champion Nidon were in a meeting in General Solis's tent, and no matter how much he demanded it, the guards denied him entry.

Orlos spotted Nidon's squire, Fress, standing nearby. He ran to him and said, "Fress, does Champion Nidon, or even King Handrin have a slate they write upon? Maybe half a stride across? I need a quill as well."

"Quills certainly, but no slate. What's it for?"

"I need it for some spiridus magic."

Fress's eyes opened wide. "Spiridus magic? Like when you turn invisible?"

"Yes! Just like that! Can I have a quill? And where can I find a slate?"

"There is a ruin just over there," Fress said, pointing off into the darkness. "There are pieces of marble everywhere. Maybe you can find a flat piece. I'll get a quill for you." Unchallenged, he entered the tent and returned a short time later with a small leather case. Inside were quills, ink, and paper. He took an old, used quill out and gave it to Orlos. "I'll need it back."

"Of course. Thank you!"

"What kind of magic are you going to do? Can I watch?"

"Spiridus magic," Orlos said and, causing himself to disappear, headed out into the night.

He found the ruins easily enough. You could hardly go a hundred strides in Belen without coming upon a piece of carved marble or a shard of broken pottery from who knows how long ago. He found a few pieces, but they were small and cracked. Then he found a much larger piece. It rested at an angle, sunk into the ground, but Telea hadn't said that it mattered.

It was getting very late, and the army's fires were starting to dim. Orlos pulled his spiridus cloak close and returned to Telea's tent. Two guards still stood by the closed front flap. He went to the rear, pulled up a stake, and slipped under the sidewall. Why even have guards for a tent if you're going to stand at the front entrance? Appearances, he supposed. *It tells everyone you're under arrest.*

Telea stood waiting for him in the darkness as he appeared. She put a finger to her lips and motioned for silence. Stepping closer, she whispered in his ear, *"Did you bring everything? The cup, the quill, and the knife?"*

He nodded.

"They think I'm asleep. Let's go."

They went to the back of the tent, Orlos under his spiridus cloak and Telea shrouded by her cloak of shadows. He slipped out first, and she followed. Then, before taking her hand and leading her off, he re-staked the tent so that no casual observer might see anything wrong.

They easily made their way through the dark camp, although Telea moved slowly and twice had to stop and rest. Eventually, they came to the ruins that Orlos had discovered. A unit of timari camped nearby, but all appeared asleep.

Telea pulled Orlos close and whispered, *"Not here. Somewhere away from people. Where they can't see us."*

"You didn't say that before. I don't know where we can go."

"We'll search along the road to Aftokropoli. We'll find something."

Orlos followed as Telea led him down along the road and past the dead. The army had worked for hours clearing the bodies from the road, but all along either side hundreds remained.

He didn't want to look, so stared at his feet. He *felt* the presence of the dead all around him, and it was only the confidence inspired by his spiridus cloak that he could walk past them.

Telea suddenly stopped and fell to her knees, visible now. She held her face in her hands. "I did this, Orlos. I killed all these people."

"You didn't mean to," he said, dropping his spiridus cloak and kneeling beside her.

She turned and glared at him, angry through her tears. "Does it matter? It's my fault! Look at them!" Her hand swept out to encompass all of the dead. "Look at them! They were innocent."

"It's done, Telea. You can't change it." The words were hard to say. How could he look out across the fields of the dead and dismiss what she'd done? But he needed her. Without Telea's help, there was no hope he'd ever see Ayja again.

She didn't reply. After a moment, she wiped her face and stood and continued down the road with him. Eventually, they cleared the great mass of the dead, although they never left them truly behind. He still saw them along the road as they walked, scattered by ones and twos where they'd fallen. They also left the last of the army's sentries as well.

"How far?" he asked. She'd led him much further than he'd expected already.

"I don't remember the journey very well," she said. "It might be some ways."

"Do you have the strength to do this?" He saw the fatigue in the slump of her shoulders and the shortness of her stride. She was still exhausted.

"I have to," Telea said. "I need something to focus on besides the great evil I've done."

They walked another six arrowflights before Telea stopped him and pointed towards the dark outline of a nearby hill. They walked across the rocky moonlit ground until they came to a fallen structure. It was impossible to say what the building had once been. Orlos saw tumbled sections of a pillar and broken roof tiles amongst the marble blocks. Together they searched through the rubble until Telea called him over.

"Here. This stone will do," she said. The block stood at the top of a small stair. Perhaps it had once been a landing at a temple entrance. Telea ran her hand across it. "It's good," she said. "The imperfections won't affect my work. Let me have the cup and the quill."

Orlos gave them to her, and she placed them on the stone, kneeling over both. "Can I have your knife?"

He nodded, taking his eating knife from the side sheath next to his dagger. "What's all this about?" he asked.

She gave him a crooked smile as she took the knife and tested the blade with her thumb, nodding appreciatively at its sharpness. Then she took the blade and slashed open her left palm. Blood welled up, and she placed her hand over the marble cup as it began to flow.

"What are you doing?" Orlos asked, reeling backward at the sight.

"Sending a message to Ayja." She grimaced against the pain. "And revealing a truth to you."

"That's so much! You should stop." Blood poured from the wound — too much blood.

She shook her head and let it flow until the cup was nearly full. Then she began to chant, and the flow of blood stopped almost instantly. Taking a rag from her belt pouch, she wiped the blood from her hand and showed it to him. The cut was gone, although a pale scar stood out in the darkness.

191

"What truth?" Orlos asked, warily eying the cup of blood.

Telea wiped the blade of his knife clean and handed it back to him, hilt first. "I never got rid of my demon."

A chill ran down Orlos's spine. "But I can see demons. Yours is gone." He took the knife from her, glancing at it to see that it was blood-free before sheathing it, certain he'd never use it for eating again.

She shook her head. "It isn't gone. I hid it from you."

"Hid it? How?"

"I've learned a lot about magic over the past six months, Orlos. One thing I learned was how to imprison my demon — to lock it away where it couldn't be seen."

Orlos drew back from her. He'd never trusted her as long as she had the demon in her. How could he? And now to learn that she'd lied and had the demon in her all along. "I thought you wanted to be rid of it. I believed you."

She shook her head. "It was too useful." Carefully, she placed the cup in the center of the stone. Then, dipping her finger in her blood, she began to write runes in a circle around the cup. "It's a shame to be rid of it now. There's more to learn."

Orlos felt a growing fear in the pit of his stomach as he watched Telea continue her blood writing. "You're getting rid of it now?"

She nodded. "I'm going to free my demon, and it will carry our message to Ayja." She wrote a few more runes before speaking again. "You have an important job, Orlos. If you see the demon reenter me, you must kill me." She didn't look up.

Orlos stared at her. She said it so matter of fact, as if her life meant nothing to her. Did she want to die?

Telea finished the circle. Then, after wiping the blood from her finger, she took her cloth and carefully wiped the drops of spilled blood from the cup. Satisfied, she picked up the quill and began to draw much finer runes in blood on its rim.

Orlos glanced over his shoulder, suddenly fearful that someone might see what they were doing. He knew it was ridiculous. It was the middle of the night, and they were arrowflights from the nearest living person.

Telea worked in silence for a long time before putting the quill down outside the circle of runes. "Finished." She took a deep breath. "Are you ready?"

"No." He glanced around again, fear filling him. Not that they might be caught now. Fear of what was to come.

"What do you want the demon to say to Ayja?"

"How can you trust it to do what you ask?"

"It will be bound to this task. It must obey my commands if it wishes to return to Dromost. And, trust me, it does. It has had enough of being imprisoned within me."

"What if it attacks Ayja?" Orlos asked.

"It could only do that after finishing its task. Even then, Ayja is much more powerful than it. The demon's only wish is to be free of me and to return to Dromost."

"You can't be certain of that."

"It's this, or no message at all, Orlos. Now, what do you want the demon to say to her?"

"It must tell her to find the Emerald Tree — the spiridus prison. She must create a working that will open the prison and let her and the spiridus free."

"How will the opening be empowered?"

Orlos shook his head. "I don't know. Her magic?"

"It isn't that easy," Telea said with a frown. "Perhaps... perhaps the spiridus." She paused then, her eyes closed. "And once opened, it must be closed again. There must be a trigger. Now, be quiet for a moment. Let me speak with the demon." Telea sat cross-legged by the stone with her hands clasped in front of her and her eyes closed.

"Ayja's parents are Hadde and Morin, correct?" Telea asked after a few heartbeats, her eyes still closed.

"Yes. Why?"

"If the demon knows her full name, and the names of her parents, it will make it easier to find her. Who were her grandparents?"

"Arno and Enna on Hadde's side. King Boradin and... I don't know the queen's name on Morin's side. I'm sorry. I'm not Saladoran, and she died a long time ago."

"It's enough."

"And you know that Ayja's real name isn't Ayja?" Orlos asked. "It's Enna. Nidon named her Ayja because he didn't know her real name."

Telea's eyes opened. "That's true? You're certain?"

Orlos nodded. "I'm certain of it. She's named for her grandmother, Enna."

"It is good you told me." Telea closed her eyes again.

For a time, nothing happened. Orlos knelt and watched Telea as she sat silently in front of him. The skin began to crawl on the back of his neck. What if the demon attacked him? Could Telea drive it off?

"Take out your dagger, Orlos," Telea said as she opened her eyes.

"Why?"

"You will see the demon. It should be bound to this circle. But I told you this before... if you see it enter me, you must kill me."

193

"I don't think I can."

"The first thing the demon will do if it possesses me is kill you. The act of summoning I am doing will leave me vulnerable. If it gets free of this circle, I won't be able to stop it."

"What if it enters me?" Orlos asked.

"I will sing *The Song of Light* and destroy it, and with it our only hope of contacting Ayja. Now, draw your dagger."

Orlos did as she commanded, hating the weight of the weapon in his hand.

The moment Telea began to chant, the runes began to glow, and wisps of smoke rose from them. Still, she chanted, and as she did, tendrils of inky, fluid, black smoke issued from her mouth, puffing and eddying with each word.

The demon! It's the demon! Orlos saw the malevolent entity within the black cloud. The smoke twisted and turned of its own volition, drawn irresistibly into the ring of runes. After a few heartbeats, the smoke stopped issuing from Telea's mouth and swirled around the cup. Orlos clutched the dagger tighter and stood, trembling.

Telea's chant changed, and the runes on the cup itself began to glow. Heartbeats later, the blood sizzled and steamed. Her chanting grew louder.

There was a flash of light, and flames shot up from the marble cup. "Obey me," Telea commanded, her voice loud and strong. The smoke spun faster and faster around the cup of burning blood. "Tell me your true name. Take my message to Enna. Do these things and be free!"

Not my name.

Orlos jerked back at the voice suddenly in his head. The demon's voice!

"Tell me your true name," Telea said again. "Bear my message to her and leave her unharmed. Do it and be free!"

There was a long pause as the demon whirled around the burning blood. Orlos felt the demon's anger. But his spriridus told him there was something else there as well. There was hope.

I am Uldamarian. Now free me from this world.

"Bear my message and be free!" Telea shouted.

The fire from the cup shot strides high, setting the entire area aglow. Smoke poured from it as well, drifting into the night sky. Within the circle of runes, the demon's shadowy form wrapped itself around the flame and then disappeared into it. As it did, the fire vanished, and an even greater cloud of smoke billowed from the cup.

"Did it work?" Orlos asked, backing from the thick smoke. "Is it gone?"

"It's gone," Telea said, backing away from the smoke.

"How long will it take to get to Ayja?"

"I don't know. It could take some time for the demon to travel to her."

"Will you know when it gets there?"

Telea shook her head. "Orlos... we might never know. You can't get your hopes up. She's probably already dead."

Chapter Nineteen

Nidon rode at the head of the column as the army marched for Aftokropoli. For three weeks, they traveled through rolling hills and one low mountain range. They passed villages, towns, and a large city, all surrounded by cultivated fields and hills covered with olive trees and vineyards.

And at every inhabited place they passed, the people spoke of the Army of the Dead. The people had been terrified as the dead had swept past them, but no one had been harmed. Nidon knew it was Telea's doing. Once she'd taken control of the host in Aftokropoli, the killing had ended. At least until they'd caught up with the Imperial Army.

Still, Nidon had Telea kept under heavy guard. Six Knights of the House and six Belenese timari surrounded her as she rode. Her fate was yet to be decided.

When the citizens learned of the arrival of the King of Salador and the Orb of Creation they rushed out to greet him, viewing him as a salvation from both the summoners and the undead alike. The dire warning of a Saladoran invasion vanished in the brilliant light of the Orb of Creation.

A day from the capital, they were greeted on the road by an imperial messenger. Nidon and Handrin joined General Solis on the side of the road as the messenger delivered her news.

The messenger was a slight, young Koromoi woman in the green of the Imperial Messenger Service. She rode a small horse built for endurance. Nidon had seen many of them coming to and from the column as they marched. She spoke rapidly in Belenese to the general, handing him two wax-sealed scroll cases.

The two conversed back and forth for a time before she saluted and rode off. "Two pieces of news," General Solis said. "One very bad. A Doomcaller army has heavily defeated the Army of the East. The Imperial Chorus has been wiped out to a man."

"This sounds bad," Handrin said. "What does this mean for us?"

"After the Summoner War, the Army of the East was greatly reduced in number. Emperor Niktonas said that a large force was unnecessary as we were at peace and that the friendly summoners had the upper hand in Drommaria — the Summoned Lands. Then, some weeks later, he sent out a proclamation that every singer in the Belenese Empire should go east, to join the army. This included the Imperial Chorus."

"If I understand correctly," Nidon said, "your singers are your greatest weapon against the demons."

Solis nodded. "It was an unusual maneuver. I thought so even then, but Emperor Niktonas had fought brilliantly as commander of the Army of the East. Now, perhaps, we know the reason for it. If the emperor was, in fact, possessed by a demon, he would have wanted any singers to be as far away from him as possible." He tapped the scrolls against his open hand. "Initial reports are that every singer was killed. It is a defeat of unimaginable proportions."

"Are the summoners invading?" Handrin asked.

Solis shook his head. "The last report is that they retreated deeper into Drommaria."

"They've crippled our strength and then retreated on their defenses," Nidon said.

"They hope to open the Dromost Gate," Handrin said. "They killed the singers to prevent us from being able to interfere with them."

"Which brings me to my other news. The emperor's sister is approaching from the north. She recently exiled herself to the College of Healers due to the erratic behavior of her brother. She is returning."

"She will be the empress?" Handrin asked.

"She is heir to the throne." Solis paused a moment and said, "She's bringing singers with her, healers from the college. They are some of the few remaining singers in all of Belen. She has also heard of Telea, the Queen of the Dead. There will be a trial."

"You know that Telea is the only person who knows how to lock the Dromost Gate," Handrin said.

"I'm certain Her Imperial Highness will take that into consideration."

The army's reception in Aftokropoli was decidedly muted, and in some cases, openly hostile. While some were fascinated and awed by the arrival of the Saladorans and the Orb of Creation, others were angry at their own army's departure and failure to protect them from the undead.

More than anger or amazement, Nidon felt an overwhelming sense of fear coming from the people. Thousands of citizens had been massacred within the walls of their own capital, a city that had been a safe haven for over a century. And just as horrifying was the knowledge that their very own emperor, a man beloved as a hero, had been possessed.

Aftokropoli's population was two thirds what it had been before the Wasting. It meant the city had more than enough space to spare for the influx of Saladorans and Landomeri. The army was sent to occupy an old army barracks and some of the nearby abandoned homes in the Military District. Fifty Knights of the House would be quartered with Handrin in the Palace District.

It was two days before Princess Kelifos arrived in the capital. It was another three days before King Handrin was granted an audience. If the king didn't appreciate the delay, the army certainly appreciated the rest. They'd been traveling almost non-stop for more than a month. Twice while they waited, contingents of Saladorans arrived in the city. More would continue to arrive each day.

Belenese tailors were brought in to make court-appropriate clothing for Handrin and Nidon. They'd be joined by all of the survivors of Ayja's expedition, as well as Satrus Exonos. Twelve Knights of the House were selected as an honor guard.

A company of Imperial Timari escorted them as they rode from Handrin's lavish villa to the palace. Citizens lined the street to watch the passing of the King of Salador and the Orb of Creation. Even as they cheered the king, Nidon saw the dark glances and pointed fingers directed at Telea. More than once, he heard the words, *vasilia necra*, Queen of the Dead.

The palace itself was a stunning, sprawling spectacle. Huge pillars held triangular pediments decorated with amazing friezes and statues in high relief. The friezes, painted in brilliant colors, depicted the legends of Forsvar, from the creation of the world to his battles with Dromost. The amount of effort that had gone into every detail awed Nidon. It made the Great Keep of Sal-Oras look like a crude stone tower, fit only for the lowest knight.

Of course, that's what it's meant to do. To awe. It worked. Outside the entryway stood ranks of the Emperor's Axes. Telea had told Nidon of them. All recruited from the Drinker Tribes who lived on the borders of the Summoned Lands. They formed the elite infantry guard of the Belenese imperial family.

"Drinkers, because they drink the blood of their enemies," Telea had told him when he'd asked. "It is a ritual, performed with runes and chants of their own devising. The magic imbues them with strength and fearlessness. Demon-fear means nothing to a Drinker, which is why they were made imperial bodyguards."

"They served a demon emperor," Nidon had said.

"The magic doesn't let them see a possessed person's demon. Only a spiridus or another demon can do that. I have no doubt they feel tremendous regret and anger at their failure to protect the emperor."

General Solis greeted them at the palace entrance, and with an escort of Emperor's Axes, they entered. *Or will they be Empress's Axes, now? Will they change the name when the princess takes the throne?* They were certainly imposing figures in their long mail hauberks and bearing their great axes.

"I noticed there are no women among the Axes," Nidon said to Telea, who walked beside him. "I've seen women among the timari and freemen. Even among the infantry."

Telea frowned. "It goes back to old superstition — the same as what keeps women from the Imperial Chorus. Officers of the court, old men, fear the women's moon blood. They think that summoners might use it to their advantage."

"Ahh," Nidon said, immediately wishing he hadn't asked. There were things a gentleman didn't speak about with women.

Unfortunately, Telea wasn't finished. "It is quite foolish. The College of Healers has proven the fear of moon blood to be baseless. Sadly, it takes time to change minds. Perhaps, with an empress on the throne, things might be different."

"There's never been an empress before?"

"Not in over a century. I won't see it, I'm sure."

"Why not?"

"I'm the Queen of the Dead. They will execute me. My fate is sealed."

Nidon knew the story of what she'd done very well now. All of Ayja's companions had told it to the king and him. As a knight he was oathsworn to do no harm to innocents. But, as a soldier, he knew hard tasks sometimes had painful, unintended consequences. Telea had to pay a price for what she'd done, but she also still had a role to play. They still needed her.

They marched down a wide, marble-floored hall lined with statues and fresco-covered walls. Pillars held up graven arches painted in gold and silver. The crossed lightning bolts of Forsvar appeared everywhere.

Finally, they reached massive double doors, thrown wide to reveal the throne room of the Belenese Empire. The escorting Knights of the House took position on either side of the door but were not allowed entry into the hall. Only the Emperor's Axes bore arms in the throne room.

The Great Hall of Sal-Oras could fit three times into the Throne Room of Belen. Massive pillars held up an impossibly high roof. Sunlight flooded the room from an arched roof that held a fortune in glass. How many people could fit into the Throne Room? Five thousand? The entire army King Handrin had brought across the mountains? The might and wealth of the Empire of Belen must have been staggering at its height, before the Great Revolt and the worst of the Wasting struck.

The importance of the East Pass hit Nidon. For all the valor of the Knights of Salador, without the mountain range between them, Belen surely would have conquered Salador long ago. The wealth and size of the empire were too much to contest.

For all its size, the great majority of the Throne Room was empty. There were no crowds, and the vast space swallowed up their footsteps. Only near the throne did they see any people, and even then, it was not many.

"They are not certain how this will go," Nidon said to Handrin. "I see more soldiers than citizens."

"I don't think it is a celebration," Handrin said over his shoulder. "It is a serious affair of state."

The Silver Throne of Belen stood atop a high dais. It gleamed in a beam of sunlight shining down from a window high above. At a distance, the elaborate details were hard to make out, but it was clearly a masterwork of the silver craft.

One feature stood above all others. Over the throne two silver lightning bolts crossed one another, each three strides in length. Red velvet seat and back cushions sat atop the throne, both embroidered with Forsvar's bolts.

The throne itself was empty. Next to the throne stood a much smaller, but still ornate, throne of dark wood embellished with silver. A young woman in a close-fitting red dress sat atop it. She had the dark tan skin and black hair of the Belenese and wore a silver circlet atop her head. She had to be Ayja's age or a little older. Nidon, for some reason, had expected someone much older.

Although no one had said it, it was clear that this was Princess Kelifos. At some point, she'd take the Silver Throne. No one, so far, had said when that would occur.

At the base of the dais stood six Axes, gleaming in their silver-adorned armor. To Nidon's right, standing on the lowest steps were fifteen men and boys, the youngest maybe ten or twelve. They wore robes of brown, red, blue, and white. Occupying the same position, on Nidon's left, stood some twenty men and women in light brown robes. Most were young, in their late teens or early twenties, although a few had graying hair at their temples.

"Those to the right are singers," Telea said, whispering to Handrin and Nidon. "Survivors of the massacre in the east, I expect. The colors are for earth, fire, water, and air singers. Those to the left are healers from the College of Healers. They must have come with Princess Kelifos."

To the left and right of Handrin's party stood perhaps fifty men and women in every manner of dress. Some wore tunics of white with stripes of different colors at the hem, collar, or sleeve. None wore trousers, just the tunics that he'd learned were the traditional attire of Belen. Others wore more colorful clothing, seemingly made up of patterned scarves elaborately wrapped around their bodies. Still, others wore kaftans and trousers like the Kiremi. All of the clothing, except for those in Kiremi style, was absurdly revealing to Nidon's eye.

The people themselves came from many races. Most had the coloring of the princess, but there were some Koromoi, a few with light hair like a Nording or a Tysk, and others dark-skinned like Telea or even like Isibindi, the Ethean warrior. He noticed too that the Etheans were somewhat separate from the others. *Rumors of war and of Ethean attacks.*

Suddenly the singers' and healers' voices rose in song. Nidon recognized it as the *Song of Light.* The demon-fighting song. Telea had sung it for him just days ago when she'd recounted her part of Ayja's story for him. He wondered at the ritual. Did the song start every royal audience?

The Throne Room of Belen seemed made for music, and the voices swelled and carried over the audience. Then, right beside him, Telea began to sing, the music of her song joining the others. Then, Princess Kelifos stood and raised her voice in song as well, her eyes on Telea the entire time.

The song went on and on until Nidon lost count of the verses. He'd only ever heard the first few before. He didn't mind. The music was more beautiful than anything he'd ever heard before. He felt the power of it running through him. Telea had told him that elementars and singers could *see* the music. He wished for a moment that he could see as well as hear the beauty of it.

The song reached its climax, and the final notes faded into the distant corners of the Throne Room. "They've purified the chamber," Telea whispered. No demon could withstand, or at least not react to, such powerful music.

General Solis stepped to the front of the dais and said, "On behalf of Princess Kelifos, we greet you, King Handrin of Salador. We welcome you as allies and as friends."

Handrin nodded to the general and then addressed the princess, saying, "In this time of need, how could we refuse the call? Helna's world is in peril. We must unite our strengths together if we are to save it."

"Princess Kelifos asks—"

"Let us dispense with the formality of court, General Solis," the princess said. Her face and voice were calm, but her hands clutched the arms of her chair. "I shall speak for myself."

She knows the importance of this meeting, Nidon thought. *She is young and trying to appear strong.*

Solis bowed and stepped aside, saying, "As you wish, Your Imperial Majesty."

"King Handrin," Kelifos said, "so much has happened, it is difficult to know where to begin. Perhaps with an apology. You were invited to Belen in good faith. I am deeply ashamed of how Kyvern Psertis treated both you and Princess Ayja. His lies fell on welcome ears when my ill-fated brother heard them and used them to his advantage. I am also investigating the role of the High Priest of Forsvar and have summoned him to court. I fear he was sorely misled as well."

Nidon pursed his lips at this but remained silent. It was his understanding that the High Priest was a willing accomplice in the attempt to steal Forsvar.

Princess Kelifos gave Telea a dark look. "Teleana Telas Tarsian. You are the one they call the Queen of the Dead."

"I am," Telea said.

"You killed thousands of my subjects and raised them from the dead as your servants. You used them against the Imperial Army."

"Everything I did, I did to save Belen and our world. The Orb of Creation must reach the Dromost Gate and bar it for eternity. Your demon-possessed brother and the Imperial Army he commanded were working to make that impossible.

"I intended to raise only the dead Etheans that your possessed brother was massacring wholesale. I lost control of my magic, and many others were killed. For the rest of my life, as short as that might be, I will be tortured by their deaths."

"We will return to this topic later," Kelifos said. She turned to Handrin. "I suppose this will sound ridiculous, but I thought the Orb of Creation would be larger."

Handrin, who'd been holding the glowing orb at his waist, raised it in front of him. It fit in his hand, just slightly too large for his fingers to curl around. A gold and silver fire burned within. "Would it shock your majesty if I thought the very same when I first saw it?"

Kelifos nodded. "Would it be inappropriate for me to touch the Orb? If I understand correctly, your daughter, Princess Ayja, allowed anyone who wished to touch Forsvar and feel its power."

Handrin lowered the Orb to his waist. "My cousin, Princess Ayja," Handrin corrected. "Not my daughter. And I wish I could let you touch it, Your Majesty, but I cannot. The magic of the two Gifts of the Gods are very different. The Godshield Forsvar cannot be forcibly taken from one who wears it. It can only be freely given. However, if I let you touch the Orb, we would have a contest of wills for who should control its power. So, in effect, I have too much respect for the power of your mind to let you touch the Orb."

Princess Kelifos smiled. "Well put, King Handrin. And I will respect your decision." She paused and then said, "I fear I might be rebuffed a second time, but might I see a demonstration of your elementar power?"

"That is not a problem," Handrin said with a smile. He raised his left hand and twisted it. A gentle breeze swirled around the room, growing gradually stronger until hair and clothing fluttered in the wind. "I can knock a man over or allow him to leap fifty strides."

Handrin knelt and touched the marble floor. With a *crack,* a piece came free, and he stood with it in his hand. The Orb of Creation flashed, and the stone reshaped itself into a ball. Handrin tossed it in the air and caught it. Then, kneeling again, he pushed the stone into the flaw he'd created in the floor, flattening it and smoothing it until it was unblemished.

No, not unblemished, Nidon saw. There was an engraving there, where there'd been none before. *HRHHII.* His Royal Highness Handrin the Second. Nidon suppressed a smile. He was close enough that only he could see what the king had done.

"I have never seen such a thing," Kelifos said, clearly awed by the display. "Your magic is so different from the magic of song."

Handrin looked past the throne and the crowd of singers beside it. "You, there," he said. "Is that wine? Could I have some?"

The princess nodded and a male servant in a red tunic embroidered with crossed lightning bolts in white made his way past the crowd. He held a silver platter with a silver pitcher and a crystal glass upon it. Handrin took the pitcher from him and poured the wine over the Orb, but instead of soaking his hand, the wine formed a second orb floating just above it.

After placing the pitcher back on the platter, Handrin brought the wine orb to his lips and drank from it. "Very good," he said with a smile. He took a second sip and then flung the wine orb above his head where it vanished into mist. Oohs and aahs came from some in the audience.

Nidon saw the princess smile and applaud, some of the tension leaving her body.

"It is fire that everyone wishes to see, though," Handrin said. He raised the Orb of Creation and it pulsed with brilliant light. A column of flame descended from the air above them, becoming a raging, spinning ball of fire a stride across. The heat washed across the crowd, many of them taking a step back from the inferno. And then it was gone.

"Your magic is dangerous as well," Kelifos said. "Such an obvious thing to say, I know."

There was a low murmur from Belenese in the chamber as they whispered to each other about what they'd seen. All but for the Emperor's Axes, who watched stone-faced.

"The Orb of Creation is a repository for the power of the aether, freeing me from tapping my strength," Handrin said. "More important, though, is the fact that Princess Ayja unlocked the power of the Orb of Creation, allowing all who touch the aether greater facility with magic."

Princess Kelifos nodded. "We saw it as well, although we didn't know the cause. The magic of song is far more visible now than it used to be. Every day we discover new magics."

"When our task is finished, and the world is free of the threat of demonic invasion, I predict a new golden age of magic," Handrin said. "I look forward to it with great anticipation."

"I wish to hear more of Princess Ayja and her journey," Kelifos said. "I wish to learn more of Salador as well."

"There are those in my company who can tell you nearly everything of Ayja's life and of her journeys. Champion Nidon raised Princess Ayja in exile and was a father to her. Hunter Calen knew her as an infant, and with her mother, Hadde, rescued Ayja and Orlos the Spiridus from a band of mercenaries. Telea, Orlos, Calen, and Sindi all accompanied Princess Ayja on her journey to the Dromost Gate."

"And they were successful? The Dromost Gate is closed?" Kelifos asked. "There have been many rumors. Including that Princess Ayja is the Bride of Forsvar — the *nafai amas.*"

"The Dromost Gate is closed," Handrin said. "However, it can be reopened again, from either side. I am here so that it might be locked forever, using the Orb of Creation as a source of power to keep it closed." He took a deep breath. "As far as the *nafai amas,* we don't have such stories in the Kingdom of Salador. We've never heard of the Bride of Forsvar. Princess Ayja is the daughter of Hadde of Landomere and my uncle, Prince Morin of Salador."

"Where is Princess Ayja now?" Kelifos asked.

"She went through the Dromost Gate to close it. She is trapped there with the Godshield, Forsvar, and the Godhammer, Dromost."

Kelifos frowned, leaning forward in her chair. "She has perished, then?"

"There are some among us who hope she still lives."

The princess leaned back in her chair, doubt writ clear on her face. "Will you dine with me, King Handrin?" she asked. "You and those who know the story of Princess Ayja and the Dromost Gate."

"It would be our pleasure, Princess Kelifos."

"Princess Kelifos," Nidon said, stepping forward. "I am Sir Nidon, commander of the Army of Salador. Are we unified in our task of locking the Dromost Gate?"

"We are," she said with a nod. "The might of the Empire of Belen is with you."

"Telea Telas Tarsian made all of this possible," Nidon said. "She was the sole survivor of your father's embassy to Salador. It was her magic, her healing, and her knowledge that allowed Princess Ayja to close the Dromost Gate. Telea is vital to the success of our mission. Only she knows how to lock the Dromost Gate forever. Will she do this under a sentence of death?"

Princess Kelifos fixed Telea with her gaze. "She is not demon possessed. I saw the magic of the *Song of Light* fill her and pass through her. She had good intentions that had ill effects. She killed thousands of innocents." Kelifos regarded Telea, drumming her fingers on the arm of her chair as she did so. "When this is all over, and the world is made safe, she shall be exiled from Belen, never to return."

Chapter Twenty

Hello, Princess Ayja, a voice said.

Sudden fear gripped her. Within her memory walk, Ayja sat up in bed, clutching her blanket to her. It wasn't Darra. It wasn't a voice she knew at all. *Who are you?*

Or should I call you Enna, the voice said. *Daughter of Hadde the Landomeri and Prince Morin of Salador. Granddaughter of Arno and Enna and King Boradin.*

Who are you? Ayja demanded again. She rose from her bed, glancing around in the darkness. There was no one inside her memory walk.

I am the demon touching your hand. So soft. Did you bury yourself under this boulder, I wonder? How did you manage that?

There was a demon touching her! She drew from her well of power and reinforced the invisible barriers surrounding her memory walk.

The voice laughed in her head. *What good does that do you? I see your shields, and I see too that you haven't awakened. Of course, you know that all sleeping minds are safe from possession. It doesn't matter, though. Shielding your spirit does no good when I could simply consume your body and take your spirit as you die.*

Ayja ran downstairs, frantically willing herself to wake up. What working could she craft that would undo the eternal *Song of Rest?* She'd thought about it before, though, and come up with nothing. Now, panicked, she could hardly keep her thoughts in order, let alone create a working.

Don't worry. Tempting as you are, I haven't come to consume you. I've come at the behest of a friend. You remember the name Teleana Telas Tarsian?

Ayja stopped and stared out the front door, her heart pounding. *You are Telea's demon?*

Telea's demon? Is that my name? Ayja caught a note of humor in the demon's voice. *Telea's demon no more. I am free.*

How are you here? What is your purpose?

So many questions! I am here because your friend Telea freed me. A tricky one she is. A trap within a trap. I never saw it.

She sang the Song of Light?

Ha! Nothing so blunt as that. I thought you were friends. Do you not even know her at all? She sent me back to find you, even though she's certain you are dead. They all think you are dead. All but for the spiridus, Orlos. He's the one who came up with the idea of how to save you.

What do you mean?

Well, how you will save yourself. They cannot save you.

Tell me!

You know of the Emerald Prison under Belavil? The place of the trapped spiridus?

They told me of it.

The Emerald Tree was a powerful creation of the demon called Landomere. The veden shattered it and used its base as a prison for the spiridus. The prison isn't in Landomere, though. The prison is here, in Dromost. The stump of the tree is simply a doorway. Orlos thinks to turn the Emerald Tree into the Emerald Gate and that you might escape through it.

Can I?

The demon laughed again. *I think it is a fool's quest. You risked so much to close the Dromost Gate, and now you risk opening another?*

Maybe it can be closed again behind us.

Us?

Ayja gritted her teeth, cursing herself for having given something away. *What will you do now, demon?*

I will tell you, Enna, whom they call Ayja. I could do nothing at all. My task is done. I could leave you here, or I could consume you. I am bound to nothing. Your friend, Telea, was kind enough to free me and not to banish me. I am a worm no longer. I am not without some power. I could make my way in Dromost. Perhaps claw myself back to the heights of power I once held. It would be hard, though. Perhaps there might be some benefit to an accommodation between us.

What do you mean?

I know where the Emerald Prison is. Or should we call it the Emerald Gate? Would you like that more? I know the demon who controls it. Ha! Not a demon at all. The veden who controls it. The last veden. King of the Veden, and oh how he hates the spiridus demons.

Within her memory walk Ayja pressed her hands against the sides of her head, hardly able to believe what she was hearing. Hope. For the first time in a very long time, she felt hope. *You can take me there? But you'll want something in return.*

Of course. I don't see Forsvar or Dromost with you here. Where are they?

Ayja paused, not certain how much she should say. But the demon would learn soon enough. *The Blade of Darra is with me. He has them.*

Ah, so you are not alone.

You should be careful. He could be close. Demons cannot sense his presence. He will kill you if he sees you here.

You warn me? We are friends now? That is good. Yes, I will keep a watch out.

And you want Forsvar and Dromost as payment for your help?

My, you are a generous one. And how will you pay Vahlah, King of the Veden? Or were you planning on killing him?

I don't know. I don't know anything.

No, you don't. For now, you and your pyren friend will pay me with the spirits of demons we take on our journey. You will make me strong. Wait! A demon comes. I will hide and watch. Tell the Blade of Darra I am here. He must wake you, and I will show myself. I must go.

With that, the demon's presence disappeared. What did it mean that *a demon comes*? Fear gripped her. Now that she had some hope in her heart, her helplessness tore at her. She wanted to be awake! She had to be able to defend herself.

Still, the bonds of the *Song of Rest* could not be broken.

Time passed. How long, she wasn't certain. She had no way to tell for sure. But then Ayja felt Darra's familiar touch in her mind as sudden warmth flowed through her. Her well of power blazed brighter behind her. She smiled with the pleasure of it.

Come in, she said, lowering her guards so that he might enter her memory walk. Getting up from the table, she ran to the front door and opened it wide. She saw him there, crossing the yard.

"I'm sorry I took so long, my queen," he said.

"A demon was here, Darra. Telea's demon. It visited me."

Darra whirled around, looking into the forest surrounding the farm. Ayja knew that in the real world, he was searching for foes. "You weren't attacked?"

"Telea sent it to bring me a message. It says there might be a way out for us. In the city of Belavil in Landomere, there is a prison in the stump of the Emerald Tree. Centuries ago, the veden imprisoned the spiridus in this tree. But, you see, the tree is a gateway to Dromost. The spiridus are imprisoned *here*."

"And Telea thinks this prison might be a way out?"

"Maybe. Darra, I think it's our only hope. The demon says it will lead us to the Emerald Gate."

"Why?"

"It wants to be rewarded with souls, with the spirits of demons we take on the journey there. And... it also mentioned Forsvar and Dromost." Ayja entered the house and approached her well of power.

"It wants them," Darra said, following her.

"A demon — a veden actually — controls the Emerald Gate. It won't let us simply pass through. We might have to strike a bargain."

Darra paced the floor in front of the fire. "Do we dare offer Forsvar and Dromost in exchange for our freedom?"

"I don't know. I hate to think of giving the Gifts of the Gods to a veden. Wake me. Then we'll find Telea's demon and speak with it."

"I'm removing the stones that hide you right now. I don't know what will happen when I wake you. I'm not certain of the loyalty of the demons I've subjugated. They might find you impossible to resist."

Ayja laughed. "Impossible to resist? Is that what I am?"

Darra surprised her by blushing and stammering, "Well, ah, in that they might want to devour you."

Ayja gave him a mischievous smile. "That's what all the boys say."

"Bah, will you stop making fun of me? This is not the time for it."

She laughed. "We have hope for the very first time, Darra! A way out! You'll excuse me for smiling, won't you?"

"Of course, my queen," he said, returning her smile.

"And, in truth, very few boys pursued me. Cam had them terrified."

"They might have feared him, but I'm certain they were thinking of you."

"That's very sweet of you, Darra."

"I...." He paused a moment and stood from the table. "The rocks are clear. You said before that I should move you, and you would awaken."

"The working I created won't move with me. It should remain where it is. If not, I'm in trouble."

"You are certainly tucked in here," Darra said with a faraway look in his eyes. "I have you now."

Ayja felt another pulse of healing warmth flow through her body. Her well of power was full, blazing brightly behind her. Was this really it? The beginning of their escape? She tried to tamp down the hope bubbling up within her.

No, I won't give up on hope. It's all I have. It is this or perish.

She was awake. Gone was her solid home in the forested mountains of the East Teren, and in its place, the dark, smoldering landscape of Dromost. Darra held her in his arms, her head on his shoulder. No longer

209

the handsome, middle-aged man of her memory walk, his pale, dead face and black eyes stared back at her. He smiled and let her down.

"How do you feel?" he asked.

"Better than I've felt since arriving in Dromost." And then she knelt double as her stomach heaved, but nothing came up but for a mouthful of bile. She choked and spat the vile stuff out.

Darra handed her the canteen. "It isn't clean," he said.

Ayja nodded and summoned her magic, cleansing the water of its poisons. Her throat was raw, and her stomach churned, but she drank anyway. Then she rinsed her mouth and spat into the dusty soil.

"I don't understand your sickness," Darra said. "I've healed you of all wounds."

"It's this place," Ayja said. "Some poison of Dromost. But I feel strong, Darra." She drank a little more. "And I have hope now."

She just had to live long enough to make the effort. Her armor was loose on her, and she was certain she must appear a skeleton. Her hunger struck her like a physical blow, tearing at her stomach and doubling her over. She didn't vomit this time, though. She drank more.

"Slowly, my queen."

Ayja nodded and took a shallow drink, rinsing her mouth and spitting the water out. "Maybe it is just hunger."

"We must get you out of here, my queen. I'm willing to pay any price."

"Let's find that demon," Ayja said, looking around. "You've filled my well of power and cured me of all my wounds. Perhaps it's time to make our big effort. Maybe we can get home."

"You are my purpose, my queen."

"This goes beyond any obligation... any expectation of service. You followed me into Dromost."

"Any of your friends would have."

"There was a time I would have killed you without a thought," Ayja said. "But now you and I—"

I am here, the demon said in Ayja's mind.

She leaped to her feet, looking around. "Telea's demon has arrived. It's here."

Darra pressed Forsvar into her hands. She slipped it onto her arm and then put her hand on her sword hilt. Darra held Dromost at his side.

Can you hear me? Ayja thought.

I hear you. I will come out. We must move. You are a brilliant fire that all nearby demons can see.

Darra has subjugated some of those nearby. Will they stay true to him?

Only as long as they fear him.

"I can hear the demon in my head. It says that we must move on and that your subject demons will only be faithful so long as they fear you."

Do you understand our speech? Ayja asked the demon.

No. I understood it only when I was within Telea. Your speech is gibberish to me now. However, I can speak in both your minds at once.

"I heard it just now," Darra said.

"I don't know if we can trust that it can't understand our speech," Ayja said. "Telea said never to trust demons. If we must talk privately, let it be in my memory palace."

Darra nodded. "And when we speak to the demon in our minds, we must remember to also speak aloud, so that you and I know what the other is saying."

Come, we have a long journey, the demon said. With that, it emerged from a jumble of rocks some fifteen strides away. The demon was a four-legged serpent, only a stride in length. Its matte black scales blended into the rocks camouflaging it. There was more to it than color, though. There was a working of the aether, making the creature hard to see. It was as if her vision wanted to slide off it and look somewhere else.

She'd seen demons like this before. They always fled at her approach. She'd also seen them battling each other. *You are smaller than I expected.*

Little more than a worm — the weakest of all demons.

But you weren't always this small.

I was once powerful. I will be again. Perhaps you will help me become powerful in return for my aid. It looked at Darra and said. *Of course I want Forsvar and Dromost. What creature wouldn't? I am not a fool, though. I do not see a result that ends with either in my grasp. More powerful demons would sieze them from me. Pay me in demon spirits. That is all I ask.* It paused for a moment and then said, *Yes, only after you have taken your share, but do not let any go to waste. I will know, and I will stop helping you. Let us go. We tarry too long.*

Which way? Ayja asked.

Over the mountains. There is a pass. Better than traversing the lava fields.

"I think you should take Dromost as well as Forsvar," Darra said. "I cannot kill demons and draw their life force at the same time."

Ayja took off her sword and belted it around Darra's waist and then took the Godhammer from him.

"This way," Darra said, pointing towards the mountains. "I've explored there."

Ayja took another gulp from her canteen and followed as they set off.

211

They'd walked several arrowflights when the demon said, *There is a demon overhead following us.*

"It might be one of mine," Darra said aloud. "I have a flying demon in my service."

Ayja looked up into the roiling, cloud-filled sky. She spotted a demon flying high above them. It was impossible to tell how big it was — certainly larger than Telea's demon. "How do you know if it is your demon above us, Darra?"

"If it flies down and attacks us, it isn't one of mine," Darra said over his shoulder. "If it flies down and lets me touch it, it's one of mine."

"Simple enough," Ayja said. "How many demons do you have pledged to you."

"Five. How many are loyal?" He shrugged. "None, I suspect. They could have run away for all I know."

They marched another dozen arrowflights before stopping at a rivulet of water where Ayja filled her canteen. The demon still circled overhead. Ayja twisted the aether and purified her water.

What is your name, demon? Ayja asked as they continued towards the mountains.

Wouldn't you like to know?

I would. I always thought of you as Telea's demon, but that isn't a name. And it isn't true.

Names have power. How do you think I found you?

I don't understand.

I had an entire world to search, and your sleep hid you. Do you think it was some accident that I came upon you, Enna, who is called Ayja, daughter of Hadde the Landomeri and Morin, Prince of Salador? I only found you because I know your true name. Even then, it would have been difficult, but it was made easier because the spiridus demon, Orlos, had a token of yours.

What token?

A stone cup you made. White marble. It was very potent. You had worked magic on it, and it was special to you. With your true name and the essence of your token, I easily found you. No, not easily. I knew where you were, but I had to be careful. I am little more than a worm. I had to sneak and to keep myself from hunting and putting myself in danger. It took time, but I made it to you.

And now you are helping us.

And now you are helping me.

Darra looked into the sky and said, "My demon is approaching. At least I hope it is mine."

They halted in the shelter of some boulders so that the demon would have difficulty swooping down on them if it attacked. Ayja took Dromost and placed it in her shield hand. It was easy enough to hold both the shield's grip and the Godhammer's shaft at the same time. With her right hand, she touched the aether. Would this be the time to test one of her new workings?

The demon swept close and landed twenty strides away. It had the fur and wings of a bat with a long serpentine tail and talons. Ayja thought it was three strides long from tail to snout. The demon folded its wings and lowered its head towards Darra. Telea's demon leaped from Darra's shoulder and hid between two boulders.

"It says many demons are coming up from behind us," Darra said. "Another of my demons is ahead of us as well."

Ayja turned and looked over the ground they'd just traveled but saw no sign of demons there. "Can we get away from them?" she asked.

"I don't know. They are approaching quickly," Darra said. "I'll send the demon back to keep watch for us. We must keep our eyes open for a good place to defend."

Darra motioned to the flying demon, and it spread its wings and took flight. It raced past Ayja, just a few strides over her head, and cast its baleful red-eyed glare her way. Then it was past her, rapidly rising overhead. Telea's demon emerged from the rocks and slithered onto Darra's shoulder.

They continued up the pass, the ground rising slowly under them. The walls on either side closed in and grew rapidly in height. *This pass will take us to Vahlah's territory,* Telea's demon said.

You've been here before? Ayja asked.

In a previous life.

You remember everything from your previous lives?

Not everything.

And you're certain this Vahlah still exists? And that the Emerald Prison is still there?

Oh, yes, quite sure, the demon said, glancing at her from its perch on Darra's shoulder.

How?

Just as I know you exist. Not because I see you, but because I know your true name. Many, many demons know Vahlah's true name. Devouring the veden's spirit would be a great prize.

Then how does he still exist after all this time?

Power.

"There's my demon," Darra said.

"It's huge!" Ayja said with a gasp. Huge and horrible. The demon was humanoid, standing upright on two legs, but over twice the height of a man — bigger even than one of Akinos's giant capcaun or urias. The demon's arms were mismatched. One was scaled and clawed like a serpent's, while the other looked like a giant crab or a lobster's claw. A smooth shell, like a beetle's, covered the demon's back. Its face, too, seemed drawn from some insect or strange sea creature.

"How is such a monstrosity in your service?" Ayja asked. The demon had seen them and lumbered in their direction, still some hundred strides away.

"I hit it with Dromost several times before it learned some respect," Darra said. "I have to say that, without Forsvar on my arm, it does seem far more imposing." Darra drew his sword.

"Really? It learned some respect? Is that another joke?"

"I'm dead, but I'm not that dead, my queen."

The demon's long strides quickly closed the distance. Ayja couldn't tell its intent and drew Dromost from her belt. The demon's pace slowed at the sight of the Godhammer in her hands.

Once again, Telea's demon slid from Darra's shoulder and hid in the rocks.

"Halt, demon," Darra called out when the demon was thirty strides from them.

That one shines brightly, the demon said, pointing towards Ayja with one talon of its serpent claw.

"She is mine," Darra said with a glance at Ayja. She couldn't read his expression. "She isn't to be consumed."

So much strength in that spirit, but I will obey. The demon glanced around. *I saw a worm near you, but it hid itself.*

"That one is mine as well. You may not eat it, either."

I hunger, master. What can I eat if you deny me everything?

"Demons are coming for the bright one. We will lure them here and destroy them."

May I eat them?

"Some. Not all. We will share."

There was a terrible screech in the sky above them. Darra's flying demon flew rapidly away, pursued by three larger winged demons. Ayja looked from them to the valley behind them and saw more demons approaching. Two dozen or more. They were still an arrowflight away but approached with great speed. Some skittered on many legs, like spiders. Others glowed brightly and flew slightly ahead — fire imps.

Darra saw them as well. "I didn't realize there were so many."

This is no wandering band, Telea's demon said from hiding. *Some powerful lord has sent them. They are after Enna.*

There are many, Darra's monstrous demon said. Was it afraid?

"The bright one is powerful. More powerful than me," Darra said. "We can defeat them. Let's defend those rocks ahead of us." They ran up the steep slope towards the narrow mountain pass. They had a lead, but each time she looked back, Ayja saw the demon host closing on them.

"Between those two boulders," Darra ordered his big demon. "Hold them there."

Ayja paused just behind the demon. Within her memory walk, she reached for one of the candles on the mantle. As she touched it, she pulsed a small fraction of her power into it, and a fully formed ring of fire appeared in her hand in the real world. It happened in just heartbeats. With a smile, Ayja hurled the ring at the approaching demons.

An orange-red streak flew from her hand and erupted in a ball of fire amongst the first of the demons. The fire imps flew through the explosion unharmed, but other imps and several spider demons were not as lucky. The imps were totally consumed, while two spiders lay curled and burning.

The bright one is powerful, the big demon said, moving to take its position between the boulders. Darra and Ayja retreated a short distance behind it.

"They will ignore me and go after you," Darra said. "I will strike them as they pass."

Ayja nodded. The big demon blocked her view of the pass below, but now she heard the scraping of clawed feet and strange, keening cries as the demons approached.

The fire imps were the first to appear, flying over the boulder and ignoring Darra's big demon altogether. Ayja knew how to fight them and was ready. As they flew at her, she sang the *Song of Light,* directing all of its strength towards them and away from Darra's grotesque monstrosity. The song's aura washed over them, and they vanished, screaming piteously in sulfurous clouds.

One imp managed to escape the song, hurling a ball of fire at Ayja as it flew away. The fire flashed at her but Forsvar's aura quenched it. Then, snatching an arrow from her quiver in her memory walk, she caused a lance of air to slam the imp to the ground, where Darra's blade sliced it in half.

More demons attacked Darra's big demon guarding the boulders. Ayja saw it snap at one with its huge crab claw while slashing at another with its serpent's talons. Two spider demons died in as many heartbeats.

Two more demons appeared on top of the boulders. One was scaled and six-legged with two tentacles growing out of its shoulders. The other, a furry beast with short hind legs and two massive arms. The head of the second one was like a wolf's, but with two long horns protruding from it.

Although the two demons could have thrown themselves down on the demon blocking the gap, they only had eyes for Ayja. She empowered another wind lance and hurled it at the wolf-headed demon. The lance caught it in the chest and sent it flying off the rock. A fierce grin crossed Ayja's face. Her workings were better than she'd dared to hope.

The spider demon made a huge leap, landing almost at Ayja's feet. It lashed out with its tentacles, but she blocked them with Forsvar and then countered with a strike from Dromost. The demon was fast. She missed its head, but crushed its shoulder, nearly ripping a tentacle free from its torso. Then Darra came up from behind it and sheared off another limb.

Still, the demon came after Ayja. Its tentacles weren't for grasping — each was tipped with a needle-sharp spike. The spikes flashed forward, cracking against Forsvar and driving Ayja back. She swung Dromost again, this time crushing the demon's head. She saw a flash in the aether, and the demons spirit was drawn into the Godhammer.

Darra's demon fell back from the gap as more attackers poured over the boulders. The big demon had a smaller spiked demon in its big claw and dashed it against the boulder over and over. A many-legged spider with a segmented tail, repeatedly stabbed Darra's demon in the chest. Venom oozed from the tail's stinger, and everywhere it struck, the flesh seemed to melt from the grotesque.

Heartbeats later, Ayja was lost in the chaos of battle. Demons came at her from every direction. For the most part they ignored Darra, only striking at him when he became an immediate threat. He stabbed and slashed at her attackers, trying to limit their numbers, but they were overwhelming.

Forsvar was everywhere, blocking tentacles, claws, teeth, and horns. A few blows got through, but her scale hauberk held them, or a parry from Forsvar or Dromost weakened them. The hammer sang in her hands. With each soul it took, it became more powerful, moving faster and faster as it wove a circle of death around her.

When the sixth circle was charged, she could contain the Godhammer no longer. She struck a demon, and the hammer flashed with brilliant purple light, and the demon exploded. Chiton and ichor sprayed everywhere as the demon was destroyed.

In the violence of the explosion Ayja felt a sudden, tremendous pain in her back even as Forsvar blocked yet another blow from her front.

216

Silver light filled Ayja's vision as strength pulsed through her limbs. With a cry of rage, she whirled and slammed Forsvar into the demon that had gotten behind her.

The pain in her back — all pain — was forgotten in the silver light of her rage. There were demons everywhere. Even overhead. She slammed Dromost into the demons surrounding her, crushing skulls and carapaces and ripping limbs from bodies. She took more wounds but didn't feel them, so potent was her fury. Still, there were too many. They pressed all around her, grasping at her and striking at her.

She saw Darra thrown against a boulder, tangled with the demons, and tumbling with them. Ayja leaped to him, twisting the aether to aid her jump. As she landed, she stove in the head of a beetle-like demon and turned to cover Darra as he stood.

More demons rushed her. She wouldn't let herself be overwhelmed by them again. Still, in her silver fury, she entered her memory walk and reached for the candles over the mantle. One by one, as fast as she could, she threw rings of fire at the demons. Explosions detonated all around her, incinerating demons and sending walls of fire washing towards her, Forsvar's aura holding the fire at bay.

She was out of candles, but still the demons came on. She reached out and touched raw aether, sending it crackling into the burning landscape to ravage any remaining demons.

Caught up in the power and the fury of her silver rage, she paid no heed to her well of power. With every passing heartbeat, her furious magical assault drained ever more energy from her well until suddenly it was empty.

Ayja stared at her hand. The power was gone, and her world began to spin. She toppled forward, plummeting into darkness. She never felt herself hit the ground.

Chapter Twenty-one

Maret walked through the forest behind her twin daughters, Quellas and Rellas. The girls scampered from one patch of everbloom to another, drinking in the soft fragrance of the luminescent blooms. Melas was off with his "grandfather" Arno learning how to craft a longbow of his very own.

It warmed Maret's heart that Hadde's parents treated her children as their very own. They were so good to them. It was good for Arno and Enna as well, having lost both their daughter and granddaughter. Doting on Maret's children most certainly helped fill a hole in their lives. *If only Enna could have visited before leaving for Belen. It would have meant so much to them.*

A wave of emotion washed over Maret. It would have meant so much to her as well. She remembered baby Enna at her breast and the devastation she'd felt when she and Hadde had been lost. Maret pushed the thought from her mind as her daughters found a babbling brook and splashed gleefully through it. It was no use telling them not to get wet. Or muddy. She'd learned that such warnings would be worthless to two sprites as mischievous as hers.

The sun shone down through the high canopy, painting the forest floor in dappled light. It was as beautiful a day as one could hope for. How many years had she been here? Seventeen? Eighteen now? She'd arrived as a pregnant, terrified fourteen year old, and now couldn't imagine leaving. It was as beautiful a place as she could imagine. And not just the forest but also the people.

"Will there be a battle?" Quellas asked. "Will father fight the demons?"

"Who said anything about demons?" Maret asked.

"Orlos!" Rellas replied, standing in the brook, her linen tunic soaked through.

"He was just making up stories for fun," Maret said, taking off her moccasins and following the girls up the brook — with somewhat less splashing involved. She carried a pack with a blanket, food, and spare clothing, of course.

"Father took his sword and his crossbow," Quellas said.

"And his armor," Rellas added. "He's sure to kill a demon."

"Your father is with King Handrin and Champion Nidon. They even have the Orb of Creation with them. He'll be safe."

"We should have brought a bow with us," Quellas said.

"Or a sword," Rellas said. "What if there's a bear?"

"Or a demon?" Quellas said, making a monster face and holding her hands over her head with her fingers clawed.

"Was that a bear or a demon?" Maret asked, smiling.

"A bear!" both girls shouted, laughing.

Maret laughed with them. "If you say so!"

They continued up the stream, the everbloom growing thick on the slopes to either side of them. She'd never seen so much of it in one place. Except... a chill went down her spine as she looked around her.

A spiridus glade.

Ahead of her, the girls squealed in delight. "A pool, mother!" Quellas shouted. "Can we swim?" Rellas asked.

"Wait for me," Maret called out. She pushed through a wall of fern and saw it then. The brook they'd followed tumbled down a steep slope in front of her, splashing into a crystal-clear pool. The banks of the pool were lined with everbloom and ferns and even, to the girls' delight, a patch of sweetberry. From the center of the pool rose a smooth, flat stone.

Maret felt the presence of the Great Spirit pass through her. Here they were safe from bear or demon. Here they were under the protection of Landomere herself.

"Can we?" the girls asked in unison, standing at the edge of the pool.

"Take off your clothes! I don't want—"

In an instant, the twins were naked. A heartbeat later, they were in the pool, laughing, squealing, and splashing one another.

"My apologies, Great Spirit," Maret whispered as she picked up the discarded clothing. As she folded them, she looked around, hoping to spot the flash of a silver spirit bird. "Are you here, Hadde?"

She wished Orlos were with her. The Lady of the Forest only ever appeared to him. She might be present, but Maret would never see her. Or at best only as a silverjay.

As the girls splashed and laughed, Maret made her way to a sunny spot just a few strides from the bank. She took off her pack and set to work laying out a picnic for the three of them.

When she finished, she walked to the edge of the pool. No trees were overhanging it, and the summer day was quite warm. "Come in! Come in!" the girls shouted.

Undoing the laces on her linen dress, Maret pulled it off, leaving her only in her under shift and braies. She shucked the braies as well and waded into the cool water of the pool.

"You didn't take your shift off," Quellas shouted.

"It will get all wet," Rellas said.

Maret sank into the water until it reached her neck, pushing down on her shift to keep it from rising. The floor of the pond was mostly pebbles with spots of squishy mud between. Small fish darted away from her as she waded closer to the girls. Maret, unlike the girls, only barely knew how to swim. It wasn't something Saladoran girls did.

"Now you're all wet," Quellas said.

"Soaked," Rellas added. "Why didn't you take it off?"

"She never does."

"Because I'm a silly Saladoran," Maret said. "We don't take our clothes off in front of other people."

"Why not?" Quellas asked.

"That's silly," Rellas said.

Maret shrugged. "It's just the way I grew up. Old rules are hard to break."

"What if they're silly rules?" Quellas asked.

"What if they don't make any sense?" Rellas asked.

"You're right. Your mother is being silly. But it's too late now."

For a time they splashed around in the pool. Maret was soaked, her hair included. Eventually, hunger drove them to their picnic, where they ate hard cheese and bread and freshly picked sweetberries. Re-energized by the meal, the girls dashed back into the water.

Maret watched them for a while before walking to the water's edge. She stared off at the brook and the splashing water as it leaped and tumbled down the rocks into the pool. Then she saw the flat rock in the middle of the pool. It seemed an even better place to sit and see the entirety of the spiridus glade.

She glanced at the girls, completely absorbed in some task that involved stacking rocks at the edge of the pool, and, in a fit of ridiculous daring, took off her shift, tossed it aside, and plunged into the pool naked. She laughed and sputtered as she came to the surface.

I really am a Landomeri now.

She walked out towards the flat rock, but the water was too deep for her to make it without swimming. It wasn't far, though, only a few strides. She could make it that far at least. Taking a breath, she started into a faltering dog paddle that took her to the edge of the rock. With some effort, she pulled herself atop the stone and sat upon its sun-warmed surface.

Now, all around her, she could take in the beauty of the spiridus glade. Her girls hadn't noticed their amazingly bold mother yet, and Maret was content to leave it that way.

They will have a fit when they see me.

Maret turned towards the falls. The girls talked quietly as they played, allowing their mother to listen to the music of the falling water and the breeze rustling through the leaves overhead. Maret lay down upon the warm rock, and before she knew it, the music of the glade had lulled her to sleep.

She dreamt of walking through the forest with Hadde at her side. Not the Lady of the Forest, or some shining spirit-Hadde, but her flesh and blood friend. They walked without speaking under the sun-dappled canopy. Maret felt both intense happiness and great loss at the same time.

Then her friend turned into a spirit bird and flew away, disappearing into the forest.

Maret woke with a start, suddenly fearful. Where were the girls? Instantly awake, she whirled to see where they were, relief flooding her as she spotted them at the edge of the pool. Her relief was quickly tinged with horror, as they were both covered from head to toe in mud.

The girls still hadn't seemed to notice her. Maret watched them for a time, curious at what they were up to. They'd built something of mud and leaves at the edge of the pond, but she couldn't make it out from her vantage point.

Curious, and too warm after who knew how long under the sun atop the rock, she slipped into the water and swam towards her daughters. Neither noticed her until she was a few strides away.

"Look what we've done, mother!" Quellas said, spotting her.

"Do you like her?" Rellas asked.

"I'm looking at the two of you right now," Maret replied. "You look like mud-people. You'd better get in the pool and wash all of that off."

"We made a mud person."

"Look at her!"

Maret turned her attention to the girls' creation. It was, in fact, a person — a mud woman. Still low in the water, Maret floated closer to the edge, propelling herself with her hands on the pebbles below.

"Tee hee! Mommy's naked," Quellas said.

"Ha ha! I thought she was a silly Saladoran," Rellas said.

"I guess I'm a Landomeri now," Maret said, her attention focused on what the girls had done. It was actually remarkably good. *How long was I asleep?*

"We made her bones from sticks."

"Look, there's her bow."

"I see, I see," Maret said. They'd given their mud woman a quiver made of bark and clothing of leaves and vines as well. "This was a lot of work!"

"It's Hadde," Quellas said.

"Your friend," Rellas said.

Maret was speechless. A surge of emotion welled through her, and she thought she might cry. *They've made Hadde. What made them think...*

She rose part way out of the water — crossing her arms in front of her for modesty's sake — so that she could get a better view of what the girls had done. It really was fine work. They were only seven after all. "Why did you make mommy's friend? What made you think of that?" She shivered in the warm air.

"Do you like her?" Quellas asked.

"Isn't she good?" Rellas added.

"Very good," Maret said. "You are great artists. But why did you do it?"

"The lady asked us to," they said in unison.

"The lady? What lady?" Maret asked as a chill crawled down her spine.

"The lady in the forest."

Chapter Twenty-two

Ayja awoke to Darra's pale face staring into hers. "I thought I'd lost you," he said.

Healing warmth pulsed through her body. She felt shattered and empty, barely able to lift her limbs. Slowly, though, life and strength returned to her. "What happened?" she asked as she raised herself to a sitting position. All around them lay the wreck and ruin of charred and broken demon corpses. Even as she watched, the flesh and then the bones and scales began to decay and sink into the earth.

She saw movement and pointed. "There's another one!" she said.

Darra spun, his hand going to Dromost. Almost as quickly, he released it. "Telea's demon."

"What happened to it?" The little serpent was larger now — twice as long as it had been before.

That was a feast, the demon said. *You were very generous. You didn't take a single spirit.*

"I have no use for their souls," Darra said. "I only needed their strength."

"Why do demons look so different?" Ayja asked. "Some look like spiders or serpents, or even creatures of the sea. Some are a strange mix of many things, like Darra's big demon." She looked around for Darra's monstrous servant but didn't see it.

That demon was a grotesque. The fastest way for a demon to grow is to subsume the essence of another demon. Take what they were and make it part of you. It is a quick way to power, but it is foolish. In the end, the many parts do not make up a coherent whole. The sum is not equal to the many parts.

It is much wiser to take the spirit of another demon and then use its potency to guide your growth in the direction you choose. That is the path I've taken. Slower, yes, but the form fits the whole. The body and the mind work together.

Darra gave Ayja a hand and pulled her to her feet. Her head spun for a moment, but then she caught her balance. Hunger tore at her, and she drank from her canteen. Her well of power was half full, maybe less. For a moment, nausea nearly caused her to lose the water she'd just drank, but she willed herself to hold it down.

"Are there other ways?" she asked the demon as she wiped her lips and sealed the canteen.

Slower, but even more powerful in the end, yes. To bind the elements around you and to become one with them — that makes for a powerful demon. I have no time for that now. I will become strong first.

Ayja's gaze took in the putrid valley of rotting demons. If not for the air-cleansing pendant she'd created, she was certain the stench would have been overwhelming. "There were so many of them."

"Our demon friend says that a powerful demon lord has been searching for you for some time," Darra said. "Its minions caught up to us here."

You upset the balance of power when you destroyed the gatekeeper and brought the Two Gifts into Dromost. There will be war.

"How many demons attacked us here?"

"Fifty, at least, I'd say," Darra said. "Only a few remained when you fell."

Ayja grimaced. "I overspent myself."

"You nearly died. I couldn't heal you and fight off the remaining demons at the same time. I took Dromost and fought them, hoping I would still find you alive."

"I'm sorry, Darra."

"I thought I'd lost you, my queen. I'm glad I got to you in time." He waved his hand past the many decaying corpses. "You wrought ruin on their attack. The valley was an inferno. I don't think we would have survived if you hadn't let your rage take you."

We must move on. We must find Vahlah, the demon said.

Ayja took a deep breath. "It's never-ending," she said. She looked around. "Where are your demons, Darra?"

"The big one, the *grotesque*, was destroyed. He fought well, though. The flying demon was chased off. I doubt it will return. The others?" He shrugged. "I doubt it will do us any good to go back and find them. We must keep going."

Ayja's first impulse was to tell Darra she was sorry for the loss of his big demon. She shook her head at the thought. The disgusting monstrosity would have consumed her in a moment, given a chance. She tried to put the image of the demon out of her mind. Even if she managed to return home, would she ever forget the horrors she'd seen here?

Her thoughts went to her memory walk. All of the candles were out. She only vaguely remembered hurling them one after another at the masses of demons surrounding her. Only a few arrows remained in the quiver by the door, ready to be loosed, but she had to take care. Darra hadn't fully restored her.

"Was that a large army?" Ayja asked the demon. "Would we ever have to fight more?"

It was a large force, the demon said. *But demon armies can be much larger. Their lord would have to be there to maintain control, though. Demon armies are not very obedient. In the chaos of battle, a demon is just as likely to attack a friend as it is a foe. It happened even in the fight we just had. When you wounded some demons with your fire, other demons turned on them for a quick meal. It only takes moments to subsume a soul.*

"This Vahlah will have a powerful army?"

Yes. And better organized than most. Vahlah is not a demon, remember. He is a veden, from your world. He brought knowledge of runes and metalworking with him. While Vahlah's physical form might not be as deadly as other demon lords, his knowledge makes him far more dangerous and their equal in power.

Ayja took a deep breath. "And he controls the only way out."

They marched on, warily scanning the cliffs above them. Demons attacked them three times as they traveled. Fortunately, it was individual demons who threw themselves blindly at Ayja. She and Darra struck down all three, with Darra stealing their strength and giving most to Ayja. Their demon companion consumed the souls of the defeated.

Time lost meaning as they marched on and on through the broken mountains of Dromost. As long as Darra could keep her well of power full and cleanse her muscles of fatigue, there was no need to stop. Eventually, though, the demon attacks became more frequent, and although her well of power was half full, Ayja could no longer think straight.

"I have to sleep," she said after what seemed an eternity. "My mind is growing distracted."

It would be a good thing, the demon said. *More and more demons are drawn to you. Hide your soul for a time, and let them disperse.*

"I'm going to use a working to make myself sleep again," Ayja said.

"I will stay and defend your hiding place," Darra said.

"But you must hunt."

We should move forward, the demon said. *Clear the road to Vahlah's territory.*

"Here," Darra said. He pointed to a hollowed out place along the canyon wall. "We'll hide you here."

Ayja gave him Forsvar and Dromost and then hid herself. It was more spacious than her last sleeping place.

"I don't want to leave you, my queen." Darra touched her hand, and she let him into her memory walk. "I don't trust the demon."

"Take it with you," Ayja said. "If you hide me well, nothing will disturb me."

Darra built a stone wall hiding her from sight while she crafted her working. "The same as before," she said. "Move me from this place if you wish to wake me." What she didn't say aloud was that she'd craft it so that she could wake herself up if she had to.

Darra put the last stone in place, and she finished her working. Sleep overcame her body immediately, and she retreated to her memory walk. She looked around the great room and at the unlit candles on the hearth. She wanted to make more of her workings but didn't think she could hold her concentration long enough. It was not enough for Darra to remove her fatigue. She needed true sleep. Retreating to her bedroom, she fell into her bed and into a deep sleep.

How long was she in her memory walk? She had no idea. She woke and slept several times. Weeks, she thought. Darra came back to her from time to time, filling her with strength and reporting on what he and Telea's demon had discovered. Sometimes they were gone longer than others, and she'd become desperate that they might never return.

She filled some of her days with workings, puzzling out the ways of magic, but always becoming frustrated with her inability to test what she'd done in the real world. She also spent time improving her memory walk, studying and refreshing the memories she'd stored there, or expanding its scope. Still, it wasn't enough to fill her time. As she began to think loneliness might consume her, she allowed herself to sleep more often. It was easy, given the compulsion of the *Song of Rest* that surrounded her.

More often than not, Darra reported that some demonic obstacle or other blocked their path as they searched for the veden and the Emerald Prison. Sometimes, when hunting was poor, or when they'd have to travel a great distance, she'd awaken within her memory walk to find that her well of power was nearly empty. It was those times when fear would fill her heart, knowing that there was nothing she could do. Even if she woke herself, she'd have no way to replenish her strength.

Her sleep was a difficult one. She ran from one dream to another, all of them unpleasant. She dreamt of demons and battle, but also of things that had happened before. Of the many friends she's lost to the ghuls and

226

of the Belenese and the summoners as well. She thought of Orlos and the love they'd never share. She tried to turn her dreams in positive directions but had no power over them.

She woke to complete darkness. Twisting the aether, she caused a small flame to appear in the palm of her hand. In the orange glow, she saw her bed surrounded by the dead. She saw Orlos and Cam, Telea and Rayne. Her childhood friends and companions from the Company of the Shield. All dead, faces and flesh corrupt, leering over her as she slept.

Ayja screamed in pain, instantly awake in the real world. The walls of her shelter were gone, and a horrible, feline head had its jaws clamped around her torso. Long, dagger-like fangs pierced her scale coat, impaling her. A clawed hand pinned her shoulder to the ground while another crushed her leg.

Claws savaged her unarmored leg as the demon dragged her from her hiding place. Silver light flooded Ayja's vision, and strength surged through her body. She pressed her hand against the demon's neck. Pure aether flooded down her arm and into it. Lightning crackled down its body and it heaved backward. Then, with a terrible jerk, it flung her through the air. As she slammed into a rock, all the air went out of her lungs, and her vision swam. The silver light faded, and with it, her strength.

The demon was bigger than a horse. Its long, scaled arms ended with clawed fingers. Its legs were short and powerful. It turned its baleful red eyes on her, its head still wreathed in smoke where her lightning had scorched its fur. It charged.

Ayja couldn't breathe. She couldn't think. The lines of the aether blurred and moved around her, impossible to touch with mind or hand. Even if she could draw it, her sword was pinned under her. But within her memory walk, a long line of candles burned on the mantle and arrows filled the quiver by the door.

She flung a circle of fire at the demon. It struck its chest, exploding in a bright red-orange ball of fire. Too close though — as a wall of flame washed over her, she threw her arm over her head and pressed her face against the ground. A wave of heat rolled over her as the demon screeched in pain.

Ayja lifted her head as the fire passed. The demon had pulled up short, blinded by the fire that had engulfed it. She loosed lances of wind into the demon, driving it back. One, two, three, four. Each one throwing the demon ten strides or more away, tumbling and rolling as the powerful blasts struck it.

Then she threw three circles of fire at the demon, each exploding within heartbeats of the last. Ayja held another ready in her hand as she lay nearly prone, barely able to support her body with her arm. Slowly the smoke cleared, revealing the charred corpse of the demon. As she watched, the demon's body rotted away.

Exhaustion overcame her. She wanted nothing more than to sleep again. To feel its dark embrace. She couldn't dare, though. She was totally exposed, vulnerable to any demon that might come along. Then the pain of her wounds swept over her body, and it was all she could do to stop herself from screaming out her agony.

Three long, deep wounds crossed her right thigh, her lifeblood pumping from them into the soil. And from her stomach, more pain, the wounds hidden under the scales of her armor. She felt the blood flowing there as well. Clenching her teeth, Ayja unbelted her sword and unfastened her scale hauberk. She eased the armor off her shoulders and, lifting her shirt, looked down at the two jagged wounds left by the demon's fangs.

She had nothing to bind her wound except her silk shirt and the halter she bound her breasts with. She pulled off her shirt, cutting it into long strips with the aid of her sword. Taking a longer strip, she bound her abdomen. Despite the pain, she tied the strip tight so that it wouldn't slip. Then she used the remaining fabric of her shirt to bind the wounds on her legs. All her wounds still bled, but the bandages slowed it at least.

If only I could heal. If Telea and I had only had more time together!

Desperately thirsty, she looked for her canteen, but couldn't find it. Darra had taken it to refill it, but he'd said that he'd returned it during one of his visits. Ayja glanced back towards her rocky refuge. It had to be there. Carefully, she drew her hauberk back over her shoulders. She wore no aketon — the hauberk's scales were sewn into a thick, silk-lined backing. After fastening the coat's clasps, she used her sheathed sword as a crutch and pushed herself to her feet. It was an almost unbearable agony.

How had it found her? What had led the demon to her hiding place? Had it been pure chance? She couldn't stay here any longer. She couldn't risk sleeping again, now that she'd been found.

Slowly, she made her way to the rocky crevasse, noting the trail of blood that led there. She saw her canteen, and also the working that had kept her asleep. With a wave of her hand, she dismissed the magic. Then she knelt and uttered a curse as she looked at her canteen. It was unstoppered. She picked it up carefully, hoping to save the little water that remained. *Less than a quarter full.*

She cleansed the little water that remained and took a long pull. She had to leave. She had to find Darra.

Every step Ayja took was an agony. She could hardly put any weight on her leg, and her abdomen burned with intense pain. She'd only gone a little over a hundred strides when the clattering of stones alerted her to her worst fears. Spiked imps, their gray flesh camouflaging them against the stones, leaped out from hiding and raced down the slope to her left. Her first thought was to reach for a candle and cast a circle of fire at them.

But they were only imps, and she only had so many empowered workings left. She was too weakened to fight with her sword. Drawing a breath, she sang, *"I sing a song of light..."*

The magic wasn't there. She couldn't find the melody. Fear washed over her.

You must be the song, Telea had told her. *You must be one with the song.*

Despite the danger, Ayja closed her eyes and concentrated. She imagined sitting in the garden at the Temple of Forsvar with Telea at her side, warm sun on her face, and a fountain streaming sparkling water just behind her.

I sing a song of light
I sing of dark dispelled
I sing of life awakened
I sing of danger quelled

By the third line, she'd found the melody and bright light flared out from her in the aether. She heard the scrape of claws as the demons raced closer, but she kept her eyes closed. Her song would protect her. She imagined Telea with her, harmonizing with her, and sang louder and with more confidence. In her mind, she directed the power of her song at the demons closest to her.

Shrieks of agony echoed off the cliffs. Ayja opened her eyes now. The closest demons were just fifteen strides away, but they rolled on the ground in agony, the *Song of Light* burning away their demonic flesh.

Heedless of the danger, more imps ran into her song, only to be thrown back. Ayja redoubled her efforts, pushing the song at the demons, even stepping closer to them so that the song would be more potent. Only three imps escaped. In leaps and bounds, they scrambled up the cliff face.

Unwilling to let them escape, Ayja hurled a ring of fire at them. The explosion consumed all three.

The *Song of Light* faded from her lips. The demons were destroyed. She took a deep breath and resisted the urge to sink to her knees and rest. Once down, she might never get up again. She had to keep moving.

One foot after the other. Keep moving. Darra is just ahead. He has to be.

Behind her, a demon bellowed.

Chapter Twenty-three

The Army of the Orb remained in the capital for two weeks, resting, resupplying, and growing in size. Every few days, more Saladorans marched into the camp, with more still on the way. Every day, Belenese reinforcements arrived as well. They'd decided not to wait for even greater numbers, however, and marched east for the Summoned Lands. A larger army would do them no good if the Dromost Gate were opened.

For three weeks, the Army of the Orb marched across dry plains towards the distant mountains of Drommaria. Slowly, the plains gave way to forested hills. Gone were the olive groves of Belen. Here they found tall pines and thick forests. The army contracted into a narrow column, winding its way higher and higher. Cloudy skies and ever-present drizzle replaced the hot sun of Belen. All along the path, they'd seen signs of the terrible war that had been fought over this ground the previous year. The summoners had made it all the way to Aftokropoli, and the people who'd lived along the invasion path had suffered terribly. Villages, if not completely burned and abandoned, held only a few citizens struggling to rebuild. And the closer they came to Drommaria, the fewer people they saw.

From the top of a ridge, Nidon looked back at the army trailing behind the Saladoran Battle. In all, they were nearly thirty thousand strong, split into six battles. The Saladorans were fourth in order of march, not exactly a position of prestige, but then they were foreigners and unfamiliar to the Belenese.

The Vanguard Battle, made up of Koromoi riders and Drinker tribesmen, led the army, followed closely by the veteran demon fighters of the Eastern Battle. Third in line came the Imperial Battle of the Empress's Axes, Imperial Timari, Imperial Foot, and two hundred Children of Forsvar. The Empress herself rode with them, knowing that her place was with the army in this time of peril. Immediately behind the Saladorans came the Aftokropoli Battle and its citizen-soldiers. The Western Battle, the rear guard, marched last.

"Where do the Summoned Lands begin?" Nidon asked Exonos as the column slowly wound its way into the hills. Although his place was with the Western Battle, Nidon had asked that the Satrus be allowed to accompany the Saladorans as a translator and advisor.

They'd slowed now, the rough track only wide enough to ride two abreast. It was cooler here, and low, dark clouds obscured the once bright Belenese sun.

"Some would argue that we've already entered them," Exonos said. "Only the Drinker tribes are brave enough to live here and in the mountains ahead of us."

"Aren't the Drinkers Belenese?"

Exonos chuckled. "The Drinkers are their own people. The Emperors of Belen might consider this land part of the empire, but I don't think the Drinkers do."

"Don't they serve as the Empress's Axes?"

"They do. They are fanatically loyal to their oaths. It doesn't matter who they serve. If a Drinker offers you his bond, it will not be broken."

"Would they do the same for a summoner?"

"*If* a Drinker offered his word to a summoner, it would never be broken. But no Drinker, no matter what the offer, would ever do such a thing. They despise the summoners and their demons. Centuries of warfare will do that. And the Drinkers consider summoning to be a sign of weakness. They feel nothing but contempt for a people who need to summon demons to do the things they cannot, or will not, do."

"I like them," Nidon said.

Exonos shrugged. "Throughout history, they've served some bad people. Perhaps not the summoners, but rebels and criminal overlords. They aren't particular as to the cause."

Nidon frowned. "Far less noble, then. Mercenaries."

The column ground to a halt. How long did it stretch ahead of them? A halfday's march? Longer? If this were the terrain they'd be fighting through, they had far too much cavalry. Their horses would be useless in the rough hills and mountains to come. The supply train for horse fodder alone was immense. It wasn't his command, though. General Solis knew his business. At least, that was Nidon's hope.

Not far away, King Handrin was deep in conversation with Telea. All of the elementars were there, gathered in a circle off the side of the road. Nidon saw Lady Wenla and her daughter Varen among them. According to Handrin the two were emerging as powerful elementars. Nidon couldn't hear what Telea was saying, but all of the elementars watched the singer with rapt attention. *She's teaching him about magic. Everything she and Ayja discovered together.*

232

From time to time, Telea would sing, and as she did, she'd make graceful gestures and movements with her hands. He knew more than most about magic — Ayja had explained it to him on many occasions — not that he understood more than the basics of it. He knew about the strands of magic and how Ayja could see them and touch them. He also knew that Telea could do the same with her voice.

The delay stretched into the afternoon, and then word came down the column that they'd halt for the night. There was no place to camp, just steep wooded hills to either side of them. Fuel for campfires would be no problem, but there was no place to pitch a tent or to corral their horses. They made the best they could in a night beleaguered by rain showers.

It was only the following morning that Nidon learned the vanguard had fought an action against a Drommarian force holding the pass. They'd won their way through, but the delay had been enough to halt the column.

They rode higher into the steep hills, passing the site of the battle near midday. Camp servants were still burying bodies as they rode by. Dozens of dead still waited, a testament to the ferocity of the action that had been fought there. Five arrowflights later, they halted again. Word came down the column that the summoners held Devil's Watch and that it would have to be stormed.

"Devil's Watch is a powerful fortress guarding the pass," Exonos said to Nidon. "While smaller trails known to the Drinkers cross the mountains, an army can only move by this road. The Devil's Watch controls the pass. It is hard news that we will have to storm it."

"Wasn't this expected?"

Exonos nodded. "There are two factions of summoners, the Gatekeepers and the Doomcallers. It was the Doomcallers who started the war. They wanted to capture the Orb of Creation so that Shulazar's Ward could be taken down and the demon invasion allowed to occur. The Gatekeepers wanted the Orb of Creation so that the gate could be sealed forever.

"After a year of terrible fighting in which the summoners gained more ground than they ever had before, they were defeated. It seemed the Gatekeepers had risen to prominence, and they sued for peace."

"And so an embassy was sent to Salador," Nidon said.

Exonos nodded. "And was betrayed by the Doomcallers. If your Princess Ayja hadn't closed the Dromost Gate, who knows what would have happened by now? I expect demons would have overrun us."

"If the Orb of Creation had been sent with Ayja, would any of this be necessary now?" Nidon asked. "Could she have sealed the Dromost Gate?"

"So I understand it," Exonos said. "The workings of magic are beyond me."

Nidon stared up the pass. The mist and trees made it a futile effort. They were far from the Devil's Watch in any case. "You won the war, but the summoners still hold the Devil's Watch?"

Exonos shook his head. "It was given back to us when peace was declared. It was a trap, though. Emperor Niktonas, may his soul rot in Dromost, garrisoned the fortress with the Imperial Chorus. With every singer he could find. And when they were all gathered there, the summoners used some demonic fire to kill them all. Our most potent demon-fighting force was destroyed in a night."

"The singers with us now, they are the only remaining singers in the Belenese Empire?"

"All who could be gathered in time. There aren't many more, though — in Belen, at least."

"Where else are they?"

"There are many in the Ethean Islands. Empress Kelifos sent word to them, asking them for aid." Exonos grimaced. "I don't think there's much hope of them arriving any time soon, though. The last thing the Etheans heard from Belen were the drums of war and news of massacred Etheans. It will be some time before they trust us."

"So we are in for a hard fight."

"We are. The good news is that we defeated the summoners heavily during the Summoner War and that they then fought a war between themselves. They are a weakened nation."

The delay stretched on and on, with Nidon becoming more and more frustrated with every passing moment. He sent word to General Solis that his Saladorans were prepared to fight but was informed that his men wouldn't be needed. Once again, they camped on the road. Nidon spent the following day with Exonos, marching up and down the road, speaking with Saladorans knights and soldiers, the Landomeri, and meeting some of Exonos's Belenese soldiers as well. All were frustrated at the delay.

Late in the afternoon, a dozen Drinkers approached. Men and women alike wore short mail haubergeons over wool aketons and had quivers of javelins on their backs and short, broad swords at their waists. All wore vests of bear or wolf fur and fur hats as well. The men had dark, heavy beards that rose high on their cheeks. They spoke with each other as they approached, one of the women pointing with a javelin to a narrow ravine off to her right.

When they saw Nidon, Handrin, and Exonos together, they approached. The woman, very tall, with piercing green eyes and a scar running from above her left eye to the bottom of her jaw, nodded to them and then spoke in Belenese. Nidon had picked up some of the language, but she spoke rapidly and with an accent he couldn't follow.

Exonos nodded and turned to Nidon and Handrin. "This is Atu, a Drinker clan leader. She says the Devil's Watch is held against us, and General Solis can't break through. He's made three assaults, but all were repulsed. The slopes are too steep, and the Drommarians are raining boulders down upon them. These Drinkers know of a path that leads behind the fortress. The ground isn't as steep, and the wall isn't very tall. Atu will lead the Drinker attack."

"It seems a poor fortress to have such a glaring weakness," Handrin said.

Exonos spoke with Atu for a few moments and then said, "The fortress is meant to defend against invasions from Drommaria. From that direction, and the road, it is nearly invulnerable, she says. Taking Devil's Watch from the rear won't be easy, but it is feasible. The path there is very dangerous and can only be passed in a single file. There is a place where a small detachment can hold off an army, but the Drommarians might not even know of it, not having held the Devil's Watch very long."

"They *might* not know about it," Nidon said.

Atu and Exonos spoke again. "Atu asks that the Landomeri join the assault. Their archery might help. She also says that General Solis sends a request for King Handrin and his elementars to join in the general assault when the Drinkers attack from the rear."

Handrin nodded his assent. "We will come."

"I will gather the Knights of the House for the assault," Nidon said. He turned to Squire Fress and said, "Find Calen and Sindi. Orlos as well. They are needed. We're storming a fortress."

Chapter Twenty-four

Ayja was utterly exhausted. Her well of power was nearly empty — only flickering embers remained. All of her empowered workings were gone. She'd killed two grotesques and a flying demon. She'd killed a dozen imps and a giant spider-demon with a dozen legs. But now she had nothing left.

She couldn't even sing. Her throat was parched, and her voice was gone. Her canteen was empty. How far had she gone? Five arrowflights? Less? Sticky blood covered her leg and abdomen. The bleeding had mostly stopped, but her wounds left her terribly weakened. Fear crept down her spine like a venomous worm inching down her back and under her flesh. She couldn't shake it.

She wasn't going to make it. She wasn't going to find Darra. She shook her head in defeat, and when she did, she caught a flash of movement out of the corner of her eye. A worm. Several worms. Following her. Normally the smallest demons avoided her. Did they sense her weakness?

Taking no action is the worst action. Never give your enemies the initiative. Cam's words came to her as if he was standing next to her. He was right, of course. She had to keep moving. Alert now for the worms stalking her, she pressed onwards.

The worms were patient, silent, and very hard to see. Lizard-like and smaller than a dog, they crept close to the ground on clawed feet. When she looked at them, their forms would blur, and they'd blend into the shadows. *Are they cooperating? Or do they think me an easier meal than fighting one another? When they devour me, do they split my soul, or does the first get it all?*

Ayja licked her lips with a dry tongue. Her head throbbed. Still, she marched on. What choice did she have? She tried to sing, but it came out a croak.

The worms were closer now. *They know I don't have much longer.* She drew her sword, knowing the attack might come at any moment.

Despite the heat and humidity, she'd stopped sweating. It was a bad sign. *Where are you, Darra?*

A rock fell behind her and she raised her sword and spun. As she turned, a wave of dizziness struck her, and she nearly fell. She desperately gained her balance and looked around but saw nothing. They were close, though. She knew it.

As she searched for them, she saw a dark stain on the canyon wall. Hoping against hope, she stumbled towards it. There, from a crack in the rocks, the barest trickle of water filled a stinking, sulfurous puddle. Ayja stumbled towards the water, desperately thirsty.

A few strides from the puddle, she forced herself to stop, remembering what happened the first time she knelt over water in Dromost. Keeping her sword at the ready, she tossed a rock into the water. It splashed, filthy and stinking, but no demon emerged.

She stepped closer and heard the scrape of claws on rocks behind her. Turning, she swung blindly, and only by the barest of luck, caught a leaping worm mid-flight, cutting it in half. Two more sprang at her, but she knocked one aside with a blow from her forearm and hacked a limb from the other.

Just as she ran the wounded worm through, another leaped onto her back, clawing its way towards her head. She spun as she felt its hot breath on her neck, then slammed her back against the cliff wall, dislodging the demon. Before she could strike it, another worm jumped at her, biting her arm. Her scale armor held, but the demon shook wildly, yanking her off balance. As she fell, she threw herself atop the demon, crushing it to the ground.

Reversing her grip on her sword, she wielded it like a long dagger, impaling the worm twice before it let go of her arm. She threw herself back as the other demon charged her. Grabbing the blade near the hilt, she thrust her sword two-handed at the worm, impaling it through the mouth. She yanked her sword violently left and right as the demon thrashed on the blade.

Ayja pulled her sword free from the twitching demon and rose to her knees to face yet another charging worm. Her head spun and her vision blurred as the demon launched itself at her. She brought her sword down on the demon's head, but the blow was weak. It struck her, throwing her against the wall. She kicked the wounded demon away from her and then cut into it again, nearly severing its head. It fell to the ground, bleeding. It twitched twice and stopped moving.

Ayja struggled to draw air into her lungs as she sagged against the rocks. She had nothing remaining to her. Her well of power glimmered with the last flickering glow of aetherial light. Blood dripped from her left hand, where she'd gripped the sword blade with her bare hand. It wasn't sharp close to the grip, but in her desperation, she'd held it too far down.

She pulled her legs under her and tried to rise, but didn't have the strength. Her wounds bled anew. She would die here if Darra didn't come for her. *Unless I put myself back to sleep. Only then can I preserve my strength.* There was nowhere to hide, though. If she slept, it would be out in the open, helpless against any wandering demon.

No. I was asleep when the demon dragged me from my hiding place. It found me anyway. Or was it just an accident? Did it just happen upon me?

No choice. I have to sleep.

She tried to clear her voice to sing but couldn't. All that came out was a rasp. She was too parched even to get a note out. Without song, there'd be no sleep. Glancing to her left, she saw the rapidly decaying corpse of one of the worms, half-submerged in the puddle. Crawling closer, she dragged it free, its flesh sloughing off its bones in her hands.

Ayja was beyond being disgusted. She needed water if she was to sing. She pulled herself to the edge of the puddle, her face just a handspan from the stinking water. It had to be cleaned before she could drink. She cupped some, the foul water burning her wounded palm and fingers. She gasped in pain but then focused her mind on the tiny amount of water she held.

She twisted the aether, careful to use just the barest amount of her reserves. The moment it was clean enough to drink, she sucked the water into her mouth. It tasted terrible, but the poisons were gone.

Now I must sing. She drew a breath but began to cough. The fit went on and on until her head began to spin. Finally, she stopped but was so weak her head sank into the mud. She tried to raise it but didn't have the strength.

Somewhere, not far away, a demon screamed. And then another. Were they fighting?

"I sing..." she started, but the words were just a mumble and had no magic in them. *"I sing a song...."*

Were they even the right words? She couldn't focus. The spike of pain through her temple was unimaginable. She closed her eyes. How close were the demons?

As she retreated to her memory walk, her mind went dark.

***

238

Ayja woke to Darra's pale face and black eyes lit in the purple glow of Dromost's runes. Warmth and life flooded through her, filling her well of power and healing her wounds. She tried to speak, but all that came out was a gasp.

"What are you doing here?" Darra asked as life force continued to pour into her. How much did he have in him? The rush of power was almost painful. She tried to push his hand away, but as she grabbed his hand, she found herself paralyzed. "You need more," he said. "Don't fight me."

Then he released her from the paralysis of his touch and removed his hand from her face. "You were nearly dead, my queen."

Ayja tried and failed to speak again, pointing desperately at her throat. Darra might have healed her, but she was still desperately thirsty. He handed her the canteen, saying, "The water is dirty."

Nodding, she twisted the aether, cleansing the water. Then she drank, chugging the water until her stomach rebelled. With a sudden spasm, she bent double and vomited. Sudden dizziness overcame her and Darra had to hold her.

"Slowly," Darra said.

Ayja nodded and took a few sips. Her stomach still rumbled, but she kept it down.

"How were you found?" Darra asked.

"A demon pulled me from hiding," she said. "Even though I was asleep. It must have been by pure accident. I think, at least."

She took a deep breath and drank a little more. From where it was tucked in Darra's belt, Dromost's circles of power glowed with purple energy, and a fine mist seemed to rise from its head. Darra noticed her glance and said. "We've seen fighting — a lot of it. But we've found Vahlah's territory."

As he spoke, a demon flew down from the sky behind him. "Darra!" Ayja shouted. She reached into the aether, and her hand glowed with power, but Darra pushed it aside as he turned towards the approaching demon.

"No," he said, "It's Telea's demon."

The demon swept close, broad bat-like wings spreading wide as it cushioned its landing. From snout to tip of tail, the demon had to be five strides long.

Ayja shook her head. "It is like the dragon, Agrep, who gave the Orb of Creation to Handrin the Great." The demon's sinuous form was lithe and strong. Long black claws, dagger-like teeth, and gleaming red and black scales told her that the small demon she'd seen before was well and truly gone. This was a dangerous creature before her.

239

There is a soul in you, the demon said as it approached.

"What do you mean?" Ayja asked as she rose to her feet. Dry blood and caked mud covered her, but her wounds were healed. Her well of power was full, as well. "Of course there's a soul in me."

The demon glanced from her to Darra and back again. It reached out with a forelimb and pointed a long, curved claw at her abdomen. *Another soul. There is another soul in you.*

Fear gripped Ayja's heart as she touched her stomach through her armor. "A demon?"

Not a demon. A soul.

"I don't understand. I'm possessed? A demon is in me?"

In your world, you call it a child.

Ayja shook her head in disbelief. "No, it's impossible. How? After so long? It's been... it's been many months!"

"My queen, what does the demon mean? You can't be with child!"

I am with child? Here in Dromost? But she'd had no sign.

Ayja felt the blood drain from her face and then choked out a sob. There had been signs. She hadn't had her moon blood ever since arriving, even though they must have been in Dromost for months. And her sickness... it hadn't been lack of food or the poisonous air of Dromost. It had been the morning sickness.

"My queen? How is it possible? It's not possible!" Darra said.

Ayja put her face in her hands as tears came to her eyes. *It was possible. Orlos-*

"My queen?"

"It is true, Sir Darra," she said. "Orlos and I made love."

"How dare he take advantage of you, my queen!" Darra shouted. "Dromost take his soul!"

"No, Darra. We are in love."

"What? You can't be!" Rage filled Darra's voice. "You are too innocent. Too good."

"Stop it, Sir Darra!" Ayja snapped, glaring at him. "He and I are in love, and now it is doubly a tragedy. I have a child in me, and I am in Dromost." She turned to Telea's demon. "Why couldn't you see my baby before?"

I do not know. I can't see your soul when you sleep, either. Perhaps it was asleep before. Or some other reason. We only found you now because the second soul was awake while you slept.

"It? A boy or a girl?"

I don't know. Male and female are all the same to me. I see a difference when I look at you, but the souls within are the same.

"Darra... when you healed me... you didn't feel another presence in me?"

"My queen, I saw only your injuries. I didn't sense another presence. I... I could look again."

Ayja looked into his black eyes. Darra's face was without emotion, but she somehow felt his unhappiness. *And why wouldn't he be? Yet another challenge. Yet another burden.* Still, she nodded. "Tell me what you see."

Darra knelt beside her and took her hand. At first, his touch was cold, and then warmth flowed through her. Darra nodded. "There is a consciousness there, but no thought. Awareness, but no memory. I don't understand. I... I wasn't looking before. Or I just couldn't see it."

Tears rolled down Ayja's cheeks. "What have I done? I cannot bear a child in Dromost."

After a moment, Darra said, "You don't have to."

"What do you mean?"

"I can rid you of it, my queen. It would be painless."

Ayja's fist lashed out, striking the pyren in the face, driving him back from her. "Don't touch my child!" she shouted, the power of the aether crackling at her fingertips. "Don't you dare!"

"I only thought... you said you cannot bear a child in Dromost."

"I can't! That's why we must escape. We must!"

"I am sorry, my queen. I will do everything in my power to help you."

Ayja looked away from the pyren, her eyes going to the valley behind him. *I'm with child.* The reality of it was too much to bear. She'd closed the Dromost Gate. Helna's world was safe. All of her efforts since then had just been to survive. She hadn't wanted to die, but if she had, she would have died knowing that her friends and loved ones were safe. Now though... now it wasn't just her. Now she had a child within her. A child that every demon in Dromost wished to consume.

"My queen, we must move on," Darra said. "More demons will come. The road ahead should be clear of the largest demons, at the least."

"Don't talk to me."

He stood and walked a few strides from her, his eyes facing up the valley. Ayja closed her eyes and imagined her home, remembering the joy she'd known growing up with Cam. Now she was pregnant with a child of her own, but her child would never know the same happiness she'd experienced. *Demons will consume her. She... I already think of her as my daughter.*

"My queen... we cannot stay. The demons will come for you."

Wordlessly, Ayja stood. Darra stepped close and offered Forsvar and Dromost to her. She felt the reassuring protection of the Godshield as she slipped it onto her arm. Dromost hummed with power, weightless in her hand. All six of the Godhammer's soul circles glowed. Even her well of power was full, or nearly so... with every passing heartbeat, her body drew strength from the well to sustain her... and her unborn child.

"How far, Darra?" she asked, not looking at him.

"Several days journey, my queen."

"And so we just walk into the veden's territory and demand an audience?"

"We do."

"And when he sends his minions to attack us?"

"We fight, my queen."

Offer Dromost to him, the demon said. *He will give you anything for it.*

"Why won't he just take it?"

You are bright with power. He will fear to fight you. Why risk it when he can have it without a fight?

"We have no other choice, do we, my queen?"

Ayja faced Darra. "Don't threaten my child again, Sir Darra."

"My life is yours, my queen. I will do all in my power to protect you and your unborn child. I am sorry I suggested otherwise."

As they started up the valley, Ayja turned to Telea's demon and said, "I must turn the Emerald Prison into the Emerald Gate. I don't even know if that is possible."

Did you see the runes at the Dromost Gate?

"I did. I have them in my memory walk." Ayja had seen both the runes that had opened the gate as well as the runes Shulazar had written in his own blood to create the protective barrier. She'd studied them in her memory walk.

Good. Very good. I didn't see them when I was there.

"Will the runes be enough?"

We don't have to create a portal. It is already there, open but blocked. Orlos's spiridus went through it when he accidentally entered the Emerald Prison. I know this. I saw it. Perhaps, with our combined knowledge, we can craft an opening that will let you through.

"We must make certain it closes behind us," Darra said. "We can't leave an opening between Dromost and Helna's world."

Of course. That can all be done in the crafting. It will be careful work.

They continued down the canyon for some interminable time. Darra caught four worms that were too slow to recognize the soulless threat approaching them. He drew their life force and gave it all to Ayja. The worms provided enough life force to sustain her and even to keep her well of power nearly full. As they marched, Telea's demon flew overhead, keeping watch for them.

The longer they journeyed, the more Ayja began to worry about what she'd do when she finally had to sleep. Would the child within her sleep as well? Did she sleep now? Then Ayja realized she could ask Telea's demon. It could sense her daughter's soul when she was awake.

Finally, Ayja waved the demon down and asked it if it could see her daughter. *You are both very bright,* the demon said. *You can be seen from far away. Your child is very often unseen, though, and for long stretches of time. I cannot see it now.*

"Her," Ayja said, convinced, somehow, that she bore a daughter. "If that is the case, I think I should sleep. While my well of power is full, my mind is exhausted. Darra, you and the demon must stand watch over me while I rest."

I should move some distance off, the demon said. *I am no longer a worm. Other demons will sense my presence and be drawn here.*

"I will watch you as you sleep, my queen," Darra said.

They found a protected nook in the cliff wall where Ayja could rest. Darra took Dromost, but Ayja would sleep with Forsvar next to her.

I will return when your child awakens, the demon said as it flew off.

"Darra," Ayja said as she curled into the crevice, "I was too short with you. Please know that I am grateful for everything you've done. I am in debt to you for both my life and that of my daughter."

"Sleep, my queen. You give meaning to my soulless life. I... I am utterly devoted to your service."

"Thank you, Sir Darra. When we escape this place, I will give you anything... everything."

"It isn't necessary, my queen. And what I want, you cannot give me," he said. She closed her eyes and retreated into her memory walk. *He wishes to be human again, but it cannot be done. How can a lost soul be returned?*

She woke moments later to Darra's hand on her shoulder. "Arise, my queen. The demon says your daughter is awake."

"So soon?" Ayja asked, her hand slipping under her armor and touching her abdomen.

"It has been many hours at least," he said, looking up at a dark sky that knew nothing of light or dark or the passage of time. The dragon-like demon perched on a boulder nearby. Was it larger than before?

"Telea's demon had a few fights while you slept, but nothing accosted you."

"Thank you for protecting me. I do feel better."

243

After gulping from her canteen, they began their journey anew. She was careful now, not to drink too much at any time. *What is this doing to my daughter? No food. Little sleep. Surviving on magic alone while I waste away. What harm am I doing her?*

Her thoughts plagued her as they walked arrowflight after arrowflight. "Why it is so different here, Darra? I want to say that I am starting to forget what a big demon looks like. We've seen only worms."

"This canyon is fairly inaccessible," Darra said. "And Telea's demon and I killed several larger demons when we passed this way before. I think the bigger reason is that Vahlah must keep this region under his control."

"I am worried, Darra. This is a desperate step we are taking."

"It is a bold step, my queen."

They traveled some time more through very rugged terrain when Ayja heard a cry from far overhead and saw Telea's demon diving for them, six smaller demons in pursuit. She raised Forsvar and held Dromost ready. Closer and closer, the demons came. Would they catch Telea's demon? Ayja began to spin a ring of fire, but suddenly, when they were only some fifty strides away, the pursuing demons veered off, rapidly climbing overhead. Telea's demon circled and landed behind Ayja and Darra.

They are from Vahlah's scouts. Look! That one flies back to report.

"How close are we?"

Vahlah is close. We will find more of his soldiers soon.

The demon was right. After only an arrowflight, they came upon a patrol of twenty demons. They were unlike any demons Ayja had yet seen. Short and hunched, but human-like with long arms, they wore full suits of armor — the first demons she'd ever seen in harness. Their armor was forged of large plates with mail covering any gaps. At first glance, she thought it heavier and more complete than any armor she'd ever seen.

The demons were very uniform in appearance, at least in their body shapes and sizes. Their faces, though, had variations. Some had tusks, while others had horns. One had only one eye in the center of its head.

These demons were armed as well. They had swords at their waists and held small, round shields. Each held a small javelin or long dart as well. They had no fabric or leather as clothing or as any part of their armor. All of the straps, buckles, and belts were made of fine metal mesh or had metal clasps in their place.

The demons halted fifty strides from Ayja before warily approaching to a distance of twenty strides. She wondered at the range of their iron darts. Forsvar would stop them, but she worried for Darra, who had no shield. She moved closer to him so that she could cover him if she had to.

"They aren't attacking," Darra said.

There are more overhead, Telea's demon said. *Twelve of them.*

Ayja glanced at the demons circling overhead and shifted her grip on Forsvar as sweat dripped from her brow. They weren't attacking. No demons had ever had such discipline before. *They were commanded not to attack.*

This was it. This was their chance. If they failed here — if they failed to parlay with Vahlah — all was lost. She and her child would die in Dromost, their souls consumed by demons.

Clearing her throat, she glanced at Telea's demon and said, "Can you tell them that we wish to speak with Vahlah? Tell them that Handrin the Great's heir is here and that she is an elementar who wields Forsvar and Dromost. Tell them that I want to speak with him and make peace with him."

Telea's demon crept closer to the line of demons. No, not a line... they stood in two ranks... like soldiers. The realization made Ayja more nervous than she'd been before. After a few moments, Telea's demon turned and faced Ayja.

Vahlah knows. Vahlah comes.

Chapter Twenty-five

Orlos crept along a narrow path through dark, steep wooded hills. He followed three Drinker warriors in short mail haubergeons and fur vests. Atu led them. She was very tall and pretty but for a wicked scar running from above her left eye and down to her chin. Behind him came Sindi and Calen and another nine Drinkers. Further back, hundreds of Drinkers and Landomeri crept silently through the darkness. A few Belenese singers and healers had come as well, the threat of demons and summoning too great to be ignored.

Orlos's stepfather, Kael, would have led them, but he'd taken one hundred Landomeri forward with the king for the main assault. Sindi had stepped into his place, leading the Landomeri detachment accompanying the Drinkers for their surprise attack. It was Orlos's place to be their silent, invisible scout.

Atu held up her hand, and everyone stopped and sank to their knees. She waved Orlos closer. "They say you sneak good," she whispered in heavily accented Belenese. "No one see you."

Orlos nodded. "That's right."

She pointed down the path. They were in a deep gorge with a cliff to their right and a rugged, boulder-strewn valley to their left. "Maybe summoners ahead? You go and see. Go to tunnel. Is blocked? Look up." She pointed to the overhanging cliff. "Maybe summoners above? Understand?"

"I understand," Orlos said, pretty sure he understood.

"Will it do any good to tell you to be careful?" Calen asked.

"Probably not." Orlos stepped ahead of the Drinkers and started down the path. After he'd gone a few strides, he summoned his spiridus cloak and felt the familiar comfort of its invisibility. It was pitch dark in the forest, the clouds and the overhanging cliff cutting off all moonlight, but Orlos's spiridus vision let him see a world of grays and blacks and whites.

Stepping carefully, he made his way forward. The forest was eerily silent. Even the scattered raindrops made no noise as they fell on the carpet of fallen pine needles. He wanted to move slowly and silently but knew that they planned to reach the back of the fortress by dawn. Five hundred men and women had to make it down the narrow trail, and they all waited upon him.

He'd only gone a short way when the path turned to the left, and he spotted a ragged cave in the cliff face. He paused and looked up, spotting a stone wall atop the cliff. Here was a natural choke point. A few soldiers hurling stones could hold an army for hours while sending word back to the fortress for support.

There was no one there. Not that he could see. And no glow of a campfire from above. The tunnel wasn't barricaded, either. Was it abandoned? Or was it a trap? Nocking an arrow to his bow, he advanced to the tunnel entrance. Rivulets of water dripped over the entrance. Ferns clung to the rock face. It seemed as if nobody had passed in ages. He glanced behind him. Go back and tell the others it was clear?

The tunnel wasn't long. Only ten strides. He'd go through and check the other side to make certain it was clear and then go back. Water dripped on his head as he made his way through. For all his bravado in front of Calen, his heart pounded. He feared at every moment that someone might spring out at him. Despite the chill air, sweat dripped down his brow as he exited the far side.

Still nothing. No sound. No movement. Off to his right, the cliff face was less steep. Rough cut stairs twisted their way up the rock face. *Go back or check a little further?* He glanced behind him, towards the safety of the column. But he'd have done them no good if an enemy still lurked at the top of the cliff.

The steps were slick with water and moldering pine needles. His steps were silent, though. Near the top, the stairs turned left and became especially steep. Then his mail shirt caught on something projecting from the rock, jabbing him painfully through the steel rings. Clenching his teeth, he turned to see what it was.

Jammed into a crack on the cliff face was a thin, sharp iron spike. Around the spike, on the stone, runes were drawn, glowing slightly under his spiridus vision. A chill of fear went down Orlos's spine, so strong that he nearly sank to his knees.

A demon spike. He's seen one before. Zaeim, the old summoner at the Temple of Dromost, had driven one into the cliff above the temple's little harbor. Orlos had watched as he'd slammed his palm onto the spike before stabbing himself with a dagger, turning himself into a sacrifice demon.

Tik-tik-tik-tik-tik. From above him, over the edge of cliff, Orlos heard a high pitched series of sounds. Then the snap of a twig. *A demon. A sacrifice demon.* He drew a slow, deep breath, shrinking deeper into his spiridus cloak. Here he was, at the demon's spike — the very center of the demon's territory.

Tik-tik-tik-tik-tik.

The sound was closer now — a little behind him. Slowly, Orlos turned, and as he did, his arrowhead scraped on the rock wall. Something moved above him, then stopped.

Tik-tik-tik-tik-tik. The sound came again — sharp clicks piercing the damp air.

Orlos looked up. Just five strides behind him, the demon crept over the cliff edge. Man-shaped, it clung impossibly to the cliff face, its fingers splayed wide as they clutched the stone. The clothes the man had once worn were just shredded fragments now, and where his skin was exposed, it seemed his flesh had been turned inside out. Exposed veins throbbed and glistened with blood. Tendons and muscles flexed and moved in plain sight.

Tik-tik-tik-tik-tik.

The demon turned to face him, and Orlos took a horrified step backward. The creature had no eyes. Two long, narrow nostrils ran from above its fang-filled maw to the top of its forehead. They suddenly flared wide, drawing in a deep breath. Then its fleshy, cat-like ears, which had been drawn against its head, flapped wide and turned to face him.

Tik-tik-tik-tik-tik.

Blind. Blind like a bat, but it hears and smells. It knows I'm close. The turn in the stairs partially hid Orlos from the demon. *How near does it have to be before it pounces?*

The demon lifted a hand and shifted closer to Orlos. Its nostrils opened wide, drawing another breath. Orlos had to be silent — his spiridus cloak meant nothing against a blind demon. The spike was right next to him. What had Telea said before? If the spike is drawn from the rock, the demon will be destroyed? Or if he threw it, the demon will have to follow? But how deep was the spike sunk into the rock? What if he couldn't draw it out?

He shifted his weight and lifted his foot.

Tik-tik-tik-tik-tik.

The demon focused on him now. It gripped the rock and gathered its haunches under it. Orlos drew his bow and loosed as the demon leaped. He reached for the spike, but the demon crashed into him, throwing him to the stairs.

They both slid on the steps, nearly falling into the gorge below, but the demon caught hold of the wall as it lunged at him. Orlos jammed his longbow stave into the demon's mouth, desperately trying to force it away. The demon twisted and pulled, trying to get its mouth free, but Orlos kept jamming the bow stave hard against the demon's face. Finally, the bow exploded with a terrible *crack*, a shard of the bow striking Orlos's brow.

For a moment, both were stunned, and then Orlos snatched his hunting knife from its sheath and stabbed the demon in its neck. Stinking, hot blood sprayed from the wound as the demon lunged again. Orlos dropped the broken bow and clutched the demon's slippery neck, trying to force its jaws away. It was far too strong, and its fangs drew inexorably closer.

Orlos stabbed again and again with his knife until the demon released its hold on the cliff to stop the long blade from striking it. The pair slid down the stairs as the demon blindly grasped for Orlos's knife hand. Orlos avoided its clutches and stabbed the creature in the chest. They were falling faster now, though, and they'd soon tumble from the cliff.

Seeing his chance, Orlos stuck out his foot, halting his descent. Then, he put his other boot against the demon and pushed. The demon clutched at him and then screeched as it fell free, toppling out of sight and landing with a crunch on the path below.

Breath heaving, Orlos peered over the edge only to see the demon righting itself. One arm was clearly wounded and not functioning well, but still, the demon raced up the wall. Drawing his sword, Orlos ran up the stairs to the spike. He drew his sword and brought it down on the spike with all his strength. There was a brilliant flash, and his sword shattered, but the spike flew from the cliff, struck the stair, and spun off into the darkness.

The demon wailed and turned, leaping after the spike. Both landed at the base of the cliff. The demon clutched at the spike, holding it high above its head, but then it wailed again and began to shimmer and collapse upon itself. The demon appeared to fall into the spike, and then it disappeared.

Orlos tossed his sword hilt aside and carefully made his way down the stairs, listening for the approach of any more demons, but hardly able to hear over the blood rushing through his ears. He had nearly reached the bottom when Calen, Sindi, and the Drinkers rushed through the tunnel.

"I'm here!" Orlos shouted.

"What happened?" Sindi asked. "We heard a demon."

"There was one," Orlos said, his heart still pounding. "Watch out; its spike is on the ground." He pointed to where it lay, glowing orange, but rapidly cooling.

"You kill demon?" Atu asked.

"I guess. Yes," he said, breathing heavily.

She struck him hard on the shoulder with her fist. "Good." She smiled. "You good Drinker."

"Are there more defenders?" Calen asked.

"No one else that I saw." He faced Atu and said in Belenese, "No summoners. Just the demon."

"If not here, no one else," Atu said. "We go rest of way and attack fort. They not know we come, I think." She knelt near the spike, and using her dagger, pushed it into a puddle where it hissed and steamed. After a few moments, she picked it up in her gloved hand. "I keep this safe. Make demon killing dart with it," she said with a smile.

They pushed on through the night. The terrain was easier here, as they followed a broad ridge leading to the back of the fortress. The Drinkers led the Landomeri through a pine forest and then stopped at its edge. Through the boughs, they made out the looming wall of the fortress ahead of them. There were no lights — just the dark mass of the walls.

Orlos crouched by a tree. His thoughts went to the demon. His invisibility had always protected him. Now he felt vulnerable in a way he'd never felt before. If he hadn't snagged his sleeve on the spike, the demon would certainly have killed him.

"Orlos!" Sindi said, making him jump at the closeness of her voice.

"What?"

"I was talking to you."

He shook his head in a futile effort to clear his memory of the demon.

"Can you go forward again?" Sindi asked. "Atu wants you to see how many defenders are on the wall and in the castle."

Orlos frowned and looked back towards the fortress. What if there were more of those demons there? What if there were demons who could see him under his spiridus cloak? "There'd be an alarm," he said. "We'd know if we'd been spotted. And we'll see them well enough in the morning."

"We might see them on the wall, but we need to know what's behind it," Sindi said. "You're the best one to do it."

Orlos didn't reply. He knew he was the only person for the task, no matter how much he didn't want to do it. He glanced around as more Landomeri and Drinkers gathered in the forest. They needed him to go forward.

He took a deep breath and nodded.

250

Standing, Orlos glanced around for his bow before remembering that it had shattered in his fight with the demon. His sword as well.

"You can take mine," Sindi said, realizing his plight.

Orlos shook his head as he unbuckled his quiver and placed it on the ground. "Share my arrows with Calen. A bow will just get in my way if I'm going to climb that wall. And this is useless now," he said as he untied his empty sword scabbard from his belt. The only weapon remaining was his long hunting knife.

Orlos drew in a deep breath. All around him, water dripped from pine needles. They were far from the arid hills of Belen now. The Summoned Lands were a strange, dark place — damp and lush and filled with demons. Well, the possibility of demons. "I'll come back soon."

Sindi put her hand on his arm. "Just see what you can see and come back."

Orlos frowned and looked away. "You ask me to sneak into a summoner fortress and then tell me not to take any risks? The two don't go together, Sindi."

"You know what I mean, Orlos. Just look and come back. Nothing more."

He nodded as he pulled away from her. Without another word, he drew his spiridus cloak over him.

Slowly, carefully, he crept out of the forest towards the fortress walls. They weren't tall, only six or seven strides. They weren't far away, either. The defenders hadn't put much effort into keeping the encroaching trees from pushing close.

There was a small gate here. At first, he spied no defenders, but as he made his way along the wall, he heard the clink of metal and then something scraping on stone. He feared a demon at first but then heard a man cough.

As he looked up, the gentle wind shifted, bringing the awful stench of death and decay to him. It was so wretched that he nearly vomited at it and had to take a knee to steady himself. He remembered that Belen's singers had been massacred here. Had the bodies not been disposed of?

The sentry above him moved off, back towards the gate. Orlos continued along the wall until he came to a corner. The wall was higher here, the ground dropping off to his right, but the wall wasn't in good repair, and he thought he might be able to climb it.

After listening for a few heartbeats, he started up. The climb was more difficult than he expected. The cracks and chinks between the stones were smaller than they looked, and it was hard to find footholds. By the time he reached the top, his forearms burned, and it was hard to stay focused and keep his spiridus cloak around him.

Still, he paused and listened before pulling himself up to the parapet. The stench of death was even worse here, but at least there were no guards close by. The man he'd heard was well down the wall, close to the gatehouse.

The fortress had no inner wall, its strength lying in the steep approaches and difficult terrain. Within the confines of the fort were a dozen buildings, some of them fortified structures of stone. Others had been wood but were destroyed by fire. As he looked closer, he saw that even the stone buildings had been ravaged by fire.

Everywhere around the buildings lay the burned and mutilated bodies of the Belenese singers who'd been massacred there.

The summoners had piled the blackened bodies in great heaps but had made no effort to bury them or to remove them from the fortress. How long had they been there? A month or more? It was more horrible than seeing Telea's army of the dead hacked to death and spread across a broad field.

I will never leave Landomere again. Please, Helna, let me get home again.

Only a few summoners were awake, most of them patrolling the walls. Across the fortress, Orlos saw summoner tents pitched in a broad, open area. There couldn't be that many of them — perhaps a few hundred. How could they stand the smell? He neither saw nor heard any signs of demons.

We can take this fortress now. The summoners had no idea that the Landomeri and Drinkers had gotten behind them. If they just rushed the wall, they'd be over it before the enemy would be out of their tents. He glanced into the sky. How far away was the dawn?

Moving as quickly as he dared, Orlos climbed back down the wall and crept back to his companions. "They're not expecting us," he said as he reappeared. Atu gave a startled jerk, reaching for her sword. She didn't draw it though, casually placing her hand on the pommel as if she'd never been surprised.

"There are only a few of them on watch," Orlos continued. "And most of those are looking out over the valley. If we rush the wall, we can easily take it. I don't think there are that many defenders in the entire fortress. We might even capture it before Handrin and Nidon can attack from below."

Atu looked up to the lightening sky. "We nearly all here," she said in broken Belenese. "We attack as soon as archers see. Maybe you right and we take fort without help."

"We will tell the Landomeri to get ready," Sindi said with a nod to Calen. "We'll clear the walls for you and then follow you up."

Atu nodded.

"I'll ask the singers to spread themselves out," Telea said. "We'll be too thin to destroy any powerful demons, but at least we'll weaken them and leave them vulnerable."

"Once the Landomeri are on the wall, the summoners will be defenseless," Orlos said. "There's little cover on the grounds of the fort."

"You've done well, Orlos," Calen said.

"Yes, good," Atu said.

The others departed to spread word of their plans, leaving Orlos to contemplate the walls ahead of them. The Drinkers had brought ropes and grapnels, and he was certain they'd quickly scale the walls. With the Landomeri loosing arrows overhead, the attack couldn't fail. *As long as no warning cry is sounded before we are ready to attack.*

Water drops gathered and fell from pine needles as the Drinkers and Landomeri near him prepared for the assault. Anxious to attack, they crept closer and closer to the edge of the woods. Orlos wanted to tell them to pull back — that their eagerness might spoil the attack. There were far too many, though, and the attack was imminent.

If some signal was given, Orlos never saw it. Silently, the Drinkers rose from the shelter of the trees and rushed forward. Most held bucklers and javelins, but many had coiled ropes and grappling hooks. Behind them came the Landomeri, arrows nocked. Orlos ran forward, realizing too late that he only had the knife at his belt.

The first shout only came when the lead Drinkers were already at the base of the wall. The cry was short-lived, as three arrows struck the sentry, killing him.

Orlos's hands shook and his heart raced. They were doing it! Grappling hooks rose and clanked on the parapets. Drinkers were already climbing. A third of the Landomeri held back, their bows held ready and covering the walls, while the rest joined the Drinkers for the assault.

Orlos ran to where he'd climbed the wall before. More shouts rose from within the fort. From atop the wall, Drinkers hurled javelins at unseen defenders. Others disappeared as they charged into the fort itself. Moments later, the first Landomeri climbed atop the wall. Soon, it was Orlos's turn. Helping hands pulled him up.

There was chaos within. Defenders raced from the front walls while more scrambled from their tents. The Drinkers were already amongst them, hurling javelins and cutting others down with swords. From their perch on the rear wall, the Landomeri loosed scores of arrows into hapless defenders. Only one small group of Drommarians managed to form themselves into a shield wall, but they would soon be surrounded.

With no weapons, Orlos could only watch. They were taking the fortress! He even forgot the stench of death.

Then his eyes fell upon a mound of the blackened, burned dead. They were moving. Not just one figure, but many. The whole mass was writhing. Soon the dead began to stand. *The dead. Silent brothers!*

"Watch out!" Orlos shouted. "The dead are rising!"

Awakened from their unnatural slumber, the dead rose and fell upon the Drinkers, grasping with cold hands, grappling them to the ground and breaking their limbs and wrenching their weapons from them.

The Drinkers were fearless demon fighters. The dead held no new terror for them. With spear, javelin, and sword, they stabbed and hacked at the undead. Their blows, though, did little to stem the tide.

From the middle of the fight, Atu shouted orders, and the Drinkers retreated for the wall.

"Swing for their heads!" Orlos shouted. "Shoot for their heads!" He ran down the wall, spreading the word. The Landomeri understood, and arrows began to pierce skulls and eye sockets. It was not easy. The dead didn't have the sense to duck and weave, but even then, shooting someone in the head during a melee was no easy shot, even for the Landomeri.

The Drinkers, however, weren't listening to him, or couldn't hear him, even though they now fought at the very base of the wall. Orlos pushed himself through the Landomeri crowding the wall until he reached a section above Atu.

"Atu! Strike them in the head!" he shouted. "Atu, do you hear me? Strike them in the head!"

For a moment, it seemed she glanced over her shoulder, and then she shouted, *"Kop! Kop torgu! Kop torgu!"*

The shout went up among the Drinkers, and as it did, the men and women stopped stabbing their spears into dead chests or hacking at arms with their swords. The sounds and sights were gruesome as swords cracked into skulls or javelin tips plunged into them. Weeks-dead brains and black blood splattered the Drinkers as the undead advance slowed.

The fight was not won, though. With only bucklers and swords, the Drinkers couldn't form a shield-wall and keep the undead at bay. The dead grasped at arms and bucklers, pulling Drinkers into their ranks where they were overcome and savaged.

Atop the wall, singers and healers raised their voices in song, sending strength and courage flowing through the Drinkers beneath them. Any other group of people, Orlos was certain, could not have stood so bravely against the stinking, rotting host of the undead. Even for all their bravery, how long could they fight?

The Landomeri next to Orlos grunted in pain and sagged to the parapet, the wooden fletching of a bolt protruding from his chest. Two more Landomeri fell nearby. Orlos looked up to see that the Drommarians had formed up behind the undead and were shooting bolts into the exposed Landomeri on the wall. Seeing the threat, the Landomeri lifted their aim and loosed arrows at the Drommarians.

It was an unfair fight, though. Pavisers stood in front of the crossbowmen and women, protecting them with their large shields, while the Landomeri stood on the walkway, totally exposed. And now, with the Landomeri arrows no longer slamming into them from above, the undead advanced even more strongly into the beleaguered Drinkers.

Orlos knelt and took the longbow from the fallen man next to him. There were only five arrows in his quiver. He looked around and saw many of the Landomeri in the same situation.

"Atu, you must retreat!" Orlos shouted. "We have no more arrows!"

The gore-covered warrior turned at his shout, only then becoming aware of the toll the Drommarian crossbows were taking on the Landomeri.

"Landomeri, go!" she shouted in reply. Then she turned to the Drinkers near her, calling out orders in her own language before plunging back into the fight.

"Loose your last arrows and then retreat," Orlos said to the Landomeri near him. "Spread the word."

They had lost. The Drommarians had both demons and the dead at their call. The Devil's Watch still stood. Orlos yanked the five arrows from the quiver and stuffed them through his belt. He nocked an arrow and looked over the heads of the undead for one of the Drommarians.

The Drommarians knew the danger. Each time they shot a bolt, they quickly dodged back behind a pavise. Orlos loosed two arrows to no effect. Below him, the Drinkers retreated through the newly opened gate. Still, many were trapped inside.

Well behind the Drommarian crossbowmen, Orlos saw a summoner in his long red robes. The man clutched his head and bent double, before rising again. He wasn't wounded but appeared in great pain. He thrust an arm towards the Landomeri, then suddenly clutched the sides of his head.

Orlos remembered Telea, bent double in pain amid her Army of the Dead. *He's controlling them.*

Orlos nocked an arrow and let fly. It was a long shot, and the arrow arced high before plummeting and striking the man through his shoulder. The summoner spun and fell to the ground. As he did, a quarter or more of the undead suddenly jerked and twisted to the side. Then they stopped moving altogether, standing and swaying instead. The Drinkers showed them no mercy, hacking into them with increased fervor.

"Aim for the summoners!" Orlos shouted to the Landomeri near him. "The ones in the robes behind the crossbows." He spotted another just behind the crossbowmen, but the woman ducked out of sight before he could loose at her. Further back, another summoner was struck and fell dead, but now they realized the danger and hid behind the pavisers.

The respite had given many of the Drinkers time to escape the fortress but not all. Many would die in the retreat. Orlos loosed the last of his arrows into the Drommarians but only managed to wound one of the pavisers. With no arrows and no sword, there was little he could do, but he was unwilling to leave anyone behind on the wall. When he saw Calen attempting to help a wounded Landomeri, he rushed to help.

"You have to get out of here, Orlos," Calen said. "The battle is lost."

"As soon as we get him off the wall."

The fighting grew closer as the two of them lowered the wounded Landomeri to waiting hands on the far side. Orlos glanced over his shoulder only to see a desperate rear-guard of Drinkers holding the dead back from the gate. Others held the stairs leading to the wall. But what if the dead pursued them? What if the summoners raised some of the dead Drinkers and Landomeri?

"We have to kill the summoners," Orlos said. Catching sight of a half-full quiver laying under a dead Landomeri, he snatched up some arrows and pushed them through his belt. "I'll circle behind them."

Calen grabbed him by the arm, jerking him back. "No! You'll leave now."

Blaring horns and shouts pulled their attention to the far side of the fortress. There was fighting at the front wall. Then Saladoran knights in their red tabards appeared. Orlos saw King Handrin and Nidon and the Knights of the House. The king held the Orb of Creation in his hand. It blazed with brilliant golden light as a wall of fire washed over the fortresses defenders.

Orlos let out a whoop as the fort's defenders were thrown into confusion by the sudden assault. So focused were they on the Drinkers and Landomeri, the defenders had let the Saladorans take the front wall.

"They're here, Calen! We've won!"

Calen gave him a grim nod. "This battle, at least."

Chapter Twenty-six

Vahlah dwarfed the demon soldiers around him. He was three strides tall, at least, and nearly human in form and shape. The closer he came, though, the less human he appeared. Two long, black horns protruded from his forehead and a shorter one from his chin as well. Enormous wings were furled at his back.

Here was a creature out of legend. One of the veden who had battled Handrin the Great and his human followers for dominion of Helna's world.

Vahlah's skin was dark gray, like stone, although a haubergeon of fine mail mostly covered it. The armor had a small round breastplate, too small to be functional unless an enemy aimed a blow at it. It was engraved with concentric circles of runes and glowed with aetherial power.

He held a long iron spear in clawed hands that, like his armor, glowed in the aether. Not with the same power as Forsvar or Dromost but potent nonetheless. Had Vahlah crafted them himself? Ayja was certain of it and suddenly feared the power of the ancient veden.

Dozens of demon soldiers in heavy armor marched with the Vahlah. Their armor was far more complete than his, but then they didn't have wings. She supposed heavy armor would make Vahlah too heavy to fly. Another dozen flying demons joined those already circling overhead.

"You have come to finish what the spiridus began so long ago?" Vahlah asked. Ayja was shocked that he didn't speak in her mind like the other demons, and even more shocked that he spoke High Saladoran, although with an odd, harsh accent.

"I don't understand," Ayja said. She stood tall and tried to put up a bold front. She wondered for a moment at her appearance. Her armor was rent and filth covered her. She carried two Gifts of the Gods, though, and the veden hadn't yet attacked. "What are you talking about?"

"The spiridus attempted to exterminate my race. Are you here to finish their work? Or have you come to free them? You will not succeed in either task."

"I came to close the Dromost Gate," Ayja said. "I succeeded. I am not here for you or the spiridus."

The veden gave her a long, baleful gaze. "I heard that the gate was closed. Why are you here then, Child of Handrin?"

Ayja stood tall. "I wish to depart through the Emerald Gate."

The veden laughed a deep laugh. "Oh, you are trapped in Dromost? Such a shame for you — and the child within you."

"If I'd known... I might have found another way." She paused. "I'm hiding nothing from you. I have no ill will for you. I did not mean to trap myself here, but it happened. I did not know that I was with child, but I am. I wish to go home, and you are my means of getting there."

"And what if I say no?"

Ayja held up the Godhammer's glowing head. The six circles still pulsed with purple light. "Do you know what happens when the Godhammer steals the spirits of the slain? Those souls are consumed when Dromost next strikes. That strike is filled with the power of the dark god himself, and the spirits are consumed, never to be reborn."

"You threaten me?" Vahlah asked.

"I come to offer you a trade. The Godhammer, Dromost, in exchange for passage through the Emerald Gate."

Sweat dripped down Ayja's brow, but she didn't dare move to wipe it away. She fixed the veden's gaze with her own, willing him to believe her words. Willing him to fear the power she wielded.

The veden laughed a long, rich laugh. "You are a bold one! What if I take it from you? Forsvar as well?"

Ayja felt her silver rage rise within her. Lightning flickered across Forsvar's face. "Then let us waste no time," Ayja said. "I hate this demon-infested world. I will leave through the Emerald Prison or perish in battle. I wield two Gifts of the Gods, and I am the most powerful elementar in Helna's green world. You will die."

Vahlah gave her a long look, no longer laughing. "To let you through the prison costs me nothing. To fight you... well, who knows what the cost would be? It certainly would be glorious." He paused a moment regarding her. "No, Child of Handrin, I think I will take your bargain. But how can you be certain what you wish to do is even possible? The Emerald Prison is not a gate. It is one way. It only leads to Dromost."

"I know the magic of the Dromost Gate," Ayja said. "I can unlock the Emerald Gate."

"A gate is not easy to open. The cost in spirits will be huge. To imprison the spiridus cost the lives of every living male veden. So powerful was our will for revenge; we were willing to do such a thing."

"How badly do you want Dromost?" Ayja asked, holding up the glowing Godhammer. "If you help open the gate, it is yours."

The veden stared at her for several heartbeats. "I will have to drain almost all the life force from the spiridus. They are an important resource for me. It will take a long time for them to regenerate."

"And how powerful will the Godhammer make you here?"

"I will rule all Dromost with the Godhammer in my hand."

"It is worth it then, isn't it? Do we have a deal?"

"We do, Child of Handrin." He paused and cocked his head to one side. "Your name? You know mine."

"I am Ayja, Elementar Princess of Salador. This is Sir Darra, my champion."

"And your demon friend?"

"Is nameless."

"A wise demon. What does it want? You will take it to Helna with you?"

"Only Sir Darra and I will return to Helna's world. The demon will remain here. It will assist in the crafting of the gate and wishes only to be paid in spirits. Darra and I will need to be given demons to draw life from as well."

Vahlah nodded. "I wondered how you sustained yourselves." He smiled. "Spirits and demons I can give you." He glanced at Telea's demon. "A demon who knows runes? Perhaps after you've departed, I might have use of a rune-wielding demon in my court. Come, join me, and we shall visit this Emerald Gate you wish to create."

Despite her trepidation, Ayja forced herself to march forward into the face of the veden and his host of demons. *Audacity. Audacity. Audacity.* She had no other choice now. There could be no half measures. Darra was at her side, and Telea's demon followed close behind.

You shouldn't have told Vahlah that I know runes, Telea's demon said in her mind.

You should have warned me, Ayja replied.

It was a mistake. I should have thought of it.

How do you know runes if demons don't know them or use them?

There was a brief pause, and then the demon said, *I learned them in the Summoned Lands. I possessed a summoner for many many years. If Vahlah asks again, tell him that.*

Is it true? Does it matter?

Very much.

259

Ahead of them, Ayja saw a massive iron gate blocking the canyon. There were two stone towers to either side of it. It was the first construction she'd seen in Dromost. There were more demon soldiers there. How many did Vahlah have in his service? Hundreds? Thousands? Even with her well of power filled, Ayja couldn't fight so many.

Did Vahlah realize it? She couldn't show him any fear. The moment he thought he could take the Two Gifts from her, he would pounce. She was certain of it.

As they approached, the gates squaled in ungreased agony as they opened. Ayja swallowed against her fear. There would be no going back now. She wasn't even sure they could fight their way out as it was.

Audacity, she thought to herself.

The canyon opened wider as they passed through the gate. Jagged cliffs rose on either side of them. Dozens of tunnels, all at various heights, entered the cliffs. There were stairs to some. She saw flying demons landing at others.

"My fortress," Vahlah said over his shoulder. "Seat of my power." Behind them, the gates screamed as they drew closed.

"Your demons are so similar," Ayja said. "They are unlike the other demons I've seen. Every other demon I've ever seen has been unique."

Vahlah paused and smiled a pointy-toothed smile. "How can one have an army with demons of every shape and size? Should I tell my armorers to make harness and weapons individualized for every demon? What a foolish waste. No, when I came to Dromost, I brought some things with me. Runes, metal craft, and stone craft. Discipline and order. I tell my demons how many spirits they may consume and how they may develop."

"And they agree?"

"They agree, or they become food."

"How have you not already taken over all of Dromost?"

"There are powerful princes out there," he said with a wave of his hand. "We are constantly at war. Against each other. Against me. To expand too quickly would invite many enemies to unite against me. Come now, we're almost to my prized possession."

They marched further up the canyon. There was a bend ahead, and a hazy green light shone off the canyon walls. As they turned the corner, the spiridus prison came into sight.

For a few heartbeats, Ayja was aware of nothing but the brilliant green glow of the prison. A column of light some thirty strides wide and forty or so strides tall, the Emerald Prison was centered on a blood-red crystal stump embedded on an island of rock. Within the column, thousands upon thousands of bright silver-green lights flashed and swirled as they flew in mesmerizing patterns. It reminded Ayja of the schools of tiny fish she'd seen swimming when she'd been aboard the *Summer Swan.*

Suddenly, like a hammer blow, thousands of voices called out to her as one. *Save us!*

Ayja stumbled and would have fallen if Darra hadn't caught her by the arm.

"Pathetic, aren't they," Vahlah said, staring into the prison. Ayja righted herself without the veden noticing. Still, the voices called out to her. They were filled with fear and pain but all cried out the same thing. *Save us!*

Ayja retreated into her memory walk, desperately attempting to escape the overwhelming waves of sadness washing over her. Darra took her hand. *What's wrong?* He asked.

Can't you hear them? The spiridus are in pain. They are crying out to be saved.

I don't hear them.

I can hardly bear it, Darra. It is crushing me.

"Do you want to take a closer look?" Vahlah asked with a smile. "Let us visit the spiridus."

Ayja didn't think she could approach any closer. *Help me, Darra. Their pain is too strong.* She felt the warmth of his life force flowing into her, strengthening and calming her. Keeping her thoughts as deep within her memory walk as possible, Ayja forced herself to follow the veden closer to the Emerald Prison.

There were no walls or guards, only the glowing cylinder of light filled with the spiridus. "Wait here," Vahlah said. "I have one task to accomplish before you can enter." He waved his hand and a score of his armored demons formed up, blocking Ayja's path to the prison.

The spiridus fled Vahlah as he passed into the prison, crowding as high and as far away from him as they could manage. From under his armor, Vahlah removed a gold ring a hand length across. He carefully placed it on a flat stone and then placed his spear's tip against it. Then he began to chant and bright light flared from his spear. Ayja saw a great emenation of aetherial power, and then it was gone.

Vahlah bent low over it, examining his work, before turning to face Ayja again. "You may enter now. Your soulless friend as well, I expect."

"What did you do?" Ayja asked.

"A little insurance," he said. "You see, demons cannot enter here. Once you enter the prison, I face you alone. What if you drive me from the prison and then use the strength of the spiridus to open your gate? I can't let that happen."

"But what does it do?"

Vahlah chuckled. "I will let that be my secret. I will only say that it will render the power of the spiridus... unavailable to you."

Ayja and Darra still held hands. Within her memory walk, he said, *I don't trust him. He's up to something.*

We knew this going in. We must be wary. Remember, he doesn't know how powerful we are. He fears us.

The demons blocking their path parted, and Ayja and Darra walked into the Emerald Prison. She felt nothing as she passed through the emerald barrier, nothing but the omnipresent fear of the spiridus.

Inside, everything was cast in an emerald hue except for the red crystal stump. Vahlah strode over and touched it. "Here is your Emerald Gate," he said. "Not very emerald, though, is it? Perhaps you should call it the Ruby Gate."

Ayja only spared the stone the briefest of glances, her attention inexorably drawn to the myriad spiridus swirling overhead. It was at once the saddest and the most beautiful sight she'd ever seen.

"They are pretty, aren't they?" Vahlah said. "Want a closer look?"

Before she could say anything, Vahlah pointed his spear upwards, and a crackling purple bolt flashed upwards, striking one of the spiridus. Even deep within her memory walk, she heard its cry of pain. Then, slowly, the spiridus was drawn down to Vahlah, and he took it in his hand.

In the aether, Ayja saw the glow of energy as Vahlah drew the life force from the spiridus. In her mind, she heard its shrieks of agony, and she knew she had to stop the veden. She had the power to do it. Dromost still thrummed with the power of its empowered circles. She couldn't take it any longer.

When she tried to raise Dromost, Darra held her fast. She tried to wrench her hand free, but his grasp tightened.

No, Ayja! Not now!

They're in pain! Can't you feel it? They are being tortured.

Not yet! You have to stay calm. All in good time.

"Here is the source of my power," Vahlah said. "An everlasting fountain of life force, not only for me but for my demons."

"Let it go," Ayja said. "It doesn't like being held."

"No? Well, my people didn't like being slaughtered." He brought the spiridus to his mouth, and for a moment, she thought he might consume it, but instead, he kissed the incorporeal spiridus and let it fly from his hands. It streaked upwards to join those flying far above.

"How is it a source of power for your demons if they can't enter?" Ayja forced herself to ask. It took all her effort not to strike the veden.

"Let me show you."

"I don't need to see. Just tell me."

"Look anyway." Vahlah went to the edge of the prison and pushed his spear through the barrier. The moment he did, one of his demon soldiers ran up to it and grasped the iron shaft. Energy pulsed down the veden's arm and through the spear to be greedily consumed by the demon. "I feed my most faithful servants this way. They love the taste of spiridus."

"How are you even here?" Ayja asked. "Shouldn't you be dead?"

"Me?" A pained look crossed Vahlah's face. "I was ready to die with the other veden. We had nothing left to live for. Our mates and children were dead. But my father had other ideas. He couldn't bear for me to die. He cast me into the Emerald Prison and into Dromost. He knew it wouldn't hold me — that I would be free and could sustain myself on the life force of the spiridus. And so I am the last of the veden — the last of my kind."

"These spiridus didn't kill your kind," Ayja said. "They live within their hosts, but they don't control them."

"What do you know, human? We slew all of the spiridus."

"I—," Ayja paused. Should she tell the veden of Orlos? That she knew of the spiridus because she knew the last spiridus?

"Come and take a look at the stump of the beloved Emerald Tree. Let us see if you can make this gate you so desperately desire."

Ayja followed the veden towards the stump, Darra at her side. As she walked closer to it, a new feeling overcame her. The spiridus' fear was overtaken by pulses of hatred emanating from the crystal. The feeling was so strong she had to stop five strides from it.

"There is your way home," Vahlah said. "Your gate. All you need to do is craft the runes to open it."

"It won't be easy," Ayja said, resisting the urge to back away from the crystal's hatred. "The runes are complicated."

"I will help," Vahlah said with a smile.

"The gate must close behind me. I don't know all the runes to do that."

Vahlah shrugged. "That is not my concern. Perhaps your pet demon knows. All I care is that in the end, I will have Dromost."

"We must have life force to do our work," Darra said.

"Ah, so the soulless one speaks," Vahlah said. "Why do you need souls? I will feed you from the spiridus here. That is their purpose."

"No. I don't want their life force," Ayja said.

"Why not?" Vahlah asked, frowning. "You have some sympathy for them? You've read some fanciful stories about them? They are killers, every one. They destroyed an entire race. Don't shed a tear for them."

"Bring us worms or some other demons," Ayja said. "I won't feed off the spiridus. In fact, I don't want their life force drained to open the gate. Use demons to do this. If you can't, I won't give you Dromost."

"You change the terms now? You have no idea how much power it takes to open a gate."

"It doesn't have to be open very long."

Vahlah paused, regarding her. "I will do it."

"Good," Ayja said. "This will take some time. Where will we stay?" Ayja asked, looking out from within the spiridus prison. She saw now that they were in a narrow dead end of the canyon. Another even narrower path led off, but she had no idea how far. She did see demon soldiers walking in that direction.

"Stay in one of my demon warrens," Vahlah said, pointing his spear at the many tunnels bored into the surrounding cliffs. "It might not be comfortable sleeping amongst my demons. They are obedient, but they do get hungry. Or perhaps you'd like to sleep here, amongst your spiridus friends? It has the advantage that no demons will enter this place."

Ayja glanced around. The Emerald Prison was open to a thousand eyes. There'd be no privacy here. But there was nothing to do for it. "Yes, we will stay here. It will keep us closer to our work."

"Excellent," Vahlah said. "You shall work on the gate itself. I shall work on gathering the life force to open the gate. The gate will only open when you give Dromost to me."

"Agreed," Ayja said.

"Your Highness," Vahlah said, giving her a wicked smile and a curt bow, "I shall begin my work."

"Where will our demon stay?" Ayja asked. She saw Telea's demon standing twenty strides outside the Emerald Prison. There were no other demons near it.

"Wherever it wishes. It will not be touched." With that, Vahlah retreated to the far edge of the prison, beyond the stump. Several of his demons approached, standing just behind the barrier. Then, one by one, they ran off.

Ayja and Darra moved to the other end of the prison, Ayja casting a wary eye at the gold ring Vahlah had placed on the ground. What manner of magic was it? If she could find a way, she would examine it.

As they reached the far side of the prison, the spiridus flew down, swarming around Ayja and Darra. Their pain and fear was overwhelming, so much so that she had to keep most of her consciousness hidden within her memory walk. There was something else there as well, though. Hope.

Save us. Save us. Save us, the voices called out. Ayja fell to her knees under the relentless assault.

"What's wrong?" Darra asked.

"They are crying out to be saved. Their voices are drowning me. I can hardly think."

"Will you save them?"

Ayja nodded, tears coming to her eyes. "I must."

"How?"

"They must come through with us."

"Vahlah won't allow it."

"We must make it work," Ayja said. Spiridus flew closer, some coming so close she could have reached out and touched them. None approached Darra, but his presence didn't seem to keep them away either. Their conflicting emotions were too much to bear. "I don't know how I can do anything in their presence."

"I don't feel what you are feeling," Darra said.

"I need them to give me some space."

"Can you speak with them?"

"I don't know how spiridus communicate. I hear their emotions, but it isn't really words. It's not like how the demons speak in our minds. It is much simpler, much more basic." She faced the spiridus and said aloud, "I will try to save you." In her mind, she pictured an open gate and the spiridus flying through it.

Escape.

The spiridus ebbed and flowed as they washed over her and around her in a glowing school of lights. Had the pattern changed?

"Sing to them," Darra said. "There is magic in your song."

"Yes! You're right! What would I do without you, Sir Darra?"

"Well, my queen, you'd be dead a hundred times over."

"Yes. There is that. When we return to Salador, I'm going to name you my Champion. For certain."

His dull black eyes looked into hers. His face was unreadable. "I am a pyren, my queen. They will kill me."

"Over my corpse, Sir Darra." Ayja uncorked her canteen and took a drink to clear her throat. Facing the spiridus, she launched herself into the *Song of Hope*. It was one of the only three songs she knew, but it certainly seemed the most appropriate.

Ayja poured herself into the song, tapping her well of power to give it greater strength. Blue-white light shone out from her to fill the entire space of the prison. The reaction of the spiridus was instantaneous. *They danced.* All of them, thousands of spiridus, moved with the music, swirling and spiraling. *Dancing on the music, riding its notes, and creating brilliant, amazing patterns all around her.*

Love. Hope. Freedom. Peace.

The pain and desperation of five thousand voices changed in a matter of heartbeats. They were filled with the joyous hope of freedom. *I will do what I can,* Ayja thought as she sang. *I will free you.*

"Stop this! Stop right now!" Vahlah commanded, as he strode towards them, his wings outstreatched behind him.

"I was only singing," Ayja said, holding Dromost ready at the veden's angry approach.

"Do not give them any pleasure," Vahlah said. "They deserve no joy. I will make them suffer if you do this again."

"I will stop, then."

Vahlah stared at her for several hearbeats before returning to his side of the prison.

"That was beautiful while it lasted," Darra said. "But what do we do now? I serve no purpose when it comes to the crafting of the rings and runes of magic."

"I suppose we start. I don't want to leave this place, but I must go out and speak with Telea's demon."

"We have a place of refuge now, at least," Darra said. "If demons truly cannot enter here."

"Let's ask Telea's demon." As she stepped up to the edge of the prison, Ayja had a moment of panic, remembering Shulazar's barrier at the Dromost Gate. It had allowed passage only in one direction. Was she a prisoner now as well?

Her fears were needless. They passed through the barrier unimpeded. Behind them, spiridus followed them to the edge and crowded the area where Ayja had passed through. Telea's demon approached. "Now we begin," Ayja said and thought.

The demon's dragon-like head bobbed up and down. *You will have to do all of the work. I cannot enter.*

"I don't know all of the runes. I need your help."

You will have to come out here so that we can plan. We can draw sketches in the dirt, but you will have to craft the circles yourself. You must be very precise. There can be no mistakes.

"I understand. I can make engravings out here and take them in. I will copy them exactly."

We must be wary. The veden will want to take both Forsvar and Dromost. The veden might want to take you as well. You would make a very powerful slave.

"I will be wary."

Show me any runes the veden crafts so that I might check them.

"I will. We have to craft the runes so that the gate will close behind me. It has to be temporary."

I will think on it. Let us start with the gate itself.

Ayja shook her head. "I know how to craft the runes that open the gate. I don't know how to make it conditional. Can you show me that?"

Yes, I can show you.

"Will you hold Forsvar and Dromost while I work on this?" Ayja asked Darra.

"I will watch over you, my queen," he said, taking the Gifts from her.

Ayja knelt on the ground and cleared a space where she could draw in the dirt. The demon crouched next to her. It began to draw on the ground with one of its long claws. Time meant nothing in Dromost. Ayja only knew that they worked for a long time by the draw on her life force as her well of power slowly drained.

At one point, Vahlah's demons came, offering three worms to them. Darra drained them of their life force and passed it on to Ayja. It was only enough to make up for what she'd lost keeping her body alive and a little more for her well of power.

Eventually, despite the infusion of strength, Ayja had to sleep. She had no idea how long she'd been awake, but her mind could no longer stay focused. She and Darra left the demon and reentered the spiridus prison. The spiridus washed over them as they entered, so thick Ayja could barely see. They made their way several strides into the prison before Ayja sat down. "I'm exhausted, Sir Darra," she said.

"Rest. I think you are safe here — safer, at least. Only the veden can enter. I will keep watch."

"Thank you." She lay back, staring up into the spiridus swirling up ahead.

"You can do this?" Darra asked. "Nothing you did with the demon made any sense to me."

"I can do it."

"I hate to say it, but this seems too easy to me. Vahlah is too accommodating. He will betray us."

"I know. I don't trust him either. But how will he do it?"

"I don't know, my queen. You must focus on saving yourself, and not the spiridus."

Ayja watched the spiridus swirl above her. "I can't, now that I've seen them. I feel the goodness in them."

"The veden doesn't share your opinion."

"I admit I don't fully understand the spiridus," Ayja said. "Orlos explained a little to me, but it is hard to understand. The spiridus is in

267

him but doesn't tell him what to do. At least not overtly. It's not like when a demon possesses someone."

"Did Telea's demon tell her what to do?"

"Her demon never took control of her. It was in her, and she could speak with it, but it wasn't strong enough to take her over."

"So you think."

"No, I know it. I've been inside Telea's memory walk. The demon wasn't there. The demon didn't control her."

"So you're saying the spiridus are innocent of the crimes Vahlah accuses them of? That they didn't wipe out the veden race."

Ayja shifted her attention back to the spiridus flowing overhead. "I know the spiridus joined the war against the veden late. At least that's what the stories say. And I know that they fought the veden. I've never heard these stories of a massacre before. And if these spiridus live within people, and if they don't control the people they live within, how can they be guilty of such a crime?"

"They were just... just riders? Riders born by a horse they couldn't control?"

"They've been tortured for centuries. I can't leave them here."

"Saving them could cost you your life."

"Cam would call it a worthy death."

"I would call it a trajedy."

Chapter Twenty-seven

Nidon stared down at the valley from the heights of the Devil's Watch. The summoners and their undead had quickly folded under their assault. The Drinkers and the Landomeri had suffered terribly, though. At least the summoners hadn't known Telea's secret – the magic she'd used that allowed the undead to raise even more undead.

He shuddered at the thought, imagining a plague of walking corpses overtaking the world. Telea hadn't understood the danger she'd unleashed at the time. She did now. Nidon believed her when she said she'd never reveal how the magic worked. There had to be more, though. What would happen if someone else discovered the technique? It was a concern that would have to wait. They first had to win this campaign.

My last campaign. I hope. Let the Rigarian situation be settled when we return. I have no desire to fight unluks and varcolac again. What would he do when it was all over? Advise the king and train young knights and squires for war? It would be a good life. He remembered his plan, years long gone, to seek out Hadde in Landomere. *What a fool I was. A romantic fool. She never thought a thing of me.*

The terrain climbed sharply after passing the empty Devil's Watch. They passed a town, the first they'd seen in the Summoned Lands. It had been recently abandoned; many belongings had been left behind. The homes here were different than any place he'd seen in Belen. Gone were the red-roofed stone and stucco villas. Here the homes were made of pine boards with second stories wider than the first. The roofs were shingled with wood as well.

Runes covered the doors and windows of every house. A rumor passed down the lines that they were meant to drive off demons. *In Drommaria, everyone's a summoner,* or so the men began to say. If there was anyone in Drommaria.

Behind the town were fields, two-thirds left fallow and only a third cultivated. Was it for lack of farmers? Had the war taken such a toll on their populace? Beyond the fields, thick pine forests grew along both sides of the road. Nidon and Handrin had just reached the edge of the forest when the column halted. They waited for a time, impatient to be moving again.

"Squire Fress," Nidon said, "ride ahead and see what the delay is."

He knew there was nothing he could do about it, but he sent the squire anyway. At least he had some news to anticipate. As the wait grew longer and longer, they dismounted and took their ease in the shade of the forest. It was a cool day, at least, under cloud-covered sky. A relief compared to the scorching plains of eastern Belen.

Before Fress returned, the column began to move again. Just as Nidon's hopes rose that they'd make some progress, they halted. Nidon was a man of great patience. He knew how to bide his anger and when to use it. He felt it starting to rise in him, unwanted and unneeded, but relentless.

Finally, Squire Fress returned. "There has been some fighting, Champion Nidon. Enemy skirmishers keep hitting the front of the column, slowing it. General Solis asks if the Landomeri might be sent forward to support his Drinkers and dismounted Koromoi."

"Fighting?" Handrin asked. "We've heard no sound of it."

"The path is this narrow all the way forward, Your Majesty. The army is strung out for dozens of arrowflights."

Nidon looked back down the road the way they'd come. The town was barely out of sight through the trees. The last battle of the army probably hadn't even made it through the gate yet. "We'll never reach the Temple of Dromost at this pace," Nidon muttered. "We have to push harder."

"It will cost lives," Handrin said.

Nidon nodded. "The Landomeri are here as volunteers. With your permission, Your Majesty, I will take the Landomeri forward with me."

"No, Champion Nidon, your role is to command the Saladoran Battle. And, to be honest, what role would you play in the skirmish line? I will take the Landomeri forward. I know many of them from when I lived among them as Sulentis. With my magic and the Orb of Creation, we'll be able to push the enemy back."

"I don't like the idea of being left behind, Your Majesty. I am your Champion."

"I know you itch to be in the middle of things, Nidon, but your place is here."

With that, the king departed. A short time later, with his bodyguard knights and Telea in tow, Handrin led the Landomeri forward.

Then, with a drizzle falling from low clouds overhead, they waited. Rumors floated down the column, but there were no messengers and no call to arms. Late in the afternoon, a messenger did arrive, calling for all singers and healers to advance to the head of the column.

"What's happening?" Nidon asked. "Is the fighting heavy?"

"No, commander," he said in heavily accented High Saladoran. "Not so much fighting. Ambushes and traps. Pits and trees across the road. No demons, though. We need singers and healers."

There'd been six healers and four singers attached to the Saladoran Battle, not including Telea. Nidon sent them all forward as commanded, although he wasn't comfortable with the order. He glanced up the wooded slopes to either side of the army, wondering what they hid. He ordered crossbowmen to sweep the hills but knew it would be hard going.

Finally, late in the afternoon, the column marched again. They made good time until night began to fall and they had to make camp. There was no open field for them to pitch tents in. They had to make due and pitch camp on either side of the road, or in some cases, on it. There was no lack of wood, though, and despite the rain, they managed to get campfires started for their cooking groups.

The night was pitch black, with clouds and mist obscuring any moonlight that would have reached them through the forest. Wolves howled in the mountains above them, but they made it through the night unaccosted. Neither men nor demons rushed out of the night to attack them.

Dense fog shrouded the morning sun. They broke camp and, damp and tired, continued to march higher into the wooded mountains. Despite the morning fog, they moved quicker than they had the day before. By late morning the fog broke, but clouds still covered the sky, a constant mist washing over them as they marched on.

Several times during the day, they passed valleys leading off to the left and right. At each of these junctures, they came upon a small village or town, and in every case, they were abandoned. On several occasions, Nidon had seen signs of the skirmishes the Vanguard Battle had engaged in. He saw broken pottery from shattered imp jars, the remains of felled trees cleared from the road, and new dirt and stone filling in pits dug into the road itself.

There were graves as well. The Belenese didn't follow the Saladoran practice of cremating the dead but buried them in graves deep in the ground. He passed perhaps fifty of them during the day. How many had been Landomeri?

Late in the day, more messengers arrived. Half of every battle was to send their horses back to Belen. The terrain had turned out to be far more difficult than expected, and the horses had become a burden, slowing the

271

army, churning the road into mud, and requiring an extravagant amount of food and support.

Nidon found Exonos, and together they decided that all of their lightly armored freemen would dismount, as would half the timari. The heavily armored Saladorans would remain mounted, although it was clear they'd fight on foot if it came to it. The decision was greeted poorly by the timari, who were very nearly as heavily armored as the knights, and certainly viewed themselves as their equals.

"You have come to our country to help us," Exonos said. "I would let you ride for that alone. But your men are more heavily armored than ours. It is right that you should ride."

"Thank you, Satrus Exonos. My knights appreciate what you are doing for them."

The following day, misty, dank, and dreary as the two previous, found two columns moving on the road. One heading deeper into Drommaria, and another, almost entirely made up of horses, heading out.

"It is a lesson to us," Nidon said to Exonos. "A fool invades a country he does not know. Our ignorance will get us killed."

Twice they came upon wider valleys with larger towns. Both uninhabited, although there'd clearly been people there within the past few days. It did seem some of the houses had been abandoned far longer.

"Three days in Drommaria, and I've only seen homes for a few thousand people," Nidon said. "Is the country so sparsely inhabited?"

Exonos shook his head. "We know little of the Summoned Lands. The western part, where we are now, is known as Drommaria. It is mountainous and sparsely inhabited. The eastern Summoned Lands are a vast plateau. There are more people there."

"You've fought them before, but never invaded?"

"The summoners have always been the invaders. We've defeated them but were always frustrated in our efforts to invade. Look at how much trouble we've had, and they've only put up a token resistance."

"And the Temple of Dromost? How far away is it?"

"Several more days. We are heading south now, nearing the coast. That is where we'll find the temple."

On their fourth day of travel, the Saladoran Battle passed through the largest town they'd yet seen. It sat at a junction in the roads where the road they were on continued to the south, but a larger, better road headed east. There'd been a battle here — the first serious battle of their journey. The unburied Drommarian dead lay stacked in the fields and ditches to the side of the road while workers first buried the Belenese.

Nidon learned that the vanguard had made way for the heavy foot of the Eastern Battle, who'd done the brunt of the fighting. Half of the enemy's survivors had retreated to the east, while the other half retreated south. They'd been a mix of professional infantry, fanatics, and summoners. And, for the first time this campaign, the Belenese had faced sacrifice demons and possessed soldiers.

"It was a short battle but very violent," Exonos said to Nidon after receiving a report. "It is a good thing the army's singers were with the vanguard, or it could have been a disaster. Your king accounted himself heroically."

Nidon's fingers clenched around the hilt of his sheathed sword. "I don't like that I've been here while others have been fighting."

"I understand the sentiment," Exonos said. "Don't fear, though, our turn is coming soon. Most of the Eastern Battle has been detached to hold the East Road. We are third behind the vanguard now, and they will make way if there is an engagement."

As night fell, Nidon made his way among the Saladorans, checking on them and wishing them well. He knew from his years of service the effect a good leader could have on the morale of his men. He also knew he was as famous as a knight could be, despite his seventeen years in exile. Seven-time winner of the Champion's Tournament — the only man to ever win so many. Killer of Akinos, at least according to many in the ranks, despite his best efforts to correct them. Behind his back, they scoffed at his denials, accusing him of modesty, and knowing that only the great Sir Nidon could have done such great feats.

He and Squire Fress were on their way back to his tent when he heard shouting from the hills above the camp. The ready watch took up their arms and rushed to reinforce the sentries, but then things became quiet again.

"I sent freemen up into the hills to scout," Exonos said, joining them. "They ran into some enemy soldiers. Refugees from yesterday's fighting hiding in the hills, I expect."

"Do we know how many retreated from the town?"

"A few thousand, but most were pursued up the East Road. We don't know how many might have headed into the hills."

"Let's double the watch and tell the men to keep their arms close," Nidon said. He turned to his squire. "Tell Sir Dalaman he has command of the first watch."

"Yes, Champion Nidon."

"I will have my men ready themselves as well," Exonos said. He looked into the sky as the mist turned into a steadier rain. "Does it never stop raining in Drommaria?" he asked as he walked away.

When Fress returned, Nidon doffed his armor, although he chose to sleep in his arming coat. It was cool enough to warrant it in its own right, but he wanted to be semi-armed as it was.

Nidon fell asleep to the patter of raindrops on his tent and woke to demon screams in the night. Their horrifying wails sent a chill through his heart as he jerked upright in his camp bed. His feet hadn't even hit the floor when the oil lamp flared to life. Squire Fress was already on his feet and moving to Nidon's armor stand.

Nidon yanked on his boots, and by the time he was on his feet, Fress was ready with his mail hosen. Nidon waved him off saying, "No time. Haubergeon." Then, facing the tent flap, he shouted, "Sir Dalaman! To me!"

While they waited for his second, Fress helped Nidon work his mail shirt over his head. The shouting grew in intensity outside. Alarm horns blared. Something huge bellowed in the woods as tree limbs shattered. "Coat-of-plates. No vambraces," Nidon said.

Dalaman, fully armed, pulled the tent flap wide. "Strong attack, Champion," he said. "From the hills to the east. The watch is holding. The men are arming."

"Hold the First Company in reserve. I'll take them and counter any breakthrough. Go."

With a salute, Dalaman disappeared into the darkness. Fress buckled Nidon into his coat-of-plates, the process frustratingly slow. Then Nidon ducked his head so that Fress could slip his mail coif over his arming cap and down onto his shoulders. Then came his helm. Nidon pulled his gauntlets on as Fress belted his sword around his waist.

"Axe," Nidon said.

"Shield?" Fress asked as he pushed the long axe into Nidon's hands.

Nidon shook his head. "Arm yourself and gather the Squires of the House. Join the First Company in reserve." Without waiting for a reply, he strode out of the tent and into the darkness.

The battle was utter chaos. Knights ran to the fighting in small groups or all alone as quickly as they could arm. There was no light at all — just shadowy shapes moving in the darkness.

A ball of fire appeared on the slopes. Then three more. At first, Nidon thought it might be elementar magic, but then remembered that they'd all gone forward with the king. The balls coalesced into fire imps, who hurled themselves at the Saladorans.

No elementars. No singers. No healers. A night for steel.

Shouts nearby. Men were running, but the wrong way — fleeing the fight. A huge form moved in the mist. A sudden image of giant urias flashed through his mind. He saw the huge hammer that had crushed him years before, nearly ending his life.

He shook the thought off. *The enemy has already broken through.*

"To me!" Nidon shouted, his battlefield voice booming across the camp. "To me, Knights of Salador."

Fleeing soldiers joined him — a dozen or so — as did a few who'd just risen from sleep. Some kept running, though. To where? There was no place of retreat in the narrow valley. It was time to fight or die.

There was no time to find the First Company. "Follow me!" Nidon called to those nearby. Not waiting to see if they obeyed, he ran in the direction of the breakthrough. "Salador! To me!" he shouted as he ran.

A naked man with glowing red eyes ran at Nidon. Screaming unintelligibly, the fanatic raised his dagger high above his head, poised to strike. Nidon's axe split the man from shoulder to solar plexus. He yanked the blade free.

Two more fanatics rushed him. With no time to recover his axe for a full swing, Nidon punched the axehead into the man's face, shattering his nose. As the man recoiled, Nidon dashed his skull open with a short strike. The third fanatic swung her sword in a sweeping arc, but Nidon parried it on his axe blade before driving the haft into her stomach.

She staggered, but then lunged at him again, hate gleaming from her red eyes. A knight next to Nidon ran her through, but she ignored the wound, and ran up the blade towards her new assailant. Nidon struck her down with his axe, but then another wave of attackers hit them.

A fanatic grabbed Nidon's axe with both hands. Instead of trying to rip it free, Nidon snatched his rondel dagger from his belt and plunged it into the man's eye. Another fanatic clutched at Nidon's axe arm at the same moment a spear scraped across his coat-of-plates. He let go of his axe and shoved the fanatic back before stabbing him with his dagger.

Something shattered nearby, and a cloud of sulfurous smoke engulfed him. A screaming imp, covered in spikes and spines, tore the helm off a knight and flayed his face with its dagger claws. The man clutched at the demon, trying to drive it off, only to have his hands impaled by spines.

Nidon could do nothing for him. Fanatics rushed him, grasping at his arms and legs, trying to grapple him to the ground. His gauntleted left fist broke noses and jaws as he stabbed over and over with his rondel.

Blinded by smoke, darkness, and blood, Nidon never saw the fanatic who slammed into him, driving him to the ground. The dead surrounding him cushioned his fall. He shoved at the fanatic atop him, only to discover that she was already dead.

As he pushed her off, he discovered the cause of her death. A huge shape loomed over him. In the darkness, Nidon saw only scales and a twisted body. The creature's arms were like thick cables, with three curved daggers for fingers. They lashed out at a knight standing in front of the monstrosity, but the man heroically held off the flailing limbs.

Nidon couldn't stand. There was a body on his leg, and the demon stood atop it, pinning him. Levering himself up as best he could, Nidon stabbed his rondel into the demon's thigh. The dagger's triangular blade was made for punching through steel armor, and the demon's scales resisted no better.

A clawed arm struck at him with a serpent's speed. Nidon blocked it with his left arm, but then it grasped him, and he felt as if his arm would be wrenched from his body. He jammed the rondel into the demon's arm, but still, it wouldn't release him. The demon raised its other arm to strike at him, but the knight fighting it struck its clawed hand from its arm with a sword stroke.

The demon screamed and let go of Nidon, turning to the new threat. It struck at the knight, but he turned the blow on his shield before stabbing the demon in the chest. Still, it fought on.

The weight lifted from Nidon's leg, and he pulled it. The demon had a hold of the knight's shield, but let it go when the knight cut deeply into its arm. Climbing to his feet, Nidon took his rondel in both hands and stabbed it deep into the demon's back. As the demon lurched and twisted, Nidon wrenched the dagger back and forth, creating the most savage wound he could.

With a serpent's flexibility, a clawed hand grasped Nidon and yanked him aside. He lost his dagger in the demon's back. Desperately, Nidon clutched at the demon's talons as they pierced his coat-of-plates. The creature was too strong, though. One of the claws slowly pushed into his shoulder.

Then the demon lurched, and Nidon was released. Once, twice, three times, the unknown knight's sword hacked into the demon's neck, until finally the head fell free from its body. Blood spewing from the wound, it toppled to its back.

"Get up. Fight," the knight said before rushing off towards the sound of fighting.

Breathing heavily, Nidon got to his knees and then to his feet. Had it even been a knight? He'd worn Belenese scale and carried a heavy, curved sword, but his shield was Saladoran and his tabard East Teren yellow.

Nidon thought he recognized the voice, though. *Sir Tharryl*. Nidon shook his head in appreciation of his skill and ferocity.

There was no fighting near Nidon, just rain falling on piled corpses. In the distance, fighting continued, but the sound was fading. He pulled his dagger from the demon's back and sheathed it but didn't even try to find his axe under the piled corpses. His shoulder burned where the demon's claw had pierced it, but he could still fight. He picked up a buckler from a dead Saladoran crossbowman, drew his falchion, and headed towards the sound of the heaviest fighting.

As he marched, he gathered soldiers by ones and twos, a spearman here, a crossbowman or two there, knights and squires as well. In the chaos of the night battle, they'd lost all formation and sense of good order. It had become a brutal fight for survival in the night.

By the time they reached the fighting, though, it was nearly over. Only a few fanatics and demon-possessed summoners remained. Nidon led a final charge into their flank, killing the last of them. Finally, all that remained were the moans and screams of the wounded.

There was no sleep that night. The dead were gathered and the wounded seen to. Men stood watch and patrolled the slopes for any sign of the enemy. They were gone, though. Nidon thought very few had survived. Retreat seemed not to have been an option for them.

By morning, word came in that the enemy had attacked all along the column. The Aftokropoli and Western Battles were cut off from the rest of the army, while the Eastern Battle was besieged in and around the town at the crossroads. The Imperial and Saladoran Battles had suffered less, only because the narrow pass had made it difficult for the Drommarians to mass many soldiers against them. The vanguard had been struck by a strong force as well but had the advantage of having all the army's singers, elementars, and fearless Drinkers with it.

"It was a mistake to push all of our best demon fighters to the front of the column," Nidon said to Exonos as night turned to morning gloom.

"The enemy let us believe they were weaker than they are," Exonos said. "We had what we Belenese call *victory disease*. We've paid for it now."

"What are your losses?" Nidon asked. "We lost close to one hundred Saladoran knights and squires, one hundred and thirty spearmen, and seventy crossbowmen. We have some two thousand two hundred Saladorans remaining in our contingent."

"I lost seventy-four timari, one hundred thirty-seven freemen, and nearly a hundred light foot," Exonos said. "I have nearly seventeen hundred remaining. It puts you at three thousand nine hundred combatants and an additional three hundred camp followers, porters, and drivers in your command."

"It was a victory, but a costly one," Nidon said. "The Drommarians are fearless. They don't know when they've lost. Their demons are as terrible as the urias and pyren I've battled in Salador."

The army didn't move that day. The Imperial Battle turned back to reestablish contact with the rest of the army. General Solis passed through, bringing half the army's singers and healers with him. A few were left with Nidon but not many. Not nearly enough.

Handrin and Telea arrived and, with the Orb of Creation as a source of aetherial power, went from place to place healing those in need of it. Kael came as well, reporting that seventy-two of the Landomeri had died in the fighting so far. He brought archers with him, and they raided the baggage train, taking the remaining stores of arrows with them, having nearly run out themselves.

That evening General Solis returned. "We've restored contact with the Western Battle," he said, "but the army has been cut off from the Devil's Watch. We no longer have supply lines."

"Do we still hold the Devil's Watch?" Exonos asked.

"I don't know. We left a thousand foot there to defend it. I've ordered the Western and Aftokropoli Battles to reestablish contact with the fortress. The Eastern Battle will hold the crossroads with the support of the Imperial Foot. The vanguard, your Saladorans, and the rest of the Imperials will continue to the Temple of Dromost."

"Until contact with the Devil's Watch is reestablished, we have only the supplies we have on hand," Nidon said.

Solis nodded. "It should be enough to get us to the Temple of Dromost."

"But not enough to get us back out again," Exonos said.

"Getting out doesn't matter," King Handrin said, joining them. He'd remained with the Saladorans throughout the day but would rejoin the van with the general. "All that matters is that we seal the Dromost Gate forever. Fighting our way free comes second."

Nidon nodded his agreement. "There is no more noble death than to give your life for a righteous cause."

Chapter Twenty-eight

A bead of sweat ran down Ayja's brow. She, Darra, and Telea's demon stood with Vahlah just outside the spiridus prison. On the ground in front of them was a full-sized model of the circle of power they would craft to open the Emerald Gate.

"Your work is exquisite," Vahlah said, staring down at the concentric rings of runes. "I am most impressed."

Ayja knelt, pointing at part of the outer ring. She had Forsvar on her arm, but Darra held Dromost, still charged with power, standing just behind her. She'd become accustomed to the safety of the spiridus prison, and now that their plan was close to coming to fruition, she was more nervous of attack than ever. More than her own life, more than the spiridus, she was consumed with saving the child growing within her.

"This is the part that was crafted by the demon," Ayja said. Telea's demon had changed since entering Vahlah's domain. It stood upright on two legs now, more human and less draconic. *More like Vahlah.* It still had a dragon's face, and its fingers and claws were much longer than Vahlah's. It had a tail, unlike the veden. And although it was bigger than before, it was still smaller than the veden.

"The emerald prison isn't really a gate," Ayja continued. "It has no physical portal to pass through."

Vahlah nodded. "Complex work. And that?" Vahlah asked, pointing to another part of the circle. "Whose work was that?"

"I did that," Ayja said, tracing her finger along a long section of work, including the section Vahlah had indicated. "Most of it I copied exactly from the circle of power at the Dromost Gate. There were some changes, but we're certain they'll work."

"Excellent." Vahlah nodded. "I see that the trigger is complete. When Dromost is in my hand, the gate will open." He pointed with his spear at the model. "I see the closing command here as well. The gate will close when you pass through?"

"Yes."

"Begin your work. I will continue gathering the life force we need to empower the gate." With that, he returned to the far side of the Emerald Prison. Just outside the prison, a long line of demons awaited him. Half were soldiers, the other half captives, waiting to have their life force drawn from them. Vahlah had been at it for days, plunging his spear into demons and drawing their essence into a steel canister at his feet.

I will be here if you have any questions, Telea's demon said. *For the most, my part is done.*

Ayja and Darra reentered the spiridus prison, greeted by a rush of spiridus. They flew all around Ayja, and even through her. "Yes, yes, I'm back," she said with a smile. "I can't even see! Please give me some room."

After a dozen heartbeats, the spiridus retreated, for the most part, at least. There were always a few hovering nearby. Ayja was becoming convinced she could tell them apart from each other, although she knew the idea was ridiculous — the spiridus were fist-sized glowing spheres of green-white light that left green trails everywhere they flew. How could she possibly tell them apart?

She and Darra went to a flat piece of rock near the glowing red stump of the Emerald Tree. With the slightest flick of her hand, she created a little dust devil that swept the area clean of dirt and debris. Her well of power was full, or near to it. Vahlah had proven true to his word and had provided Darra with worms and imps to feed upon. It was only once a day, though, and just sustaining herself was a constant drain.

"I'll create the circle here," Ayja said. "Would you hold Forsvar?" After Darra took the Godshield from her, she knelt on the ground. The rock was rough and filled with imperfections. She knew it had to be a perfect surface to function as a source of power for the gate. Any flaw might alter the runes she placed there and lead to disastrous results.

Twisting the aether, Ayja passed her hands over the rock face, fusing cracks and smoothing out ridges and ripples. She'd make a circle one stride across, plenty large enough to contain the runes she needed, and, more importantly, large enough to contain the tremendous power that would open the gate.

Sweat gathered at her brow as she worked. Despite how much she'd learned and how large her well had become, stone was the most difficult element to work with. Finally, she had a cylinder of stone a stride across and half a hand high. It was embedded in the surrounding bedrock, rising slightly out of it.

Ayja stopped and admired her work, taking a long pull from her canteen. Her tremendous hunger was a terrible constant that she couldn't escape. Water helped, but only a little. As she stoppered her canteen, she noticed how drawn her hand had become. *Skeletal.* She was glad she had no mirror in which to look at herself. Darra was keeping her alive, but at what cost to her body? And at what cost to her child? She was wasting away. Her well of power drained faster and faster. Even without the ability to judge the passage of time, she knew it was true. At some point, her well would drain faster than Darra could fill it, and she would perish.

I'll be gone before that can happen, she thought as she stared down at her work surface. *We'll escape soon. Very soon.*

"What are you thinking about?" Darra asked.

"You can tell when I'm thinking? We've spent too much time together, I think, Sir Darra." She managed a small smile to soften her words.

"I saw your forehead crease — like when it does when you're deep in thought."

"Yes, definitely too long. We're like a long-married couple now, aren't we?"

Darra nodded and looked away.

"I was just thinking about what I'll eat first when we return home," Ayja lied, not wishing to burden him further with her hopelessness.

"Which is?"

"Roast beef and asparagus followed by apple pie."

"A good choice."

Ayja sighed. "It will probably make me sick. I should probably start with chicken broth and let my body recover first."

"A wise choice."

She glanced at him and smiled. "I couldn't have done this without you."

"The Dromost Gate couldn't have been closed without you."

"We make a good pair, Sir Darra."

He paused a moment. "We do, my queen. I'll remind you, we haven't made it back yet."

"We will." Ayja knelt by the circle again. "My well is much drained."

"I can give you some of my strength."

Ayja shook her head. "I don't want us weakened too much. In case Vahlah turns against us."

"Just a little," Darra said, holding his hand out to her.

Smiling her appreciation, she took it and soon felt the familiar warmth streaming through her, filling her limbs with strength and healing and then pouring into her well of power. Too soon, it stopped.

"Thank you, Darra. That will keep me going a little longer." Looking into her memory walk, she peered at the copy of the magic circle she'd placed on the floor in front of the fireplace. In the real world, she placed her finger on the stone and twisted the aether, so that her finger sank into the stone. Ever so carefully, she drew the first rune.

She stopped and appreciated her work. It was good. She moved on and carved three more runes, creating the first phrase of the working that would open the gate. As she paused a second time, exhausted from the effort, a spiridus flew down and touched the circle. As she watched, green light flowed from the spiridus and into the runes.

"Hey! What are you doing?" Ayja tried to swish it away. Her hand passed right through it, but the spiridus apparently got the idea, zipping off to join the others circling overhead.

"What happened?" Darra asked.

"The spiridus attempted to empower my runes. They're not ready yet, though."

"Why did it do it?" he asked, staring up at them.

Ayja's eyes followed his. A chill crawled up her arm. "They know what I'm doing. They want to go home."

"They told you this?"

She shook her head. "Just an impression I have." She paused a moment and very quietly said, "Do you know what this means?" She glanced across the prison at Vahlah, but he was occupied drawing the life force from another victim. "The spiridus can voluntarily provide life force. I thought it had to be drawn out of them."

Darra glanced at Vahlah and then down at the stone tablet. "If the spiridus can empower the gate, we don't need him. Can we work this to our advantage?"

"I'm not sure how," Ayja said. "I'd need to change the runes very quickly, before he noticed. And I'd need the spiridus to understand what I intend. There's also the golden ring he placed on the ground. I don't know what it does. So many unknowns!"

"Still, we know something now that we didn't know before."

Ayja nodded. "I've had it, for now, Darra. I need to rest my mind and think for a bit."

"I will watch over you, my queen," he said. He took off his tattered kaftan and rolled it into a bundle. "A pillow, or as close to one as we have. I'm sorry it's not more presentable."

Ayja took it from him with a smile. "You are too good to me, Darra. And I imagine I'm barely more presentable than your kaftan." She was certain it was far worse than that. She'd barely managed to wipe the worst of the dirt from herself with a scrap of cloth and a little water in the entire time they'd been in Dromost. How long had that been? It felt like months.

"You are beautiful, my queen," Darra said, his black eyes unreadable.

"Flattery, Sir Darra? I've already made you my Champion. What else could I give you?"

He looked down at his pale hand and said, "What I want you cannot give me."

Ayja sighed. It was true. She couldn't turn him into a man — a living, breathing man. "Well," she said, "when we get out of here, I will give you everything it is in my power as a Princess of Salador to give you." She laid down on the hard ground, placing Darra's kaftan under her head. He stood nearby, Forsvar on his arm and Dromost in his hand. Above, the spiridus flowed and swirled in mesmerizing patterns.

I imagine King Handrin wouldn't appreciate my giving two Gifts of the Gods to a pyren, she thought as she closed her eyes and entered her memory walk. She was in the kitchen, near the fireplace. There were only a few burning sticks in there now. The fire wasn't dangerously low, but weak enough to give her pause.

In her memory walk, she wasn't starving or disheveled. She smiled at the freedom of her kirtle and the feeling of her bare feet on the polished pine floors. Taking out a cutting board, she sliced off a piece of dark bread and slathered it with butter. She wanted eggs and bacon as well but was in too much a hurry to bother. She could cheat, of course. It was her memory walk — but to destroy the illusion would destroy some of the potency of her walk.

She sighed with pleasure as she ate, savoring the sweetness of the butter and the nuttiness of the rich bread. *I will never stop eating when we escape this place. I will become as big as a house.*

Walking into the great room, she glanced at the quiver by the door. She still had a few unempowered workings there. They were useful, but what she really needed were more empowered workings. Those had devastated the demons who had attempted to overwhelm her. She glanced at the fireplace mantle where the candles had been. How quickly she'd hurled them at the demons!

Ayja felt a strange sensation. A warmth coming from within her. At first, she was alarmed, but the warmth was life-giving. Was Darra touching her and giving her life force? He had little to give, and she wanted him strong in case they needed to fight. But this was different. Within her memory walk, she had a sudden feeling that something was nearby — touching her mind.

Walking quickly to the door, she looked out into the evening twilight. She saw motion in the woods and called out, "Darra? Is that you?"

There was no response. Even though the warmth within her was life-giving, fear gnawed at her. If it wasn't Darra, who was it? How could they have passed her wards?

Then, out of the forest came a green-white light. It flashed across the yard and disappeared behind the house. *A spiridus.* Ayja stepped out the front door and looked in the direction the spiridus had gone. It wasn't supposed to be possible. Her wards were supposed to block any entry into her memory walk. Were they flawed? Had Telea not told her the correct way to construct them? Had Ayja been open to possession all this time?

As the questions filled her mind, she walked out onto the front yard, looking everywhere for the spiridus. She still *felt* its presence. Then it streaked towards her from behind the opposite side of the house and hovered in front of her at eye level.

It was real. It was physical. Ayja didn't know how she knew — she just knew it. She reached out her hand towards the spiridus, her palm up, and the spiridus settled onto it. It was as light as the lightest bird, almost insubstantial, and warm to the touch.

Escape?

Ayja drew in a deep breath. "I will take you home," she said.

The Great Spirit awaits. Your mother awaits.

A cold chill ran down Ayja's spine and the back of her arms. "My mother is dead, long ago."

With the Great Spirit, she waits.

"What do you mean?"

She speaks through the tree. Escape. Home. The spiridus flew from her hand and disappeared through the open door of her house.

Ayja ran through the front door, catching sight of the spiridus as it flew into her fireplace. *My well of power.* She dashed across the room, fearing what the spiridus might do. Then she stumbled and nearly fell as a surge of green energy passed from the spiridus and into her fire. Then the spiridus vanished up the chimney.

Ayja ran to the hearth and knelt there, staring into the green-hued flames. The fire was noticeably bigger. The spiridus had given its strength to her. She cried out in surprise as the spiridus flashed over her shoulder and settled into the flames again. More life-force poured into the fire and the flames rose even higher. It was only a matter of heartbeats, and again, the spiridus flew up the chimney.

No — not the same spiridus! She felt it, but she didn't know how. She yelped and then laughed as another flew past her head and into the fire.

"Ayja! What is going on?" Darra's voice called to her from outside. "They keep entering you. I don't know if I can stop them."

"Come in! Look what they are doing!" By the time Darra walked through the front door, three more spiridus had arrived and departed. Her fire blazed emerald, silver, and golden flames now. "Look what they've done!"

"This is wonderful," he said, watching as a spiridus flew three laps around the room before departing out the front door. "Look how strong your well of power is!"

The spiridus kept coming until Ayja's well of power was full to overflowing. The last one rested on her hand again. *Home. She waits.* Then it vanished out the door.

"Thank you!" Ayja shouted in its glittering green wake. She couldn't contain her smile. "Do you know what this means, Darra? My work will be done so much faster now! I wonder, will they keep giving me more strength each time I deplete my well of power? I hope it isn't hurting them."

Darra walked closer to the fire and stared into the green flames. He smiled. He was handsome for an older man. It was hard to reconcile his appearance in her memory walk with the pale, gaunt, black-eyed pyren she knew. Of course, the same could probably be said of her, now. "Before you finish the circle, you should create more of those, what did you call them? *Empowered workings.*"

"If I work on those, it will take longer for us to escape."

"I'm afraid you see only the end of the road and not the path we must take to get there. It might be harder to escape than you think. We must be ready for a fight. We must be careful and think of everything that can go wrong."

"You're right. Of course, you're right. I can't let my hope blind me."

"What do we think is going to happen?" Darra asked.

Ayja paused and thought a moment before replying. "When I give Dromost to Vahlah, the Emerald Gate will open. When I step through it, it will close. You and the spiridus must go through before I do."

"He'll try to stop the spiridus from going through. He might try to stop you as well."

"He has that gold ring he placed on the ground. He's forbidden me from examining it, though. I don't know what it does. All we know is that it can do something to the spiridus."

Darra looked out the door and into the forest beyond. Ayja knew when he did this that he was looking at something in the real world. She kept her own consciousness in her memory walk. *Let Vahlah and the demons think I'm sleeping.*

Darra turned back to her. "So what happens if the ring acts as some barrier, blocking the spiridus from leaving? And maybe Vahlah turns on you in an effort to take Forsvar from you."

"We fight. If we win, either by driving him off or by killing him, I can work to free the spiridus from whatever effect the ring is having upon them."

"I imagine that, if we gain the upper hand, he'll retreat out of the prison," Darra said. "Outside, he'll have the support of his demons. And if we escape with the spiridus, he'll still have Dromost. But what if he gains the upper hand? My queen, if we are losing the fight, you must retreat through the gate, even if it means leaving the spiridus behind. If you are killed, the gate won't close."

Ayja shook her head. "It will close upon my death. I wrote it into the runes."

"What? You didn't tell me that before. I hate the sound of it. Still, if we are losing, you must escape. We might not be able to save the spiridus. Can the two of us together defeat him if he wields Dromost? I've held both Gifts but can't tell."

"Neither can I. I'll have my magic and you by my side, but he has his spear and armor." She frowned. "Cam always warned me against going into a fight without knowing your enemy first."

"We'll have to fight with our backs to the gate. We have to keep our retreat open. It's a shame we have only your sword and my dagger for weapons. I will try to close with him and paralyze him with my touch, but it won't be easy. Do you know how powerful his spear and armor are?"

Ayja shook her head. "Not as strong as the Two Gifts, but still potent. I can't read the runes on them. I'd have to examine them much more closely. But... you just gave me an idea." She went to the door and took down her sword from where it hung from a peg. Drawing it, she said, "I can make some improvements to my own sword. It won't be Dromost, but I can empower it with some magic of my own."

"Do it, my queen. We must have every advantage."

She took her sword and placed it on the table. "I'll figure everything out in my memory walk," she said, "but the actual work on the sword must happen out there in the real."

"I know the delay pains you, my queen."

"I won't be able to live with myself if I don't make every effort to save the spiridus."

Darra looked away from her. "I see Vahlah. He's coming."

Ayja withdrew from her memory walk and rose to her feet. Darra gave Forsvar and Dromost to her as the veden strode closer, scattering the terrified spiridus. He glanced at her stone circle as he landed and grinned at her. "Taking our time, are we?"

"I only have so much strength in my well of power," she said, lying. Her well of power was bright with the green energy of the spiridus. "Trust me. I want this finished more than you do."

"I don't know about that," he said, glancing at Dromost. "I'm looking forward to it as well." The veden was armored as before and still carried his iron spear. He pointed the spear outside the prison and said, "Here, I've brought you a gift. Perhaps it will let you get back to work."

Six armored demons approached the prison, each holding a squirming worm in its hands. Darra went to draw the life force from the demons. Ayja cringed as the captive demons screeched nearby. She didn't turn her eyes from Vahlah, however.

Vahlah took a few steps away and settled himself onto a large rock.

"What are you doing?" Ayja asked. The demon had never taken a seat before.

"This is my domain," Vahlah said with a sweeping motion of his spear. "I can sit anywhere I'd like. I think I'll stay and watch you work. I grow tired of sucking the life from helpless demons."

Darra returned and touched Ayja's hand. Her well was full, but Vahlah didn't know that.

He isn't leaving, Ayja thought to Darra as a trickle of power flowed from the pyren to her, refilling the small amount she'd used in the brief time since the spiridus had left her. *He wishes to see me work.*

Ayja pulled her hand from Darra's and gave him Dromost. She would keep Forsvar. She had to with Vahlah staying so close. Kneeling by her stone circle, she twisted the aether and touched the surface. Slowly, exactingly, she traced the runes of power into the stone. Her mind raced, but she had to stay focused on what she was doing. It was hard, though. Vahlah sat nearby, watching her. She wanted to think about the artifacts he carried with him. She wanted to know what he was planning.

As she came to the part of the circle where the trigger was, she paused. If she continued, it would mean the gate would only open if she handed Dromost to the veden. She stopped and sat back on her haunches, wiping the sweat from her brow.

"Tired already?" he asked. "I could feed you if you just asked." Vahlah stood and, raising his spear, sent bolts of purple energy into the spiridus above, striking them and drawing them down to him. Ayja felt their pain, their searing agony, and couldn't take it. She stood and pushed Forsvar's aura outward, overlapping the veden and breaking the spear's link to the spiridus. They fled high above, all but for one that Vahlah held in his hand.

"Petty. So petty," Vahlah said.

"You don't have to be cruel about it," Ayja said.

"You make me laugh. You don't want the spiridus hurt in any way, while I massacre demons to open your gate for you."

"The spiridus don't devour souls to sustain themselves or to make themselves more powerful."

"So they are better than demons? What about the cruelty of the spiridus who massacred my people?"

I know a spiridus! Ayja wanted to shout. *I know the truth!* She didn't dare, though. What might Vahlah do if he knew a spiridus still lived in Helna's world?

"You saw the massacre of your people?"

"No, I was away. I saw only the results. I was there when the spiridus were imprisoned, though. I helped. I was proud of my part." He held the spiridus in his hand high above his head, and Ayja watched as he drew its life force from it. The spiridus's light faded until it was only a pale shadow. She felt its pain and its longing to be free. Vahlah laughed and released it. "Now, do you wish to stay here forever? Or will you return to work?"

He knows why I stopped. He doesn't trust me. Ayja knelt by her stone circle. She twisted the aether and began shaping the stone. She didn't want to create the runes that would only trigger the gate if she handed Dromost to Vahlah. Now that she knew the spiridus could power the gate, she only wanted to escape.

She paused — a dozen heartbeats — longer. *I have no choice.* Slowly, carefully, she carved in the commands. It was a long, slow process. "Very good," Vahlah said as she finished the phrase. "That's what I wanted to see. We are bound together now, you and I. You wish to leave, and I wish to possess Dromost. Our goals are shared."

Ayja stared down at the work she'd just completed. She could change it. She could make it so that the gate would open without giving Dromost to him. Then, with the spiridus providing the life force, they could open the gate and escape. If only Vahlah would leave them alone for a time. But of course, he wouldn't. He knew. Of course he did.

And so I will have to fight him.

"This is the tricky part," Vahlah said. "Turning the prison into a gate."

"Will you stop talking, please?" Ayja said. "This is difficult work."

"Of course it is. I've carved my fair share of runes. I won't disturb you any longer."

She returned to work. It was a slow process, but even then, she dragged it out. She needed time in her memory walk. Time to work on her sword and to empower more workings. Finally, she paused, saying, "I must rest. Humans must sleep from time to time."

"Rest briefly, then," Vahlah said. "I will gather more of the life force we need to open the gate."

As he withdrew, Ayja gave Forsvar to Darra. "Watch over me, Sir Darra. I have a lot of work to do."

"Of course, my queen."

Then, despite her fatigue, she drew her sword and sat down. Placing the sword across her lap, she inspected the blade. It had seen hard use in Dromost. There were nicks in the blade, and it looked somewhat worse for wear. It was a magnificent weapon, though. Laying down, she held the sword in both hands and rested it on her chest as she let her conscious mind sink into her memory walk.

It was time to make her sword a little more magnificent.

Chapter Twenty-nine

After two days of unending battle against the elements, felled trees, and summoner ambushes, Nidon was summoned to see King Handrin. As he approached the waterlogged tent, he saw six Knights of the House and six Empress's Axes standing at attention outside. Inside, he found General Solis with King Handrin and Empress Kelifos.

"We are cut off, General Nidon," Solis said without preamble. "The enemy has retaken the crossroads in force, and they are marching on us. I am going to take the Imperial Timari and the remaining Imperial Foot and attempt to defeat them and reopen our lines of communication. The Vanguard Battle, the Empress's Axes, and the Children of Forsvar shall remain here and serve under Empress Kelifos. King Handrin shall take command of the Saladoran Battle and Satrus Exonos's Belenese contingent." He paused a moment and took a breath. "We have decided that you, General Nidon, shall have overall command of the attack on the Temple of Dromost." He paused and looked out the tent flap. To Nidon, it seemed a pained look crossed the general's face. "I think we all understand at this point there is not much hope that we will be able to withdraw back to Belen when this is done. I will do the best I can to open a way home. It is up to you to seal the Dromost Gate. General Nidon, do you accept this task?"

Nidon glanced at Handrin and Kelifos. Both stared expectantly back at him. Nidon had twice before commanded armies. He hadn't expected this, though. To come to Belen and command their soldiers as well as his? But the Saladoran contingent was the largest remaining to the army, and King Handrin bore the Orb of Creation. It made sense that Nidon, as captain of the Saladoran contingent, should be offered the honor.

This would be the most important battle in all of history. If he succeeded, he'd be remembered as the general who sealed the Dromost Gate. If he failed... the world would end, and it would be his fault. The fact that no one would remain alive to blame him did not make him feel any better. But who would do it if not him? He'd trusted General Solis to get them here even if he hadn't agreed with every action the Belenese general had taken. Could he let some other man command now, when the stakes couldn't be higher?

"It would be my honor," Nidon said. "I will command the attack."

Solis shook Nidon's hand and said, "I wish you well, Saladoran. If I fail to break through, I will at least hold them off as long as I can. I wish you good fortune. May Forsvar smile upon you."

"I trust you, General Solis," Nidon said. "Win our way home."

Solis bowed to Handrin and Kelifos before saying, "I must see to my soldiers. I wish you all well." With that, he departed the tent.

It was only then that Nidon realized Solis had been relieved of his command. He'd escaped punishment for his involvement in the massacre of the Etheans in the capital and for marching against King Handrin. Nidon didn't know the reason. Had the young empress been unwilling to challenge the veteran general? Or had the Belenese belief in the absolute authority of the monarch absolved him of responsibility? In either case, he'd been kept on to lead the invasion of the Summoned Lands.

What Nidon did know was that the fighting through the mountains had been frustratingly slow. Stuck deep in the column, he'd been unable to take part in much of the action or any of the decision making. "This was unexpected, Your Highnesses," Nidon said. "I am honored, though."

Empress Kelifos glanced at Handrin, and he gave her a nod. "We decided this together," she said. "Solis was an able general under Emperor Niktonas, but he made several mistakes that caused us to lose our confidence in him. His frontal attacks on several positions, including the Devil's Watch, were poorly planned. He brought too many horses into the mountains. He is, I think, a better defensive general than an offensive one."

"With much of the army trapped behind us," Handrin said, "the Saladoran Battle is now the largest contingent. Empress Kelifos suggested I take command of the attack, but I deferred to you, Champion Nidon. You've led an army on the attack before. The men have faith in you."

"Thank you, King Handrin. Your faith will be justified."

"We have six elementars in the van," Handrin said. "Twelve singers and eight healers as well, including Telea and Empress Kelifos."

"My Axes, the Children of Forsvar, and many of the Saladoran Knights have been spared from the heaviest fighting so far," Kelifos said. "With the support of the Orb of Creation, King Handrin's magic, and our song, I am certain of victory. If none of us return, but the gate is closed, so be it. My reign shall have been the shortest but most glorious in history."

"We will do this together," Nidon said, hoping it was true.

For two days, they pushed into ever greater opposition. Nidon was eventually forced to pull the exhausted Vanguard Battle into reserve. He placed Exonos's freemen and the Saladoran crossbow companies at the head of the column in their place, supported by Saladoran spearmen. It left him with Exonos's timari, his Saladoran knights, the Empress's Axes, and the Children of Forsvar to make the final assault.

It was another three difficult days before the Temple of Dromost came into sight. Twice they'd seen the ocean through gaps in the mountains. And then the trees disappeared as they exited the mountain pass they'd been following. Ahead of them was a barren, rocky landscape leading to a promontory pushing out into the wide, green sea. High atop the cliffs stood the massive, pillared black marble temple.

Gulls flew overhead, and the sun shone for the first time since they'd entered the Summoned Lands. Nidon's spirits would have lifted if he hadn't seen the obstacle that was the fortifications guarding the temple. A tall, strong wall ten strides high and three arrowflights across cut the temple off from the mainland. Sheer cliffs fell off from either side and into the sea. The only way in would be through the front gate or over the wall.

Banners and flags flew from atop the fortifications, flapping their defiance in the ocean breeze. Defenders crowded the walls. Orlos had told him that there was a town behind the walls and then another line of defenses before the temple proper would be reached.

Nidon had been surprised that the enemy had decided not to face them in the narrow pass beyond the gates. It would have been a bloody battle forcing their way through. Did it mean the enemy were few in numbers? Or did they simply have great faith in the strength of their walls? Nidon had no siege machinery, but he did have King Handrin and the Orb of Creation.

Nidon stood on a low hill overlooking the Temple of Dromost, Empress Kelifos and King Handrin at his side. The army's captains gathered in front of them.

"Through your valiant efforts, we have arrived," Nidon said. "Now, one last great task lies before us. We must capture the Temple of Dromost so that the gate can be sealed. We will attack tomorrow. For now, we will take defensive positions in front of the walls. Saladoran foot companies and Belenese freemen are to deploy two arrowflights from the walls. We don't know what artillery they have, so be wary. The Knights of Salador will establish their camp to the left. Satrus Exonos's timari will camp to the right. The Knights of the House, the Empress's Axes, and the Children of Forsvar will take the center. The Drinkers, Koromoi, and Landomeri, will set up blocking positions in the pass to prevent us from being attacked from the rear. Engineers and camp followers will begin manufacturing ladders for the assault. I will call for you again once I've examined the enemy position and planned the assault. Before you go, Empress Kelifos would like to address you."

The empress stepped forward. She was dressed as a timari, wearing her magnificent scale hauberk and bearing a gilded mace. "Brave Belenese and Saladorans. Koromoi, Drinkers, and Landomeri. Etheans even, despite the indignities forced upon your people. We come here, united for one purpose: to close the Dromost Gate for all eternity. The route home is closed by our enemies. General Solis is doing all he can to clear our path home. But today, that is not our route." She raised her mace and pointed it towards the Temple of Dromost. "That is our path. We will carve a path through our enemies and to the very Gate of Dromost. Only then can we turn our thoughts to home. For if we fail, all our efforts come to naught. Our homes and everything we know will be destroyed. Have faith, though. Our path has been difficult, but the Knights of Salador are with us, as is their king who bears the Orb of Creation. How can Forsvar not be with us in this task? By our might and song and magic, we will demonstrate to our Lord that we are worthy of his return!"

As she spoke the last words, King Handrin raised the Orb above his head and brilliant light flared from it. "Know this," he said. "You are part of something great. There has been no event in history that can compare to what we are about to do. Let us finish what Princess Ayja began. Let us close the Dromost Gate forever!"

Again the Orb flared, and the soldiers and officers around them cheered.

Nidon hadn't planned on the display. He hadn't expected the royals to say so much. But their effect buoyed even his own hopes, and he found himself grinning as he cheered along with the others. Still, deep in his heart, he hoped that some way might be found to save Ayja. He knew it was impossible, but he wouldn't give up his hope that she still lived.

As the cheers subsided, Nidon called out, "Officers, see you to your units! Victory will be ours!"

The army deployed carefully, fearful of some trickery by the enemy, but as the day wore on, they were unaccosted. Tents sprang up, horses were corralled, and wagons were laagered. It was all done smartly and in good order, despite the many sleepless days and half rations. The sun was overhead, the sea breeze was cool, and their final destination was in sight. Despite all of their travails, it finally seemed they'd get their chance to complete their mission.

That evening, as the sun set over the ocean, Nidon again invited the survivors of Ayja's expedition into his tent. Empress Kelifos, King Handrin, and a few ranking officers were there as well.

Nidon spotted Sir Tharryl by the tent flap. Unlike other Saladoran knights, he wore a fine scale hauberk and had a heavy, curved sword at his waist. Over it, he wore a tabard of plain yellow. "I never got the chance to thank you, Sir Tharryl. Three or four nights ago — when we were attacked in our camp. You fought the scaled demon. I was pinned under a pile of dead. You saved my life."

Tharryl crossed his arms. "Wasn't really trying to save you, Sir Nidon. Was just trying to kill the demon. Didn't even know you were there at first." He shrugged. "Saw you stick it with your dagger a couple of times."

"I did my best, good sir," Nidon said, wondering at Tharryl's grim mood. "You haven't picked your coat of arms yet?" He nodded at the blank tabard.

"Don't think I'll get a chance, seeing as I'm going to die."

"We don't know that, Sir Tharryl," Handrin said. "We may win our way free."

"Not me. I'll be the first over the wall, and I'm going to kill every one of those fuckers until they finally get me."

"Sir Tharryl," Nidon said. "You are in the presence of your king, the Empress of Belen, and two good women. You will watch your language."

"What are you going to do? Kill me? I'm a dead man."

Nidon was about to respond when Telea said, "Isibindi is dead, Champion Nidon. She was an Ethean warrior in my service. She was Sir Tharryl's, ah, fiancee. She died in the fighting the night you spoke of."

"I am sorry to hear that, Sir Tharryl," Nidon said.

"It is what it is," Tharryl said. "I'll join her as soon as you get this attack underway. Someone's got to be the first over the wall, and it's going to be me."

Nidon nodded. "I'll give you that honor, Sir Tharryl."

"It is an honorable choice for a Knight of Salador," Handrin said. "You will be remembered."

"Don't really give a shit, Your Majesty. Just want to kill them for what they did."

"You'll get your chance, Sir Tharryl," Nidon said. Then he turned to the others and said, "But before we attack, I need to know what we'll see beyond this wall."

"There is a small town between this wall and the next," Calen said, stepping forward. "The Doomcallers had already captured this first wall and the town when we were last here. We defended the second wall."

"The town is mostly destroyed," Sindi added. "They've left fifty strides of clear space before the second wall. The second wall is higher and one third the length of this one."

"They had no siege weapons," Tharryl said. "No need for them at such short range. The attackers had two rolling towers they used in the assault, but I'm certain they've been dismantled. I see no trebuchets or heavy catapults on the towers in front of us."

"They could have ballistae or light stone throwers," Nidon said, "but I see no heavier weapons. Still, it will be a difficult assault. Ladders and valor."

"What about making our own siege towers?" Orlos asked.

Nidon shook his head. "The terrain is too rough in front of the walls. We'd have to move too many boulders and fill in pits with gravel and fascines. We don't have the time. I'm sure they built their towers using the wood from the buildings in the town. We might be able to do the same when we get inside."

"Time is pressing," Handrin said. "If General Solis cannot hold the pass, the enemy will be upon us from the rear. We are short on supplies as well."

"We have water and wood and can slaughter the horses if need be, although it would pain me to do so," Nidon said. "You are correct, though, Your Majesty. We must press the attack. We will assault tomorrow."

"I will use my magic and the Orb of Creation to assault the wall," Handrin said. "I am concerned, though. I see in the aether that there are arcane wards placed upon the stone. I'm not certain how well they'll resist my magic."

"They will resist the magic of song," Telea said. "I don't know what they'll do to elementar magic."

"We have no time for subtlety," Nidon said. "We will hit them hard and fast. We have the Orb of Creation, elementars, singers, and healers. We have the finest soldiers in the world. We will take this wall."

They set down to planning the attack. All through the night, the sound of hammers and axes was heard as dozens of ladders were assembled for the coming assault. Soldiers were fed full rations for the first time in days, and despite how much he dreaded it, Nidon ordered some of the horses slaughtered to feed his hungry soldiers. He couldn't send soldiers weakened by hunger into battle, and without a supply train, the horses would soon begin to starve in any case.

The morning dawned clear and bright, lifting morale. The enemy had, for whatever reason, made no attack during the night, despite the warnings of the Belenese that the summoners often attacked under cover of darkness. Was it because of weakness? Did they not wish to lose any of the few defenders they had?

Nidon's Saladoran crossbows, with the support of Exonos's timari, would shower the walls with bolts and arrows, covering a general assault by Saladoran knights and spearmen. Sir Tharryl and a group of volunteers would lead the assault on the gate. He would be joined by spearmen, squires, and men-at-arms, each promised a knighthood by King Handrin should they reach the walls.

While that assault was going on, King Handrin and the Knights of the House would head for a small tower a third of the way down the wall. Due to a kink in the wall, the tower was less vulnerable to missile fire from other parts of the wall. Handrin would breach the tower with magic, allowing his elite knights to storm the stairs and take the walls.

As the soldiers moved into position, Squire Fress pointed at the gate keep and said, "Look there, Champion Nidon. It looks like the Banner of Salador."

Nidon didn't see it at first. Then he saw it, flapping boldly in the breeze above the gate keep. Fress was right. The Banner of Salador fluttered amongst the Doomcaller war flags. Blood rushed to his face. It was the banner Ayja had taken with her on her mission. It had fallen with Sir Lyam in the Temple of Dromost.

Taking a deep breath, he said, "Tell Sir Tharryl and his men that whoever takes that banner shall be made a Knight of the House and will be known forever as a Hero of Salador."

Fress saluted and ran off towards Tharryl's company of volunteers.

"Are we ready?" Exonos asked as he joined Nidon.

"We are. What is the word from our rear guard?"

"Nothing new. They received a messenger from General Solis. He continues to push towards the crossroads."

"Good. Our rear is secure, at least." Nidon turned his attention back to the army in front of him. All seemed in order. They'd taken no effort to hide what they were doing. It was a daylight assault. Years of experience had taught Nidon that night attacks were filled with confusion and peril. Better to make the attempt in the light of day. And he'd been warned how the summoners and their demons liked the night.

Nidon's heart thudded heavily as he prepared to order the advance. Never had he been more nervous before an attack, and he wasn't even in the front lines. If all went to plan, he'd never even draw his sword. His frayed nerves weren't out of fear. They came from the weight of command. This was his attack. Victory and defeat were on his shoulders.

He drew a deep breath and said, "Give them a wave, Sir Dalaman. Send them in." The knight raised his flag over his head and waved it boldly left and right. The banner was an exact match for the one brazenly displayed over the keep. Beside him, a trumpeter blared out the call for "attention."

All across the line, horns blared their reply as company flags waved left and right. "Signal the advance," Nidon said. Sir Dalaman thrust his flag forward as the trumpeter made another call.

Saladoran crossbowmen and Belenese timari advanced within an arrowflight of the walls, but still, the enemy didn't reply. Behind them, the knights of Salador kept pace. Most of the crossbow and timari companies halted one hundred strides from the wall. Some began to loose at unseen targets, and one entire company loosed a volley that cracked and shattered against the wall to no effect whatsoever.

"Please tell the commander of that company to refrain from shooting bolts at invisible enemies," Nidon said to a messenger, who immediately mounted and rode off.

Columns of knights and spearmen began to pass through the crossbowmen. They carried their long ladders with them as they made their way across the broken terrain. Finally, when they were fifty strides from the wall, bolts and arrows flew from arrow slits in the wall's towers and men began to fall. Still, the walls themselves appeared empty. Where were the defenders?

Then, with a cheer, the knights rushed towards the walls. Just as the first companies began to raise their ladders, a shower of objects flew over the wall to land amongst the attacking soldiers. There were puffs of smoke and flashes of fire as dozens, and then hundreds of imps appeared. At the same moment, figures suddenly rose all along the crenellations. Defenders hurled more imp jars, stones, and firepots down upon the knights.

Ladders that had started to rise now fell as knights fought the imps among them. Nidon heard voices rise in song as Belenese singers attempted to drive the demons back to Dromost. There were too few of them, though, and their voices couldn't reach the entire battlefield. Then, after just a few heartbeats, a wave of arrows and bolts rose up from the attackers. Nidon was certain the walls would be scoured clean by the tremendous volley, but the defenders hardly seemed to notice the barrage.

"How is that possible?" Nidon asked. He'd seen the missiles fly true. They'd struck the enemy full force. Was it some magic? No one near him could explain.

As knights and singers killed and banished the imps, the ladders began to rise again. A few resisted the defenders' attempts to knock them clear, and knights began to climb. Nidon had done it before — climbing a ladder in an assault. It was terrifying. There was no more courageous act than climbing a bouncing ladder into the face of a determined enemy.

Some of the knights were knocked off the ladders by thrown stones. He saw one struck by an imp jar, the helpless knight burned by the fire imp that clung to him until he could take no more and fell to his death. Others were impaled by spears or knocked off their ladders by heavy blows.

Nidon looked to where King Handrin had advanced with the Knights of the House. They were at the base of the small tower, but Nidon couldn't tell if they'd made a breach in the wall. He saw Empress Kelifos there as well, surrounded by a bodyguard of Empress's Axes.

A ladder reached the gate keep, and Nidon saw Sir Tharryl climb it. He held his shield ahead of him, warding off bolts and stones. He reached the top, and standing on the highest rungs, attempted to force his way between the crenellations. Three defenders hammered him with swords and axes, but they couldn't drive him back. Squires and spearmen clung to the ladder behind him, waiting for him to break through.

Nidon took two steps forward, his hand on his sword hilt before he realized what he was doing. He wanted to be on that ladder. They had to take the wall. *You're a bastard, Tharryl, but you're a tough bastard. Get off that ladder!*

Bodies began to plunge from the wall to the left and right of Tharryl's ladder. They fell, crashing amongst the attacking soldiers. At first, Nidon wondered if they'd been shot. But why had they fallen forward? And why so many at the same time? Then he heard terrible, inhuman roars. The men and women who'd fallen from the walls rose as demons among the ranks of the attackers, raking them with razor claws and gnashing teeth or grasping at them with long tentacles and crushing the life from them.

And still, the defenders on the walls hurled stones and imp jars, ignoring the arrows and bolts that impaled them. Nidon had seen the fanatics. He knew they were brave. He also knew they died just like other men. But these men were impaled by six or more arrows and kept on fighting.

No more ladders rose, and only Tharryl's remained on the wall. Even as Nidon watched a demon on the ground below broke it, casting Tharryl and everyone on it to the ground. And still, Handrin had not breached the tower.

Fighting raged all along the wall. One by one, the demons fell, but each at terrible cost. Not only were the demons killing his men, but the defenders above them were wreaking havoc upon them.

A bloody messenger ran to Nidon. "A message from the king, Champion. He cannot break the wall. It is guarded by summoner magic. Also, the singer Telea reports that the defenders on the wall are silent brothers — they are undead."

That is why our missiles are having little effect.

"Fall back," Nidon called out to his messengers. "Call them back. Starting positions! Messengers go." He turned to his banner-bearer and said, "Give the signal." At his word, Sir Dalaman began sweeping the banner in large circles around his head.

Here was the moment of greatest danger. Would the retreat turn into a rout? Word spread among the officers and soldiers, and ever so slowly, they disengaged. Spearmen hastily formed shield walls under the cover of the crossbowmen and timari. And then, step by step, the spearmen retreated. Demons threw themselves at the Saladorans, but one by one they were dispatched. And, to Nidon's great relief, no more bodies fell from above to become demons. Even the silent brothers on the wall sank out of sight and no more imp jars were thrown.

Those who were able helped the injured, leaving only the dead behind. They'd lost hundreds in the attack. The defeat had been total. Nidon had never in his life been on the side of such a complete disaster. *And I commanded it.*

At least there was no pursuit. The army was still intact. Nidon held them at the ready for a time, just in case the enemy might sally from the gates, but the attack never came. *They are willing to wait for us behind their wall. Why shouldn't they? Time is on their side.*

"The walls are enchanted," Handrin said when they met later. "Each stone has runes engraved upon it, and when my magic touched them, the power of the aether rose up in them and countered me. I damaged a single block. I've never seen anything like it. There is no going through this wall."

"We lost nearly five hundred soldiers," Nidon said. "I'm waiting for the final count. The men fought heroically, and yet we only put three ladders up on the wall, and only one man reached the top. Sir Tharryl wished to carve a path through the enemy, but I don't know that he killed a single foe before he fell."

"He will get another chance," Telea said. "He lived."

Nidon stared at her. "How is that possible?"

"He broke both legs, but he was brought back. He can be healed. So can the other wounded."

Handrin nodded. "I will share the power of the Orb with the healers. The Orb of Creation is not limitless, however. Once drained, it takes time to recover."

"It is a well of power beyond anything I could have imagined," Telea said. "I understand now how it will seal the Dromost Gate."

"But we must get it to the gate first," Nidon said. "How do we accomplish that? Another assault like we attempted today will end just as disastrously. I have failed you, my king. I am honor bound to offer my resignation."

Handrin shook his head. "We didn't know what we faced. Now we do. You will continue to command, Champion Nidon." He looked towards the wall. "I could call down a curtain of fire atop the wall, destroying the silent brothers and summoners there."

"I don't think it will work," Telea said. "When we were last here, and Calen and Sindi helped defend the second wall, the Doomcallers didn't use any magic on them. The Doomcallers knew their magic wouldn't work."

"I can try it," Handrin said. "Under cover of darkness, I can approach the wall and call down fire. We would know soon enough."

"We also don't know how much harm we did to them," Empress Kelifos said. "We took losses, but so did they. Perhaps another assault would work."

Nidon paced. "We don't have enough information. How many defenders do they have? Only what we've seen, or are there thousands behind the walls?"

"Orlos could scout for us," Handrin said. "He can scale the cliffs." The king turned to a squire and said, "Find Orlos. Tell him I need him."

"Your Majesty, those cliffs can't be scaled," Nidon said.

"Orlos and I climbed the Great Keep of Sal-Oras," Handrin said. "We can do this."

"King Handrin," Kelifos said, "this is too dangerous. We can't risk you. You must close the Dromost Gate."

"Who else will do it? Fendal is back at the crossroads. Only Lady Varen and Lady Wenla are up to such a task. I don't wish to send them into such danger."

"But you'd send a man?" Kelifos asked.

"Your Majesty," Nidon said, looking at Handrin, "I know that it isn't the Saladoran way to send women into such danger, but we sent Ayja to the Dromost Gate, and she closed it. Her mother slew Akinos. Lady Varen and Lady Wenla must attempt this."

Handrin held up his hand. "You are both right. I would send a man but balk at sending a woman. And I think of myself as forward-thinking. Old thoughts die hard. Call for them."

Chapter Thirty

"Help me, please," Ayja said, her eyes raised to the spiridus circling around her. She still sat with her sword across her lap. "I need your strength." How long had it been since she entered the Emerald Prison? Days at least. Longer maybe. Eternal twilight made judging the passage of time impossible. The end was near, though. The final runes that would turn the Emerald Prison into the Emerald Gate were nearly finished. She'd worked slowly, though. In the time that it had taken her to carve the runes, she'd also managed to create many empowered workings within her memory walk.

She'd also had time to work on her sword. The blade's nicks were gone and it was as sharp as the magic of the aether could make it. It only needed a few final touches. And now she had her chance. Vahlah was busy drawing life force from his captives. She had to finish before he came back to inspect her work again.

Entering her memory walk, Ayja placed her sword on the heavy oak planks of the kitchen table. She focused on the base of the blade near the hilt and imagined the runes she'd place there. Runes that would give the sword its own well of power. Then she flipped the blade and on the other side imagined more runes. Her sword would do more than cut; it would be an artifact of elemental power.

She could do this. She'd studied the Godhammer. She knew its runes and how they worked — at least for the most part. Her sword wouldn't match the Godhammer in brute power. It wouldn't steal the souls of those it slew. Those workings were beyond her. But while its well of power held, the sword would be a fearsome weapon.

A small circle began to glow on the sword's blade. Ayja stared at that spot and focused her will, pouring power into it and etching the blade with her magic. The steel resisted her working. It was far more difficult to work than any other substance she'd ever attempted. She was stronger now, though, and understood magic better than she ever had.

"Help me," she called out to the spiridus again. She didn't look up but felt the spiridus as it approached. Then, one after another, they entered her, filling her well of power even as she drained it.

The effort tore at her. Sweat poured from her brow and down her back as she focused on the searing point of white light on the sword blade. The whole world went dark but for that one point of light. Still, the spiridus entered her, pouring their life force into her well. Within her memory walk, the fire burned emerald green.

Ayja flipped the blade and worked the other side. Her breath came to her in great gasps, almost as if she'd run a sprint of two arrowflights. Still, she pressed on, not knowing how much time she had. If not for the spiridus, she would have had to stop a dozen times over for want of more power.

Finally, soaked through with sweat and exhausted, Ayja stared down at the rings of power she'd crafted. There was one last step to complete. Taking another of the silver clasps that had broken from her armor, she held it to the sword and inlaid the silver into the runes. Within her memory walk, she twisted the strands of aether and placed her workings onto the sword.

Dizzy with the effort, she touched her well of power, ready to transfer some of her strength into the sword, when something flew into her line of sight. A spiridus landed on the sword's blade, obstructing her view. She was about to shoo it away when the spiridus disappeared into the blade.

You bring hope.

Ayja lifted the blade and looked under it to see if the spiridus had passed through, but it was gone. Then she looked at the blade again and saw the shimmer of emerald light on the steel.

"What did it do?" she asked aloud.

"What do you mean?" Darra asked from where he stood guard nearby.

"The spiridus entered my sword." Ayja raised the weapon for him to see.

"Is it giving its own strength to the sword?"

Still partially blinded by the afterglow of her working, Ayja peered at the circle of power she'd created. "It did," she said, her voice filled with wonder. "I think it is still there."

"I know nothing about your magic. Nothing about the spiridus either. Perhaps it will leave when it is ready."

"I don't know," she said, regarding the blade. "Perhaps." Ayja took her canteen and drank until it was empty.

"Should I refill it?"

Ayja shook her head. "I want you nearby. I must rest for a bit." She looked down at the blade again and touched the still-warm runes. *Are you in there?*

Hope.

For what? Freedom?

Hope.

"I don't understand," Ayja said aloud. "It only says, 'hope.'"

"Then name it Hope and let it be, my queen. I can think of nothing else. If the spiridus wants to leave, it will."

Ayja lay down. She placed her sword so that the hilt was near her face and she could see the runes. Darra once again placed his ruined kaftan under her head. She smiled her thanks as she closed her eyes. Within her memory walk her fire blazed green, but the room was lit by golden light. There was so much she wanted to do. She glanced at the mantle where her unlit candles sat.

With a sigh, she went to them and filled the empowered workings from her well. The fire dimmed as she drew from it, but even then, a spiridus entered and filled it again. She smiled at it as it darted for the door. "Thank you!" she called after it.

She saw her quiver by the door. With so much strength, she could create more empowered workings. She was so tired, though. Ayja went to her room and fell asleep the moment her head hit the pillow.

Dreams filled her sleep. Dreams of a forest of giant oaks with sunlight streaming down through their leaves. Beautiful white flowers covered the forest floor while bright streams made music as they fell over rocky waterfalls. She smelled the earth and moldering leaves and the delicate scent of the little white flowers. And everywhere she looked, she saw spiridus flitting through the branches or hiding behind flower petals.

Home. Life. Hope.

Ayja walked through the forest. It was the most beautiful place she'd ever imagined. She was looking for something but wasn't quite certain what it was. Or was something looking for her?

Come to me, Enna.

She knew the voice. She walked a little faster. There was a slope ahead. She heard rushing water beyond.

"Ayja, wake up," Darra's voice said. She felt him shaking her. For a few moments, she refused to open her eyes. She wanted to stay in the beautiful dream and find the voice. "Vahlah is coming."

She opened her eyes. She saw Darra's deathly pale face and black eyes staring down at her. Some of his lank, black hair had come loose from the tail he kept it in and partially covered his face. Behind him, lightning crisscrossed Dromost's dark skies.

Darra offered Ayja his hand and pulled her to her feet. She sheathed Hope, and Darra handed Forsvar and Dromost to her. Vahlah marched up to them and glanced down at the circle of power and frowned. "No progress?"

"I had to sleep," Ayja replied.

"I brought more gifts," Vahlah said. "So that you might work more quickly." He pointed with his spear to where more demon soldiers were bringing up captive worms. "Send your soulless friend to collect your strength."

Ayja nodded to Darra and turned back to the veden. She saw something new. Vahlah wore an iron chain across his body. A round stone tablet and a steel canister hung from it. Runes covered the tablet and it had a hole in the center that the chain passed through. When she looked into the aether, she saw no lines of power radiating from it. The still canister was the size of a quarter keg, and radiated immense power — so much that she was nearly blinded in the aether.

Vahlah saw her looking at the tablet and smiled. "You have your secrets and I have mine," he said. "Do not betray me."

What would happen if he empowered the tablet? She had no way of knowing without examining it. "I want to see the tablet," Ayja said.

"No. We have a deal. Give Dromost to me, open the gate, and leave. It is as simple as that. You don't trust me and I don't trust you. I know you did something to your sword. I know your pet demon was working on a project of its own as well. So you'll forgive me for preparing my own defenses. Now finish your work, and let's be done with this."

Ayja glanced toward's Telea's demon. It was preparing something as well? She'd conferred with it several times recently but had seen nothing amiss. But then again, she and Darra kept most of their attention on Vahlah. The demon lay on the ground, curled around itself, with its wings spread over it like a tent. It looked asleep, but she knew they didn't sleep.

Ayja drew a deep breath. Too many secrets. Too many unknowns.

"Finish your work," Vahlah said again. The veden paced impatiently in front of her.

Ayja gave Dromost to Darra. As their hands touched, she passed him warnings of both Vahlah and Telea's demon. Then, drawing on her well of power, she began to mold runes into the stone. The work was easier now. The more practice she had, the easier it became.

As she worked, Vahlah stalked nearby. She tried to put the veden out of her mind. After a time, she paused to stand and stretch. She took her canteen and went to drink from it before realizing it was empty.

"I need more," Ayja said, holding the canteen out to Vahlah.

"I am not your servant. Have the soulless one do it."

"No. He must remain with me. Send one of your demons."

Glowering, Vahlah took the canteen and strode to the edge of the prison. As soon as his back was turned, Ayja raised her hand, and several spiridus flew down and entered her, filling her well with strength. They fled before he turned back.

"It will return shortly," Vahlah said.

Ayja nodded and went back to work. She had only one last section to complete — the closing commands. She completed everything except the two final runes, waiting for her canteen before she'd touch it. Finally, it was returned and she spared some of her strength cleansing the water within. She took a long drink as Vahlah glowered over her.

Kneeling, Ayja started the final inscriptions.

Suddenly it came to her how close she was to home, and her hand began to shake. She pulled it back from the stone and clasped both her hands together. *Would this really work? Am I going home?*

"What are you waiting for?" Vahlah asked.

"This isn't easy," Ayja said, composing herself for the last effort. *He will try something.*

Ayja touched the stone and carved out the final line of the last glyph.

"Done! It is done!" Vahlah shouted. "Well done, Daughter of Handrin the Great. Given other circumstances, we could be friends."

Ayja stood. "We both get something we want," she said. "I hope you enjoy ruling your demon world."

"Oh, I will. I certainly will." Vahlah stepped up to the circle of power and placed the spiked butt of his spear in the center of her intricate carving. He began to chant, and a dark aura rose up towards the spiridus crowded at the top of the prison.

Pain. Fear. Death. The suffering of the spiridus struck Ayja like a physical blow.

"What are you doing?" she shouted. "Use the demon blood you collected!"

Vahlah continued chanting, and slowly spiridus were drawn down to the spear. They resisted, but the veden's magic could not be denied. When they were a stride from the end of the spear, brilliant emerald light was drawn from them and into it. The light flowed down the shaft and into the circle of power, where it slowly filled in Ayja's carvings.

"You promised not to use the spiridus for this," Ayja said, raising Forsvar and hefting Dromost in her hand.

"Look, Ayja!" Darra called out.

She turned at Darra's warning. Behind her, near where Vahlah had placed the golden ring on the ground, a huge, shimmering gate had opened. Unlike the Dromost Gate, she could see through this one. There she saw a brilliant emerald tree set in a magnificent stone chamber. Vahlah had opened the gate!

Above her, Ayja saw the spiridus that had already given their life force streaming towards the gate and freedom. "Go! Go!" she shouted. She ran a few strides towards the gate and then stopped.

It wasn't right. The gate couldn't have opened. Her gate, the one Vahlah was empowering, would only open when he had Dromost in his possession. And the Emerald Tree — wasn't it shattered and only a stump?

She turned back to Vahlah. His spear glowed emerald with the life force of the spiridus. At his feet, the circle of power erupted with green fire. Beneath the flames the runes shone brightly. The circle was empowered.

"What is that?" Ayja demanded, pointing at the shimmering gate the spiridus streamed through.

"Before I met you, I didn't know much about gates, but I did know a lot about prisons. The spiridus are mine. You cannot take them."

The gold circlet is a prison!

"Stop!" Ayja shouted to the spiridus. "Don't go there!" But the spiridus continued to race towards the portal.

Vahlah removed his spear from the circle of power. In a heartbeat, the emerald light faded from the spear, and it was black iron again. The spiridus, however, continued to stream towards the false gate. "Flee!" Vahlah shouted, laughing. "Freedom awaits!" He faced Ayja. "Give Dromost to me, and you can save them. You see, it is a special prison. In a short time, it will utterly consume your precious spiridus. Give Dromost to me and leave. It's the only way you'll save them!"

How many spiridus would perish in the time it took her to defeat him in a fight? No, it was more than that. She had to defeat him and figure out how to nullify the prison. Or she could give him Dromost and save as many spiridus as she could.

Ayja looked over her shoulder at the spiridus racing towards their doom. She threw Dromost to the veden, who caught it in his free hand. The circle of power flashed brilliant green, and next to the stump of the Emerald Tree, another gate appeared. Smaller than the false one, and opaque green, its edges wavered and shifted. It was there, though. The gate home was open.

Vahlah held Dromost high over his head and unfurled his huge wings. "It is mine!" he shouted.

Ayja ran for the false gate.

"No, Ayja!" Darra shouted. "This way!"

She shouted up to the spiridus, "Turn back! Fly for the other gate. That's the way home!"

A few heeded her words. Those closest to the false gate continued to stream through it. What magic had Vahlah devised to kill them?

She ran to the false gate, still shouting at the spiridus to turn back, but no more listened. The sight of freedom after half a millennia of imprisonment was too great a lure. Ayja searched the ground for the golden ring Vahlah had placed there. She found it, hidden, behind the gate.

From behind, the false gate didn't exist at all. There was just the golden ring lying on the ground. Hundreds of spiridus streamed into the middle of the ring and disappeared. Ayja fell to her knees and read the runes.

It was a prison. Only a prison. There were no runes that would cause death. "Where is Vahlah?" she called out.

"Gone," Darra replied.

Ayja searched the sky for any sign of the veden. The spiridus streaming past her obstructed her view, though, and she saw no sign of him.

"I don't know where," Darra said. "I was watching you. Come, Ayja, we must go."

"Not yet." She turned her attention back to the gold ring. She grasped it with her free hand and tried to lift it, but it wouldn't budge.

"Ayja, we must go!"

Ayja slung Forsvar on her back and grasped the ring with both hands, but Vahlah's magic bound it to the stone. She pushed her vision into the aether, but before she could start, there was a crack and a clatter nearby as if stone or metal struck stone. As she looked up, the hundreds of spiridus streaming towards the prison fell to the ground, unmoving.

"What happened?" Ayja asked, looking up.

"Telea's demon threw something into the prison," Darra said.

Ayja saw it then, in the aether. A deep blue-black haze filled the area. Some working of magic she didn't understand. Just outside the prison, Telea's demon paced, snarling towards Ayja. What new betrayal was this? The spiridus were no longer entering Vahlah's prison but now lay on the ground. Still alive, but unable to move.

Not all of them, though. Those near the Emerald Gate flew through it.

"What did the demon throw?" Ayja asked. "Where is it?"

"It landed somewhere over here," Darra said, pointing towards the ground nearby and running that direction.

Ayja saw it. A smooth black stone. "There! Take it!"

Before Darra reached the stone, the green light that had filled the Emerald Prison disappeared. Ayja looked around in confusion. The stump of the Emerald Tree was no longer blood red. It was pure emerald.

In the distance hundreds of shapes moved. Demons streamed out of the caves dug into the canyon walls. Flying demons dove from the heights. The prison was gone. The barrier was gone.

"Hurl it away!" Ayja shouted. It was all she could think of. The stone, whatever magic the demon had placed upon it, only affected those spiridus near it. They had only moments before Vahlah's demons would be upon them.

As Darra touched the stone, a blast of dark, magical force erupted from it, throwing him ten strides through the air. He crashed to the ground but rolled quickly to his feet. "I can't approach it," he called to Ayja.

The spiridus still lay upon the ground, unmoving. The stone's malevolent magic still filled the air, undiminished after hurling Darra away. Immobile, the spiridus would be massacred.

Ayja sprinted towards the stone. As she closed on it, Forsvar's aura touched it and the stone's magic was quenched. She picked it up and hurled it as far as she could. As it flew, the stone's magic returned, but it was too far away to affect the spiridus any longer. Heartbeats later, the spiridus began to rise.

"Behind you!" Darra shouted.

She turned and saw the pyren charging Telea's demon. It held the gold ring in one claw. *It has the spiridus!*

Even as she watched, the dragonlike demon unfurled its wings to launch itself into the air. With barely a thought, Ayja hurled a wind lance at it, knocking the demon over.

It was just enough time for Darra to reach the demon. As the demon righted itself, Darra reached out with his bare hand and touched it. It was too big to immediately paralyze though, and recoiled from his touch. Then it lashed out with a claw, long talons raking across Darra's chest and driving him away.

The demon knows Darra too well, Ayja thought. Drawing *Hope,* she charged. Again the demon unfurled its wings, but before it could take flight, Ayja summoned a blast of wind to hurl her forwards. As she fell she raised her sword for a tremendous stroke. *Hope* blazed with green fire.

The sinuous demon leapt away from her, and her blade only slashed its neck instead of decapitating it. Ayja swung again and severed one of its arms at the elbow. Shrieking in fury, the demon buffeted her with its wings, the wind driving her back. In that moment of freedom, it gathered itself onto its haunches, and threw itself into the air.

Ayja leapt forward and swung again but only managed to slash the demon's tail as it flew out of reach. She knew she had only heartbeats to spare before it escaped and she hurled a ring of fire at it. Flames erupted all around the demon, but it flew out the other side of the inferno unaffected.

With another stoke of its wings, the demon flew higher. Too high for her to even leap. It still clutched the gold ring. How many spiridus were trapped inside?

One more wind lance! A powerful one. It was her only hope. But even as she summoned strength from her well of power, the demon twisted and contorted in the air and suddenly plummeted toward the ground. In her head, Ayja heard a terrible scream. *NOOOOO! Not now!*

Before the demon hit the ground, its physical form vanished and it became a creature of mist. And then the mist shrank into a shimmering ball and disappeared. The golden ring fell to the ground below.

"We must flee," Darra said. He stood near her, dagger in hand, pointing at the winged demons diving at them from above.

"I have to get the ring first," Ayja said as she ran past him. Demons charged them from every direction. She and Darra had only moments before they'd be overrun. Ayja snatched up the ring and slipped it onto her arm like an oversized bracelet and then slid Forsvar over it. The prison was as safe as she could make it. Whatever force had felled the demon, it had given her the chance to free them.

All around her, spiridus rose into the air, their flight steadier now. The false gate was gone. "That way!" Ayja shouted, pointing towards the Emerald Gate. It was then that she saw that not all of the demons were coming for her. Some were flying for the Emerald Gate. *They mean to enter Helna's world.*

A flying demon swept through the spiridus like a hawk through a flight of songbirds, snatching up two of them in an instant. Another flying demon approached and she hurled an empowered working at it. With an explosion of fire, the crippled demon crashed into the ground, breaking its back and wings on impact.

Ayja and Darra ran for the Emerald Gate. A demon struck at the spiridus, but the spirits were faster now and evaded its attack. They would make it! The spiridus would escape. It was too late for Ayja and Darra, though. The demons were closing in too fast. They'd have to fight their way through.

Ahead, two flying demons swept through the Emerald Gate. Another flew at Ayja, slashing at her with its claws. She turned the attacks on

Forsvar and sheared off the demon's wing with a stroke of her sword. Then, from every direction, Vahlah's armored demons struck them. Vahlah himself was still nowhere to be seen.

Ayja pushed ahead, knocking demons aside with blows from Forsvar and cutting them down with her spiridus blade. The sword blazed with green fire, cutting through demon armor and slaying them with every stroke. But for every demon she killed, two took its place.

Darra followed her, stabbing demons with his dagger and drawing their life with his touch. The final few spiridus streaked through the gate, but demons were streaming through behind them.

"Go!" Darra shouted from behind her. "Close it!"

Blows hammered her from all sides. She and Darra fought back to back now, making no progress. From within her memory walk, Ayja took a candle and hurled it at the ground. Light flashed and demons screamed in agony.

They gained another five strides. But the demons hurled themselves forward, and Ayja and Darra were hemmed in again.

"Leave me!" Darra shouted. "Close the gate!"

Ayja threw another ring of light at the ground, incinerating the demons closest to her. Again they surged a few strides closer to the gate. She had only four candles left and too far to go. Demons crowded the space between her and the gate, while others continued to pour through.

Ayja hurled a ring of fire at the demons in front of her before they could close in. She held Forsvar's aura close to her, and the flames washed over its protection. Even as she charged into the inferno, she hurled another ring of fire. She cut down burning demons as she ran through them, knocking others aside with crushing blows from Forsvar.

The gate was so close, but there were still demons blocking her path. She threw her last ring of light. Its brilliant flash incinerated the demons closest to the gate and blinded those further off. Ayja dashed through the gaping hole her working had left in the demonic forces. As she reached the gate, she stepped aside for Darra.

He wasn't there. Fifteen strides back, the demons had him surrounded. She barely made him out in the chaos of battle.

"Darra!" she shouted. She took a stride towards him, but several demons rushed her. She cut one down and another took its place. She had no way of protecting Darra. Blows hammered against Forsvar, driving her closer to the gate.

She had her silver fire. The rage of battle, the chaos, and the pain, had it boiling close to the surface, ready to erupt. Her silver strength would give her the power she needed to save him.

"Go, my queen!" Darra shouted.

She couldn't abandon him. Her sword flashed emerald as she beheaded the demon in front of her. But before she could advance, a massive abomination loomed in front of her. The armored, bull-headed demon lowered its horned helm and charged. It plowed into the backs of the demons in front of her, throwing them into Forsvar. Ayja stumbled backward, swept up by the onslaught of the giant demon, and the press of the soldiers it drove before it.

There was a green flash, and Ayja toppled backward, falling over an emerald stone. She was in a large, domed chamber, dimly lit by the stump of the Emerald Tree and by the remaining emerald branches connected to the vaulted ceiling above. A demon roared and thrashed nearby. Figures moved at the edge of her vision.

Darra!

Ayja rolled to her feet. The gate was still there. It hadn't closed. *But it should have! I've gone through!*

The giant demon was in the gate, thrashing about, bleeding from wounds in its neck as it struck the bright edges of the gate. It was too big to pass. Was that why the gate hadn't closed?

Forsvar warned her of an unseen threat behind her. She spun around, raising the Godshield. And there stood Vahlah. The veden swung Dromost in a wicked arc, the runes erupting in a brilliant flash as they struck Forsvar. The blow, stronger than any she'd ever felt, sent her hurtling through the air. She lost her grip on her sword as she flew towards a wall. With barely a heartbeat to spare, she twisted the aether and summoned a blast of wind to cushion her. Even then, the impact was crushing, the air driven from her lungs. She fell to the floor on her hands and knees.

She looked up in time to see more demons charging at her. Behind them, Vahlah's wings opened wide, propelling him in a giant leap towards her. Ayja flicked one of her two remaining fire rings at the rushing demons.

The explosion consumed several demons, but Vahlah swept through unharmed. He swung Dromost as he landed, but she was already away, her summoned wind propelling her across the chamber.

There were at least a dozen demons in the room with Vahlah. All turned and rushed her.

Ayja raised Forsvar as the demons hurled a volley of steel darts. They cracked and thudded against the Godshield, none getting past. And still, the gate was open.

Ayja hurled her last ring of fire, incinerating more of them. Again Vahlah swept towards her. She leaped away from him, but he corrected his flight and struck out with his iron spear. She took it on Forsvar, but the impact threw her flight off course, and she landed hard, stumbling and falling prone.

As she got to her feet, a single demon attacked her. She parried its hammer, then struck it with the Godshield, knocking it aside. Her well of power was low.

She needed *Hope.*

Then, near the tree, she saw the ring of power Vahlah's father had crafted long ago. The ring that supported the spiridus prison. Rays of red light emanated from the ring to the stump and then to the gate. Now, though, atop the ring sat a stone tablet — the same tablet Vahlah had carried. Both the tablet and the ring were covered in smoking, black ichor. Vahlah's steel jug lay cast aside on the floor, red-black fluid dripping from its open top.

He's blocked the gate open. That's what the tablet and the jug were for.

A dark form swept over her, and there was a thundercrack as Dromost smashed into the Godshield again. The power of the blow rocked her back, and she retreated a few paces. Vahlah lashed out with his spear, but it glanced off Forsvar's rim. From her left and right, more demons approached. Still, she gave ground under Vahlah's assault.

The Emerald Gate flashed. The bull-headed demon was gone, and one after another, demon soldiers came through. There was no sign of Darra.

Vahlah grinned as he hammered at Ayja. He knew she was finished.

And she was. Her well of power was nearly empty. The candles on her mantle were out. And, while she might hold off one assailant for a time, the never-ending onslaught would take her. She was going to die. Before she did, though, she had to close the Emerald Gate.

As Vahlah recovered Dromost for another blow, Ayja struck him with a wind lance, driving him back. In the brief moment it gave her, she ran to *Hope* and swept it off the floor. As soon as she had it in her hands, she let her silver fire consume her. Rage-fueled strength flooded her arms as Ayja's vision went silver.

Aiming her sword at the charging demons, Ayja channeled the raw power of the aether through *Hope* and sent a crackling bolt of silver fire through them. They cried out as the fire savaged them. Vahlah struck her again, but this time Ayja countered. *Hope* burned with the brilliant white fire of the aether as she swung it. Vahlah barely caught the sword on his iron spear. Arcane energy exploded at the clash and he nearly lost his spear with the force of it. Ayja pressed him with a relentless series of attacks, driving him back.

More demons charged her. Again she reached into the aether and blasted them with silver fire, incinerating them. Then she turned the fire

313

on Vahlah. The aetherial bolt caught him on the chest and the runes on his armor flared. The veden recoiled under the assault, spreading his wings and hurling himself away from the attack.

Ayja let her fire go, unable to sustain it. She had earned the space she needed. She ran to the circle of power and raised *Hope* high above her. The ancient blade still cracked with the aether. She glanced at the gate, hoping against hope that Darra would come through.

It flashed emerald green as another demon arrived.

I'm sorry, Darra.

She brought *Hope* down upon Vahlah's tablet, channeling all the power of the aether within her into the strike. Splinters of stone cut into her flesh as a fiery explosion hurled her backward. Ayja hit the floor hard but managed to roll to her feet. She was dazed and weak. Her silver fire faded and a wave of exhaustion flowed over her.

When she looked over Forsvar's rim, the Emerald Gate was gone.

Vahlah leaped at her again, and Ayja staggered under the Godhammer's crushing blows. Only Forsvar saved her, the Godshield turning aside the greatest part of what Dromost dealt.

With every blow, she retreated until he backed her against the wall. Only embers remained in her well of power.

"You failed," Vahlah said, leveling another strike on her. There were demons behind him, Ayja couldn't tell how many. "Most of your spiridus are trapped in Dromost and will never escape." He swung again. "I would have liked to have them to feed me."

Clang!

"Yes, I would have liked to have my demon army."

Clang!

"But, you've brought me an even greater gift."

Clang!

"Now I will have Forsvar."

Ayja barely had the strength to raise Forsvar. Her silver fire had taken everything she had remaining. Closing the gate had been her final, defiant act.

"You thought I wanted to be King of Dromost?" Vahlah laughed and struck her again. She slammed into the wall behind her.

Within Ayja's memory walk, the last ember of her fire went out. *Hope* slipped from her hand as she slid down the wall to the floor.

"Centuries of exile are over," Vahlah said, leaning close to her. "All I've ever wanted was to return to this world and to take my revenge upon it. And thanks to you, it will all come true."

Chapter Thirty-one

Orlos crept close to the cliff edge and peered over. Waves crashed against the rocks far below, visible even in the near-total darkness. Close behind him were Wenla and Varen, both shrouded in dark clothing and with lamp black covering their faces and hands. Not far away stood the walls of the Temple of Dromost. There were no guards to be seen. Nor any light at all. But he knew they were there, summoners and their silent brothers, waiting with imp jars and stones. *The walls can't be breached. We have to do it this way.*

"I'm not sure about this," Lady Wenla said, peering over her shoulder to the safety of the camp they'd left behind. She'd long ago left behind the kirtle and gown of a lady and now wore the trousers and tunic of a Saladoran soldier. "Let's get this over with."

"Not yet," Orlos said, peering back towards the camp. "Telea is coming."

"I thought only you were going," Varen said. Her appearance had also taken a dramatic turn. Even through the difficulties of the campaign, she'd always managed to somehow look pretty, prim, and proper. Now she wore men's trousers, had a face smeared in black streaks, and had her hair pulled back into a commoner's ponytail.

Telea appeared out of the darkness, drawing a gasp of surpise from Varen.

"This isn't what we planned for," Wenla said. "Didn't King Handrin tell her not to come?"

"Of course the king knows," Orlos lied.

"I just spoke to him," Telea said. "That's why I'm late."

The two had come up with their plan after the officer's meeting. *"We can end this, Orlos,"* Telea had said. *"We can turn the tide of this battle."*

"How?"

"Not everyone in the temple is one of the living dead. There are Doomcaller summoners and warriors in there as well. If we get inside, I

315

can create my own silent brothers. And, unlike the Doomcallers, I know how to make my undead create more undead. They will destroy the defenders from the inside."

"What if it gets out of control like before?"

"Not this time. I'll keep them under control. Once we're inside and see what's there, I want you to return and tell Champion Nidon what I've done."

"Why not tell them now?" he asked.

"How do you think they'll react to the idea that I'll raise another army of the dead?"

They had to take the risk, Orlos had realized. Time was against them. He glanced at Telea. Wrinkles creased the corners of her eyes, and white streaked her hair. There were still many in the camp who would not speak with her and who called her *Queen of the Dead*. The Belenese healers and singers in particular would have nothing to do with her. Her strength, at least, had returned, after the ordeal of the previous weeks. She no longer had to stand up to the crushing weight of the undead souls linked to hers.

"We don't have to go far," Orlos said, kneeling and peering over the cliff edge. "It's hard to see, but there's a rough ledge about half way down. We climb down to it, walk along it, and then climb back up beyond the wall."

"It's a lot of stone work," Varen said. "I don't know if I have the strength in my well of power."

"I will share my strength with you," Telea said.

"You just have to get us across the ledge," Orlos said. "Your mother will get us up the other side." Although Varen was the stronger of the two elementars, Lady Wenla had insisted that she take the more dangerous task. She would get them back up the cliff and inside the temple.

Telea tied intricate rope harnesses around their waists and their thighs. "I grew up with Drinker mountaineers," Telea replied. "If you're going to climb a cliff, you should do it properly. This will keep you safe. You're ready now." Telea fastened a rope to the harness and then looped it around an iron spike Varen set into the stone with magic. "We will stop your descent any time you wish. Go ahead."

To her credit, Varen went over the cliff without complaint. Telea slowly let the rope out as Varen worked her way down. Wenla peered over the cliff edge and reported to them on Varen's descent. "Very good," she said. "And she is down now. She's on the ledge."

Orlos regarded the temple walls as Telea lowered Wenla. There'd been no sign they'd been seen.

"Your turn," Telea said. She tied the rope to his belt and he stepped over the edge. Telea let him down and then rappelled after him.

"I made some improvements to the rock on my way down," Varen said when they joined her. "To ease our climb back up."

"Thank you," Orlos said. "Can you do the same for the ledge?"

"I'll do my best."

Telea tied a rope through all of their harnesses to catch anyone who might fall. It was difficult work on the narrow ledge, but she managed it well enough.

On several occasions, Varen created handholds for them to get past narrow parts of the ledge, but finally they reached the end and could go no further. Sweat beaded from her brow, plastering her hair against her temple.

"So now it is my turn," Wenla said, staring upwards. "Go back, Varen. Wait for us."

"Thank you, Varen," Orlos said. "You have the strength to get back?"

"Yes," she said, but Orlos saw doubt in her eyes.

"I will help," Telea said. She took Varen's hand and began to chant. The young woman's eyes widened at the touch.

"You've restored my well of power!" she said.

"It's in my interest as well," Telea said with a smile. "When you return, do what you can to make the climb as easy as possible for us."

"I will," Varen promised. "And good luck! Come back soon, mother." Telea untied her from the rope binding them together, and Varen began to make her way back down the ledge.

Wenla watched her daughter's progress for a few moments and then turned her attention to the cliff. Orlos watched as the elementar molded the rock, making handholds for Telea and him to use. He remembered how difficult it had been for Handrin to create handholds up the Great Keep of Sal-Oras and hoped the baroness had the strength in her.

Telea followed Wenla soon after she started in case she needed to loan her strength. Orlos waited until she was a third of the way up before following himself. In many places, natural cracks in the wall made alterations unnecessary. In other places, Wenla was forced to make deep pockets in the sheer stone. The climb was easier than the Great Keep had been, but, if anything, he was more afraid. Here, an alerted enemy waited for them, and a single dropped stone would knock him off the cliff. He glanced down, quickly realizing he wouldn't hit the ocean. Jagged rocks would dash the life from him. He didn't look down again.

He reached the top and clambered over a low stone wall. Nearby, Telea and Wenla sheltered in the shadows of a ruined building. Orlos crept close to them. "I... I wish you good luck," Wenla whispered, wiping the sweat from her brow and streaking her lamp black in the effort. "I would stay, but—"

"Your daughter is waiting for you," Telea said.

"Tell General Nidon that we've made it," Orlos said.

"I will."

Orlos glanced at Telea and then back at Wenla. "The king and Sir Nidon don't know Telea is here," he admitted to her. "They wouldn't have allowed us to do this."

"So what do I tell King Handrin and Champion Nidon?"

"That Orlos and I will attempt to destroy the summoners from inside," Telea said. "And that they should be ready to attack when the fighting starts. You will hear it. Now go, Lady Wenla, and thank you for what you've done. Many lives will be saved."

"I hope you know what you're doing," Wenla said.

"I know exactly what I'm doing. I know the price I'll pay."

Wenla took a piton and sank it deep into the ground, her magic allowing it to penetrate the solid rock. Then Telea wrapped a rope around it and lowered Wenla down the cliff. When she finished, Telea tied the rope off. "I'll leave it like this in case we need to escape," she whispered to Orlos.

"Best to just hide it," Orlos said. "A sentry might find it there and know that someone has climbed up."

Telea pursed her lips and then quickly pulled the rope up into a neat coil. "Here," she said, placing it in the shadows next to the building that hid them. "Remember this spot."

Orlos took Telea's hand and pulled his spiridus cloak over him. A heartbeat later, shadows gathered around her and she faded from sight. They were perhaps half way between the outer town wall and the inner temple wall. There'd been no effort made to restore the town since the last time Orlos had been here — it still stood mostly destroyed. Hand in hand, so that they might not lose each other, they crept into the ruins. They passed another building, this one smaller and intact, and then could see the main street leading between the two gates.

Telea suddenly grasped his hand tighter. He looked past her and gasped. Ranks upon ranks of silent brothers stood behind the main gate. There had to be hundreds of them, if not a thousand. They filled not only the open space behind the gate but every street and alleyway as well.

He felt Telea's other hand brush his face and then drew his head closer to hers. He felt her warm breath on his neck as she whispered, "Nidon cannot fight this. They'll never take the wall."

"What do we do?" he whispered back.

He felt her pull away, still holding his hand. "More are coming," she whispered, drawing close again.

Down the main street marched a robed summoner and three undead, two women and one man. Looking back to the ranks behind the gate, he saw that the majority in the front ranks were armed as soldiers or fanatics, but those in the rear had no armor and just simple weapons. He whispered what he'd noticed to Telea.

"Still too many, even if they are poorly armed," she said. "Let's look beyond the next gate." Gently pulling him along, they moved down a side alley and up another street until they could see through the open area in front of the temple gate.

The siege towers that had been there were destroyed, completely burned to the ground. The wall, narrower but taller, stood impregnable, with soldiers standing sentry atop it. "They aren't silent brothers," Orlos said. The undead had a herky-jerky way of moving that set them apart from the living. Once you'd seen them, you could tell the difference in a moment.

"The gate is open," Telea whispered. "We should sneak through and see what's beyond."

Orlos watched as four more undead walked through the gate, again escorted by a summoner. He didn't relish the idea of attempting to sneak through, invisible or not. "Nidon needs to know what lies beyond."

It was strange speaking to someone who was also invisible. He felt her breath and knew her face was close to his, but in the darkness, which normally meant little to him, she was unseen. "Yes, that would be better," she whispered into his ear.

He felt her pull as she led him towards the gate. They paused for just a moment at the opening, and then Telea led him rapidly through. As they exited, she pulled him hard to the left. Only then did he see the two guards speaking quietly to each other. Orlos and Telea passed a tower entrance, and then she led him behind a small temple building.

There were no ruined structures here. Black marble temples were randomly scattered across the grounds. Some were small, like the little offering temples he'd seen at the Temple of Forsvar. Others were quite large, although none so great as the actual Temple of Dromost looming over all of them.

"Do you hear that?" Orlos asked. From a few buildings ahead of them he heard the rhythmic chanting of many people.

Telea turned her head to the side and said nothing at first. "It's a ritual of sacrifice," she said.

"Because they're making silent brothers?"

"I don't know — I can't tell. Let's go closer."

319

Keeping off the main avenue, they advanced closer to the courtyard and the ramp leading to the temple itself. Creeping to the edge of a building, they peered out and saw hundreds of people there, kneeling in long lines facing the ramp leading to the temple entrance. The iron gates were open at the top of the ramp. Nearly a hundred silent brothers stood guard along the short cliff leading to the temple's little plateau.

Then, beyond the guards, he saw the glow of blue light emanating from the temple doors, and his heart dropped into the pit of his stomach. "They've opened the Dromost Gate!" he hissed to Telea.

She nodded. "It's the same light."

As they watched, a summoner led someone from the kneeling crowd up the ramp. At the same moment, an undead woman departed the temple and descended the ramp in the opposite direction.

"Not yet," Telea said, gripping his hand tighter. "They're still making sacrifices. If the gate was truly open, I think we'd know it."

"But look at the blue light! It's just like we saw when the gate was open."

"There'd be demons coming out the door if it was open, not silent brothers. They're sacrificing these people for their blood and then animating them as temple defenders. I think they're close, though."

Orlos drew a deep breath. "What do we have to do?"

"I'll make undead from them," Telea said, nodded towards the crowd in front of the temple. Half men and half women, all wore simple clothing or even rags. There were no soldiers among them.

"They're just peasants, Telea. They aren't soldiers. You can't use them."

"Who else can I use?" Telea asked. "My working must spread quickly. Attempting it on soldiers is much too risky."

"But they're innocent."

"They're not innocent," Telea whispered, her voice more urgent now. "Look at them. They're volunteers. They want to be here. They're taking part in the ritual."

"They don't know better."

"Orlos, don't be a fool. The gate is almost open. It must be done this way. Don't let Ayja's sacrifice go for naught. She closed the Dromost Gate. We must keep it closed, or everyone will perish. Everyone."

Orlos looked out over the throng. Telea was going to turn them into the undead. It was wrong, but what other choice did they have?

"You don't have to do anything, Orlos," Telea said. "Just stay here. When the fighting starts we'll head to the temple itself and see what we can do there."

Orlos glanced over his shoulder towards the gate. "Should I tell Nidon?"

"We'll have to put our faith in Wenla. I need you with me."

He wanted more than anything to leave. To run back and tell Nidon what they'd seen. To not see Telea create her army.

"Please, Orlos," she said.

"I'll wait," he said.

Suddenly his hand was empty. He scarcely heard her depart.

The chanting continued as, one after another, victims were led up the ramp and undead walked down it. Was the light within the temple growing in brightness? Dozens of heartbeats passed and nothing happened. Where was Telea?

Shouts rang out from the back of the crowd. Orders? Warnings? Then cries of fear and pain.

Footsteps rapidly approached, and then Telea blindly blundered into him. "Follow me," she said. Grabbing his hand, they ran to the edge of the cliff and then along it. They passed behind a small temple and came to a clear space near the ledge where the Temple of Dromost stood. Shouts of fear echoed off the temple walls.

Chaos reigned in the courtyard. The hundreds of waiting sacrifice victims mobbed the ramp, fleeing Telea's undead. At the same time, the summoners atop the ramp ordered their silent brothers to counterattack. Trapped between the two undead forces, the peasants were easy prey for Telea's creations. One after another they were killed, only to rise as her minions.

Orlos and Telea ran to the bottom of the temple ledge. It was only a little over two strides high. Fleeing peasants ran towards them, oblivious of the two invisible invaders. "We must hurry," Telea whispered as they pressed themselves against the rock. "My undead will be outnumbered by the silent brothers."

"I don't understand. How can we do this without your undead?"

"They're just a distraction. Come, we have to climb here." In just heartbeats they were atop the ledge. Looking down, he saw some of the peasants at the back of the crowd throwing themselves atop others, dragging them to the ground and choking the life out of them. Moments later, the newly killed rose to fight. Still, the tide of battle turned against them.

Silent brothers from both the temple and the outer wall rushed into the courtyard, hacking and stabbing at Telea's undead. In the swirling melee, it was nearly impossible to tell one side from the other.

Telea led him up the temple stairs to the very door of the temple itself. They leaped out of the way as two summoners rushed out. After they passed, Orlos leaned forward to look inside. There were still two summoners there. A peasant knelt between them, bent over a glowing circle of glyphs on the floor. Behind the group, the stone ring of the Dromost Gate swirled with brilliant blue light.

The blue field wasn't complete, though. Black patches swirled within the blue, but they were only a fraction of the whole. The Doomcallers were close to succeeding. Telea pulled Orlos away from the door. They turned the corner of the temple and ran back along its side, finally stopping in the shelter of a huge pillar. The sounds of fighting and screams of fear blended into the waves crashing hundreds of feet below.

Telea became visible and sank to her knees, pulling him down with her. "Let me see you," she said.

Orlos let his spiridus cloak drop. "What are you doing, Telea?"

"Listen carefully," she said, cutting him off. "I am going to stop this. I will destroy the summoner defenses, but I need you to command me. I am going to summon a demon inside me — a sacrifice demon. It will be incredibly powerful. My well of power is full, and my knowledge of these secrets is great. But you must control me, or I will run rampant."

"This is mad."

"Shut up, Orlos. This is the only way. This is my choice. My undead are failing as it is. The summoner silent brothers are destroying them. I will give you the power to command me. When it is all over, you must remove the dagger and command the demon to leave me and return to Dromost."

"And what will happen to you?"

"If all goes well, I will be as you see me. You must command me. Be strong, and no harm will come to you. You must bare your chest."

She drew her short dagger and sliced the laces of his tunic and ripped it wide. Then she pulled apart her kaftan and tunic, exposing her chest to him.

"What—"

Telea began to chant. As she did, she took his left hand in her own and drew her dagger across his palm, cutting it deeply and causing him to cry out in pain. He couldn't pull away, though. He panicked. Her chant paralyzed him. Ice flowed through his veins as fear gripped him.

She put her dagger aside, and dipping her finger into his blood, drew something on his forehead. Then she slashed her left hand and drew strange symbols on her own forehead. Orlos closed his hand against the pain, only realizing then that he could move again. His blood poured from between his fingers and onto the temple marble between them.

Telea took his bloody hand in hers, and their mingled blood fell together. With her right hand, she mixed their blood and then began to write on his chest. As she wrote, he felt a searing pain and smelled burned flesh. He pulled back, but despite the slickness of his hand in hers, she wouldn't let go.

"Telea, there has to be another way!"

She shook her head as she dipped a finger in their mingled blood and then wrote on her own chest. Smoke rose as the glowing glyphs burned themselves into her. She showed no sign of pain, chanting and writing without pause. Then, when she was done, she picked up her dagger, looked him in the eyes, and said, "Remember, when it is all done, remove the dagger and command the demon to return to Dromost. Command it by name."

"Remove from—"

Before he could finish, she reversed her dagger and plunged it into her chest.

Even with the dagger in her heart and her lifeblood pumping from her chest, she began to chant again. Inky black smoke began to issue from her mouth. After a few heartbeats, it began to ooze from her nose and eyes as well.

"Uldamaran, I command you!" Telea shouted, her voice filled with power. "Come back to me. Take my body and obey Orlos!"

Suddenly, her voice changed, becoming deep and guttural and not hers at all. Soon she was completely wreathed in smoke. Then the smoke rose and took shape, growing larger and larger as it rose over him. Blazing red eyes shone from the swirling smoke.

Terror washed over Orlos. Unthinking, unknowing, all-powerful terror. He collapsed onto his back as long flaming talons emerged from the smoke, reaching for his naked chest. Suddenly, searing pain erupted on his brow and his chest. The talons retracted, and a voice said in his head said, *Command me.*

Orlos scrambled backward from the huge demon. From Uldamaran. Telea's demon. Wings of smoke spread high above it, almost to the temple roof above.

The terror was still there, but he knew now that the demon could not harm him. Telea's magic protected him from the demon she'd become.

Command me, Uldamaran said again.

"Kill," Orlos muttered. "Kill the summoners at the Dromost Gate. Kill them all!"

In an instant, the black cloud washed over Orlos as the demon raced for the front of the temple. Cold engulfed him, and for a heartbeat, Orlos knew death. Moments later, bloodcurdling screams filled the air, echoing off the temple buildings.

Orlos just lay on the ground, his hand covering his face. He *felt* the connection he had with the demon. Uldamaran was bound to him. He felt the thrill of death as the demon slaughtered the summoners and their guards. Through the demon's eyes, he saw flaming talons shred living and undead alike.

The living fled the demon's approach. The undead fearlessly attacked, only to be cut down in swaths. Uldamaran raised its hands and mist flowed out from them, washing over the fleeing peasants and soldiers. They fell, choking to the ground, rising moments later as the demon's own undead servants.

It knows Telea's magic, Orlos realized. He pushed himself to his knees and stood. Telea lay on the ground in front of him, her eyes wide open and staring, the dagger still in her chest. She wasn't dead. She twisted and turned on the bloody marble, and through her lips, he heard a muttered chant. He knelt beside her and nearly grasped for the dagger. She was in horrible, horrible pain, and he could release her. All he had to do was to pull the dagger from her chest.

In his mind's eye, though, he saw what Uldamaran saw. It was flying towards the wall. Doomcaller summoners started their chants, attempting to drive it off. Two of them created a barrier the demon's claws couldn't penetrate. It flowed away from them, sending its undead minions instead. The summoners' demon shield had no effect upon the undead, and, too late, they turned to flee, only to be run down and killed.

Orlos felt his grip on Uldamaran begin to fade as it swept through the gates and into the village. What if he lost control of it? Would it go after the Belenese and Saladorans?

Kill them all, the demon's voice said in his mind.

Should he pull out the dagger? The demon had slaughtered the temple priests and guards and had killed the sacrifice victims that would fuel the opening of the gate. But there were still summoners and a thousand silent brothers on the outer wall.

"I'm sorry, Telea," he said. "Just a little longer." Orlos scrambled to his feet and ran after the demon. As he turned the corner of the temple, he tripped on one of the dead and fell into a pile of corpses. The ramp and all the ground around it was a slaughterhouse. He got to his feet and ran. The demon was amongst the undead army now. Orlos felt them fall as Uldamaran swept through them, its own host of undead charging into the battle behind it.

Orlos tried to draw his spiridus cloak around him as he passed through the second wall's gatehouse. It wasn't there. Whatever foul magic Telea had done to him, he couldn't summon his spiridus cloak.

324

For an instant, he feared she'd driven his spiridus from him entirely, but it was there, deep within, blocked by his link with the demon.

As best he could, Orlos hid behind the corner of a half-destroyed wooden structure. The demon was just behind the first wall. Doomcallers hurled imp jars at it as summoners raised their chants to fight it off. The imps didn't last long against Orlos's demon, but they did it harm, unlike the undead who threw themselves uselessly against it.

A man fell from the wall, screaming out a terrible cry. When he struck the ground, he rose again, but as a grotesque, scaled demon. The demons squared off against each other, and for the first time, Uldamaran took serious wounds as the demons slashed at each other with their long talons. The fight did not last long, though, as Uldamaran was more powerful, and with a triumphant roar, destroyed its rival.

Desperate, the Doomcallers threw more imp jars, buying themselves enough time to create two more sacrifice demons to fight it. *Where are you, Nidon? Attack!*

Footsteps approached from behind Orlos. He spun just as someone slammed into him, throwing him to the ground. Cold dead hands grasped for his neck as Orlos desperately fought them off. Dead eyes stared at him from above snarling, snapping jaws.

Orlos jammed his forearm into the man's neck, preventing his slavering jaws from biting his face. He grasped the man's wrist with his other hand, stopping him from raking Orlos's face with his nails. The undead's free hand grabbed Orlos by the throat, choking him.

Orlos tried to roll him, just as Kael had taught him, but was wedged against a fallen beam and couldn't get any leverage.

They have to be struck in the head.

Letting go of the undead man's wrist, Orlos reached for his dagger. Instantly, the undead had both hands on Orlos's throat, choking him with incredible strength.

He couldn't find his dagger. His belt had twisted and thedagger was caught between their bodies.

Blood pounded in Orlos's temples as his vision began to narrow. He bucked as hard as he could and his hand found his dagger hilt. Orlos drew it and stabbed at the living corpse's head, but the dagger only slid along the man's skull, creating a horrible gash. He stabbed again, but the man lurched, and the dagger sank deep into his throat under his chin. Thick blood poured from the wound, but still, the undead fought on.

Blackness overcame Orlos as the dead man crushed his windpipe. Orlos stabbed one last time, his strength failing him even as he struck. Through the darkness that enveloped him, Orlos saw a bright light. It shimmered and glowed and seemed to move in the darkness above him. No, not above him. In him. His spiridus.

Wake. Your friends need you.

Help me, Orlos thought and then released his body to the spiridus as his consciousness faded and his world went black.

Orlos choked and sputtered as his eyes flickered open. His throat burned savagely and a coughing fit overwhelmed him. Through it, the sound of battle raged nearby. A demon roared, but he heard the sound of music as well. A terrible weight pressed down on his chest. He looked down to see the motionless undead atop him, a dagger in his temple.

Orlos pushed the body off of him and then rolled onto his knees and vomited. He could hardly breathe, the pain in his throat was so intense. For the longest time, he coughed and choked and sputtered until he vomited again.

Horribly weak, Orlos crawled over the dead man and pushed himself onto a pile of rubble. Bright light flared at the top of the gatehouse. King Handrin was there. Nidon, as well. But so was his demon.

Kill them all, Uldamaran's voice echoed in his head.

Handrin hurled a blast of fire into the demon, tearing into its shadowy form. It screamed in pain but then struck at the king. Nidon stepped in front of the blow, his shield held high, but was driven to his knees. There was another knight with him — Tharryl. The former man-at-arms wielded his tulwar two-handed, hacking at the huge demon.

Again Orlos heard singing. It came from somewhere behind the king. The demon reeled back from it, but then launched itself forward again. *They don't have enough singers for such a powerful demon.*

Orlos forced himself to his feet. "Come to me," he croaked. His throat was on fire and the words barely crossed his lips. Staggering forward, he called out again, "Come to me."

The demon paid him no attention, lashing out at King Handrin again. Again Nidon threw himself in front of the blow, his shield shattering as flaming talons raked across his body. The Orb of Creation flashed as Handrin aimed a mighty blast of fire at the demon, striking it and driving it back.

The demon surged forward, but Empress Kelifos appeared on the wall in front of it. Orlos heard her voice as she sang the *Song of Light,* even across the battlefield. The power of her song drove the demon back, but her voice couldn't hold it off for long.

Orlos had to get closer, but there were too many undead between him and the demon. He only had moments before the demon killed Kelifos, Handrin and Nidon. And once they were killed, who could stop Uldamaran from rampaging through the army?

Orlos turned and ran for the temple, his only thought to pull the dagger from Telea's chest. The entire path to the temple was strewn with massacred temple defenders. Orlos ran up the ramp and then along the side of the temple, feeling the demon's rage at being held at bay all along. Not much longer, though. The Orb of Creation was nearly spent and the demon knew its victory was near.

Telea still writhed on the ground, her dagger in her chest. What would happen when he removed it? What had she said — *I'll return to how I was?*

Orlos ran to her and knelt at her side. "I'm here, Telea," he said, barely rasping out the words. She moaned and muttered, her eyes staring blankly up at him.

He grasped the dagger and shouted, "Go back to Dromost, Uldamaran!" The words burned and tore at his throat. He pulled the dagger from Telea's chest. "Go back to Dromost! I command you, Uldamaran! Give Telea back to me!" With a horrible scream that echoed across the Temple of Dromost, the demon's smoky form dissipated, shredded by the ocean winds.

Blood poured from Telea's wound now, flowing freely. Orlos tossed her dagger aside and pressed his hand against the wound, trying to staunch the flow of blood. "Telea!"

"I die now, Orlos," she whispered.

"You said you'd return to the way you were."

"I lied." Her face twisted in pain. "I deserve this for all I've done."

He looked around, desperate for help, but they were alone at the back of the temple. Handrin's knights would have won the wall by now. They were on the way but would be too late. With each heartbeat, Telea drew closer to death. "Healer," he tried to shout, but his voice was barely a whisper.

"Goodbye, Orlos," she said as her eyes closed, and she went limp on the blood-soaked marble.

"Help!" Orlos shouted, but his voice cracked, and nothing came out. Telea just lay there, still under his hand. Nobody would come. She could not be saved. He'd been angry at her at times. Jealous at others because of how close she was with Ayja. He'd hated the demon she'd willingly borne within her for so long. But through all her pain and loss, she'd always been true to Ayja. She'd saved them so many times. And now they were going to lose her.

There was nothing he could do.

Spiridus, can you save her? Can you save her as you saved my mother? he thought, hoping against hope it might reply.

His spiridus never spoke with him. Not true speech. His spiridus communicated through emotion and memory and dream. Most of the time Orlos was unaware of the separate presence of the spiridus within him, so close was their relationship. But at that moment, he suddenly became aware of the living spirit within him. He felt the spiridus move and saw a golden-green glow travel down his arm and to his blood-covered hand, still pressed on Telea's wound.

Must leave you...

A vision flashed in Orlos's mind. He saw a stone room lit by candlelight. A crowd of people. He saw a horribly wounded young woman on a table and knew that it was his mother. He also saw an ancient and bent man leaning over his mother. The man touched her and his spiridus entered her, saving her life and entering her womb to become one with the unborn Orlos.

I understand, Orlos thought. *Return to me when she is healed.*

I cannot...

Again an image flashed before Orlos. He saw within Telea... an ancient temple... a beautiful ruins filled with flowers and walkways. *Her memory walk,* he realized. But even as he watched, the ruins began to fade and turn to smoke, drifting away. A bright golden-green light appeared, and the ruins became whole again.

I must remain, the spiridus said.

If you leave, her memory walk will disappear?

Her soul. It is sundered. It perishes.

The image crushed down upon Orlos, and he sagged atop Telea. She'd sacrificed her soul when she'd summoned the demon. "Why, Telea? We could have found another way!" he rasped.

Choose, the spiridus said.

Must I give you up to save her? Forever?

Choose.

Spiridus were eternal, undying. But souls... when a person died their soul returned whole to Helna. But not a soul sacrificed to a demon. Not a soul consumed by a demon. That soul was gone, destroyed forever. Orlos looked down at Telea. Her soul would know no peace. There'd be no eternal reward for her. She would not live on in the memories of a spiridus.

Unless I let my spiridus save her.

"Go," Orlos whispered. "Please save her."

The bright light of his spiridus left his hand and entered Telea. The moment it did, she gasped, drawing a deep breath and opening her eyes wide. But at the very same moment, a moan escaped Orlos's lips as the enormity of what he'd done struck him.

He was a spiridus no longer. Darkness fell upon him like he'd never imagined, and it terrified him. He'd never, ever truly known darkness. Now, in the middle of the night, under a cloud-filled sky, sheltered behind the black marble of the Temple of Dromost, he knew true, pitch black darkness.

His first thought was to draw his spiridus cloak around him, but it was gone. Not blocked, as it had been when he'd been tied to the demon, but truly gone. He felt naked, defenseless against the dangers of the world. A world of fear that he felt more intensely than anything he'd ever felt before. Hunger, fatigue, and pain all crashed down upon him. With an anguished cry, he threw his back against the temple, feeling some security in the solid safety it provided.

He shouted out in fear as a hand reached out of the darkness, grasping his wrist. In his mind, he saw one of the undead coming for him, but the hand was warm, and he suddenly found himself pulled into an embrace.

"What have you done, Orlos?" Telea said, burying her head in his neck as she wrapped her arms around him. "What have you done?"

In her embrace, Orlos felt the presence of his spiridus again. All his fear melted in the comfort of Telea's arms. His spiridus wasn't gone, not truly. "I had to save you," Orlos said, sobs wracking his body. "I couldn't let you die. You gave up your soul."

"I know what you've given up, Orlos. I *feel* it."

Tears poured down Orlos's face. He hadn't known — he hadn't truly understood — the cost. He was no longer the person he'd been. He didn't know who he was anymore.

"I know you, Orlos," Telea said. "I understand you now, better than you can imagine. The spiridus binds us together. You are a good person. Better than I realized before. Better than you knew yourself. I can never repay you for what you've done, but I will always be here for you."

She pulled him closer and held him even tighter in her embrace. He felt the presence of his spiridus and realized that what he had lost wasn't truly gone. That through Telea, he could still touch the magic of the spiridus and know what he'd once known.

Chapter Thirty-two

The spirit bird flew through the forest, the sunlight glimmering off its silver feathers as it passed between the shadows cast by giant trees. It entered the spiridus glade and circled twice before settling on the branch of a Landomeri Oak.

It is time for you to return, the forest said to the bird.

Return?

Awake! Evil arises. A threat beyond me. I need you to heed my call again.

What evil?

Awake! Your daughter needs you.

The bird cocked its head, peering into the pool and the sparkling waterfall leading into it. Everbloom grew all along the pool and the stream flowing out of it. *My daughter? I... I remember a daughter.*

Awaken! She comes, and evil pursues her.

That life is behind me.

It is yours again. Take the form beneath you and make it yours.

The spirit bird looked down at the edge of the pond. There was a body there — a body of sticks and mud and grass. Hopping from the branch, the spirit bird drifted down, and then, just before it hit the ground, it transformed into a shimmering, ethereal woman, becoming the Lady of the Forest. She knelt by the figure of mud and reached out a tentative hand to touch it. *This is to be my body?*

The danger is a mortal one. You must have a body again.

A body of clay and sticks?

Clay and sticks will become flesh and bone. For a short time, at least.

The Lady of the Forest lay down upon the clay body, merging with it and becoming one. The body would not move, though.

There is no life here.

Wait.

The sun poked out from behind a cloud and shone down upon the Lady of the Forest. Slowly, warmth filled her body. The mud began to shift and move, and fingers emerged where there'd been only clumps of dirt. Within her body, the sticks grew, forming bones. A smooth river stone became her heart.

From under the Lady, plants grew up into the body, spreading throughout and creating muscle and tissue, organs and veins. More plants grew over the body, forming clothes of vines and leaves. Mud became flesh and skin. Within her chest, her heart beat once, then twice. Blood flowed through her veins, and her eyes opened.

Hadde stared up through the rustling leaves of Landomeri oaks and into the sunny sky. Bright white clouds floated by, propelled by a fresh breeze. She took a breath and gasped. She sat up and stared at her naked legs where they emerged from beneath a tunic of leaves — legs of flesh and blood. Real legs. Living legs. She held her hands in front of her face and flexed her fingers.

Memories flooded back to her. At first, they seemed like half-forgotten dreams. Shadows of things that had happened. Her childhood. Her parents. Riding Lightfoot. Shooting a bow. Then they became clearer. The Wasting. Salador. Prince Morin. She remembered giving birth.

I am Hadde from Long Meadow. I am a mother.

She remembered fighting varcolac. They surrounded her. It was raining. She held her daughter in her arms and then placed her on the ground.

Enna. My baby.

She fought them. She killed two — then three. But then their chief had thrown a javelin at her. Hadde touched her breastbone where it had entered her. She'd fallen. Her last sight had been one of Enna, lying wrapped in a blanket on the ground beside her.

She lives. The Great Spirit's voice was gentle, but there was urgency behind it. *Your daughter lives and returns.*

"My baby," she said. "Enna lives?", speaking with a voice she hadn't known for many years.

A baby no longer. Many seasons have passed. A woman now. She saves the spiridus.

Time had meant nothing to Hadde for so long. She'd been a spirit, sometimes a bird, sometimes a shadow of her former self — the Lady of the Forest. Her former life had meant nothing to her, just the faintest, fleeting dream.

"Where is she?"

Find her at the Emerald Tree. There is danger there. She brings my children, but she also brings demons and a veden. Save my children, Hadde of Landomere, Lady of the Forest.

Hadde stood. A bark quiver filled with leaf-fletched arrows hung from a belt of braided vines. She held a living bow with leaves springing from its tips and a string of twisted plant fibers. Her long hair — hair that had once been midnight black but was now highlighted deep green — was braided with white everbloom flowers.

She held her hand in front of her face again. "I am truly alive?"

For a short time. I give my life to you, again, so that you might save my children.

"I will die?"

Save your child. Save my children. You will return to what you were. Go now. It opens. They come.

Hadde ran from the spiridus glade. She knew to run north, towards Belavil. Her bare feet flew over the forest floor. She knew every step, every twig, every rock. Nothing slowed her as she raced over fallen leaves, barely making a sound. Everbloom lined her path — she was on a spiridus road — as she had been once so long ago.

There was strength in her limbs — more than she'd ever had in life. Fatigue meant nothing to her. Was the Great Spirit sustaining her for her final battle? Through a break in the trees, she saw the slopes of Belavil. There were people outside the open gates. They saw her and waved. The smiles on their faces showed they clearly didn't realize the danger they faced.

Hadde dashed through the gates and into the city, following the paved street as it wound upwards. How much time had passed? It was so strange to see the ancient city full of people and life. There were new homes built amongst the ruins, old stones given new life. Everywhere there were fountains and gardens, window boxes full of herbs and everbloom, and ivy growing up marble columns.

"Lady of the Forest!" someone shouted — a young girl. Enna's age?

No, Enna's a woman now. How many years have passed?

"Danger!" Hadde shouted as she ran. "Sound the alarm!"

Looks of concern crossed people's faces. She heard them calling out to each other.

"Demons come to Landomere," Hadde shouted. "Veden! Arm yourselves!"

She didn't dare pause to explain more. She wasn't certain herself what they faced. She was halfway up the twisting streets when she saw the first spiridus. Gold, silver, and emerald green, they flashed through the air. People shouted with joy at the sight of them.

Hadde called out her warnings again. The people were genuinely confused now, seeing her, seeing the spiridus, and then hearing her dire shouts. Some followed her, but none were armed — just curious and joyful Landomeri following the physical embodiment of the Lady of the Forest.

Spiridus flew alongside her now. She felt their joy but also heard their warnings. *Demons come! Save her!*

Alarm horns sounded from above, followed by cries of fear. Hadde ran faster, the pace still effortless. How long could the Great Spirit sustain her?

The thought of her infant daughter in her arms filled her mind. *Just a little longer.*

Men and women emerged from homes with bows and spears. Seeing Hadde, they set off after her as she ran up the road towards the threat above. Soon they came upon people fleeing in the opposite direction, many with children in their arms. Terror filled their eyes as they called out warnings of demons.

Hadde passed through an archway and onto the terraced garden that made up the highest point in Belavil. There was a ruined temple here, as well as a beautiful marble home.

A flying demon, gray-skinned and bat-winged, swept down and sank its long claws into a fleeing man's back before lifting him into the sky. As it flew, the demon's fangs ripped out the man's throat, spraying the ground beneath them with a rain of blood. Then the demon hurled the lifeless body to the ground where it hit a marble block with a sickening crunch. In a single smooth motion, Hadde drew an arrow, nocked it, and let fly. The arrow struck the demon mid-flight, impaling it. Long-thorned rose-brier vines exploded from the arrow, coiling around and tearing into the demon's flesh. With a terrible cry, the demon plummeted to the ground, dashed to death against a fluted column.

More demons flew overhead. Landomeri archers loosed arrows at them, keeping them at bay for the moment. More demons charged out of an arched tunnel entrance near the ancient temple. A few already ranged across the gardens, charging the Landomeri wardens who were there. A huntress drew her bow and loosed, but the arrow bounced off the demon's breastplate. Before she could loose again, two demons hurled iron darts at her, killing her.

Near the marble house, a hunter loosed arrow after arrow at a charging demon. One of three punched through the demon's armor, but it charged on, hurling itself at the man and ripping into his flesh with long talons. From a balcony above, a woman in a long green kirtle stepped out with a crossbow. She shot the demon in the back, the crack of her bolt passing through its armor audible across the gardens.

Maret. My friend, Maret.

Hadde pulled four arrows from her quiver and placed them in her bow hand as she leaped atop a fallen block of marble. She nocked an arrow and loosed it at a charging demon. She'd aimed for the demon's face, its open helm leaving it vulnerable there, but at the last moment, it raised its steel shield. The arrow shattered against the shield, but then exploded in a tangle of rose-brier vines.

The vines wrapped themselves around the demon's limbs and head, causing it to topple to the ground. Dropping its sword, the demon clawed at the vines, but long thorns ripped into its hands. A vine encircled the demon's neck and forced itself down the demon's throat. Even as it died, red roses sprang from the vines.

Another demon charged towards the house as Maret cocked her crossbow for another shot. Hadde's arrow caught the demon mid-stride and rose-briers erupted from the arrow, entangling and engulfing the demon. From above, Maret's crossbow bolt pierced the demon's helm, killing it.

Four Landomeri joined Hadde, loosing arrows. Their heavy armor made the demons hard to kill, though, and all four Landomeri had to focus their efforts to take down a single demon.

Hadde loosed a dozen arrows without pause. The living bow was a wonder to hold. The draw was a feather touch, but the arrows flew fast, flat, and true. Each arrow that struck slew the demon it hit with a tangle of rose-briers.

Hadde's eyes went to the dark tunnel entrance. Spiridus raced out of the exit, bright even in the sunlight. As they raced across the garden, she heard them call, *More below! The gate is open!*

"Defend your people," Hadde said to the Landomeri near her. She jumped down from the marble block and ran for the tunnel entrance.

Enna is there.

As she approached the tunnel entrance, she drew another handful of arrows. She slowed and nocked another as she drew close to the steps leading under the temple. No more demons had exited, although a few still ranged the gardens or flew overhead. She couldn't stay to fight them — her battle was below.

Peering into the darkness, she saw no sign of demons. Silently, on bare feet, she ran down the steps two at a time.

All her life, she'd heard stories of the beauty of Belavil and the ancient ruins there. She'd even been there — with Belor — many years before. She'd never heard of tunnels beneath the ruined temple. As Lady of the Forest, she'd heard whispers of the discovery of the Emerald Tree. It was poisoned, though, by the dark magic of the veden and what they'd done there. When she'd tried to visit, the darkness had been too strong for her to pierce.

Not now. She ran through the darkness, its twisted magic unable to stop her living, physical form. A few spiridus suddenly joined her, and they lit her path with their light. Behind her, she heard the footfalls of the Landomeri.

Clang!

She heard the distant sound of a heavy blow. She ran down another flight of stairs.

Clang!

She ran faster, fearing that she'd arrive too late.

Clang!

She was close now. She heard a triumphant roar as she emerged into a huge, vaulted chamber. Bright green branches arched into the ceiling, and a huge emerald stump lay on the floor. All around her, an acrid, sulfurous smoke drifted in a haze. Through it, she saw the demons. Six of them stood behind their huge, bat-winged master at the far side of the room.

A woman in scale armor huddled against the wall beneath the winged demon. She wore a round shield on her arm, its rim crackling with power. A heartbeat later, though, the lightning flickered and went out.

Enna!

"I will have everything I ever wanted," the demon said in a powerful voice. He raised his warhammer high over his head.

Hadde drew and loosed. Her arrow struck the demon in the back between its great wings. Its armor flashed with purple light. Rose-brier vines wrapped around the demon's body, but they couldn't take hold. Thorns ripped into the demon's flesh, but they withered under some magical assault.

With a roar, the demon turned and faced Hadde. "Slay her!" he commanded. The demon launched itself at Hadde. He thrust his long iron spear forward like a lance as he flew at her. Hadde loosed another arrow at the demon's unarmored wing. The arrow impaled the wing and erupted, long thorns shredded the leathery membrane. The demon crashed to the floor and skidded to a halt.

Hadde turned her attention to the demon's charging companions. She dashed out of their path, fast-drawing and loosing her arrow. The arrow struck a demon in the chest and engulfed it in slashing vines. Still running, she loosed another arrow, striking a demon in the leg. It toppled to the floor, its legs constricted together. The vines crawled up its body as it frantically tried to rip them away.

The Landomeri who'd followed her into the chamber loosed arrows at the demons as well, but the steel plates of the demon-armor turned most of them aside. One struck a demon in the helmet, throwing off its aim as it hurled an iron dart at Hadde.

She'd almost made it to Enna's still form. Forsvar dangled lifelessly from her arm as she leaned against the wall. Two demons raced at Hadde. One fell with an arrow in its neck and another in its leg, both arrows loosed by her Landomeri companions.

The remaining demon leaped at Hadde before she drew another arrow. She ducked as its curved sword flashed over her head. It lunged at her and cut her shoulder. Hadde jammed an arrow into the demon's shield, leaping backward as vines exploded from it.

She dropped to the ground and rolled away as the vines engulfed the demon. As she stood, the big demon got to its feet across the chamber from her. It looked at her and then at Enna. Without a pause, it charged Enna.

It wants Forsvar.

She shot an arrow at the demon's feet as she ran to her daughter. Rose-briers sprang up and wrapped around his legs, sending him crashing to the floor.

Hadde knelt at Enna's side. Her daughter lay motionless on the floor. Just strides away, the demon ripped through the vines with the warhammer's spike. Blood covered his ankles and legs where the long thorns had torn into his flesh.

Hadde shook her daughter's shoulder. Enna was thin and pale. Her head lolled to one side. "Please, Enna, get up." One of the spiridus who had followed Hadde swept down from above and entered Enna's chest. Still, she didn't move.

The demon rose to his feet, one leg still entangled by vines. "I will not be denied," he said. He chanted in a harsh, foreign tongue and the iron spear glowed with a deep purple aura.

Hadde reached for an arrow but knew she was too late. Just as the demon began to throw, two spiridus streaked past and flew into the demon's eyes. The demon screamed as brilliant green light blinded it. Hadde threw herself atop her daughter as the spear flashed overhead, slamming into the wall. There was an explosion of purple light as stone shards tore into Hadde's back. She threw her hand over her head as larger rocks fell upon her.

Bleeding and battered, she forced herself upwards, pushing the rocks aside with her unnatural strength. Nearby, the demon began to chant again, raising his free hand towards its face and the spiridus there.

Hadde drew another arrow and shot the demon in its arm. Thorns embedded themselves deep into the demon's flesh. The purple fire that had begun to glow in the demon's hand winked out as the demon shouted in fresh agony.

She shot the demon in the leg, the vines wrapping around both legs again and forcing him to his knees. The fall pushed needle-sharp thorns even deeper into the demon's flesh.

Hadde stood and nocked another arrow. She had three left to her.

"I will kill—" the demon started, but Hadde's arrow punched through his throat and out the back of his neck. He choked for a moment before rose-briers exploded from the arrow, tearing through his flesh and bursting from his skull.

The two spiridus flew free as the demon toppled face first on the floor, the warhammer clanging on the stones as it skidded towards Hadde. She turned to Enna and brushed debris from her. "Enna, wake up," Hadde said. "Please wake up!" She touched her daughter's face, but there was no life there. Her skin felt cold, and when Hadde felt Enna's neck, there was no heartbeat.

"The Great Spirit will save you," Hadde said. She didn't cry. There was no need for tears. The Great Spirit wouldn't let her daughter pass. She couldn't. Not after all that had happened. She touched Forsvar, barely recognizing the pulse of power that washed over her, and removed the Godshield from her daughter's arm.

Putting the Godshield aside, she lifted her daughter in her arms. Even in her armor, Enna weighed next to nothing. Her skin was pulled taut over her bones. Blood and grime covered her face, which was peaceful in death.

No. Not death. She will not die.

Even if her daughter had been twice as heavy, Hadde could have lifted her. The strength of the Great Spirit still filled her arms. She turned and saw three Landomeri approaching. She didn't spare them a moment as she ran past them towards the entrance. How far did she have to go?. How long did her daughter have? *How long do I have?* The Great Spirit hadn't promised her eternal life.

Hadde ran up the long tunnel under the temple. She took the first set of stairs two at a time, despite her burden. Another long, dark hall stretched out in front of her.

This isn't fair, Enna. You are too young to die.

She reached the last set of stairs and pushed upwards. Still, the strength of the forest sustained her. Enna was a feather in her arms. She couldn't be dead. The Great Spirit would not allow it. Not now. Not after all they'd been through. Not after all they'd done.

Finally, the end of the stairs appeared, and she saw the bright outline of the sky in the tunnel's entrance. There were many armed Landomeri there now, rushing towards the tunnel entrance. She saw no sign of demons.

People ran towards her, but Hadde ignored them, her only thought to return to the Spiridus Glade. It was Enna's only hope. She dashed through the terrace entrance and down the city streets. People watched her pass, their eyes full of wonder and fear.

As she ran out of the city gates, sweat began to pour from Hadde's forehead, and her breath came in gasps. Her incredible strength drained from her limbs. "Not yet!" she gasped out.

She stumbled into the forest, her arms burning with the effort of holding her daughter, her thighs on fire with each stride. She slowed to a jog and then to a walk.

Lights swirled around her, catching her by surprise. The very sight of the spiridus raised her spirits, and Hadde pushed deeper into the forest. Mighty Landomeri oaks towered overhead. Ferns brushed her legs as she ran amongst them.

Faster and faster the strength fled her body. Then, one of the spiridus touched her shoulder, and some of her strength renewed. As it retreated, Hadde saw that its light was diminished.

"Thank you," Hadde gasped as she ran forward again.

Twice the spiridus had to revive her with their life force, or her strength would have failed. Even with their efforts, her hopes faded. Her strength was leaving her faster than it could be restored.

Then, out of the corner of her eye, Hadde caught a glimpse of white flowers. *Everbloom.* Their scent wafted over her, sparking hope in her again. More and more the glimmering white blooms lined her path.

She heard the waterfall before she saw it. Bursting through a veil of fern, Hadde ran into the spiridus glade. A stream rushed down a rocky slope and into a small pool. Ferns and glowing white everbloom grew everywhere. And all around her were the spiridus. They streaked over the pond, their reflections mirroring them in the water. They twisted and turned, winding their way through the everbloom, seemingly playing a mystical game of hide and seek. Even more spiridus floated gracefully amongst the cathedral arches of huge oak branches soaring high above.

Unable to go on any longer, Hadde set her daughter down in the ferns beside the pool. "Save her, Landomere."

The spiridus swirled overhead, more and more joining as they formed a circle rotating above Hadde and Enna. *You once brought the last spiridus back to me and gave me strength again. You saved Orlos the Spiridus when he was stolen away. Your daughter brought my children back to me. But she has been gone too long. Long ago, I brought you back from death's gate. She has already passed through.*

"Save my daughter!"

What you wish is beyond me. Some day it might be within my power, now that my children have returned, but not today.

"I will give my life for her."

You have no life to give. What you have is temporary. Fleeting. Even now, it fades.

The voice went silent. Hadde looked out over the spiridus glade and saw only the reflection of the spiridus in the water, spinning and swirling. Slowly, Hadde bent forward and placed her forehead on her daughter's chest, above her heart. How much had Enna suffered to bring the spiridus out from Dromost? Tears finally came to her eyes. To be truly alive again, if only for a short time... to see her daughter, but only in death. How she wished only to have a few moments together.

I cannot give you the life you want, but I can give you a life.

Hadde jerked upwards at the voice. She'd thought she'd been abandoned.

You and your daughter shall share a life, and this spiridus glade shall be your home. Sleep here each day and be restored, or perish.

"Yes! Please!" Hadde called out.

You shall have the day, and sleep at night as a Landomeri Oak. Your daughter shall have the night and sleep each day in this pool.

"But I must see her! I must speak with her. Can't we have that?"

Each dusk and each dawn, there shall be time that you share.

"Yes! Bring her back!"

The sun sets. The spiridus within your daughter keeps her soul in this world. You must accept one as well. Without the spiridus, your soul shall depart this world.

"I will take one," Hadde said. "Anything to be with my daughter."

From the cloud of spiridus circling overhead, one descended and hovered in front of Hadde. She reached out her hand and the spiridus settled on it, light as a feather.

I am yours, the spiridus said. *Will you take me?*

"I will," Hadde said, and with those words, the spiridus sank into her hand. There was a glow for a moment, and then it faded. She felt a warmth within her, a comforting presence. *Love.*

It is near dusk. If you wish to speak with your daughter before dawn, remove her armor and place her in the pool.

As hastily as she could, Hadde unbuckled the scale armor her daughter wore. As she removed it, she found a golden circlet wrapped around Enna's arm. It was engraved with strange runes, but Hadde had no time for it and placed it upon the armor. Beneath her armor, Enna wore only tattered rags.

Hadde lifted her daughter, who now appeared more skeletal than before. She weighed nothing. Hadde carried her into the pool. She held Enna there, just resting at the surface. "Please bring her back," Hadde said. *Please.*

The spiridus descended. They engulfed the two women, coming so close and so tightly packed that Hadde could see nothing but bright green and silver light.

Life. Love. Light.

Hadde held her daughter in the cool water as the spiridus circled all around them, pouring their life force into the two women. Hadde saw nothing and felt only the water and the weight of her daughter in her arms. Then her daughter moved, and the cloud of spiridus expanded away from them.

Hadde looked down and saw her daughter transformed. Still painfully thin, her face and body were healthy and full of life. She was clothed not in rags, but in lilies and water plants, with flowers in her silver-highlighted hair.

Then Enna opened her eyes and smiled. "Mother," she said.

Hadde drew her into a fierce embrace. "I'm sorry, Enna. I tried to save you, but there were so many varcolac. And then I found you, after so many years and the demon had—"

"Shhh, Mother. Cam told me what happened. I know what you did to try and rescue me. And we are here now. Alive. Together."

"Cam?" Hadde asked, pulling back just a little so that she could look her beautiful daughter in the eyes.

"Nidon. He rescued me. He raised me."

"I don't know how I knew, but I did know that you were alive. Enna, you do know that I would have come for you if I could have?" Hadde asked, taking Enna by the shoulders. "I was here, in Landomere, but I was a spirit of the forest — the Lady of the Forest. I couldn't leave — you must understand that. I would have come for you. I would have, Enna. My beautiful Enna. You are so big. You were just a tiny baby when they took you. And now! And now, look how tall you are!"

Enna laughed. "Mother, I didn't even know that you were alive. Cam — Nidon said that you were dead. He saw you die."

"I was. I did. I was just a spirit. There's so much to tell you."

"We have time now, Mother. Although... you do know we're standing in a pool of water."

"I don't care," Hadde said, crushing Enna to her again.

"We could sit on the bank," Enna said after a time.

Hand in hand, they exited the pool and sat down amongst the ferns and the everbloom. Everywhere, like fireflies, the spiridus flew about, joyful in their newfound freedom. Hadde frowned in confusion as her daughter made odd gestures with her hands, and then she felt a tingle and warmth spread across her lower body as the water flowed off of her and disappeared into the ferns surrounding them.

"Did you do that?" Hadde asked.

Enna smiled. "I'm an elementar."

"You are?" Hadde took a deep breath. "I have to learn so much about you." She couldn't help it and began to cry. Bending forward, she put her face into her hands as sobs wracked her body. She felt Enna lean close and hug her. For a long time they sat together like that, both crying in their happiness.

"We are a pair," Hadde said, finally pulling back from Enna. "Landomere has clothed us in the vestments of the forest."

"It is less than I'm used to wearing," Enna said, smiling down at her clothing of lilies, flowers, and vines. "Not quite the Saladoran attire I grew up in."

"We don't wear much in Landomere," Hadde said. "Not like the horrible dresses they make women wear in Salador." She drew her legs close and wrapped her arms around them. She smiled. "I was once called Hadde the Naked."

"I know!" Enna said with a laugh. "Cam told me. I mean, Nidon."

"You keep calling him Cam. What happened? He raised you?"

"He saved me. When the varcolac... when they... I can't even say it."

"When they killed me."

"He slew the last of them and took me to safety. He knew Queen Ilana would hunt for me, so he took me deep into the East Teren and raised me in the mountains there. He didn't even know my name. He named me Ayja."

"Ayja? It's a pretty name," Hadde said. "Is that what you wish to be called?"

Enna shook her head. "Not by you, Mother. You named me Enna."

Hadde smiled. "It's for your grandmother. She still lives. Your grandfather, as well. You will see them soon, I hope. But tell me of Nidon. How was he even there to save you? How did he even know what had happened?"

"He was coming to see you when he heard of the plot to capture me," Enna said.

"To see me?"

Enna smiled. "He never forgot you. He loved you dearly."

Hadde remembered the big knight clearly. He'd rescued her from Earl Waltas and had always been kind to her even when few other Saladorans had been. She'd only had thoughts for the gallant Prince Morin back then and had no romantic interest in Champion Nidon. So strange that he'd thought of her that way. "Nidon loved me?" Hadde laughed. "I had no idea."

It was almost full dark in the skies over the glade, but the many spiridus lit the warm spring air with their soft light. Enna laughed. "That's what he thought. *She didn't even know,* he said. *I was such a fool. But if I hadn't been a fool, I wouldn't have found you.*"

"He raised you like his daughter?"

"We told everyone he was my uncle. In truth, he was my father. He is a great man, Mother. He taught me well and raised me to be strong." Enna's eyes shone with fresh tears. "I want to see him again."

Hadde's heart suddenly thudded in her chest. "It's starting to happen," she said, the Great Spirit's words coming back to her. She felt the change rush through her body — a tingly, prickly sensation. She had little time.

"What's wrong?" Enna asked, her brows knitting with concern.

"You know... you know we are changed," Hadde said, standing. She didn't want to stand, but she couldn't help herself. "We share a life now. The Great Spirit said so. We have spiridus within us as well."

"She told me," Enna said. "You have the day and I have the night. We meet only between the two."

"Night is falling," Hadde said, lifting her arms to the sky. A wave of drowsiness overcame her and she struggled to stifle a yawn. "Not yet!" she pleaded. "I want to see you more. Please, just a little longer." She couldn't move, though. Her feet were rooted to the ground and her arms seemed to stretch further and further to the sky. "Just a little...."

She felt her daughter's warm hands on her. "In the morning, Mother. I'll see you with the dawn. Oh, and I'm going to have a baby."

Chapter Thirty-three

Ayja watched in awe as her mother transformed into a tall, beautiful oak tree. It was, at the same moment, utterly beyond belief and perfectly natural. *Of course she turned into an oak tree. What else would she do?*

And, Ayja knew, in the morning, she would enter the pond and become one with it and with the Great Spirit of Landomere. She was alive, but there was a price.

Half a life, shared with my mother, and always within reach of the spiridus glade. She knew, deep in her core, that she must never find herself away from the glade when the sun broke the horizon.

She sat at the base of her *mother tree* and put her hand on a root there. For a moment, she expected it to be warm, but it was cool and solid. She was a tree. But there was something else. Whether it was the spiridus within her or the magic of the glade, Ayja sensed her mother's presence there.

Ayja put her hand to her stomach, feeling the bulge of her baby. *So small... smaller than she should be.* Had her experience in Dromost done some harm to her child? She hadn't eaten anything in so long, her life supported only by Darra's magic. Ayja shifted the lilies and water-vines aside so that she could see her stomach. She'd never really had a chance to look at her own changing body while in Dromost, not wanting to draw attention to her unborn child in front of the demons. Or even Darra, for that matter, although that had been her Saladoran modesty more than anything.

I have a child in me. Please, please, let her be healthy after all I've put her through.

Ayja took a deep breath and stared up through the canopy of leaves at the star-filled sky. To breathe clean, beautiful air, scented with the fragrance of everbloom. To see a clear sky full of stars again. To feel life all around her. She never imagined such joy.

The moment would have been perfect if not for the hunger that still gripped her. The spiridus and the Great Spirit had restored her well of power, but with every passing heartbeat, the well was reduced as her body drew upon its strength to sustain her.

She *knew* this spiridus glade, though. She was part of it. And she knew that there was food here. Skipping from rock to rock, she crossed the babbling brook. She didn't fear getting wet. Water was part of who she was now. It was part of her essence. She did it only for the joy of it. She found a patch of raspberries growing on the far side of the stream. Not all were ripe, but most were. She knelt next to them and picked one. Never, ever, in her life had she eaten anything more delicious.

Finally, she had to force herself to stop before she overdid it. Her stomach had been empty so long she feared what would happen if she gorged herself. So, reluctantly, she turned away from the berries and cast her eyes upon the glade that was now her home. She walked around her pool, touching the white everbloom flowers and feeling the ferns brush up against her bare legs. She felt soft moss and rich soil under her feet and felt the warm spring breeze on her skin.

It was absolutely peaceful. Then she realized someone was approaching. Ayja didn't know how she knew it, but she did. There were three Landomeri coming through the forest. Two women and one man pushed through the screen of ferns and stopped in awe at the sight before them. Spiridus flew everywhere, lighting the darkness, as the falling brook made music in the background.

The man carried Dromost, while one of the women held Forsvar and the other had Ayja's sword. They carried their own weapons as well, and the women bearing Forsvar wore a mail haubergeon. Their eyes settled on Ayja, and they froze.

"Hello," Ayja said. "Welcome."

The woman with Forsvar fell to a knee, and the others followed suit.

"There's no need for that," Ayja said. "I am Ayja."

"Are you a spiridus?" asked the woman with Forsvar.

"Did you save the spiridus?" asked the man.

"I helped free them from Dromost," Ayja said. "But I'm not a spiridus. I mean, I have one within me, but I'm not a spiridus."

"If you have one within you," the woman with Forsvar said, "then you are spiridus."

"I'm very new to this," Ayja said. "It only just entered me tonight. Please stop kneeling. Tell me your names."

"I am Samara," the woman with Forsvar said as they rose. "This is my husband, Dama," she said, motioning to the man at her side. "My friend, Cirenne." She nodded to the other woman. "We saw the Lady of the Forest fight the demon in the Chamber of the Emerald Tree and then take you out, but these Gifts of the Gods were left behind. The spiridus guided us here."

"The sword is my mother's," Ayja said. "I've had it for many years. I wonder if she'll want it back again."

"Who is your mother?" asked Cirenne.

"Hadde."

Cirenne's mouth dropped open. "Hadde? The Lady of the Forest is your mother? But her daughter was taken from us long ago!"

"I was saved and taken into hiding. I just met my mother again."

"Your name is Ayja?" asked Samara.

"I was named Ayja in hiding. My mother named me Enna."

The three shared knowing glances. "Where is the Lady of the Forest?"

Ayja gave her mother's tree a quick look and then said, "She's with the Great Spirit. She will return with the dawn."

"You've been blessed by Landomere," Samara said.

Ayja nodded. "I think the veden killed me." She frowned. "My soul was ready to depart, but a spiridus entered me and kept me here. My mother brought me to this place, and Landomere restored me."

"What do we do with these Gifts?" Dama asked, looking down at Dromost. The spirit circles no longer glowed, having been exhausted when Vahlah struck Ayja when she came through the gate.

Ayja walked up to Cirenne and said, "I'll take my mother's sword and give it back to her when she returns in the morning." Cirenne offered it to Ayja hilt first, and as Ayja took it, she heard the word *hope* in her head. She stared at the blade. Was the spiridus still within it? *Are you there?* She asked in her mind.

Hope.

You are free now. The spiridus are free.

Hope protects. Hope serves. Hope lives.

Ayja took the sword to where her armor lay on the ground. She didn't know what to think about the spiridus within her sword. She couldn't imagine that it would want to stay there when it had the freedom of the forest. Kneeling, Ayja placed the sword upon her armor. Then she let out a gasp as she saw the golden ring there.

The spiridus prison.

She reached out and touched it. There were thousands of spiridus trapped within the ring. Far more than had escaped out the gate. She'd forgotten them — forgotten the ring itself. Ayja stood, holding the prison. She was surprised that she could see the runes engraved upon it even in the full darkness. Was it a trick of the spiridus light in the air? Or was it the spiridus within her granting her its sight? Still, she wanted the

345

writing to be perfectly clear. She didn't dare make a mistake with what she was about to do.

Within her memory walk, her well of power burned with bright green fire. It was as full as it had ever been. Ayja twisted the aether and caused a fire to spring up in her hand, lighting the golden circle. The three Landomeri gasped at the sudden display of magic. Ayja smiled at them and twisted the fire into a ring and let it hover in the air, lighting her work. She stared down at the prison, reading the runes engraved there.

"What is it?" Samara asked.

"A prison," Ayja said, deep in thought. She committed the runes to memory, placing them in a clay pot in the kitchen of her memory walk. "Not for long, though." She smiled as she drew deeply from her well of power. Twisting the aether, she molded the gold in her hands. She spent her power frivolously, knowing she no longer had to worry about restoring it. The single rune she focused on slowly faded as the gold rose to fill it in.

With a brilliant flash of silver-green light, spiridus erupted from within the ring. Ayja was blinded by an explosion and nearly dropped the ring as thousands of spiridus streamed out. The joy of their release struck her like a physical blow, and she flinched back from it, raising the ring high above her head. For heartbeat after heartbeat spiridus fled the prison, flying high into the sky above Landomere.

Free! Hope! Happiness!

When the last one was gone, Ayja lowered the ring. The three Landomeri stood in front of her crying. "What did you do?" Samara asked.

"That is the last of them," Ayja said. "All of the spiridus who were imprisoned in Dromost."

For the first time that Ayja had seen, the spiridus departed the spiridus glade, flying out over the forest in every direction. She felt the joy in their departure as they returned to the forest that had been their home so long ago.

Ayja took the gold ring and placed it atop her armor again. The three Landomeri looked around in wonderment at the sight of the spiridus glade. It was a magical place. Ayja felt it. Everything about it was perfect. She'd seen incredible, beautiful sights in her journeys, but nothing had ever moved her as profoundly as this. She looked over to her mother tree and wondered if she felt it as well.

After a time, Ayja wasn't certain how long, Dama said, "The Gifts, Ayja, what should we do with them?"

"Leave them here," she said. "They are too powerful to be let out into the world." He nodded, and along with Samara, they placed Forsvar and

346

Dromost on the ground next to her sword and armor. Will you do something for me?" Ayja asked. "Will you go back to Belavil and let everyone know that Hadde and her daughter have returned to Landomere? That we are alive and well?"

"We will," Samara said.

"Can you send word to King Handrin of Salador and Champion Nidon that we are here as well? Nidon won't know me as Enna. Make certain that he knows Ayja is safe."

"We will."

Ayja looked at the two Gifts of the Gods. "Did anyone see you take them from the Chamber of the Emerald Tree?"

Cirenne glanced at the other two Landomeri. Dama nodded, and Cirenne shrugged and shook her head. "It was chaotic. A lot was happening. I'm sure some saw us."

"I'm sure they did," Dama said, "but I don't know that they knew what they were looking at."

"Tell no one of them," Ayja said. "Please. It is best for the world if they are thought lost. And lost they shall be. I shall make certain they are never found."

"But what if they are needed?" Dama asked. "What if some great evil arises?"

"If the need is great enough, Landomere will make their presence known. Let them remain here, hidden and safe until such a time comes."

"I don't want to leave this place," Cirenne said. "It is too wonderful. I've never been to a spiridus glade before."

"You will find it again," Ayja said, knowing it was true. "Bring my mother's family. And please, please make certain Sir Nidon knows I'm here."

"We will," Samara said. With one last long gaze at the spiridus glade, she said, "Thank you for bringing the spiridus back to us." Then the three Landomere turned and disappeared through the screen of ferns.

Ayja returned to her possessions. She took the golden spiridus prison and set it aside. Her belt was wrapped around her scabbard and rested atop her armor. Both were dirty and heavily worn from her time in Dromost. It was spring in Landomere, and she'd entered Dromost in late fall. She'd been there for months. Four? Five? Far too long.

She picked up the belt and her sword. *Hope,* it said to her. She smiled at the gleaming green blade. "Let's put you away so that no one gets hurt." The sword *snicked* home as she sheathed it. As she set it aside, she saw that her small belt pouch flap was unbuckled. Lifting the flap, she saw a bundle of rags stuffed in it.

Ayja bit her lip as she pulled them out. The carefully wrapped strips of cloth were the best pieces they'd salvaged from Darra's kaftan. Sitting, she spread a piece across her lap. He'd done so much for her. He'd given everything. She had to blink away the tears that came unbidden to her eyes.

She discovered one last little bundle in the pouch, and when she took it out, she felt something hard wrapped within it — a flat stone a little smaller than her palm. There was writing carefully carved into it.

My love.

Ayja frowned and turned the stone over. There was writing there as well. *My queen is.*

My queen is my love.

This time she couldn't choke back a sob, nor the tears streaming from her eyes. He had loved her. All he'd done for her he'd done out of love. She'd never realized it. She'd never known. He was a pyren! He was so much older than her!

My queen. He'd said it over and over even after she told him to stop. *My queen is my love.* All those times he'd said *my queen,* he'd been saying, *I love you.*

And I left him behind. I left him to die in Dromost. After all he did for me. He kept me alive for all those months, and I abandoned him.

Ayja pressed the stone against her forehead so hard it hurt. What could she have done? How could she have saved him? She should have fought harder. She should have seen Vahlah's betrayal. *I was such a fool. I was so desperate to leave. I wanted all of my plans to come true. I willed them to be true instead of thinking them through.*

The glow of the nearby spiridus grew brighter.

Peace. Love. Savior.

"I left him behind," she said. For a long time, she knelt there, holding the stone cupped in her hands. Over and over, she thought of those last desperate moments in Dromost, trying to think of what she could have done differently.

Darra was certainly dead now. Truly dead. Even with his magic, he would have been overwhelmed. At least he felt no pain. No physical pain, at least. *He loved me, and I never knew it.* She wouldn't have — couldn't have returned that love. In no way did she feel any romantic love towards the pyren. She could have appreciated him more, though. She could have let him know how much she recognized what he'd done for her.

Finally, very late in the night, she took the stone, Forsvar, and Dromost, and walked with them into the pool. The moment she was in the water, she recognized it as her home. It felt natural. It felt like the one place in the world she most wanted to be. Smiling, she walked deeper and then submerged herself.

She saw perfectly clearly in the water, and holding her breath took no effort at all. No, it wasn't that. She didn't feel the need to breathe. The pool was far deeper than it appeared from above. She drifted to the bottom and placed Forsvar and Dromost atop a large flat rock. Then she placed Darra's stone on it as well.

When she was done, she rose back to the surface and walked from the pool. She returned to her armor. She found her silver pendant there — the one she'd crafted to cleanse the poisonous air of Dromost. Taking it, she put it over her head. It did nothing in Landomere. The air was as pure as air could be. It was a reminder, though, of what she'd gone through, and what she'd seen. Her canteen was there as well, miraculously unbroken.

Her armor was rent and worn. Scales were missing, and in places there were long gashes that reached through the lining beneath. It had served her well, protecting her from many blows that would have killed her. She looked at the armor and her sword. Would she ever need either of them again? She was safe now and would never leave Landomere again. She couldn't even leave the vicinity of the spiridus glade.

Placing her sheathed sword and canteen inside the armor, she folded the scale coat closed and did up the clasps. Taking the entire bundle in her arms, she entered the pool and took them to the bottom and left them with the Gifts of the Gods. She'd felt the magic of the pool. The water would not harm those things she placed here.

Let none of them ever be needed again.

Returning to the surface, she went to sit at the base of her mother tree. "If I speak, will you hear me?" Ayja asked. "Should I tell you the story of my life? Tell me in the morning if you heard me. If not, I'll tell it to you again."

And so she sat for the rest of the night, recounting everything she could remember, going back to her earliest memories. As she spoke, the few spiridus who remained in the glade darted back and forth over the pool and through the treetops overhead. How long had it been since she'd been in a place of such utter peace? It had been less than a year since her father's ghuls had arrived to terrorize her home. She'd known moments of peace since then. There'd been times of laughter and joy, but always, over everything, the looming threat of the Dromost Gate.

Now there was peace. Simple peace. There were dark memories, but maybe over time, she could put them behind her. She looked into the sky and saw lightness growing there. She stood and faced her mother tree, waiting for her to appear. For a moment, she felt a wave of fear. What if she didn't come back? What if....

No. Her mother would return. And Ayja would enter her pool for the day. To sleep? To... what? What would happen to her? What had her mother experienced?

Then it began. The tree grew smaller. The many branches turned into two. The trunk split into legs. Vines grew over her and sprouted leaves. And then, in heartbeats, her mother stood in front of her, clothed in nature's attire. Hadde blinked at her daughter and then smiled and threw herself forward to embrace her.

"Good morning, Enna," Hadde said.

"Good morning, Mother."

For a time, they just held each other. Ayja extricated herself from her mother's embrace and said, "Did you hear me? I talked to you all through the night."

Her mother shook her head and smiled. "I'm sorry, Enna. I knew you were nearby. I felt your presence." She looked around, motioning to their surroundings. "I felt the presence of all life. I felt the spiridus and all of the living creatures. Even the plants. I felt the breeze on my branches and the earth on my roots, but I couldn't hear you."

"I worried that you might not. I'll tell it all to you again. Or you can share your story with me first. There's so much I want to know about you. Cam only knew so much, although he cherished every memory he had with you."

"I wish to know your story as well," Hadde said, touching the side of Ayja's face. "But perhaps you can tell me this story first — the one that begins with you telling me you're pregnant."

Ayja laughed. "Oh... that!" She touched her slightly rounded belly.

"Yes! Oh, that! I somehow don't feel old enough to be a grandmother."

"You certainly don't look it, Mother. You barely look older than me."

"The past, how long has it been?" Hadde paused. "I don't even know. Once I became the Lady of the Forest, I lost all track of time. How old are you, Ayja?"

"I think I turned eighteen in Dromost," Ayja said. "Time was hard to track there."

Hadde shook her head and sighed. "I missed out on seventeen years of my daughter's life. And now my daughter is going to be a mother! Who is the father?"

"Orlos the Spiridus."

"Orlos, but he's just a...." Hadde paused. "I was going to say baby. But he's your age. Was he in Dromost with you?"

Ayja shook her head. "I went through the Dromost Gate in Drommaria — the Summoned Lands. I had to leave him behind. He would have died in Dromost — he couldn't breathe there. I could, because of my magic. I hope... I hope he is well. If anyone could have escaped, it would have been him."

"Tell me, Ayja. Tell me your story."

They sat at the edge of the pool, and Ayja told her mother a different story than the one she'd started the night before. She hadn't gotten very far when sunlight brightened the horizon. Ayja felt the change. She had to enter the pool.

"I have to go, Mother, and I've only just started," she said with a frown.

Hadde took her hand. "We have a lifetime together now. Even if we can't always speak, we'll know that the other is near. And, little by little, we'll learn each other's stories."

They embraced one more time, and then Ayja walked into the pool. This time, as she submerged herself, her clothing of lilies, flowers, and vines disappeared from her body, leaving her naked in the cool, inviting water. She turned one last time and waved at her mother before sinking under the surface and becoming one with the pool.

Chapter Thirty-four

As Ayja emerged from the pond, garments of water lilies and green vines formed over her. The last rays of sunlight glimmered through the highest treetops as she awakened for another night. Her mother waited for her at the water's edge, and they embraced.

"Hello, daughter," Hadde said with a smile.

"Hello, mother," Ayja replied.

Four months had passed since Ayja had leaped through the Emerald Gate, and her mother had greeted her every dusk in the same manner. And in a very short — too short — a time, Ayja would say goodnight to her mother as she made her transformation into a tree.

They had precious little time to share, and Ayja cherished every heartbeat of it. Each dusk Hadde told Ayja of her life, and every dawn, Ayja told her mother of hers. Slowly, ever so slowly, they learned more of each other and Ayja's love for her mother grew.

"You have guests," Hadde said, taking Ayja in hand as they walked from the pond's edge.

"Grandmother and grandfather?"

"No, not tonight. These visitors are from much further away."

Ayja frowned, and then her heart skipped a beat in her chest. "Has Cam arrived? Is he well?"

"Not Nidon, but others from beyond the pass. Nidon had to go to Sal-Oras and see the king, but I've been told he's on his way."

"Who is it, then? Orlos? Telea?" Ayja couldn't help the smile that crossed her face.

"They have news for you. Things to share."

"It's them! Ha!" Ayja touched her round stomach. Her body had rapidly transformed in the few months since she'd escaped Dromost. She was no longer a skeletal figure, and her baby was growing nicely within her. She could even feel her move from time to time, an event that always filled her with wonder and love. "I think I have bigger news. Has anyone told them?"

Ayja's heart suddenly thudded in her chest at the realization of what she was about to tell Orlos. *He doesn't know. He has no idea!* She'd rehearsed what she'd say over and over but was now suddenly filled with panic.

"No, they don't know about your baby. And, remember, Ayja, until very recently they thought you were dead, or at least that you would never return. And a lot of time has passed. Things have changed."

Ayja frowned, suddenly concerned. "What do you mean?"

"They'll explain. It's not my place."

"They're well, though, right? They aren't hurt."

Hadde shook her head. "No, they're fine, but... they'll explain."

"Mother—"

Hadde held up her hand. "They are waiting at the cottage. They'll explain. Do not worry."

Ayja glanced into the forest and then back at her mother. "I should stay. We have so little time together."

"Go, Enna. See your friends. I will see you again at dawn."

"I love you," Ayja said. "I'll see you in the morning." She turned and headed for the cottage. The home wasn't for Ayja or her mother — they were creatures of nature now, with no need for a roof over their heads. The cottage was for Ayja's child and her caregivers. She, for Ayja was certain she was a girl, would need a home and someone to take care of her when Ayja was in her pond. Her mother would help, of course, but the baby would need a wet nurse and contact with other people. Grandmother Enna and Maret had offered their help as well. Ayja had no doubt her daughter would be well cared for.

What kind of mother will I be? Only awake at night. How will my little girl react to a mother clothed in lilies, and who sleeps every day in a pond?

Of course, her daughter had a father... a father who didn't yet know she existed. Ayja swallowed hard. How would Orlos react to seeing her? What would he think about being a father? Would he disappear and vanish into the forest?

She shook her head. He might be reckless, but he could be counted on when she needed him. Ayja walked silently through the gathering darkness, although gaining a spiridus made the dark mean much less than it once had. She parted tall ferns as she followed the stream towards the cottage. Overhead, three spiridus shone brightly as they flitted through the branches and leaves. She smiled at them despite her nervousness.

Ayja's belly was not so great yet that it hampered her movement, although it was certainly large enough for her to notice. She placed her hand on her stomach as her daughter kicked, smiling at the pressure, as she lifted one last fern to glance into the cottage's clearing.

She and her mother had done much of the work, Ayja using magic to shape the stone of the walls, her mother using her bond with nature to cause a living roof to grow overhead. They had help from others as well; Ayja's grandparents came from Belavil to work and to visit. She saw Orlos and Telea, sitting together on a bench of stone Ayja had smoothed and molded. It sat beside a boulder she'd turned into a table standing just outside the front door.

There were no lights in the cottage, just moonlight shining down through the trees. Orlos and Telea sat close to each other, hand in hand, their heads close together in murmured conversation too quiet for Ayja to hear. It was odd seeing them hand in hand. They'd never been close. Orlos had always mistrusted Telea's demon. But as her mother had said, a lot of time had passed. Ayja had spent months in Dromost, and more time had passed since she returned. Telea's demon was long gone; it only made sense that they'd grown closer.

Orlos's head turned in her direction, and Ayja felt a wave of nervousness, certain she'd been seen, but then he turned back to Telea. What would he think, seeing her dressed in living clothing and very clearly pregnant? She suddenly wished she was wearing a Saladoran kirtle and gown that might hide her better.

Too nervous to approach, Ayja just stood and watched them for a dozen heartbeats. They were very comfortable together — something Ayja hadn't seen before. There'd always been a wall between them. The demon was gone now, though, sent to Dromost to find Ayja. And the two had certainly shared enough experiences that they could be friends.

Then a chill crawled down Ayja's arms as she saw something that couldn't possibly be true. Just as she saw the spiridus flying overhead, she spotted another, this one residing within Telea. For the briefest moment, Ayja thought it might be the demon still within her, but then, with absolute certainty, she *knew* it to be a spiridus.

And there was no spiridus within Orlos. "How?" she gasped, the word barely escaping her lips.

Telea looked up, and her mouth opened wide. She spoke to Orlos, and he leaped to his feet, banging his hip on the stone table and wincing in pain.

There was no hiding any longer, and Ayja stepped free of the ferns and into the dark meadow.

Grimacing, Orlos limped towards her, calling out, "Ayja! You did it! You're back!" But then he turned and took Telea's hand before

354

approaching. Ayja walked closer, trying her best to walk tall and keep her breath steady — neither of which was easy.

Telea was the first to truly notice Ayja. She dropped Orlos's hand and halted in place. Orlos paused and looked at Telea before turning back to Ayja. His eyes went to her abdomen and he gave out a gasp.

"Ah, surprise," Ayja said, everything she'd rehearsed for weeks fleeing her mind

"I, um, oh," Orlos stammered, his mouth working like a fish on land. "Is it, ah—"

"Ours," Ayja said, stepping closer to him. A few strides separated them, and her heart fell when he didn't rush to embrace her. Instead, he again looked back to Telea.

"A child is joyous news," Telea said, but Ayja saw a look of concern writ on her face. Telea stepped past Orlos and hugged Ayja. "Ayja, we are so glad you are alive. We'd lost hope."

As Telea let her go, Ayja looked past her to Orlos. "What's wrong, Orlos? I've never seen you at a loss for words."

"It's so much to take in," he said. "I'm going to be a father. You're going to have a baby."

"We're going to have a baby," Ayja said. "Our baby."

"I'm so glad you're alive," Orlos said. He stepped closer and finally embraced her, but his arms were stiff, and he didn't sink into her. As he let her go, he stared down at her stomach.

"What's going on?" Ayja asked, close to tears at the odd behavior of the two of them. "I thought you would be happy to see me. Are you upset at my being pregnant?"

Orlos and Telea shared a glance, and then Telea said, "A lot has happened to us, Ayja."

"To you? I went to Dromost, pregnant, and returned!" Ayja said, crying now, not understanding their behavior.

"Ayja, Orlos has lost his spiridus," Telea said. "No, not lost. He *gave* his spiridus to me to save my life, just as Orlos the Ancient gave the same spiridus to him."

Orlos shook his head. "You don't *give* a spiridus," he said. "I asked the spiridus to save you." He looked up at the spiridus flying overhead and then back at Ayja. "I'm sorry, Ayja. I'm not the person I was before. I'm not Orlos the Spiridus any more. I'm just Orlos."

Ayja took his hand in hers. "You aren't any different! You look just the same."

"I'm different," he said, his face twisting in anguish.

"I'm sorry, Orlos. I was thinking only of myself. I didn't think of what you have been through."

"We thought you were gone, Ayja," Orlos said. "We gave up hope."

"Of course you gave up hope," Ayja said, wiping her tears away with her free hand. "Who wouldn't have? But you did send Telea's demon to me. Without it, I surely would have been lost. But I'm back. And the fact that your spiridus is in Telea doesn't change how I think about you."

"But it changed how I think about her," Orlos said.

"What does that mean?"

"We are connected now, through the spiridus."

Ayja looked from one to the other. "What does that mean?"

"We love you, Ayja," Telea said. "Both of us. You never even suspected how deeply I cared for you. And Orlos was despondent at your loss. Both of us are overjoyed at discovering you are alive here."

"But..."

"When I'm with Telea, I am with the spiridus again," Orlos said. "When I touch her, I can feel my spiridus again. I feel whole again."

"And I feel the spiridus's love for Orlos," Telea said. She paused then and added, "And I feel it as well."

Ayja's heart sank as she looked at the two of them holding hands. "You are in love."

"It's more than that," Orlos said. "Different. We are connected."

"More than love? But I love you, Orlos. I thought we'd share a life together. We'd raise our child together. And Telea, you are my closest friend. I wanted us to study magic together. To do all those things we talked about before. I know it's different now. I — I'm different now. I spend my days as one with the forest. I disappear into a pond. But it doesn't change how I feel. It doesn't change the life I want to have with you."

"We understand that Ayja," Telea said. "Everything has changed, and nothing at all. Both of us want to be with you. Orlos wants to be your husband and father to your child. I want to be your friend. I want to explore magic together."

"We want to do it together," Orlos said. "The three of us."

Ayja looked past them towards the stone cottage. "Can't you ask the spiridus to return to Orlos?"

"Telea would die," Orlos said.

"The spiridus binds my soul to this world," Telea said. "My soul is shattered without the spiridus."

Ayja drew a deep breath. "It wasn't going to be a normal life anyway, was it?"

"Did any of us ever have a normal life?" Telea asked. "By any stretch of the imagination?"

"No... I suppose not." Ayja glanced back at the cottage again. She'd imagined something like a normal life there, with Orlos. But how would that have ever worked, with her returning to her pool every morning? No, it was never going to be normal. "The two of you will live here? Together?"

Telea nodded. "And you and I shall study the ways of magic, just as we always talked about. And Orlos will be father to your child."

Ayja drew a breath and sighed. "And I will visit each dusk and depart each dawn. I will sleep in a pond and be a stranger to my child."

"Not like that," Orlos said. "You might sleep apart from us, but we will be a family. We will keep your hours. Telea might take half the night so that you can make magic together, and I take the other so that we can be together. Despite all that has happened, all that has changed for all of us, I still care deeply for you."

With his free hand, Orlos reached out and took hers. And then Telea did the same so that they all stood together in a circle. "We have been through a lot, the three of us," Orlos said. "Telea and her demon, Ayja in Dromost, and I..."

"Gave up part of who you were, so that I might live," Telea finished. "We can't change these things that have happened to us. We survived, but we didn't do it unscathed. Ayja, I've only heard the smallest part of what you've been through, and you did it all while carrying a child. But despite all we've been through, we made it alive to stand here together tonight. Our future together won't be normal in any sense of the word, but who says it can't be happy? It might take time to adjust to our new circumstance, but we have each other."

"Cam always held out some hope that I'd emerge from the East Teren and take my place as Queen of Salador," Ayja said. "I don't think I ever believed him. It was too fanciful a dream ever to come true. I thought I'd marry and live out my life among the hillfolk. How very, very wrong we both were." She squeezed the hands of her friends. "Nothing has turned out as I imagined, even my imagining of the last few days as I awaited your arrival. I thought things might be different...

"But, you're right, Telea. It doesn't mean it can't be good. We can make a life for ourselves here. And it isn't just us. We have a family — my mother, my grandparents, and Orlos's family. This can be a joyous life. So many died so that we could accomplish our tasks. We lived through it all, and should take every advantage of what that life offers us."

Ayja let go of their hands and drew them both into an embrace. She couldn't help the tears that came to her eyes or the sob that escaped her lips. Memories washed over her, memories of ghuls, pyren, and lyches.

Of her father and of his minions and of all her friends who had fallen. She also thought of Darra and the horrors of Dromost. The weight of the memories seemed likely to crush her beneath them, and she might have fallen to her knees if Orlos and Telea hadn't been there to hold her up.

Then, very close and very quiet, Telea began to sing the *Song of Hope*. The melody washed over Ayja, driving the fear and sadness from her. Her thoughts instead went to her friends and the laughter they had shared. Even those who had passed away had enriched her life and made her a better person. She had Orlos and Telea. She had her mother. She had a family in Landomere. Soon Cam would return to her. And then, not too far away, she'd have a child of her own.

Through her tears, she began to smile. Orlos, who'd been under a dark cloud ever since he'd arrived, looked at her face and smiled as well.

"Thank you, Telea," Ayja said, kissing her friend on the cheek. "When we have time, I'll tell you how your music lessons saved me in Dromost. Later, though. Come, let me take you to my spiridus glade."

Chapter Thirty-five

Nidon walked through the Forest of Landomere just behind Orlos and Telea. Orlos's mother, Maret, walked at his side, with the rest of their party following silently behind. Nidon's hands shook uncontrollably, and butterflies filled his stomach. He should have eaten earlier, but for perhaps the first time in his life, he hadn't been able to eat a bite.

The welcome feast had been held in Maret and Kael's home high atop Belavil. Nidon had never seen a more beautiful city or met a more welcoming people. Orlos's younger brother and twin sisters had been there, as had Hadde's parents, Arno and Enna. The gathering had been a joyous one, and the food had looked and smelled fantastic, but Nidon had been too overcome with anticipation to touch it.

Maret and Kael had invited them to get a night's rest after his long journey, but Nidon couldn't bear the thought of it. He wouldn't have slept a wink in any case. So now they strode a forest path lined with luminescent white flowers. Overhead, the moon peeked out between scattered clouds and the leaf-filled branches of the largest trees Nidon had ever seen. Somehow, the dappled light of the moon and the glow of the flowers gave enough light for them to travel by.

"We were under siege for five days," Orlos said to his mother, continuing a story that had gone most of the night. "But now the rune-covered walls helped us against the enemy assaults. From the cover of the walls, our elementars brought fire down upon them, and our singers banished the imps and the possessed men and demons.

"King Handrin and Telea went to the Temple of Dromost to seal the gate. I wasn't there. Kael and I were on the walls — there was no shortage of arrows or bolts within the temple."

"I hope you kept safe," Maret said, and then paused. "I suppose that sounds kind of dumb at this point."

Orlos laughed. "I was safer then than I had been at some points in the previous days. Anyway, we gave King Handrin and Telea time to seal the Dromost Gate. The Orb of Creation sits on a pedestal in front of the

359

gate surrounded by a glowing shield that nothing can penetrate. The Dromost Gate can never be opened. It is sealed by one of the Gifts of the Gods."

"Does it sound ridiculous if I just said that I'm happy you're home again and safe?"

He glanced over his shoulder at her and smiled. "You'd be singing a different tune if we'd failed."

"You should be proud of your son, Maiden, ah, Lady Maret," Nidon said. "He's a hero. We couldn't have succeeded without him. Telea, as well."

"Thank you, Champion Nidon," Maret said. "And it's just Maret now, if I haven't mentioned it before."

"Perhaps once or twice," Nidon said with a smile. "It is hard for me to think of you as the mother of four children and not the child I used to know. Your family is beautiful. Your husband, Kael, is a good man."

"Thank you, Champion Nidon. It is kind of you to say so."

"Just Nidon will do," he said with a grin.

Maret stopped and looked at him. "What? Just Nidon? Not even Sir Nidon?"

"It doesn't seem right here," he said, motioning to the dark forest surrounding them.

"This is quite the rebellious change for such a paragon of order," Maret said.

He shrugged. "Perhaps over fifteen years as an outlaw and exile changed me."

"Well, Landomere had that effect on me." She turned back to Orlos. "But how did you get home if you were under siege at the temple?"

"The Etheans came for us," Orlos said. "Despite the evil that the demon emperor had done to their people in Belen, the Etheans came. Before we'd left Aftokropoli, Empress Kelifos sent word to the Etheans asking for their aid, not really expecting it. They sent a fleet!"

"There was a terrible sea battle," Nidon said, "but the Etheans were victorious. They brought us from the Temple of Dromost. Not everyone escaped, though. Someone had to hold the wall while the last of the army boarded the ships. The Empress's Axes and the Children of Forsvar stayed behind."

"Perhaps they—"

"None survived," Nidon said. "There was no hope for them. They knew it when they volunteered."

"That's terrible," Maret said.

"They died so that others could live. Theirs were noble deaths."

"We're close now," Telea said.

Nidon's heart lurched at her words. They'd explained it to him, but no matter how many times he heard it, he couldn't get his mind around it. *Ayja and Hadde live but share one life. They split the day and night between them. And my little Ayja is pregnant.* He drew in a deep breath. All that mattered was that she was alive and well. The rest he'd just have to get used to.

Glancing over his shoulder to see if the others were still following, Nidon followed Telea and Orlos through a maze of giant ferns. As the ferns thinned, he heard the sound of water rushing into a pool as the fresh, enchanting scent of everbloom grew even stronger.

The full moon shone down atop a glimmering pool from an opening in the canopy above them. Fern and everbloom surrounded the pool and covered the slopes leading down to it. A bubbling, babbling brook tumbled down a fall and into the pool. And then he saw her, dancing from stone to stone, a wreath of everbloom on her head and a bouquet of it in her hands.

She saw him at the very same moment and cried out, "Cam!" Then, in a single leap and a rush of air, she landed at the edge of the pond and raced towards him. Nidon didn't wait for her but ran to her and caught her as she leaped into his arms.

"Ayja! My Ayja!" He wrapped his arms around her and did not attempt to hold back as sobs wracked his body. Slowly, he fell to his knees, taking Ayja with him, and not caring that there were others there to see. "I thought I'd lost you forever."

Her embrace was as strong as his. "I'm back. All is well. We're together again."

"I'm never letting you go again."

Ayja laughed in his arms. "I don't think you have to worry about that."

Nidon pulled back and looked her in the eyes. She was crying as well but smiling just as broadly as he was. Then he looked her up and down to make certain she was really, truly there. She wore a shimmering gossamer gown that sparkled with water droplets reflecting the moonlight. There was a bulge in her belly, but it hadn't slowed her down. "They say you turn into water and are only you at night. I don't understand."

"It is the magic of Landomere," she replied. "The magic of the Great Spirit. This is my home now. I know you don't want to hear it, but I died. The Great Spirit brought me back, but... but there are limitations. During the day, I am part of this spiridus glade — part of the Great Spirit. At night I am as you see me. It is the opposite for my mother."

"And your... your baby?"

361

Ayja touched her stomach. "Yes. The Great Spirit and the spiridus together saved us."

"Ayja and the baby both have a spiridus in them," Telea said. "The spiridus kept them alive, just as Orlos's spiridus saved me."

"Giving up my spiridus to save your life is a decision I'd make a hundred times over," Orlos said. He forced a smile, but there was loss in his eyes. The young man was making a good show of it, Nidon thought, but he hadn't been the same ever since the battle at the Temple of Dromost.

"Cam, I hope you're not upset that I'm... that I'm having a baby," Ayja said.

Nidon smiled. "Let's say it was a surprise when I got the news. It's not the Saladoran way, but I'm ready to give up Saladoran ways. Orlos is a good man. And good people surround you. People who love you and think of you as family. You will be a good mother. Your child will have a good life. Better than I gave you. It saddens me that for so many years, I was your only family."

Fresh tears sprang to Ayja's eyes, and she hugged him close for a very long time. Then she said in his ear, "My mother is here."

Nidon took in a deep breath and pulled back from Ayja. "I don't understand. She's been gone so long, how is it even possible?"

"She lived on all those years as the Lady of the Forest — a spirit guardian, not conscious of who or what she was. She'll tell you. She'll explain it better. But then the Great Spirit gave her life so that she could fight the demons at the Emerald Gate."

"You can explain it all you want, but I don't think I'll ever understand." Just then, a flash of light caught Nidon's eye. He turned to see several spiridus enter the glade and race across the top of the water. He'd seen a few of the spiridus since entering Landomere but none so close. They were beautiful and filled his heart with joy. The spiridus flitted overhead, dancing through the branches of the trees.

"Your mother... she is here?" *A tree,* he wanted to say but couldn't bring himself to say the words.

Ayja pulled herself back and motioned to a tree, standing closer to the pool than the others. "She'll wake in the morning."

"You can speak with her?"

"Only at dusk and dawn when we are both awake for a short time. It isn't enough."

He stared at the tree, still not quite believing it.

"I call it sleeping," Ayja said, "but no force of nature or magic can wake us. We are not conscious of the world."

Ayja extricated herself from him and helped him to his feet. Nidon wiped the tears from his face, trying not to be too obvious in front of the others. It shouldn't have concerned him, he knew. Maret, Orlos, and Telea had tears in their eyes as well.

"We brought a few more friends, Ayja," Orlos said, walking back towards the ferns and parting them. From them, Sindi and Calen emerged. Smiling, the two Landomeri strode up to Ayja and embraced her.

"We are never leaving Landomere again," Sindi said, taking Calen's hand. "We've had enough adventure for a lifetime."

"And we don't think it would be safe for our baby," Calen added.

"I'd be lying if I said I was surprised," Ayja said with a smile.

"Our children will be near the same age," Sindi said. "They will grow up together."

"That will be wonderful," Ayja said.

"We are happy that you made it, Ayja," Calen said. "And about your mother as well. It is a joyous time in Landomere."

"My mother is very proud of you, Calen," Ayja said. "She said that you were very brave when the two of you tried to save Orlos and me so long ago."

"I was terrified. Your mother was the fearless one. I was always sorry that I wasn't there when she needed me at the end."

"You did everything you could. You didn't let your fear stop you. She knows it. Come and see her soon."

"I will. Can I bring Sindi? She very much wants to meet her."

"Of course."

"We brought a couple of other friends," Orlos said from the edge of the glade.

Ayja smiled. "More surprises?"

Orlos stepped through the ferns and then soon returned, leading Sir Matus and Sir Jaek behind him. Both wore Belenese attire, baggy trousers under bright kaftans. Jaek had a patch over one eye and Matus a long scar running from forehead to cheek.

Nidon watched Ayja race up to them, hugging both at the same time. "I'm so glad to see you! You made it!"

"We were captured and taken as slaves when you passed through the Dromost Gate, Your Highness," Matus said. "They put us on a Drommarian war galley."

"The Etheans saved us," Jaek said. "If we can come back, we'll tell you our story, Your Highness."

"I want to hear it! I'm so happy that you lived. And I'm just Ayja now."

Jaek touched his eye patch. "You can tell us apart now."

"I always could," Ayja said. "You're Matus."

"Jaek."

Ayja laughed. "I knew that!"

"My brother's just happy he's the better-looking one now," Matus said.

"You both look dashing and daring," Ayja said. "Please, come and visit. I want to hear your tale." Nidon saw Ayja look past them and towards Orlos. "There's someone else, isn't there?"

"How did you know?" Orlos asked. "Did the Great Spirit tell you there was someone outside the glade?"

Ayja shook her head. "No, you're still standing by the ferns."

Orlos parted the ferns and called to someone beyond. Tharryl walked into the glade, his eyes wide with wonder. Then the hulking knight saw Ayja and walked towards her, taking a knee in front of her. Unlike the twins, he wore a fine Saladoran tunic and trousers. Nidon still had a hard time believing the man had survived. He'd fought like a man demon possessed after Isibindi's death. Even the dozens of wounds he'd taken hadn't slowed him down. But despite his own best efforts, he couldn't be killed.

"I owe you an apology," Tharryl said without preamble.

"Why?" Ayja asked.

"Because I didn't behave like a knight. I was crude to you and cruel. I mocked you when I shouldn't. But I was a fool. You fought the demon at the gate and won. You were willing to sacrifice yourself for all of us when you walked through that gate, knowing you'd never return. And, despite the way I treated you, you made me a knight."

"You deserved it, Sir Tharryl. You were faithful to the very end. Nothing could bring you down. Rise, Sir Tharryl, you don't have to take a knee before me. You are my friend."

Tharryl stood, looming over everyone but Nidon, who had to admit the young man had him by a handwidth. "I don't know what to do," Tharryl said, shifting his weight and looking around the group. "I don't know my place in the world. I miss Isibindi."

"You are a good man, Sir Tharryl," Nidon said. "I'll put in a word with the king. I'm certain he'd make you an officer in the Knights of the House. He'll grant you an estate for what you've done."

"I, ah, don't want to leave my friends," Tharryl said, glancing around the group and then down at the ground.

Then Ayja stepped up to him and wrapped her arms around him and embraced him with her head upon his chest. "Then stay with us, Tharryl. Stay with your friends."

"I'm very sorry for how I treated you, Your Highness."

"Ayja. And you can hug me back. We're friends, Tharryl. And you'll stay here in Landomere with us."

The big knight wrapped his thick arms around Ayja and held her close. Nidon saw tears well up in Tharryl's eyes. "Thank you, Ayja," he said. "I think I will."

Then he let her go and stepped back among the others, only to have Sindi punch him in the arm. "I always thought you were soft," she said.

Tharryl laughed and said, "Only when compared to you."

"Thank you all for coming to see me," Ayja said. "I'm so relieved that you survived your many ordeals. And that you came to visit me here. Please, come and visit us again. And my baby when she arrives. Tonight though, I'd like to spend some time with my Cam."

One by one, she hugged them and sent them on their way back into the forest until only Nidon remained. She looked up at him when they were gone and said, "Are you hungry?"

He laughed as he looked down at her vibrant, living face. "I am now! Maret offered up a feast, but I couldn't eat. I was so nervous about seeing you. I really didn't think it was true."

"I can't offer you much, but there are sweetberries — that's what they call raspberries here — growing by mother."

Nidon looked at the tree again, shaking his head. "It just can't be true."

Ayja took his hand and led him to the tree. "It's her," she said with a smile. "You'll see in the morning. You're staying, aren't you?"

"If I can."

"Of course! You can stay as long as you like."

Nidon stood just a few strides from the tree. "She... can she hear us?"

"You asked that before!" Ayja said with a laugh. "No. At night she's a tree." Ayja stepped up to it and put her hand on the bark. "Would you like to climb her?" she asked with a mischievous smile.

"No!" He looked up into the tree's branches. "Don't you think this is so very, very strange? We're talking about a person becoming a tree."

Ayja shrugged. "It is the magic of the Great Spirit. Come, let's have something to eat."

A few strides away, a sweetberry patch full of plump red berries grew. He ate one and found it to be the most delicious thing he'd ever tasted.

"They are all different," Ayja said as she picked berries. "Calen and Sindi are happier. Matus and Jaek seem more serious. Tharryl wasn't an ass. Telea is full of regret. And I worry about Orlos. He's given up so much."

"Difficult times force us to change," Nidon said. "We see the world differently than we did before. I'm not the man I was before I plucked a crying baby from the mud and took her to be my daughter. I'm not the man I was before I met your mother."

"You were a great father, even if we never used the word between us," Ayja said, taking his hand and squeezing it. "I couldn't have wished for better."

"I'm so very proud of you, Ayja," Cam said. Blood rushed to his cheeks and he had to fight back tears. "I'm so glad you made it."

"We'll never be separated again," Ayja said to him. "Landomere is our home now. And, in the morning, you'll see my mother again."

Nidon glanced up into the branches of the tree. "She's well? How does... how does she look?"

"She's beautiful. She has those three radiant suns on her cheeks like you told me about. And she has piercing gray eyes. She hasn't aged. I think she'll look the same to you as the last time you saw her. She only looks a little older than me. And yet she'll be a grandmother."

Nidon sighed. "She'll think me an old man."

"You're not *that* old."

"Thanks. I'm just past forty. Still fit, right?"

"She'll think you're handsome and charming."

"Now, that's a lie. No one has ever called me charming. Or handsome for that matter."

"Well, you are. And she spends half of each day as a tree, so you have that on her."

Nidon laughed at the ridiculousness of it all. How different life had turned out from what he'd imagined as a young squire whose only hope had been to be knighted someday. For a time, he and Ayja ate their fill of berries, and then they sat down at the bank of the pond and watched as two spiridus danced over the water. They talked about all that had happened to them since they'd last seen each other.

"It was worse than you're letting on," he finally said.

She didn't reply.

"You don't have to tell me. Trust me. There are things in my life I wish to forget."

"There were people who made great sacrifices to save us," she finally said. "Sir Darra was one of them. Don't remember him as the pyren who served Morin. Remember him as the hero who saved me in Dromost."

Nidon nodded. "I will." He laid back in the ferns, making a pillow of his hands and staring up into the night sky. The moon had moved on, but the stars were nearly as bright. He smiled as a spiridus zipped past his view.

"Hey, Ayja, where are Forsvar and Dromost?" He turned his head so that he could see her. She sat cross-legged in the ferns next to him, looking out over the pond.

She smiled. "The Dromost Gate is closed. The Emerald Gate is closed. The Great Spirit thinks Helna's world is better off without Forsvar and Dromost for now."

Nidon stared back up at the sky. "King Handrin will disagree."

"Tell him to take it up with the Great Spirit."

Nidon chuckled. "I will... next time I see him."

He took a deep breath. Had he ever been in a more wonderful place? He never wanted to leave. He woke some time later to Ayja saying, "Goodnight, father," as she kissed his cheek.

"Goodnight, daughter," he replied, rolling onto his side and falling fast asleep again.

The sun was in his eyes, and something was tickling his nose when he woke again. He tried to brush the irritant away. After a moment's reprieve, he tried to find sleep again, but the tickle came back.

And a woman's giggle.

Nidon opened his eyes, and she was there, sitting beside him. The years had not touched her. Her long, black hair framed her beautiful face. Three sun tattoos decorated each cheek. And she was smiling as she ran a fern frond down his nose.

"Hadde?"

"You sure like to sleep, Sir Nidon," she said with a smile. "I hope you don't mind, but I got tired of waiting for you to wake up. There are only so many hours in a day."

He sat up and brushed the hair from his face. "Is it really you?" She was clothed by nature, wearing just leaves and vines and a necklace of everbloom. Her wiry, strong arms, and lean, muscled legs were exposed by the scant clothing she wore, but he hardly noticed anything but her face. A face he thought he'd never see again. A face that had filled his thoughts for years.

He glanced over to the tree, but it was gone.

"It's really me, Nidon."

"I tried, Hadde. I tried. I was heartbeats too late. I saw the varcolac. I saw you...."

"I heard your horse's hoofbeats. They sounded like thunder."

"But I was too late. I saw you there. You were... I cannot bear to say it."

"There was a part of the Great Spirit in me, Nidon. When I died, the Great Spirit took my soul to Landomere, where I lived on as the Lady of

367

the Forest. I don't remember all those years or all that happened to me. It was a dream to me.

"But when Ayja returned, and the Great Spirit's need was greatest, she saw fit to give me life again. By all rights, both Ayja and I should not be alive."

Nidon shook his head with wonder. "It is all beyond me." He looked at the pond. "Ayja's there?"

Hadde shook her head. "She isn't *in* the pond. Don't think you'll find her sleeping at the bottom. Ayja *is* the pond. She is one with it and one with the forest. Until night falls and she wakes again."

She paused, looking into the water. "We don't have much time together each day," Hadde said, "but Ayja has told me about your life together. She couldn't have had a better father."

Nidon looked away from her and stared back at the pond. Tears came to his eyes, but he wiped them away. "I love her with all my heart. She is my daughter, at least to me. She is everything to me."

"You helped her become the woman she is. She would not have lived without you. She would not have endured without what you taught her." Hadde reached out and took his hand in hers. Her hand was warm and strong, and a thrill went through his chest at her touch. "I wasn't there for her, but you were, Nidon. I am eternally grateful. Because of you, she's with me, and I can get to know her. My heart breaks with the joy of it."

Nidon nodded. "I'm happy that you're happy." He looked her in the eyes. "I'm glad that you're here."

Hadde smiled. "She told me that you often thought of me. I didn't know that when we were acquainted."

Nidon blushed and looked away for just a moment. "I, ah, perhaps Ayja shouldn't share quite as much as she does."

"I always thought very highly of you. There were many things I didn't like about Salador, but you weren't one of them. You defended me from Earl Waltas and respected me as a warrior."

"You deserved it."

"I was, perhaps, smitten by a charming prince. Perhaps I should have known better. He turned out not to be the man I thought he was."

"He and I weren't on good terms."

"And now I see why not. You were the better man. You proved it over and over."

Finally, Nidon summoned up the courage and said, "I did think a lot of you over the years. You were, and are, an amazing woman. I wish — you don't know how much I wish — things could have been different. Over fifteen years lost!"

"And what are you doing for the next fifteen years?"

368

Nidon didn't say anything for a moment. "I wish to stay here. I wish to live in Landomere, where I can be with Ayja." His heart pounded in his chest as he added, "And where I can be near you."

Hadde paused and looked at him and smiled. Squeezing his hand, she said, "I'd like that very much."

Acknowledgements

The Orb series was made possible through the generous help of my friends and family. I'd like to take a few moments to thank them for their contributions.

Mike Shultz is my critique partner and first round editor. He's been with me for every step of this ten year odyssey. I can't thank him enough for all the help he's given me over the years.

The Emerald Gate had a large cast of Alpha Readers. These first-round readers help, not only with editing, but by giving story advice. A huge round of thanks to James Latimer, Dan Merenich, Dan Joyce, Bob McDaniel, Carol Heppe, and Helen Heppe.

Beta Readers help with editing and proofreading. I am continually stunned at the number of errors I manage to make while writing. Many thanks to Bonnie Keagy, Cindy Kirschenmann, Caymus Ruffner, and Harvey Lapp.

Shelley Uthgennant is my volunteer proofreader. Slowly, but surely, she's teaching, me how, to use, a comma.

Dallas Williams is again responsible for the fantastic cover art for the entire series. His work is fantastic.

Writing *The Orb* was a long and wonderful journey. It was at some moments a joy and at others a torture. It is with mixed pride, happiness, and sorrow that I write these last words. If you've read this far it means that you've experienced *The Orb* in its entirety. I hope you've enjoyed the journey you've taken with my characters and me. My thanks to you, the reader, for the support you've given me over the years.

The Emerald Gate is dedicated to my daughter, Amelia.

Made in the USA
Coppell, TX
16 November 2020